POWER

USA TODAY BESTSELLING AUTHOR
CASSANDRA ROBBINS

POWER

Copyright © 2022
Power by Cassandra Robbins

All rights reserved. No part of this book may be reproduced, distributed, or scanned in any manner without written permission of the author, except in the need of quotes for reviews only.

This book is a work of fiction. The names, characters, and establishments are the product of the author's imagination or are used to provide authenticity and are used fictitiously. Any resemblance to any person, living or dead, is purely coincidental.

Edited: Nikki Busch Editing
Cover Design: Lori Jackson
Formatting and proofing: Elaine York, Allusion Publishing, www.allusionpublishing.com
Cover Photo: Michelle Lancaster
Cover Model: Richard Deiss

PLAYLIST

Unholy- Kim Petras and Sam Smith
Happier Than Ever- Billie Eilish
Rude Boy- Rihanna
Super Freaky Girl- Nicki Minaj
Heroes- David Bowie
Slave To Love- Bryan Ferry
Ring of Fire- Johnny Cash
CUFF IT- Beyonce
Unstoppable- Sia
I See Red- Bonnie Elizabeth Sims
Best of You- Foo Fighters
Cherry- Lana Del Rey
Ceremony- New Order
Touch Me- The Doors
God's Plan- Drake
Sadness- Enigma
King of Pain- The Police
Love The Way You Lie- Eminem and Rihanna
Bad- U2
Angels Walk- Paul Westerberg
Can't Help Falling In Love- Elvis Presley
Just Like Honey- The Jesus and Mary Chain
Endless Love- Lionel Richie and Diana Ross

One

JETT

Beverly Hills, CA

"**H**and me my coffee." I finish buttoning my starched white dress shirt and stare into the bathroom mirror.

"What?" My fiancée screeches at her phone and sits up. Her fake tits barely move when she tosses the covers off and stands, showing me her phone, as if I can see it from where I'm standing.

Reaching for my tie, I can't help but grin. Whatever is on there is unleashing the legendary bitch. My cock hardens. Not gonna lie—seeing her be a cunt does something for me.

"Is the governor's fundraiser tonight?" she snaps.

"Coffee," I demand right back. Her dark eyes narrow. Licking her lips, she dramatically reaches for my mug, then sashays toward me.

My erection instantly deflates, not because Rachel isn't beautiful. She is. At forty-eight, she looks damn good. She eats nothing but salmon and salads and exercises every day. Along with her dermatologist's and plastic surgeon's help, my fiancée could easily pass for mid-thirties.

I'm just a dick, I guess. Thankfully, Rachel's on the same page. Makes things easy, uncomplicated. I get to have zero guilt that I don't love her.

POWER

And she gets to have me. All my money, connections, power, *all of it*. That's what turns Rachel on. That, and the fact she enjoys watching other women suck my cock as much as I get off watching her eat other women's cunts.

We belong together, both selfish, workaholics, into making money and climbing the social ladder. Hell, at the rate I'm going, the sky's the limit. And Rachel knows it.

Smirking, she invades my space and places my mug on our large marble sink. While I smooth my tie, the flowery perfume she favors makes my nose twitch. I need to discuss switching her scent. That, and her straight black bob. I'm sick of the Uma Thurman-*Pulp Fiction* look on her.

"So." She holds her phone up again. "Jennifer just texted me. Apparently, it's the governor's fundraiser tonight, and Emily does not have it on my calendar." She stares at me like I can actually do something about this.

"Did you text *Emily*?" Already thinking of other stuff, I reach for my coffee.

"Of course," she says tightly. "I hope she doesn't think she can slack off because I let her blow you." Her eyes caress my face.

I grin, setting down the coffee. "*You*, allow her? Rethink your words, Rachel." I cock my head. The morning rays from the bathroom skylight aren't doing her any favors. Yeah, that hair color and style have to go.

"Jett, she's my assistant—" Her voice trails off and she tries to touch me.

Not in the mood, I grab her wrist, stopping her. "If Emily doesn't have it on your calendar, there has to be a reason. Before you get unreasonable, wait for her answer."

Tossing her wrist aside, I reach for my suit jacket. Her eyes narrow on me, and she glances down at her vibrating phone.

"Be polite," I warn.

She rolls her eyes. "You're so obvious, Jett. Don't worry. I won't fire her until she fucks us both again." She shakes her head.

2

I place my hand over my heart. "Aww, Rachel, you get me." The look she throws me makes me burst out laughing.

"Emily," she says curtly into the phone. "Please explain to me why I had to find out from my friend that the governor's fundraiser is tonight." She purses her borderline-duck lips.

"Shit. That's today?" Rachel straightens, her eyes finding mine. The look of aggravation makes me pause.

"No, I forgot." Sighing, Rachel rubs the back of her neck and starts to pace. "Okay. Well, I still don't understand why Jett and I are not confirmed for tonight. It's not like my daughter is a child." She moves the phone to her other ear.

"No, I'll send fucking Maria to pick her up. Confirm that Jett and I will be attending the fundraiser tonight and make sure we're sitting with the governor. Also, get ahold of Stephen for a gown. And Emily?" Her eyes dart to mine as I walk past her to grab my phone from the dresser. "Don't ever assume anything. I don't change my plans simply because my daughter is flying in. I do have a business to run." She hangs up and tosses her phone on the bed.

"Un-fucking-believable. I will fire her ass if we are not sitting at the governor's table." Her voice grows louder and her chest flushes.

I nod and pocket my phone, not quite sure what to make of this. "You forgot that your daughter is flying in today?"

Her eyes dart back to mine. "I'm busy. You're not the only one who works," she grumbles, twirling a strand of her hair. It's an annoying habit of hers. Bugs the shit out of me. One time, I actually saw her sucking on the ends.

"How does this happen?" I demand, pushing that distasteful memory away and focusing on the fact that Rachel has not once mentioned her kid coming to visit.

"How does what happen?" she retorts and marches past me toward the bathroom.

I grab her arm. "Your daughter is coming, and you forgot to tell me? Or yourself, apparently, if that phone call is true." Her hazel eyes narrow on mine.

"Raven and I don't get along." Her voice is flat. "I was hoping she was going to spend the summer with her father like she usually does. But shitty Frank has impregnated his stupid girlfriend, so yes..." She takes a breath. "It appears my daughter will be spending the next couple of months with us."

Letting go of her arm, I frown. This is wrong on so many levels. I have great parents. My mother adores me and my brother Brett.

"Rachel, you forgot your own child? What the fuck is wrong with you?" I almost start laughing because I knew she was a cutthroat, shallow bitch, but this is... well, I'm not really sure what this is.

"Don't judge me," she snarls. "You don't have kids—"

"Exactly. I don't. For this reason. But I think I'd remember if my kid was coming home for the summer."

"Stop." She sighs. "Raven is... different from me. We have zero in common." She walks toward me. Rubbing her hands up and down my dress shirt, she playfully tugs on my tie. "I did mean to tell you. I really did, but with work and the wedding..." She closes her eyes, then opens them. "This sounds bad, but I just forgot."

I look down at her. I'm no saint, but if my mom had forgotten that I was coming home for the summer...

"I'm late." I remove her hands. Christ, her flowery scent is now saturated into my suit.

"Jett, I'm telling you this is not a big deal. She has a boyfriend, and she should spend most of the time with him," she calls after me. This would be a major red flag if I wanted anything more from her than what she already gives.

"Please don't be mad at me. This is nothing but a slight inconvenience." She smiles but her lips twitch.

I raise a brow at her, shaking my head. "Whatever, I don't care." *Because I really don't.*

She nods, then goes into wife mode. "Do you want me to have your tuxedo sent to your office, or will you come home first?"

"Office. I have a full day. And, Rachel?"

She looks up from her phone.

"If you need to stay and maybe... bond with your daughter tonight—"

"Stop, Jett," she whines.

I snort and shake my head. "You just keep being you, my love." Looking at my watch, I head down the stairs, needing to get the fuck out of here. I'm in court this morning, defending my client, a pro bowl player. Jeremy is being mistakenly charged with possession of cocaine at a party. It's nothing but a jealous girlfriend trying to get back at him, a cliché setup... and that is exactly how I'll spin it.

With a grin, I turn sleep mode off, loving the feel of my phone's nonstop vibration as it tries to catch up with all the texts sent from my many assistants.

"Mr. Jett?"

I'm so involved in reading my messages I barely register the small, middle-aged Hispanic woman who stands over in the corner of the foyer. Maria? Mary? I know it starts with an M. She's the only person Rachel insisted I keep on my payroll.

"Yes?" My voice is cordial. She takes a step forward, her face looking miserable, as if I'm the last person she wants to talk to.

"I'm sorry, but Ms. Rachel needs me to pick up Miss Raven." She holds up her phone.

"Who?" I look down at my own phone to view the latest text from Rebecca, my secretary.

"*Raven*... Ms. Rachel's daughter." Mary sniffs and straightens her shoulders. I cock my head at her, then text Rebecca to hold on.

"Sorry, Mary? I'm a very busy man—"

"Maria." She corrects me with a disdainful sniff. This does get my attention. She's got balls—no one corrects me.

I grin while she continues to frown at me. Clearly, she doesn't find my smile as charming as most. "Maria, yes. What is it that you need?"

POWER

"My car is not starting," she states flatly.

I look up the stairs, wondering why she's decided to bring this to me and not Rachel, but fuck it. "That's unfortunate. Please take one of mine."

She nods but doesn't move.

"Is there something else?" I stare down at her, her brown eyes flashing as if she's angry with me. If Rachel hadn't thrown a fit about having her, I'd fire her ass. Instead, I plaster on a smile.

"Yes. Ms. Raven... is not like Ms. Rachel." I blink at her. Am I getting a lecture from the help?

"Excuse me?" I raise a brow. There's balls, and there's full-on recklessness. Does she not know who I am? Screw this, I'm gonna fire her ass.

"Oh, Maria, thank goodness I caught you before you go." My fiancée descends the stairs, wearing a tight, navy pin-striped skirt and white blouse. The relief in her face at seeing Maria makes me pause.

"Can you and Raven pick up Jett and my dry cleaning on the way back from the airport, please? I'd send Darcy, but she's doing damage control for one of my clients." She runs her hands through her black bob. Her stilettos echo on the floor.

"Yes, Ms. Rachel." Maria's voice is almost monotone.

I cross my arms, fascinated at this play of events. Rachel Stewart, the badass bitch who came from nowhere, who clawed and fucked her way to the top, creating one of the most successful PR firms in the country, is desperate for Maria's help.

Why?

Maria is not even hiding her disapproval. It's literally oozing out of her.

"You know what?" I start to text. "Why don't I have Iain drive you, Maria?"

Both Rachel and Maria stare at me, mouths agape. "Honey, don't be silly. Maria has a car."

"Apparently not. Seems it's broken. I'll take the Tesla today. Maria, you go get Ms. Stewart's child." I smile, watching Maria. Apparently, she's not impressed by my generous offer if the narrowing of her eyes is any indication.

Interesting.

Rachel reaches for her purse. "I've been telling you for years that car is unsafe, Maria. I'm shocked it's lasted as long as it did," she says and pulls out her sunglasses with a sigh. "Also, I know this is bad timing what with..." She waves in Maria's direction. "But I may have to do a quick trip to New York." She holds up her hand as if to stop any conversation from us.

"Okay, well, I'm off." She nods at Maria. "Jett and I will be home late tonight." She dramatically puts on her sunglasses, then turns and leaves, her overpowering perfume following her.

I look back at the maid, nanny... whatever she is. "How long have you been working for Ms. Stewart?" My eyes take in her face. She's tiny but her frame is strong. Her frown lines make her appear older than she probably is.

"I've been with Ms. Rachel for twenty-five years." She gives me a curt nod. "Where is this Mr. Iain? I don't want to be late for my Raven." She looks at her watch. My mouth twitches at her audacity. She's starting to grow on me. Clearly Rachel is a shit mom, and her kid needs Maria.

"He's waiting outside. I've told him to take you wherever you need to go." I grin again at her. If it's possible for her to frown more, she does.

"Thank you," she mumbles and walks over to one of my original Chippendale tables for her purse.

"Maria?" My voice stops her.

"Yes?" She turns.

"Please put Raven in the guest room that faces the backyard. The view is beautiful." She blinks at me, but nods.

Turning, I move toward the back of the house and grab the key fob for my Tesla.

POWER

For a split second, I wonder what this Raven looks like. Is she tall and reconstructed by plastic surgery like her mother? Christ, Rachel doesn't even have a picture of her daughter anywhere. Isn't that some kind of requirement for a mom? My parents' house is piled with photos of my brother and me.

Whatever, with Rachel as her mother I'm sure she's either a spoiled brat or a scared mouse. Either way, none of it concerns me. The girl is here for the summer; then she'll be back in New York. To be honest, I'll be surprised if I say more than ten words to her while she's here.

My phone vibrates as I start up my Tesla.

"Talk to me, Rebecca." And all thoughts of Rachel and her kid vanish as I start my day. There's a reason I am the best defense attorney in the world, and it's not just because of my personality and looks.

No. I live, breathe, and eat my job. The more demanding and challenging a case is, the harder it makes my cock.

I don't lose.

I don't believe in chance.

And I make my own fucking luck.

I love my life.

two

RAVEN

LAX Airport

"I hate my life," I gripe at Cher, my bestie and the traitor who's leaving me to go to Florence, where she'll spend the entire next month with her family in their incredible château. Drinking wine, sunbathing nude, and—knowing Cher—meeting some hot Italian guy who speaks no English but doesn't need to because his giant cock says it all.

God.

"Take it easy. And stop throwing me the death glare. I'll be back in no time. Besides, you need to deal with Brody." She points at me, then turns to flash the barista at the Starbucks a million-dollar smile.

"Thank you." She takes both the coffees, the guy grins, and I fight the eye roll. I don't want to be a jerk, but... come on, does he really think a girl like Cher would be interested in him?

"Why do you do that?" I demand as I take my coffee, praying my mother has sent Maria, or better yet has forgotten, and I can take an Uber.

"What? Be a pleasant person?" She smiles at me as we walk.

"Um, no. Be a phony and lead guys on." I mimic her smile.

"Wow." She shakes her head, then says, "You need to get fucked, Raven. *Hard.* I don't care if it's Brody or someone else.

POWER

At this point, anyone with a hard dick will do. Get your V-card punched and maybe you can go back to being the best friend I know and love." She wraps her tan arm around my shoulder as if giving me support. Which only bugs me, because she's right. I do need to have sex. It's all I can think about lately.

"You're gonna spill our coffees," I grumble, trying to shake off her arm.

Cher is beyond gorgeous: a cliché California girl. Long blond hair, big brown eyes, and tall, with a body to die for. We've been friends for as long as I can remember. My mom is Cher's father's PR person.

"Look, it's all gonna work out. I'll be back before you know it. And, we can escape back to New York if it's not copacetic at your new daddy's house." She says this looking straight ahead as she bites her lower lip trying not to laugh.

"I'm not participating in this conversation," I snip.

We step out into the mayhem of LAX and I take a deep breath. Besides the slight smell of smoke and exhaust, it feels good to be home, or whatever Los Angeles is to me. I mean, I despise that I miss it, because my mom loves it so much. Hence why I picked New York for college. The farther I'm away from her poison, the better.

"Los Angeles, I love you." Cher dramatically tilts her head back and closes her eyes as a bunch of people maneuver around her. They stare but stay quiet, unlike people in Manhattan, where they'd curse and plow into her.

"Really?" I grab her arm, causing her eyes to pop open and her coffee to spill, and jerk us over to a metal bench so I can get my phone out of my large handbag and figure out a plan.

"Watch my boots," she whines and dramatically pulls out a pack of cigarettes. Cher's decided that she's now a smoker. Whatever, they're her lungs, not mine. I look around at the never-ending lines of cars and the drivers being told to keep circling. For them, it's loading and unloading only.

"Do you think I can be lucky enough that she forgot I'm coming today and I can take a cab?" I wave the smoke out of my face as I power on my phone.

"Nope." Cher snorts and blows smoke up in the air as she points her cigarette to the right. "Isn't that Maria?"

About ten cars down, there's Maria frantically waving me over to a giant black SUV.

I sigh. "Yes, at least it's not Mommie Dearest. I don't think I could stomach the car ride," I deadpan, then glance at Cher, who's smiling.

"What?" I dump my phone in my bag and wave back at Maria. "Wish me luck. Let's pray *Jett Powers* is better than we think."

"Daddy Powers? Oh, he's better than alright." Cher inhales and grins at my stare.

"Please stop calling him that." I roll my eyes.

"You know I'm right. He's fucking hot." She sighs and points her cigarette at me. "Your bitch of a mom is actually lucky I'm going to Florence."

I burst out laughing as I pull her in for a tight hug. As inappropriate as she is, she really is the best.

"You be good." I swallow the lump in my throat. "I'm going to miss you."

"Shuddup. You're going to make me start crying and I need to go to my gate. I'll call you when I land." She pulls back and looks directly at me.

"You be you, Raven. You're kind of my hero, you know?" She pulls me in for another tight hug.

Shaking my head, I reach for my luggage and laugh. "I have no idea why." I sniff. She's only going away for a month. I have zero idea why it feels so monumental. I'm sure it's just everything going on right now. The unknown is never my friend. Smiling, I approach Maria and a man in a black suit.

"Because you're beautiful inside and out," Cher screams after me.

POWER

"You're crazy," I yell back at her, then hug Maria who squeezes me tight.

"Mi amor, let me look at you." She holds me at arm's length. Her warm, caramel-colored eyes sparkle, but her mouth is downturned.

"Oh dear." She sighs, and I have to laugh. Maria is never happy, but I don't even care what's upsetting her. I'll find out later, I'm sure. Right now, I'm just genuinely happy to see her.

"Come on, Maria, no frowning. I promise I'll be good. You have nothing to worry about. Cher is going to Florence." I hug her again. Maria's way more my mother than my biological one.

"I'm not worried about Cher," she grumbles. Taking my luggage, she shoves it at the man in the suit and dark sunglasses.

"Hi, I'm Raven…" I go to hold out my hand, but Maria stops me. I frown. *What the heck?*

The man doesn't seem offended. If anything, his attention is on everyone and everything but me. When I look back to where Cher is standing, she waves and blows me a kiss; then I slide into the back of the vehicle.

Maybe all this dread about coming home is silly. I mean, so my mom is dating Jett Powers, a man nine years younger than her who is supposed to be a genius and is to-die-for hot. Oh, and one other problem… I can't stop fantasizing about him.

I settle into the soft leather seat, wondering if I'll even see him that much.

If all the tabloids are even slightly true, the man is a workaholic who demands that everyone bow to him and do his bidding.

An egotistical asshole. Everything I despise, so why is my stomach doing flips at the mere thought of meeting him?

Because you need to get laid.

Brody better be home from Stanford. Hopefully the debacle of our last visit will be forgotten, and his dick will actually work this time.

I can't think about that—I seriously can't. Brody is wonderful. He had some anxiety issues and that's all. I've waited, saved myself for him, because he's a solid guy, and I love that. He's also someone my mother would never in a million years want.

God, I can't believe that's how I choose a guy these days. The first thing I do when I see a man is think, *Is this someone my mother would want to sleep with?*

If the answer is maybe, I move on.

Sad, pathetic, but true. This is what happens when your mother fucks your high school boyfriend. The one guy you think is the be-all and end-all, only to be slapped awake that he's not.

She never would admit it, but Darren did. In fact, he did more than just tell me. He viciously showed me. She'd been texting him, sending him naked pictures of herself, begging him to stop by her room before he left.

Yeah, all the time I thought I had the perfect boyfriend, he was hanging around to have sex with my mom, by far the most traumatic and humiliatingly painful experience yet.

It still haunts me, his handsome face mocking me when I told him I wanted to wait a little bit longer, that I wasn't ready yet. He laughed, calling me a dried-up, frigid bitch. And not to worry because my mom was more than willing to put out. I remember barely making it to the toilet before I threw up after he showed me the pictures and texts.

That was the day I changed.

I acknowledged the truth that I hated my mother... and that I wasn't having sex until I found a man who was kind and good.

So here I am. Nineteen and still a virgin.

Not only do I have to spend my summer with the very woman I despise, but there's the uncomfortable fact that she is now engaged to Jett Powers.

Yeah, not happy. Not happy at all.

I take a deep breath as my mind goes to the infamous Jett Powers. He's considered a god in the news. I've been tossing around the idea of pursuing environmental or constitutional law. So I've heard his name *a lot*. He's fearless and confident. One of my professors even used the term *legend* to describe him. Whatever, so he's a master at convincing people.

He's still human, with flaws, big ones if he's marrying my mother. I take a deep breath and try to slow down my racing pulse. This has to be nerves and curiosity, nothing more.

I'm making this a way bigger deal, honestly. If I see the man at all, it will be in passing.

I cross my leg and toss my giant bag to the floor. Smirking, I muse that he's probably short, with hair plugs and a flabby gut that his expensive suits have to cover.

Turning, I smile reassuringly at Maria while she puts on her seat belt. Great, she's still frowning, and suddenly I shiver, and it's not because of the air conditioner.

Maria seems worried. That's never a good sign. Fantastic. All the energy I've put into convincing myself that I'm being ridiculous evaporates.

"What's wrong?" I reach for her hand. This dread I'm having is exhausting, and my head is pounding.

"You just stay in your room and study, okay?" Her voice sounds harsh as she squeezes my hand back.

Okay, this is absurd. I'm a grown woman. I refuse to be any more uncomfortable than I already am.

I clear my throat and recross my legs, preparing to tell Maria that it's summertime and I'm not spending two-and-a-half months hiding in a room.

Instead, I squeeze her hand back, smile, and say, "Of course. Trust me, Maria, no one will even know I'm there."

three

JETT

Beverly Hills, CA

"**C**hrist." Although it's scorching hot, I still went for a run. Now I'm trying to catch my breath. After placing my thumb on the scanner to open my gate, I stretch and admire the backyard.

"Hi, Mr. Powers." My head gardener smiles at me.

"Max." I nod.

He motions to the other gardeners to stop working as I pass. Thank fuck, because the noise from those blowers is making my head go from dull ache to full-on pounding.

Cracking my neck as I walk up the steps, I glance around at my huge backyard. Six months ago, I had it completely torn up and made drought efficient. Hired the best landscape architect, who removed almost all the grass. I live in Los Angeles, we're in a drought, and I'm sick of being a drain on the water supply. Now it's covered with desert rocks, succulents, and drought-resistant flowers. I had a huge outdoor kitchen and bar built to the left by my pool, which I decided to leave. I use it, and the tile in it was hand-painted by a famous artist in the 1950s. Hundreds of tiny bistro lights hang over it, and several cabana-style couches complete the look.

POWER

Too bad I'm the only one who sees it. I don't think Rachel has been back here unless it's to sneak a cigarette. I have no idea why she thinks she's hiding that disgusting habit. It's not like I don't have a nose and security cameras.

Yeah, I need to throw a party. What's the point of having an incredible house if you don't show it off?

"Hot out. Right, Mr. Powers?" Max smiles again, adjusting his straw hat over his eyes.

I grin at him. He's probably the same age as me, although the sun has taken a toll on him. Max has worked for me for over ten years. He shows up on time, always seems happy, and loves his family. Last week after my run, he showed me a bunch of pictures on his phone of his granddaughter.

"Should have done laps this morning," I say, running my hand through my hair, which is starting to curl from sweat.

"Yeah." He nods as if that is obvious, and I almost laugh.

My theory was I needed to sweat out the poisons, though that's BS. If my day wasn't packed, I'd have Sam come over and give me an IV full of electrolytes and fluids. But I'm needed in court in two hours, and after that I'm meeting some of my Harvard buddies for dinner.

"You take care, Max. If you need water, you know where it is." I motion with my head toward my pool house.

"Thanks, Mr. Powers. See you next week," he calls out, but I'm already entering through the French doors, tugging up the bottom of my T-shirt to wipe my face and let the air conditioner do its magic. I make my way toward the kitchen. I'll down a few cans of Still water. Not as good as the hangover infusion, but it will have to do.

Fucking Governor Dorsey. He knew as soon as he brought out his private stock of twenty-three-year-old Pappy Van Winkle bourbon I wasn't going to say no. I sat and drank the nectar, then indulged in Cuban cigars, as the politically entitled tried to convince me that my future lies in politics.

It doesn't.

No matter how many times I tell everyone this, they seem to keep hoping. I'm not naïve. They know I have the stomach to fight dirty. And we need that in a candidate. Someone who will go toe-to-toe with the most corrupt. Unfortunately for them, my passion lies in what I already do.

I'm the best defense attorney in the United States, and I love the law. What other occupation lets you argue your idea and win?

I'm a master at making people bow to my words, twisting the truth to get my way. Christ, I just got a Disciple off for triple murder charges. The man was the enforcer, part of the infamous one percent MC. Not only did I get him acquitted, but at the end of the day, the Disciples also looked like heroes.

I fucking love my job.

So I told them until I get a hard-on at the thought of running for office, like I do every time I step into a courtroom, I'll go to my grave as a defense attorney.

"I didn't have time to let you know my schedule. My main focus is Jett and my career now." Rachel's voice goes up a notch, causing me to grit my teeth. I guess along with water, I should take some Advil.

A loud snort and a bored "Thanks, Mom" makes me stop right at the entrance. Christ, the daughter. I forgot about her.

"Oh please, you're fucking nineteen. My job is done. Did you expect me to lie to you?"

"Well, since that's what you usually do..." I can't help but smirk at the sass coming out of the daughter's mouth. Not that I blame her. Fucking snakes make better mothers than Rachel.

"Knock it off, Raven. I will not let you ruin things for me. Now go get dressed. Jett should be back—"

"Ruin things for you?" the daughter interrupts, her voice raspy as if she just woke up and rolled out of bed. And that's when my cock decides it's time to wake up.

Perfect.

POWER

"Look, clearly I cramp your style. So why don't you just buy me the apartment in Manhattan, I'll go back to New York now, and it will be like I was never here."

Again, clever...

I adjust my erection to the other side before I enter, my headache completely forgotten, now replaced with a need to meet my future stepdaughter.

"No. Jett would think it's weird," Rachel snaps.

A flash of dark hair and laughter is all I see and hear as I enter. Rachel's back impedes my view.

"Wait. Let me get this straight. You want me around because *your boyfriend* needs to think you're actually a good mother?"

"He's my fiancé," Rachel corrects her. "And I'm done discussing this. You'll stay the summer. Now, I have to pack and go to New York. I have to hold Courtney's hand. She's reinventing herself. I have her scheduled to do *The Late Show with Stephen Colbert* and *Live with Kelly and Ryan* this week." Rachel moves to the refrigerator.

And fuck me...

Long legs greet me. The girl is leaning her elbows on my island holding a cup of coffee in nothing but a white T-shirt that barely covers her ass. Her long dark hair is swept over to the side allowing me to see her perfect profile.

My eyes travel the length of her. What the fuck? I do not like being surprised and this... Jesus, there's no way *she* came out of Rachel.

The refrigerator shuts with a snap, forcing my eyes to leave our visiting Lolita and focus on Rachel who's pouring creamer into her coffee, her vibe not happy. Not that mine's any better, but it's for completely different reasons. I'm starting to piece together that the reason my fiancée has never talked about her daughter is because she's jealous of her.

Which is beyond screwed up, but then again, Rachel is fucked up...

"Oh, Jett. I was just telling Raven that I have to go to New York for work. Now, don't worry. She has a boyfriend, so I'm assuming she'll stay with him." Her voice makes her sound like she's talking about a kindergartner.

I cock my head, and for a split second I visualize myself beating the shit out of the poor soul who happens to think he can touch my Lolita.

"Oh my God," Raven hisses. Her eyes widen as she bolts straight up. The coffee mug she was holding clinks on the marble, but it's her tits that hold my attention. The white tee she wears clings to them, causing my eyes to narrow as she breathes in and out.

"Pleasure to meet you, Raven." I grin at her as I walk in and hold out my hand, watching her nipples harden as if they know it's only a short amount of time before I bite and suck on them.

She looks down at my extended hand, then straight up into my eyes.

And time stops.

Neither of us blinks as I drown in the deep blue pools of her eyes.

Sapphires.

She needs to have them spilling all over her, running down her tits in a sparkling river of gems.

The fuck am I doing?

She licks her lips, and I'm reminded that we are not the only ones in the room, nor has she taken my hand.

"I'm Jett, but you can call me Mr. Powers."

Her smirk fades and eyes narrow. Now that I stand over her, she's smaller than I originally thought.

"Nice to meet you," she says in a rush, taking a step back as her cheeks pinken. Again, I'm struck at just how stunning she is.

"Raven." Rachel sets down her coffee. "Shake Mr. Powers's hand. What's wrong with you?"

Raven's eyes flash to her mother's, then back to mine. I cock my head and flash her a smile as she purses her lips, then goes to shake my hand. Turning, I walk to the refrigerator saying over my shoulder, "I work all the time, so the house is yours. Just no parties, please."

"I'm not the party girl type. So you have nothing to worry about." Her voice sounds dry, almost bored.

Almost.

But her eyes give her away. That, and she's now biting the bottom fleshy part of her cherry-stained lips. She has this intoxicating aura of innocence and bitch.

It works for her. But at the end of the day, she's off limits, and not only because she's Rachel's daughter, which, let's be honest, should be the main reason. That is, if I was good.

I'm not.

Not even a little. But I don't do drama. And this Lolita staring daggers at me is nothing but trouble.

"Good, then we have nothing to worry about." I walk over to Rachel and kiss her forehead. She smiles up at me and places her hands on my chest.

"I'm sweaty, my love," I state and move away. "Make yourself at home, Raven." I walk out, drinking my water, my eyes doing one more head-to-toe appraisal as I pass.

I'll rub one out in the shower, and all thoughts of Raven will be gone. As soon as I come, I won't even remember that she's going to be living with me *alone,* for days...

Yeah, I won't remember that at all.

Four

RAVEN

What just happened? No, strike that. What *is* happening? I can't stay in this house alone with that man.

He's awful.

Arrogant.

And heart-stoppingly hot. I take a deep breath and slowly release it, yet almost start laughing. Poor Cher. The tabloids don't do him justice. She'd literally freak if she saw his beautiful face. My eyes remain on him as he leaves. Of course, he's tall, with thick, dark hair. God, it even curls slightly around his ears. And his body... The man doesn't have an ounce of fat on him. I mean, his T-shirt was sticking to his six-pack, maybe even an eight-pack...

Too bad he's an asshole, telling me to call him Mr. Powers. I should have said, *Sure, as long as you call me Ms. Stewart.* Why do I always think of great comebacks afterward? I hate that.

Mr. Powers.

Suddenly all I can think of are his full, delicious lips on mine as he picks me up and slams his big dick inside me. Because if he's this perfect in real life, his penis has to be giant-size, too. Right? What is wrong with me? I'm mortified, but my panties are gooey and wet.

"Go put some clothes on." My mother's voice makes me almost scream. How did I forget she was still here?

I swallow and nod at her since I can't look her in the eyes. Jett Powers is her fiancé. Yes, my mother is a terrible person and a bad parent, but she's still my mother. I have to stop lusting after her boyfriend... fiancé. He really might end up being my stepdad.

That's sick. And yet I almost squirm as my pussy throbs. Would he want me to call him Daddy?

Jesus Christ. I need sex, *now.*

Tonight.

Brody has to come over, or I need to go to him. Either way, the job needs to get done.

I clear my voice and finally look up at my mother who's frowning at me. With the amount of Botox she's had injected into her face, that's quite a feat.

"So." I nod at her. "Have a good trip." I turn and almost run. God, talk about awkward and guilty sounding.

"Raven?" Her voice stops me, and I slowly turn.

"Yes?"

"Do you think I'm stupid? I saw you eyeing Jett." I go to open my mouth to deny it, but she holds up a hand, stopping me.

"Stop. You're like a bitch in heat. Let me give you some motherly advice." I almost groan because I can feel this is going to be ugly. Wow, I haven't even been in LA for twelve hours and here we go.

"Just because Mr. Powers was nice to you, it means absolutely nothing. It's his job to make people think he likes them." She walks toward me, and any guilt that I might have had evaporates as I stare at her.

"Do you think I don't know that *every* woman wants him? But I'm the only one he put a ring on." She smirks. "Because *we* belong together." She licks her fat duck lips. "So don't get your hopes up. The only thing Jett Powers likes is a warm willing hole."

"Oh my God." I gape at her, watching her eyes go up and down my body, her lips turning into a sneer.

"I'm the only one who can truly give Jett what he needs."

I blink at her. *What the hell?* I know we're not close, but that was horrific, mortifying. I don't even know what to say. How do you defend yourself against that kind of venom? Thankfully, she saves me and decides to leave, her heels making an annoying clicking sound on the stairs.

"The fuck?" I whisper, rubbing my forehead. I need my phone, but of course, it's charging upstairs in my room. Do I chance another run-in with my mother? Or worse, *Mr. Powers?*

"Screw it." She's even more erratic than before, if that's possible, and I refuse to let this mess with me. I take a deep breath, straighten my shoulders back, and march out of the kitchen.

His house is amazing. Not that I would expect anything less from someone like him, but I am surprised at how eco-conscious it is. His entire backyard looks drought efficient. This morning, I went out on the bedroom's balcony and saw a huge *rain barrel.* Not that Los Angeles gets much rain, but the fact that he cares about our environment enough to have one bugs me. He has to stay a dick in my mind: a man so horrible he invests in corporate greed and gives millions to lobbyists—an energy hog who doesn't believe in global warming.

An entitled asshole.

Grabbing the glossy wooden banister, I dart up the stairs, my bare feet *tap-tap-tapping* on the cold bluestone-paved tile. Not gonna lie. The main room is lovely. Open floor plan, with pale-yellow walls and giant windows, large glass French doors, along with a whitewashed brick wall and an ornate fireplace and mantel.

Either he's an art lover, or he hires someone who is. That's an original Jackson Pollock hanging to the right.

Yeah, this place is sophisticated and eye-catching, but at the same time it feels good, welcome, like you want to grab a cup of coffee or tea and sit down and just be.

POWER

Disarming, like him.

That should be on Jett Powers's tombstone: Here lies a beautiful, dangerous, disarming man. I almost burst out laughing. This has to be my mind blocking out that that my mom is a vile and hurtful person.

Why would she say those things?

"Leave it alone, Raven," I whisper, shaking my head as I swing open the door to my room, then shut it so I can lean against it and catch my breath.

Brody. I need to call Brody. I can't deal with my mom, but Brody *can and will* ease my pain.

At least that's what I'm telling myself right now. This is what I do when my mom traumatizes me. I either act out like a child, or I do the opposite.

Pushing off the door, I move toward my phone and sit on the edge of my bed, trying to catch my breath. Clearly, I'm more freaked out than I want to admit. And I'm not sure it's my mom's words that are entirely causing it.

My eyes drift around the room. It's lovely, with light teal walls and ornate windows. French doors lead out to a nice-sized balcony overlooking his massive property. This room is more elegant and luxurious than the rest of the house.

I reach over and snatch my phone off the charger and press on Brody's picture.

"Pick up, Brody," I snap, my mind replaying the way Jett's veiny forearms made my tongue tingle as he held out his hand for me to shake it. All I could think of was licking them...

"Hello? Raven? Can you hear me now?" I bolt up at Brody's voice. *Shit, what am I doing?*

"Tell me you're home?" I demand.

He laughs. "It makes me happy to know you missed me." His kind, mellow voice used to make me relax. Today, though, the opposite is happening.

"Are you here?" I snap.

"Um... yes, I got in this morning—"

"Good, when am I seeing you?" I don't care if I sound needy. It's Brody, and *I am* fucking needy. I'm sick of fantasizing about a man I should never ever think about.

"I need to have lunch with my parents. Can I pick you up tonight?"

My eyes dart around the room and I wonder what time it is. "I guess." I sigh, then silence. "Brody?"

"Yeah, I'm here. Are you okay?"

"I'm fine," I snap. He's getting that nervous voice, which I really can't deal with.

"Raven, I don't know what's going on with you, but I have to go to lunch with my parents. My grandmother is coming."

I look down at my nails and almost want to scream, *At least you have a grandmother and parents who want to take you to lunch!*

So much for not having issues. Whatever, he needs to get over here and pick me up and fuck me against the wall, pound into me hard. Actually, the wall might be uncomfortable for the first time...

"My mom is out of town, so I have the house to myself. I'll text you the address. Plan on spending the night, okay?"

Silence again. "Brody?"

He clears his throat. "Yeah, that sounds great. I don't know about staying the night. I mean, I live in Manhattan Beach, so it might be easier with traffic if I leave after dinner."

I close my eyes, trying not to snap again and make him nervous. He's starting to sound scared and unsure.

"Brody?" My voice cracks.

"Yeah?"

"Do you want to see me?"

"Yes, I can't wait to see you. Please believe me." His words sound fine, but the tone sounds unsure, and to be honest, I don't know how to help him.

Nodding, I walk to the window and look down.

POWER

Perfect. Just fantastic, it's my mom talking to Jett. I lean closer. She looks angry as her skinny arms fly animatedly in the air.

That same guy in the suit from yesterday who picked me up from the airport is putting her bags in the trunk.

Jett laughs, then grabs the back of her neck, bringing her in for a kiss. I must let out some sort of noise because Brody's voice makes me jump.

"Raven? What's going on with you?" he demands, but I can't turn away while watching my mom cling to Jett. That's when it dawns on me: she loves him.

Or at least *believes* she loves him.

My hand reaches out to touch the cool glass on the window, wanting to feel him if only for a second...

"Brody? Are you coming tonight?" My voice sounds almost robotic as I watch my mother get into the car, and the man in the suit shut the door and walk around to the driver's seat.

"I'll try to be there around six. And, Raven?"

I drop my hand and watch Jett back up as the car pulls away.

"Yeah?"

"I love you," he says. Two days ago, I would have told him I loved him back. Two days ago, that was true.

But I'm not my mother. I don't lie. Instead, I say, "I need you." My voice shakes a little because I'm not sure my words are for Brody or the dark-haired man from below. As if he knows I'm watching him, he turns and looks up at me.

My heart stops, then starts to race as he robs the very breath from me. What the hell? I need to move, but I stay exactly where I am.

This time Jett Powers is not grinning. If anything, the look in his eyes makes me shiver and goose bumps appear on my arms.

Prey. He looks at me like I'm his.

"Oh my God," I whisper.

"*What?* You're scaring me, Raven." Brody. Sweet Brody, having absolutely no idea what's happening to me. I swallow and take a steadying breath while I stare down at the man I need to stay away from.

He's not good. But, then again, maybe I'm not good either. It's almost as if I can feel him, like he's calling to me.

Wow. I'm losing it. Maybe I should ask Brody if I can stay with him? That's what I'll do. After we finally have sex, I'll ask him to get us a hotel room for a couple of days. He's loaded. His dad is a TV executive, for God's sake.

"Raven? Talk to me." His voice is shaky, and he sounds scared.

"Sorry, I'm fine. I'll see you tonight." I lower the phone and continue staring down at him.

Look away, Raven. Look away. My heart is pounding so fast I can feel it in my temples. But it's not me who breaks our stare; it's him. He turns, his gray suit accenting his broad shoulders, and walks away from my view.

I don't move, just keep looking out the window as I try to rationalize it all.

Because I'm in crisis mode right now, and if I'm not careful, I'll go over. I breathe deeply and take a step back. Exhaling, I lift my phone again.

Cher.

I'll call her, tell her everything. Confess all my sordid thoughts, get them out so they're free and then they can't hurt me.

But I don't.

For as long as I live, I'll never understand why I toss my phone on the bed and walk into the bathroom pulling my T-shirt off.

Maybe it's because he's forbidden and that excites me.

Or maybe it's because everything about this is wrong and dangerous, and for some reason, I like that.

Yeah, I'm not calling Cher.

I'm not calling or confessing anything.

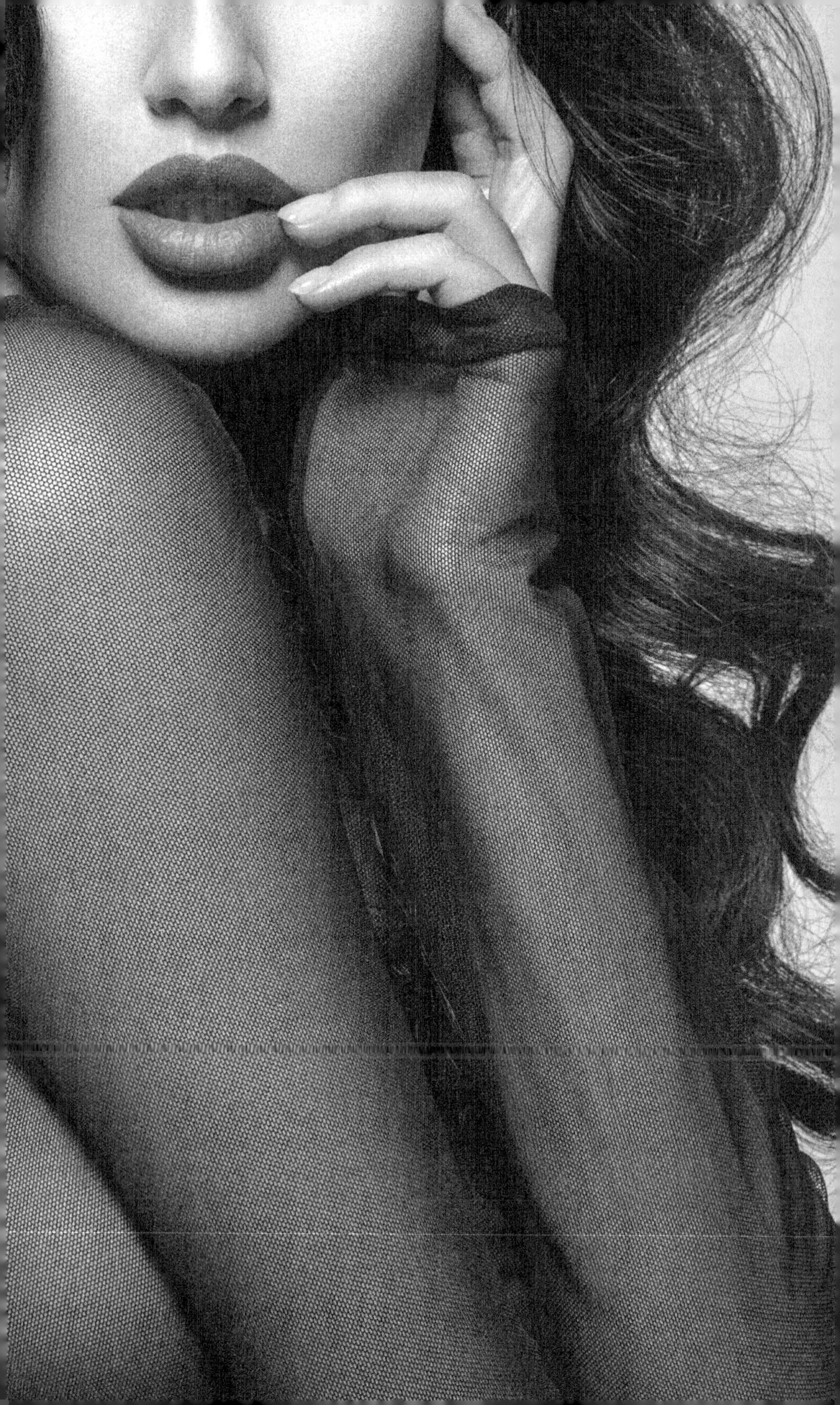

Five

RAVEN

I'm pacing in my new Chanel ankle boots, an impulse buy right before I left New York. I know you're technically not supposed to wear boots in the summer, but these are white leather with a jeweled C and circles, and I need to look fantastic tonight.

I look at my phone. Seven p.m. "Where is he?" I've literally spent the day getting ready for this. I feel like a bride in the 1700s waiting for my new husband to deflower me.

Ridiculous.

I sit down on the edge of the long white couch, then jump up as I hear the beep alerting me that someone is at the gate.

"Finally. Okay, calm, you're calm," I tell myself, then look around the room for cameras. Thankfully, I don't see any. That would be the icing on the cake since I've been pacing and pretty much acting like a crazy person for hours.

I push on the button. "Yes?"

"It's me. I'm sorry, traffic was bad, and I got los—" I beep him in, cutting him off, not caring for his stupid excuses as to why he's an hour late.

God, if this doesn't go well, I'm done. "I'll let him in," I call out to some guy named Larry. I'm still meeting everyone. It's not like Jett has a huge number of people in his house, but I am starting to see a few familiar faces.

POWER

"Mr. Powers knows this man is coming?" Larry looks at me like he knows he doesn't, but is covering his ass by asking.

"Yes, he's my boyfriend." I smile at him.

He rolls his eyes but nods and walks toward the area of the house I haven't seen yet. I smooth my dark blue slip dress and open the huge door.

Brody bounds up the stairs holding a bouquet of flowers in his hand and a bottle of wine under his arm.

He's about six feet and has always been on the thin side, and if it's possible, he looks like he's lost weight. For a guy who grew up on the beach, his pale skin just screams vitamin D deficient.

"Raven. You look so beautiful." I go to take the flowers, trying hard not to be disappointed. So he doesn't have Jett's striking looks or body. Brody is a good man, though. He's on track to become an architect.

"Aww, thank you." I go to hug him, then realize I'm acting like his friend, so I get on my tiptoes to touch his lips. He looks a little surprised. I guess he thought I was just going to hug him.

"I missed you." I smile again, pushing all thoughts of anyone but him to the back of my mind as I take his hand and drag him inside.

"Wow. So this is the famed Jett Powers's house. How is he?" He looks around, then down at me.

"He's a dick. But perfect for my mom. She's a bitch, so..."

"Raven." His brown eyes widen. "You don't mean that." I stop walking and turn to look at him.

"I do. Is that a problem?" He stares at me then shrugs, staying quiet, and I almost start laughing. What was I thinking? Whatever. He's going to take my virginity, and then if he doesn't like that I can't stand my family, he can leave.

"Come on, I'll show you the kitchen. Are you hungry?" I head in that direction only to have him move forward and grab my hand.

"I'm sorry. I'm nervous." He smiles, and I almost sigh in relief, because he does have a nice smile.

"I'm nervous too." I wrap my arms around his neck, but he clears his throat and backs away, holding the wine.

"I took this from my dad's private stock. It's amazing." He grins, and for a moment warning bells go off. Is he fucking gay? I'm not an arrogant person, but I know I look amazing, and he's more worried about the wine than my tits, which, I'm sorry, are fucking perfect.

Full, not too big, with big nipples, come on...

"Sure. Wine sounds perfect." I take the bottle, not waiting to see if he follows me. Memories of the last time we were together make me falter. He did get hard, but then he'd lose it. Yeah, he's not gay; he's just a little timid.

I reach for the electric wine opener as he saunters in and looks out the windows.

"I'm starving. You want to order some food?" My voice gets louder as the hum of the opener quickly opens the bottle.

"Nah, I ate earlier. I'm vegan now, did I tell you that?" My hand freezes and I look over at him.

No wonder he looks so pale and gaunt. The man needs a steak, something bloody to get the color back in his skin.

"Um, no. Last I heard, you were a vegetarian." Turning the wine opener back on to finish, it dawns on me how uncomfortable this is. I know we haven't talked as much since we both were slammed studying for finals. But we still talked. You would think he would tell me this. It's kind of a big thing. It would be for me. But I love food, including meat.

He turns and looks at me, then at the wine. "Yeah, the health advantages of being vegan just seemed right. I mean, I really want..." And I tune him out as I look around for some wineglasses. Brody is passionate about animals. Hence, I understood the vegetarian thing, but vegan... that's a whole 'nother level. I know it's trendy, and I've tried vegan restaurants several times. It always gives me horrible acid reflux, and I have bloat for days.

"I can't find wineglasses, so these will have to do." I talk over his preaching. He looks a little startled, but nods at the two glasses I hold in my hand.

"As long as you feel good," I say lamely because he has his hands in his pockets looking like a kid who's just been scolded. For fuck's sake, he's two years older than me. Why does he seem so immature all of a sudden?

I take a deep breath and pour us both a lot of wine. Assuming we're not going out to eat, we might as well have sex. Then, if it's as bad as I suspect it might very well be, I'll break up with him. We can still stay friends, because that's what we really are anyway. Or, if the way he's looking at me as I approach is any indication, he might break up with me. I can't help but grin. *He* is going to break up with *me*.

Oh, where is Cher when I need her? I should have listened to her. She warned me this isn't typical, in quotes, "Straight guy behavior."

Still, he's so sweet and smart, and not that he was ever buff, but at least he looked healthy last time I saw him. Now he looks like he might fall over if a gust of wind blows on him.

"Here." I hand him the wine and completely invade his space because I saved myself for him, and I'm going to get drunk and get this albatross of my virginity off my neck.

"Thanks." He grins, and my heart picks up. He does have a nice smile: straight, white teeth and full lips.

"To tonight," I say brazenly and don't wait for him. I just clink my glass with his and start chugging.

Brody watches, but must sense that I'm not backing down, so he also starts to drink. Thank God his dad has good taste in wine. This is a delicious Bordeaux. It's like a thick mouthful of flavor. I think I taste oak, maybe chocolate or berries. All I know is it went down way too easy, my head already feels better, and Brody's skin is starting to have some color.

"Shall we sit?" I smile and lick my sweet-tasting lips.

He nods. His eyes dip to my breasts, and I almost scream to the ceiling, *Thank you, God.*

I don't. Instead, I take his hand, he grabs the bottle of wine as we pass the island, and we walk out into the main room that's now pretty much dark.

Little glittering lights from outside spill in. Otherwise, we're all alone in our own cocoon of dark red wine and us.

I set my glass down and reach to take the bottle from him. He quickly drinks the rest of his wine, then grabs me and shoves his tongue down my throat.

I almost gag, but I'm so happy he's taking the initiative that I moan and pull back enough so our tongues are twisting together, rather than having his be like a swab that tests you for strep throat.

His hands move to my ass, and he pulls me closer. We're both thin, though, and I twist slightly so our hip bones aren't touching. *Screw it, might as well get this going.* I slide my hand to cup his dick and start to rub. Again, I almost say a prayer of gratitude to the big man, and I'm not religious, but Brody Moore is definitely hard.

And all I can think of is it's finally happening. I'm going to get laid. It might not be fantastic, but what first time is? And it's with Brody. He's gonna be gentle and sweet, which I assume will mean less pain. To be honest, I simply don't want to be a forty-year-old virgin, and at the rate I'm going, I can see it happening.

"Raven?" My eyes pop open and I stare up at Brody. Shit, how long have I been drifting, not responding?

"Yeah?" I moan.

"Can I... can I go down on... you?" His voice trails off, and I decide right now that I hate when guys ask. My next boyfriend will not be an asker, that's for sure.

"Yeah." Trying to sound sexy, confident, I reach for the bottle and pour us some more wine. He takes his and downs it like a shot, then smiles.

POWER

I smile and follow. In the back of my head, I can't help but think we're kind of pathetic. I'm nineteen and he's twenty-one, and we need a bottle of wine to give us enough courage.

I shake my head, mostly to clear those thoughts, but also to entice him as I pull down one strap of my slip dress, then the other, letting it shimmy down to my boots.

Then I stand, waiting for him to touch me. He doesn't. In fact, he stares, so I step out of the dress, dramatically kick it aside, and drop down onto the white couch, absently wondering if we should go upstairs. I mean, this couch is really white. What if I bleed? But the comforter and sheets on my bed are also white... *Jesus, Raven, focus.* He's still standing there.

"Brody..." Again, I moan. That seems to be working, so why change it up? He nods and nervously rubs his hands up and down his jeans.

Is he sweating? Thank God it's dark. "Everything okay?" I say, still using the sexy voice.

"You're so pretty." He drops to his knees, and again, it shouldn't bug me, because I'm grateful and all, but can't he say beautiful? Stunning? *Pretty* might as well be *cute*.

"Oh God." Then I bite my lip because that was not my sexy voice. That was a real, *Oh God*, because his hands, which are touching me, trying to pull my tiny G-string down, are definitely moist. I arch up to help him, but of course the string gets caught on one boot.

"Stop." I take a breath and sit up, then gentle my voice. Even in the dark I can see the panic on his face. "Let me help." I almost take my boots off, but with this tiny slip of fabric, it's so easy to kick them off and toss them in the corner. I do that and lie back again.

Slowly, he inches forward. Looking up at the ceiling, I wonder if now is the time to close my eyes and think about *him*. His dark head with thick hair would make me want to run my hands through it. I arch a little since I can feel his breath on my clit, and for the first time I really do moan. And then my eyes pop open.

What the fuck is he doing? Or better yet, what is he not doing? He's literally slobbering on my crotch and avoiding the most important spot.

Do I tell him to suck on my clit? What do I do?

"Does that feel good? Do you like it?" He looks up at me, a big smile on his face, like he just received an award at doing a job well done.

Wait, does he think I'm done? I swallow, then moan again and arch like a cat. This time I really do wrap my hands in his hair and shove his face back down. He gasps but tries again. It's wet, from him, sloppy, and all around bad.

I can't. I have to tell him. I go to open my mouth, but a voice stops me. My body freezes because, *no!*

Not him.

He can't possibly have seen this.

"I don't know who the fuck you are, but get your pathetic face out of Raven's cunt."

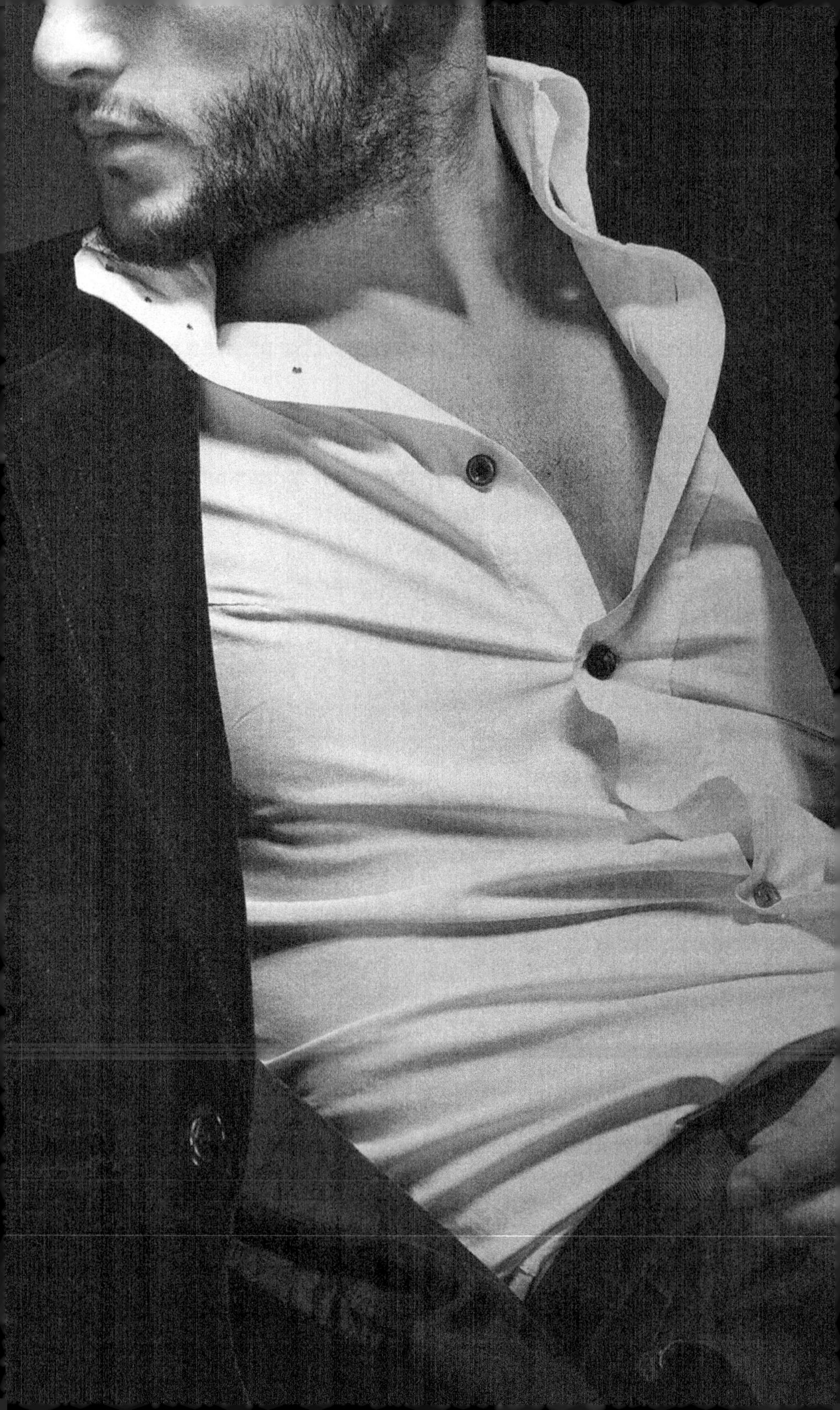

Six

JETT

I shut the door to my Tesla and look out at the BMW parked in my front driveway.

"Who the fuck is this?" Pulling my phone from my suit pocket, I check my messages. I've just finished having dinner with a few friends. They wanted to continue, but after last night, and the fact that Raven is home alone, I decided to pass.

I scroll through the two from Emily wanting to know if she should stop by. I saw those at the restaurant. I'm looking for one from my assistant Larry. He basically runs my personal schedules and keeps an eye on the house. And here it is:

Larry: The daughter's boyfriend is here.

The fuck? How am I just seeing this text? I look up at my house. No lights are on. Maybe they left, although his car is here.

Christ, if I have to deal with some punk wandering around my house freeloading off Raven... I turn my handle and the door opens.

Perfect, I'm gonna kill Larry. What's he thinking leaving the door unlocked? It doesn't matter that I have cameras and massive security; this is a fuckup, and he'd better have a good explanation.

"Does that feel good? Do you like it?" I stop as I set my phone and key fob down, adrenaline shooting through me so fast the hairs on the back of my neck prickle. I walk straight through the kitchen and stop.

There she is.

My fucking Lolita.

Naked, on my couch, legs spread open with some skinny fuck's head between her legs. For a moment, I feel as though I'm in a tunnel, and all I see are her full tits and his head, trying to eat what is clearly not his.

I take a breath, deciding whether to rip his head off her by force, or with my words. I choose words. The last thing I need is a scandal.

"I don't know who the fuck you are, but get your pathetic face out of Raven's cunt."

Raven bolts up, and the boyfriend stumbles to his feet.

"I... Oh God. I... was just—"

I take off my jacket, tossing it on the chair as I command, "Lights on." The room floods with light as I unbutton my bottom sleeve, and Raven tries to cover her full tits.

"Jett... I mean, Mr. Powers." Her eyes are giant balls of deep blue; her lips are red yet not swollen from having a cock in her mouth.

"If you want to live"—my eyes lock with hers as I spit out orders to her pale-faced boyfriend—"I'd get the fuck out of here."

"Yes, sir. I'm sorry." I don't watch him run out of the room. The sound of the door slamming is enough. Jerking my tie off, I sink to my knees and grab her ankle boot.

When I jerk her cunt forward, she gasps. I'm beyond thinking. Consequences don't apply right now.

My cock wants her, and I have no intention of denying myself.

"You don't come unless you ask," I hiss, then latch onto her swollen pink nub and suck. Her fucking pussy tastes like mangoes, sweet as sugar. She moans loudly, and I reach down to unbuckle my belt.

"Oh my God." Small gasps come from her mouth as her hands and nails dig into my couch, and I spread her legs wider.

"Mr. Powers... I, need to, I'm going to..." My cock jumps at her calling me Mr. Powers. I like it *a lot*. I keep sucking on her clit, sensing when she starts to pulse and becomes wetter. Still, I need to see her beautiful face as I make her climax.

I lift my head and look down at her. Her breasts are flushed, her cheeks are pink, and her pretty pink pussy is glistening.

"That's it." Using my thumb, I rub her slickness back and forth so I can watch her come undone.

"You come for me, my pretty baby." And she does. Screaming my name, she lets go, head thrown back, nipples hard and red. Her body jerks, her core pulses, and I watch it all.

"I... holy fuck." She flops back as if she's too drained to move.

Smiling, I stand and unbutton my slacks and free my large, aching cock.

"I..." Her eyes widen at my erection, which is already leaking. Christ, I'm glad she's ready for me because I have no intention of waiting. I drop down onto the couch next to her and lift her up to straddle me. She grips the back of the couch.

"We can take our time later. I need to be inside you." And I'm not lying. It's as if I've been possessed by the way her pussy tasted, how pink and wet she is, how her eyes look at mine as if this need, this hunger that's ravaging me is the same for her.

"Fuck me," I say and grab both her hips, slamming her wet cunt down onto my cock. In one moment, the universe changes. Her tight, slick core envelops me, and I feel everything, including that barrier I broke through without even knowing. But I don't care that she's probably in pain. This is a pleasure that knows no bounds.

"Fuck." I close my eyes and let her adjust to me.

"Talk to me," I murmur, trying my best not to lift her up and slam her down on me again. But I'm losing the battle. Her cunt feels way too good.

"Thank you." She smiles down at me as I grab the back of her neck, bringing her lips close to mine.

"You should have said something, not that it would have mattered." I slap her ass and she gasps, and I take her lips roughly.

I've kissed probably hundreds of women. They all taste good, they all have a unique smell... but this one.

This Lolita is going to be my downfall because she tastes like a nectar I was born to drink, and has a cunt she's saved only for my cock. Our tongues twist and I deepen the kiss while I prompt her to rub her clit on me.

"Oh God," she whimpers and bites her bottom lip.

"Jesus Christ. You're so tight, so fucking tight. You feel so good. You like having Mr. Powers's cock inside you?" I pick up speed, digging my hands into her hips as I guide her, teach her how to fuck.

"Yes, I love having Mr. Powers's cock inside me." She growls most of it, but as soon as she says *Mr. Powers*, I let go. My stomach muscles tighten, and with one last hard thrust, I'm fucking gone, exploding into her warmth as my cock jerks my milk into her.

Staying deep inside her, I let us both catch our breaths and come back to earth and try to ignore that I not only just fucked my fiancée's daughter, I took her virginity.

Hmm, not quite sure how I'm going to deal with this. I lift her up and ease her off me. We both groan at the loss. Well, I moan, and she hisses.

"You okay?" I stand with her and jerk my slacks up, zipping up but not bothering with buttoning. I take her hand. She seems a little stunned.

"Hey." I force her to make eye contact.

"I'm fine." She nods, then looks around, I'm assuming for her dress. But I like her naked.

"Come on." I lace my hand with hers. "Let's take a shower and sleep."

"But my dress." She tries to break free to get it, then stops and stares down at the couch.

"I... *oh my God.*" I look at where she stares, her face pale as if she's just seen a murder.

"I'll have it replaced." I smirk. Not gonna lie—seeing that giant wet cum stain and her blood is a huge turn-on. I feel like a king who just conquered a country and now gets to enjoy the treasures of my pillaging.

"Wait, we... I... just slept with my mother's fiancé." She whispers the *slept* part and covers her mouth, and I can't help it. I let out a laugh.

"Oh, Raven." I pull her into my arms and whisper into her ear, "You fucked your mother's fiancé *hard*. Such a naughty girl you are. Tomorrow I'll see about punishing you." She shivers, and my cock hardens again at the thought of training her to do what I like.

"But my mom..."

"Rachel won't find out." I pull her up the stairs with me, and into the very bedroom that I share with her mom.

"This is... bad, right?" She stands, looking like a fucking goddess, naked with only her boots. I start to unbutton my shirt. I don't need to reassure her this shouldn't have happened.

It shouldn't have, but as soon as I saw her, I knew I was gonna fuck her. I didn't know she'd be, without a doubt, the fuck of the century.

That's probably not good. Well, hopefully I can get enough of her delightful body while Rachel is gone. Worst case, we can always sneak.

I toss my shirt in the hamper while Raven just stares as if she's fighting a battle. That is noble, but pointless.

Kicking off my shoes, I strip off my slacks and grab my hard cock, stroking it.

"Come here, Raven," I command.

She jumps and licks her lips, but moves toward me right when my cell phone starts ringing. We both look at my slacks, which I've just discarded.

"Get my phone." My eyes trail up her body and stop at the dried blood on her thighs. She shakes her head no, as if she knows it's her mother.

"The phone, now," I remind her.

Slowly she reaches for it, sighing when it stops ringing, her eyes looking at the screen as she hands it to me.

"Thank you." I smile at her. She gazes at me, then at my hand, which is picking up speed as I jack myself off.

"Kneel," I order. The phone starts ringing again.

"I can't." She swallows and tries to leave, but I grab her arm.

"Raven. You're gonna obey. Now take my cock in your mouth. I need to talk to your mother."

Her eyes grow huge, but her nipples are rock hard. She hesitates, and the phone stops ringing again.

She walks toward me. "You can't be serious."

"Open your legs."

"Why?" She groans as I approach her and waits, then opens her legs. My fingers slide right into her.

"That's why. It feels good, doesn't it?" I slide my two fingers in and out of her while pushing on Rachel's number.

"I've been trying to get ahold of you," she grumbles.

"Hold on, my love. Let me put you on speaker."

Raven gasps, but her pussy gets wetter. Smirking, I remove my fingers and she moans. I cock my head and push the speaker.

"How's New York?" When I push her head down, she drops to her knees and I shove my cock in her mouth, closing my eyes at how good it feels. In an instant, she starts to gag.

"Tiring. I've been pumping Courtney up all day. She's super nervous about changing her look. I'm going to charge her double since I'm holding her hand through all of this."

Rachel continues to talk, but I'm done listening. I toss the phone on the bed so both my hands can better guide Raven's head. Smiling, I caress her cheek with one hand while wrapping the other around the base of her hair. She tries her hardest to stay quiet while she takes my giant cock.

"Fuck." I gasp for breath. As twisted as this is, my cock has never been harder. What is it about this one? From the second I laid eyes on her...

"Exactly. Fuck is right. I mean, musicians are so insecure. She's a giant star."

Raven's eyes dart up to mine at her mother's bitchy voice. Have to hand it to Rachel—she truly believes the world revolves around her.

I grin, pulling Raven's hair back as she pops off me, saliva dripping down her mouth, and I almost growl like a caveman at how fucked up I am. This is hot, and I have zero intention of stopping.

"Suck," I demand, grinning at her small gasp as my thumb rubs back and forth on her full, pouty lips and dips in and out of her mouth.

"It really does suck. And, oh my God, I ran into Gigi. I almost didn't recognize her. She's gained probably thirty pounds. I was embarrassed being seen with her." Rachel continues to badmouth a friend, spewing ugliness.

Tilting my head, I stare down at Raven, wondering if she's like her mother. Not that I care. I'm satisfying a craving, and I guess helping her out. Who stays a virgin at *nineteen*? My hand tightens on her hair, and I jerk her head back, looking into her sapphire eyes as if I can find answers. They swim with desire and something else, but I'm not the one who should figure that out.

Despite how much of a bitch Rachel is, I am going to marry her. "Breathe through your nose." I smirk as I remove my thumb and replace it with my cock.

And I forget everything else. No more listening to Rachel tell me she is breathing. All I want is to watch Raven suck and try to take my giant cock as far as she can.

She gags, but her blue eyes stay locked with mine. Back and forth, I guide her head as my balls, slick with her saliva, tighten.

"Fuck, that's it." She sucks harder and it feels so good, so right, that I don't try to hold back. I shove her head onto my pulsing cock as it hits the back of her throat.

"Jesus Christ." I hold her head tight and fucking come, my cock jerking till I feel the pleasure all the way to my toes.

I let up enough to watch her swallow my cum. She keeps sucking on me like I'm a Popsicle on a hot day, licking the tip as she takes every drop.

Then she stands and smiles as if she's proud, and she should be. She's made me forget everything but her, a feat that I can't remember ever happening.

"Jett? Are you there?" My eyes stay on hers, but I walk to the bed and grab my cell.

"I need to take a shower. Talk tomorrow." Hanging up, I look back at my Lolita. She doesn't move, just stands naked in her fucking Chanel boots, my cum on her chin and breasts. Never have I seen anything more magnificent.

With a smile, I walk toward her, vaguely realizing that Rachel's annoying floral scent is gone, replaced by Raven's scent.

Orange blossoms and coconut? Whatever it is, I want to bury my nose in her neck and inhale.

As I step closer to her, fuck, she looks almost feral, with the evidence of me being her first on her thighs.

When I take her hand, she blinks up at me, and that jolt of energy almost makes me tell her to leave my room.

Because I should be satisfied.

Done.

I came. This is when I lose interest.

Instead, I walk us into my shower, push her against the glass wall, the water spilling down on us, and lower myself to eat her cunt.

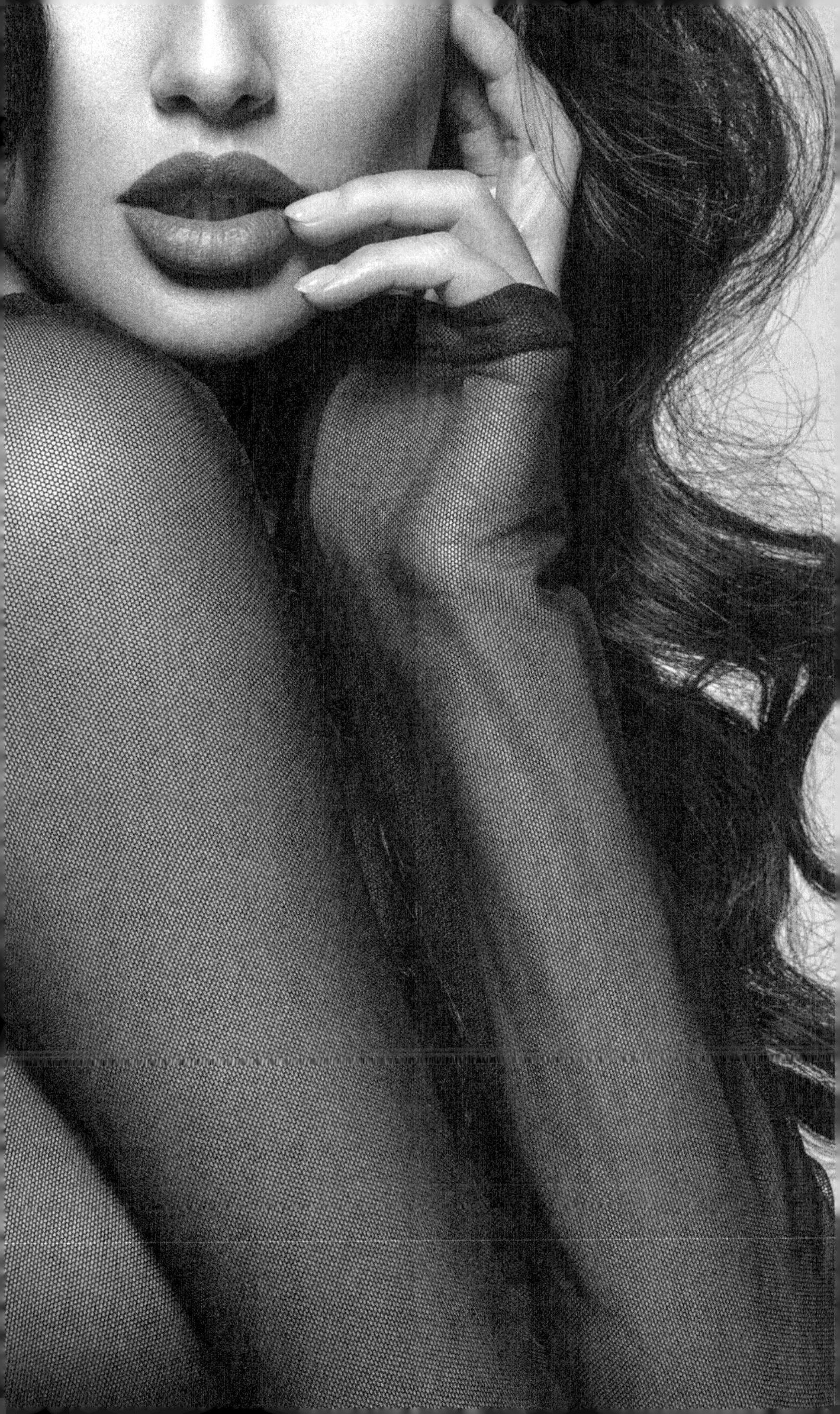

Seven

RAVEN

My eyes blink open, and for a moment, it takes me a second to figure out where I am: it's morning, not my apartment...

"Holy shit." I bolt up, bringing the silk sheet with me as I look around for him. I'm alone, and every single filthy thing we did last night comes flooding back to me. I almost pull the sheet over my head.

"Pull yourself together." I bite my lip, listening to make sure I don't hear him before I get out of the bed.

Their bed.

Oh my God. I had sex, numerous times last night, in my mom and Jett Powers's bed. I kick off the sheet and my leg muscles almost scream in protest when I try to stand.

"Okay," I whisper, sitting back down on the edge, trying to think. Jesus, this was not what I had planned. It was supposed to be Brody, not my mother's fiancé!

"*Brody.*" I stand again and almost trip over the bottom of the comforter on the floor. "Shit." I look around, trying to find my dress, but all I see is a massive room with lots of windows allowing you to see the view from three different spots.

My cheeks heat up and I sigh, trying not to replay last night and this morning. *Oh God.*

Nasty.

POWER

Filthy.

And scarily addictive. I might be a terrible person, but I'm not going to lie to myself. Last night will go down as the best night of my life.

But it's morning, and I must call Brody and break it off officially with him. And, as far as my mom goes, I have no guilt.

I thought I might, but nope, *none*. I almost start laughing. A bitch like her does not deserve my guilt, nor my remorse, for that matter.

Now Brody... Sighing, I grab Jett's suit jacket, which is draped over a large leather chair, and slip into it. It dwarfs me, literally hangs on me longer than most of my dresses.

I wrap it tight around me, because it smells like him. Fresh and clean, with a touch of mint? Maybe the ocean breeze? I don't know. Whatever it is, I love it. I need to use the bathroom, but I should get out of this bedroom. The last thing I need is poor Maria catching me in here naked, with nothing on but Jett's suit jacket.

I move toward the large door, as I peer out purposely ignoring the picture on the wall of my mom and Jett kissing.

Nothing. I see nothing. I do hear activity, but it's downstairs, so I run straight to my room and slam the door.

Since I didn't sleep here, everything is exactly like I left it. Again, I sigh and step into the bathroom. My phone starts to ring, and I freeze.

"Shit, it's Brody," I say, not caring that I'm talking to myself. First things first, I need to pee, then brush my teeth.

I'd love a cup of coffee, and wonder if I can slip downstairs and get one before I try to somehow break it off with Brody and keep him as a friend. I'm just washing my hands when my phone starts up again.

"Screw it, let's get it over with." Running, I grab my phone from the dresser. "Hello?" I cringe at how guilty I sound.

"My cock has been hard all morning, thinking about you in my bed." The deep, gravelly voice makes me puff out air. I try to steady my breathing because I sound like I'm panting. Wait, am I panting?

"I'm up." And then I close my eyes at what an idiot I am when I hear Jett start to laugh.

"No, baby, I'm up. And uncomfortable as fuck. I'm going into court soon, but I'm sending Iain with some packages for you. I need you to be ready for him to bring you to me at three p.m., Raven."

I nod, because I can't breathe.

"Raven, words. Use them."

"Yes, I can be ready." My voice sounds breathy, and this time I'm not even trying. My head is spinning, and my body is almost achy with need.

"My name, *say it,*" he demands, and I can feel the thick, erotic intensity through the wire. I squirm as my sensitive pussy gets wet and slick.

"Yes, Mr. Powers. I'll be ready for you." Licking my lips, I bring a hand to my neck and touch my cheeks. They're burning as if I have a fever.

"Good girl," he growls, and goose bumps appear on my arms and legs.

"I have a full staff. They are there for anything you want. I pay them a lot of money to make sure I'm happy. And that now includes you."

My heart skips a beat at his words.

"Thank you." I bite my lower lip hard. This is crazy. *Am I starting to like him?* Of course, I like him. He's gorgeous, experienced, and can make you come so hard you can barely walk.

"Talk to me. I can tell you want to say something." Great, now add he's a mind reader?

"I just..." Looking up at the ceiling, I continue, "Do you feel bad that last night happened? You know, since you might be marrying my mom?"

I can almost see him grinning. "No. Your pussy was the tightest I've ever had. Any other questions?"

Again, my stomach flips and dips. Not exactly the answer I was expecting, but since I don't know him that well, I'll take it.

"Raven, I need to go. If you have something else you want to tell me, now's your chance." His meaning is clear: *this is it.* I need to tell him if I want this to continue or not.

Am I really okay with this? I mean, he's probably going to be my stepdad. To be honest, this feeling I'm having about him is probably nothing more than a big fuck-you to my mother. So screw it—you only live once. And Mr. Jett Powers has a giant cock, a magical tongue, and muscular, porn-star arms.

"Raven?" His demanding voice makes my nipples instantly harden.

With a deep breath, I take the plunge.

"No. I'm perfect, Mr. Powers," I respond, straightening my shoulders. Good thing I don't believe in hell. Clearly, I'm a sinner.

"Good. I'll see you soon." The line goes dead, and my legs almost give out.

"Ms. Raven?" My eyes dart to my door.

"Yes?" I call out. If it's Maria, she cannot come in. She'll freak if she sees me in his suit jacket.

"Hi, it's Patty. Mr. Powers wanted me to bring you coffee and some breakfast," the voice yells through the door. I hesitate. What if Maria is with her? *Stop it, you're being paranoid.* If Maria was here, she'd already have come in.

"Just a second." I look around the room, trying to calm myself. No one knows anything. I'm sure Patty is just thinking Jett is being nice to me because I'm Rachel's daughter.

"Hi." I peek out to see a tall woman holding a large tray loaded with food and a silver coffee pot.

"Oh, thank you." I look down at myself and sigh. Whatever, so she sees me in his suit jacket. When I open the door fully, she smiles at me. If she notices, she doesn't show it. Just marches in, goes straight to the balcony door, and sets the tray down.

"Let me know if you need anything else." She nods and smiles.

I like her. She has kind eyes.

"Thank you. This looks amazing." I go to show her out, but she holds up her hand, stopping me and quietly, closes the door behind her.

"Good God." I groan. *What the hell am I doing?* I take a deep breath and sit down, pouring myself some coffee as I think.

The goal was to lose my virginity.

Check.

And then some. Again, I groan and almost cover my face, remembering Jett walking in on Brody going down on me last night... the look in his eyes as he rolled up his sleeves. I thought I would die of humiliation, but then he grabbed my ankles, lowered himself, sucked on my clit.

Jesus, Brody was barely out the door, and I was coming. I take a sip of the dark roast coffee and wonder if it's just coincidence that the coffee is black. Maybe Patty forgot to bring cream and sugar, but she looks pretty efficient, considering all the goodies she brought.

Bagels, croissants, with what looks like homemade jam. Pineapples and mangoes, along with cream cheese and lox.

If I didn't have Brody hanging over my head, I'd really enjoy this. Who doesn't love living first class every day? I take another sip of coffee, grab my phone, and push on Brody's number.

It barely rings once and he picks up. "Raven, I'm so sorry. Are you okay? That was horrifying. I already called and apologized to Mr. Powers." And I almost choke on my coffee.

"Brody? Tell me you didn't." My cheeks heat up again.

"I did. I had to. He caught us... you know." And I almost roll my eyes.

"Wait, did you actually talk to him?"

"Yes. He thanked me and said you needed a little time to be alone, but that you would call me in a couple days. He was actually pretty cool about it. I mean, I had heard all these stories about him being th—"

"Brody. Just stop." I have to interrupt him. This is so wrong. "Look." I close my eyes, then say, "We need to not see each other anymore. I love you, but as a friend."

"What? Raven, I know last night was—"

"It's not about last night. I mean, it is, but it's not." Cheeks on fire, I take a deep breath and rub my forehead. "I'm not the right girl for you, and the last thing I want to do is hurt you. I hope we can stay friends."

There. I did it. I reach for my coffee, then decide I'll probably choke again, so I put it down and pick up a silver fork to play with.

"I… Raven, are you sure?" He sounds sad, but not as sad as I anticipated. Again, I wonder if he's secretly as relieved as I am.

"Positive. You're amazing, Brody, you really are."

"I'll always be there for you. All you need to do is ask." He blows out some air. "Wow, okay. Well, my dad is going to be disappointed." He laughs, but it's forced. "Honestly, you were always out of my league, Raven."

"Brody, that's not true." *Great, I feel like crap.*

"It's true, and you know it. And if I'm honest, I need to work on my head. I'm kind of confused about stuff." He sighs. "I'm gonna go. Take care, Raven."

"Okay, bye, Brody." But he's already hung up.

Grabbing my coffee, I walk to the edge of the balcony and toss it over, then sit and pour a fresh cup. I pull my legs up and let Jett's scent lull me into a better frame of mind. Leaning forward, I grab a croissant. A light knock makes me stuff my mouth with half the buttery deliciousness before I go to answer it.

"Yes?" I clear my throat as I swallow and peek out again. The driver, Iain, stands with three black lacquer boxes.

"I'll be back in a couple of hours for you." When he hands them to me, I smile at him, but he doesn't return it. Hmm, maybe he likes my mom, but he'd have to be actually insane. She doesn't discriminate when it comes to who she's a bitch to.

It's pretty much everyone, unless she thinks she needs you. Which is why Maria has always had job security. She needed Maria to raise me, and Maria is smart enough to never let her forget it.

"Thank you," I say to his back. Whatever, he doesn't have to like me.

Kicking the door shut, I bring my boxes out onto the balcony and set them on the lounger. I stuff the rest of the croissant into my mouth, wipe my hands, and open the small box first.

It's lipstick. Red. Yves Saint Laurent. I think I already have it, but it says special edition so... maybe not.

I flip open the next box and gasp. Fucking Jimmy Choo heeled sandals covered in crystals that wrap up the ankle, literally to die for. My fingers caress the hundreds of tiny crystals and I check the size: thirty-six. He had to have looked at my boots. How else would he know?

I lick my lips and lift the lid to the last box. It's the largest, and I pull out a silk, strappy dress. The waist fits like a corset, and the rest is see-through chiffon.

"Holy fuck." I stand up and drape it over me. I thought it was black; it's not though. It's a deep, dark sapphire that shimmers in the sun, and by far the most gorgeous dress I've ever owned. All of this had to have cost him a fortune. I know he's rich, but still.

After I place the dress back in the box, I sit down to eat some more pineapple and start my transformation.

I have zero idea where he is taking me, but I intend to look the best I ever have.

A ripple of adrenaline snakes up my spine. Reaching for my boxes, I step back into my room and drop them on the bed.

A small card falls out of one.

"Oh God," I whisper as I open it, my hand slightly shaking.

Raven,

POWER

Do you dare?

I flip it over, but that's it.

Do I dare? Dare what? The dress? Him? All of the above? I drop it. Again, that ripple of adrenaline, maybe unease about what's happening, fills me as I walk into the bathroom and strip off his suit jacket, letting it fall to the floor.

I smile.

He's just so nasty.

Exciting.

And for the first time ever, I do dare.

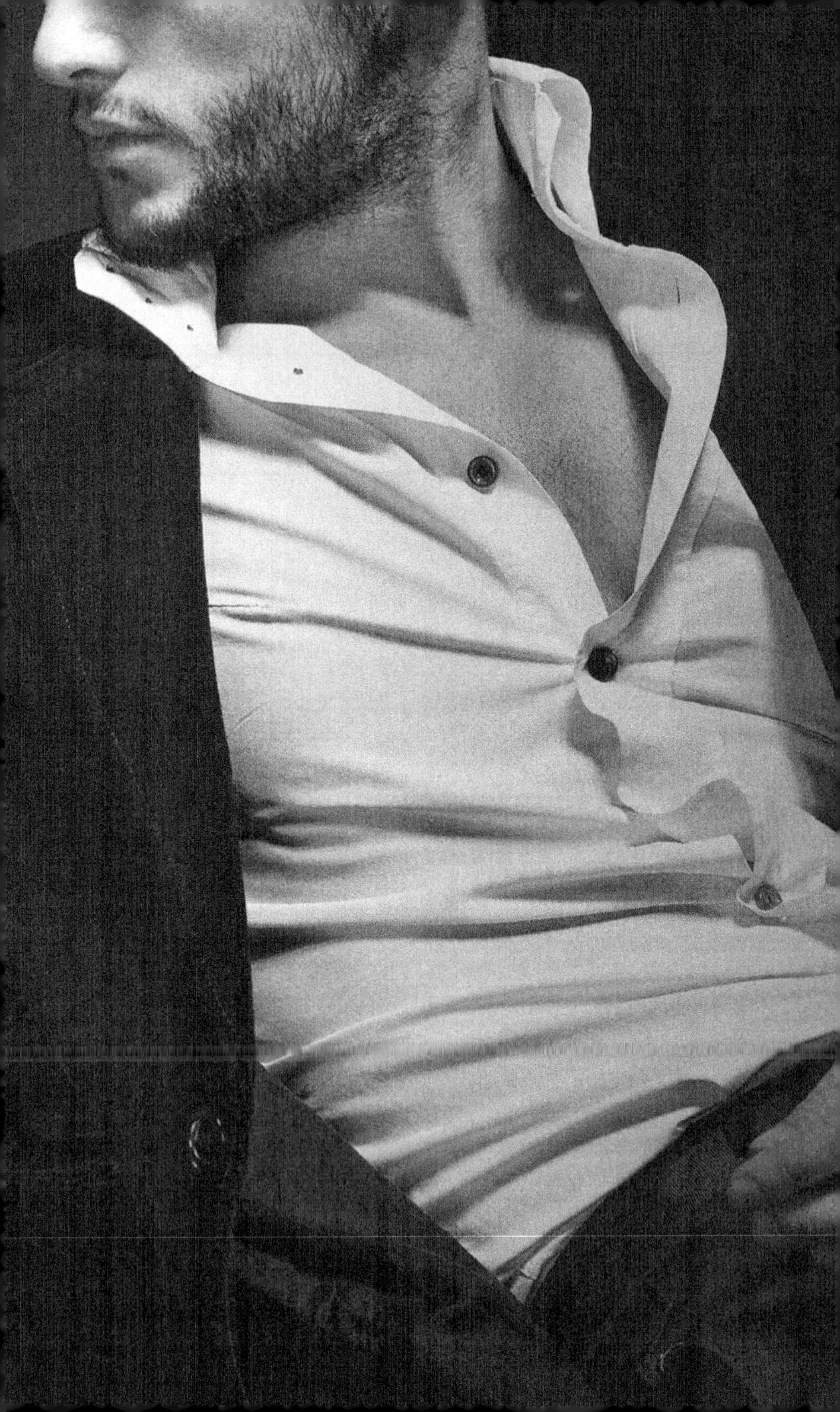

Eight

JETT

"Mr. Powers?" Rebecca's voice comes in through the speaker.

"Yes?"

"A Ms. Stewart is here."

"Thank you, Rebecca, send her in, and you can take off early." I grin. The reason I'm in a good mood is here.

I didn't jerk off in the shower I took a few minutes ago, nor did I excuse myself at my daily meeting to relieve my blue balls. No, I adjusted myself, letting my hard cock ache and throb, knowing the longer I wait the more pleasure I'll get.

My mind goes to that first thrust. She was tight and wet and hot. I felt that virgin barrier rip, and it was as though I were possessed after that.

Best fuck I've ever had.

And I've fucked a lot of women. Still, I hope she's fine when I'm done. I'm not a man who confuses great sex with love.

But I do like spoiling her. She kept a smile on my face all day. It's the least I can do until Rachel comes back.

Rachel.

It's funny, when Raven asked me if I had guilt, it was an automatic *no*. To have guilt you need to know that you're doing something wrong and actually care enough about that person to experience that feeling.

POWER

I don't have that with my fiancée.

I asked her to become my wife because I'm turning forty, and socially and career-wise, marriage is the right choice. That, and Rachel checks off most of my boxes.

I walk over and pour myself a bourbon as my door opens.

"You want a drink?" I call out, then look up.

Time stops—it ceases to exist as I watch her walk toward me. Slowly I bring the expensive scotch to my lips.

"Hello, Mr. Powers." Slightly raspy, her voice does it for me. My cock almost throbs as if he needs to remind me that the object of his obsession is here.

"Hello, beautiful." My eyes take her in. Stunning can't even begin to describe this creature who's walking toward me.

Breathtaking... that's close. She truly is exquisite, and it's not the dress or shoes; it's the way she holds her head up, her shoulders back. Her air of confidence, it's like an aphrodisiac.

She takes my breath away. My eyes dip to her red lips that smirk as if she knows. I bring the drink to my lips and shoot my fifty-year-old liquor, which is supposed to be savored, letting the sting and burn add to the ongoing pain merely thinking about her has brought me.

But now she's here, in my office, and I'm not gonna wait anymore.

I almost growl as I set the glass down with a loud thud and reach for her, jerking her to me.

"Jett." She gasps as my hand snakes into her thick, dark hair and pulls her head back.

"What did you call me?" I unbutton my belt with my other hand.

"I..." Her eyes are like giant-sized saucers, and suddenly all I want is to wake up every morning seeing them. *What the hell, Jett?*

I'm wound up too tight. I should have jerked off, released the poisons, because I'm not thinking straight as I take her lips and growl into her cherry mouth. My tongue instantly tangles with hers as she digs her nails into my forearms. Electric energy zings through us, and for some reason this angers me.

"Fuck." I lift my head. Her lips are already swollen from my bruising kiss, but her eyes... they sparkle like gems in the sunlight.

She likes it rough, not that I even care. I'm not in the mood to be anything but what I really am. I spin her around, and she instinctively grabs the edge of my desk.

"You don't talk, you don't come until I say so," I hiss and jerk my slacks down, releasing my swollen, angry erection. I try to breathe, which is not easy—by just looking at her ass in this dress and her long legs in those heels, I'm gonna humiliate myself like a teenager if I'm not careful.

"Lean forward." My hand lowers her chest to my desk. She takes in small, fast breaths.

"Scared?" I lean over her, grabbing both hands to place at the end of each side.

She shakes her head slightly and I almost smile. "That's a good girl. Spread your legs. I hope you're ready because I've been thinking about this cunt all day." Leaning in, I jerk up the layers of chiffon and dump them around her waist.

I stop for a second to look at her fucking perfect ass. My fingers almost tingle as I reach to caress it. Not sure if that's because I want to spank it over and over, heat it up, so I can feel its warmth as I fuck her, or if it's because I want that small rosette hole.

I have every intention of fucking it. Maybe not tonight, but before this is over, I will have been in every hole she has before I let her go.

"So smooth and soft," I tease as her lips spread into a smile; then I spank one perfect cheek. She screams in shock and instantly rises up. But my hand goes to her neck, holding her down.

"Ahh, baby, you're not trained, and right now I don't have the patience." Moving her G-string aside, I kick her legs open wider, and in one hard thrust I'm deep inside her.

POWER

"Hot and slick...yeah, you were made for me," I murmur as I rut in and out of her, leaning forward to thrust as deep as possible.

"What's my name?" I grunt and look down at my hard cock going in and out of her wet, pink pussy.

She smiles and digs her nails into the wood as if she's bracing herself. "Jett..." She pants. "I mean, Mr. Powers."

She cries out as I pound into her hard and fast, grinning at her audacity.

"Sassy girls don't get to come." I pick up speed. "But I'm gonna fill this tight pussy up. And you're gonna wait." I grunt out each word, breathing through my nose, the pleasure so intense, I feel everything tighten.

"Jesus Christ." I go over, my body jerking as I come in thick waves of pulsing ecstasy. I hold her hips and pull my still-hard cock out almost all the way, then plunge back in. Her core is so wet and tight and ready for her own release.

But she can wait.

And learn.

I lean forward with my hands on either side of her head, as I say into her right ear, "Name? What's my name, beautiful?"

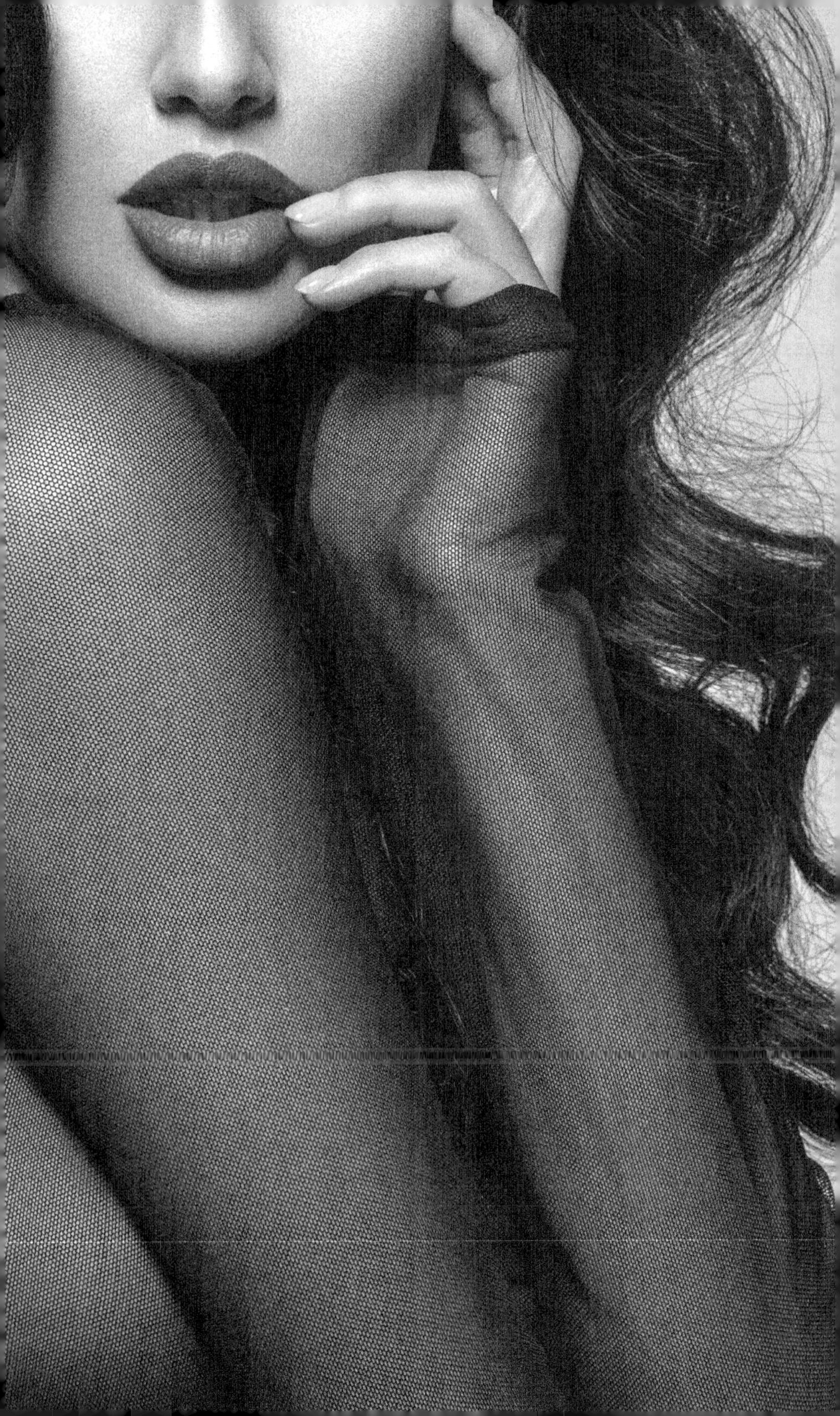

Nine

RAVEN

I puff out some air as his body jerks into mine. *No*, he was right there, his massive dick was hitting that spot. I was ready to come...

"Name? What's my name, beautiful?" I stop breathing. He's not serious, is he? My mind is racing, my breaths coming fast, and I groan as he slowly moves in and out of me.

"Mr. Powers," I whisper, and then almost scream when he pulls out and turns me around facing him.

"Oh my God." For a moment, I almost touch myself, but reach back and dig my nails into his desk as I try to breathe and not humiliate myself further by begging.

His blue eyes narrow as he watches me with that smug smirk on his handsome face. My hands are starting to ache from clawing the wood. It's either that or claw him.

His eyes dip to my breasts and lower. His sperm slides down the inside of my thigh. With my panties soaked and my dress still around my waist, I've gone from looking magnificent, to a drowned rat in a matter of minutes. I can only imagine my makeup.

"Baby, my pretty baby." His voice makes my eyes dart back to his as he reaches for my chin and softly whispers into my lips, "You look desperate."

"Why are you doing this?" I almost want to cry. I was perfect, and if I'm going to be ruined, you'd think he'd let me come.

"Why do you think?" He brushes his lips on mine, and this time I do feel tears in my eyes.

"Because you're some kind of fucked-up control freak who only cares about himself?" I burst out.

He watches me with that stare of his that I'm beginning to hate, yet love. Then he throws his head back and laughs.

Laughs.

"Whatever, asshole." I try to move away because I'm done. But he grabs my arm.

"Easy, Raven. I like your sassy mouth, but if you keep it up, those tears of frustration you're having are going to be because my cock is so far down your throat you're gagging." He easily lifts me up under my arms and sets me gently on his desk.

I go to slide off, because I'm done. I'm clearly out of my element, my core is swollen and throbbing, all I want to do is come, and *I hate Jett Powers.*

"Look, you're my mom's fiancé. I should never—"

"That's right, Raven. I am your mother's fiancé. Who was just *inside you.* Now, I asked you to do one simple thing, and you can't seem to handle that."

"Holy fuck," I hiss, trying to jump off the desk. I have to get away from him. He's way too powerful up close.

"You can't talk to me like that," I fire right back, even though that was a terrible comeback, and he raises a dark brow at me, not even offended. If anything, he looks like my words make him want to laugh.

"We're late, my beauty." He takes my other ankle and I moan, then want to die, because he heard that.

"You can't win." It's a statement, not a question and I glare at him.

"Mr. Powers?"

Again, his lips twitch, and I visualize one of my five-inch Jimmy Choo heels he spent three-thousand dollars on stabbing him in the heart, *if* he even has one.

"Yes?" He places my legs on each shoulder as his strong tan hands start at my ankles and move upward. All sarcastic questions fly out the window. Thank God, he's going to finger fuck me. I drop back onto his desk as he holds my gaze with his eyes, his nostrils slightly flaring as if he loves my scent.

"Please." My breathing sounds harsh, and my eyes widen, because that was the last word that was supposed to come out of my mouth.

He grins as if he knows it, then backs up. "Stay still, beautiful. I have something that is gonna take care of all that neediness you're feeling." He places both my heeled shoes on his desk as he buttons and zips his slacks, tucking his starched white shirt in as he walks around to the other side and opens a drawer, bringing something out.

"Now." He flashes me a smile as he walks back, moving in between my legs again. "Let's see how bad you want to come? You think you can be a good girl for Mr. Powers?"

"Wait. What is that?" I'm trying to see what he's holding: it's small and pink.

"Raven. Let me enlighten you on me. I have a very limited amount of patience, and you're testing it. Do you want to come?" His tone seems rather bored, but his blue eyes are almost black as they hold my gaze.

"Yes." I slowly nod, biting my lip. Why am I fighting with him? We're not in a relationship. He really is my mother's fiancé.

Jesus Christ, Raven, what is wrong with you? This is a game. That's why he only wants me to call him Mr. Powers. This is nothing more than sex. It's like a lightning bolt has struck me, and I get it.

This man is going to marry my mother. *Of course, he is.* God, what an idiot I am. I let orgasms and his pretty face distract me into thinking this was different. I almost start laughing. What was I thinking? Just because he took my virginity and bought me nice clothes doesn't mean he's going to dump my mom.

POWER

He's brought me here to have fun, play this forbidden, naughty game. I must remember this. Otherwise, I need to hop off his desk and go back to the house. He'll let me. I can feel him already pulling back. *It's now or never, Raven. What's it going to be?*

"Fine." I take a deep breath and lean back, spreading my legs open, the spike of my one heel digging into his wooden desk with a satisfying scrape.

He cocks his head at me. "Fine what?"

"Fine, Mr. Powers." A small shiver goes through me. I can feel him watching me even as I look up at the ceiling. Then I feel his two fingers ease in and out of me in a slow, tortuous rhythm.

"That's it, baby. I don't even need lube, you're so creamed up." His fingers leave me, replaced by the small, ball-like vibrator that he leaves inside me.

"Now, go fix yourself up." He removes my drenched panties, then helps me off the desk. For a second I hold on to him, barely able to stand, more from shock because I thought he was going to use the vibrator to make me come, *now*.

"Wait, you want me to go out with…" My voice trails off as he turns and casually pockets my panties, then walks over to refill his drink.

"Bathroom is there. Hurry up, Raven. I don't like being late." He motions with his head for the door to the right.

Taking a breath, I feel full. I can tell it's inside me, but I can walk, and maybe if I squirm…

"You can't," he announces, taking a sip of whatever brown liquid he's chosen. I smile and grab my small clutch, marching into the bathroom. I flip on the light and almost scream at the reflection that stares back at me.

"Jesus." I reach for a Kleenex to rub the mascara off from under my left eye. My lipstick is smeared all the way up to my nose, making me look like a clown. I take a breath and start to repair myself.

Jesus, my hands are slightly shaking as I quickly reapply everything. I take a step back and look at myself. I don't even need blush since I'm completely flushed and was already going for smoky eyes. I'm actually shocked at how good I look. A little red lipstick and *boom*.

Spinning around, I grab a bunch of tissues to clean myself up as much as I can, almost moaning as I touch the vibrator. Then I toss the wad into the dark wicker trash basket and straighten my dress.

I take another deep breath and walk out, forcing one foot in front of the other.

He must have made a deal with the devil; no one can be this beautiful otherwise. My breath stutters as my eyes take in his tan skin, beautiful dark hair looking more so with that starched white shirt. He's removed his tie and unbuttoned the first two buttons, allowing me to see his neck. With that black suit jacket, he just screams danger and power.

"You look exquisite, Raven." His voice sounds deep and gravelly, causing a shiver of excitement as he holds out his hand for me to join him. Unlike the first time we met, this time I take it.

Swallowing back a gasp, a jolt like liquid heat zings into my hand—it's like I've been injected just by holding his hand. He walks us out of his lavish office and into the elevator.

We don't talk.

I barely breathe.

When his hand squeezes mine, I look up at him, admiring his profile, which is as perfect as his full face.

And suddenly, I understand his note. The ding of the elevator distracts me. He guides us to the waiting Mercedes.

"Careful when you sit." His voice is warm, and he watches me slowly slide in. I cross my legs, and he moves next to me, a knowing grin on his full lips.

"Thanks, Iain." He settles back and the car moves smoothly forward.

POWER

I lick my lips. "I guess this"—I look down, then over at him—"is what your note meant this morning?" The car is dark, but the lights from the city still allow me to see part of his face.

"What are you studying?" I blink at him. Did he just completely ignore my comment and ask me what I'm studying?

The car is quiet, save for the driver putting the blinker signal on.

Clearing my throat, I turn slightly, so I can see his face better. "I haven't decided, but I'm leaning toward environmental law."

"Really?" By the tone of his voice, he sounds genuinely interested, which throws me. I was expecting him to laugh. No one, not even Cher, really cares about my interest in law.

"Yes, I find it fascinating, and with everything going on, I think the world needs people like me." I cock my head at him, waiting to see that famous smirk.

Instead, he says, "Agreed. You'll be brilliant." His gaze holds mine. He leans back. "You're at Columbia, right?"

What the? I recross my legs and try to focus on the fact that he is done playing, and now we are having a polite conversation.

"No. I'm at NYU."

There's the famous smirk I was waiting for. "So you're not really serious about the law?" He looks out the window, and for a second, it's as though I'm a disciplined child who feels shame that Daddy doesn't approve. Which is absurd and fucked. Granted, NYU might not be Ivy League, but it's an excellent school.

"Excuse me?" I snap.

"Why NYU? It's average, at best. Your mother has the connections and money to get your foot into a much better college."

"That's exactly why. I try to avoid her help on most things." My face heats up.

He turns his head and looks at me, then back out the window. "Well, good for you." His tone is dismissive, and I visualize kicking him again, or at the very least, taking this vibrator out since it seems he's forgotten about it.

74

"You want me to drop you off at the front, Mr. Powers?" The driver breaks into my thoughts as I look out the window at the large crowd milling around what looks like a gallery.

"Yeah, I'll text you when we're ready." The car pulls over, and a valet runs over and opens the door. Jett steps out, but doesn't hold out his hand for me. Simply waits for me to slide out. I'm two seconds from leaning over to tell Iain to take me home when I feel it: a light vibration on my clit and up on my G-spot as I dig my nails into the leather seat.

"Raven?"

I grit my teeth and almost slap his hand away, which he now holds out for me to take.

"Just a second," I snap, closing my eyes. Of course, he's stopped it as he pockets his phone.

"You okay?" Jett leans in so he can see me. I ignore his handsome face and step out onto Melrose Boulevard. It's been a trendy street in LA for a long time. When I was in high school, I used to get most of my wardrobe up and down this street.

"What are we doing?" I ask, looking at the paparazzi snapping pictures and screaming at someone as they enter the large, mostly cement building.

"Is that Ammo from the Stuffed Muffins?" Feeling his hand at my lower back, I move forward.

"Where's your fiancée?"

"Mr. Powers?"

"Smile." He grins and waves but stays silent. I wasn't prepared for this. *Press?* What is he, the king? What if my mom sees us? Jesus, are people gonna know her in there?

"What are we doing?" I hiss, putting my clutch in front of my face.

"You ever hear of Gia Fontaine? This is her collection."

I turn to look at him. "Gia Granger?" My eyes widen. "As in married to the Rock God?" Because, besides Jett, Granger is fucking hot. I've seen the Stuffed Muffins twice in New York.

POWER

"Well, she goes by Gia Fontaine with her work, but yes." His lips twitch as I drop my clutch to really look around. Is he in there?

"Untouched" by the Stuffed Muffins spills out of the speakers as we walk up to the gallery's glass front door. Beautiful people mill about. Wait, is that a Kardashian inside?

"You can go in, Mr. Powers." The woman in red flashes him an almost blinding, white-toothed smile, as one of the two suited men, who I assume are security, opens the glass door.

Is this his life? Going from the courtroom to the rich and famous? Of course, it is. Why do I see him on all the tabloids? Oh my God, now I'm going to be on them...

"What if my mom sees us?" I look up at Jett, somewhat shell-shocked at everything he really is. And not only his career, but him, in general. Like is there nothing he's not a master at?

"Thanks, Patricia, you look gorgeous." He winks at her as we pass, and an irrational spike of jealously shoots straight to my heart, which is kind of distressing—I'm not a jealous person. If anything, I'm the opposite. Like, I could not care less.

But when it comes to him and that wink? I want him to wink only at me.

Get a hold of yourself, Raven. He's not yours, or hers, he's your fucking mother's.

"What if she does?" He smiles at someone across the room. Does he seriously not care?

"Jett Powers. Welcome." A woman carrying two glasses of champagne approaches us, and for a second, like most of the room that seems to follow her as if she walks on water, I stare.

She's beautiful, and that's saying something because you really have to be lovely for me to think that. She's tall, but she's in heels, wearing a silky white wraparound dress that clings to her breasts, displaying a perfect body as she walks. Her long brown hair is off her face, so you can see her features. I want to stomp my foot at how I hate being short or petite, as my father lovingly puts it. I can't compete with someone like her.

"Mrs. Saddington, you look stunning, as usual." Allowing her to kiss his cheek, he flashes his signature panty-melting grin.

She laughs, and it's rather musical, infectious really, and I find myself smiling at her.

"Such a smooth talker." She shakes her head, smiling at him. "If I didn't have Reed—"

"But you do." A tall man who walks up behind her, wearing a black suit much like Jett's, wraps a possessive hand around her front, jerking her to him as he extends his other hand to Jett.

"How are you, man?" Jett shakes his hand, and the conversation starts to flow easily, casually. As if it's no big deal that he's one of the wealthiest men in the world.

My head is spinning. This is Reed Saddington. *The* Reed Saddington, billionaire bad boy who finally married his childhood sweetheart, and if the gossip rags can be believed, he's a devoted husband and doesn't cheat. The way he holds his wife, possessive and strong, tells me he would kill any man who dares to touch her.

"Tess, Reed, this is Raven." My eyes dart up to meet Jett's amused ones as I swallow and smile.

"Hello, so nice to meet you." It's my automatic response, been saying the same thing since childhood. They both smile back, but the slight flash in Reed's eyes, and the look of confusion on Tess's beautiful face... Yep, they know my mother.

"Can I get you a champagne..." Tess's voice trails off. Maybe she's waiting to see if I'm of age.

"She's fine. So it looks as though this is a huge success? Gia must be thrilled." Jett draws Tess's rather stunned attention back to him, and thankfully away from me.

"The exhibit starts in that room, and it travels around like a spiral up the stairs." She points with her glass.

My eyes follow to where she's pointing. Jesus, it's like out of a movie. When I say celebrities, we are talking A-list. I wish it wouldn't be completely tacky to take pictures. Cher is going to freak.

Ammo and Rhys Granger stand, laughing and drinking, Granger with a casual arm slung around Gia, who's smiling and talking to the fans surrounding them.

"And, Raven, there's a bar over on the back side of the gallery if you're thirsty. It has everything. Enjoy." She smiles as Reed drags her toward a man who has to be a basketball player. He's a head taller than Jett, who's at least six three.

"You got a thing for rock stars?" His voice is at my ear as he places both hands on my hips, guiding us into the room with all the celebrities.

"No," I say way too quickly. My face heats up.

"Liar." I feel his breath on my neck. "I can introduce you, although Granger likes his wife. There's Ammo." His voice sounds almost bored. I look up at him, horrified. I know we're not a couple, but I had no idea he'd be fine setting me up.

I take a deep breath. His eyes are focused on the photographs, and if it wasn't for his clenched jaw and hands digging into my hips, I'd think he'd already forgotten about me.

"Sure. I love Ammo," I gush. He nods, and his pulse beats strong in his temple. Maybe he's not as casual as I thought?

Jett propels us toward them, pulling me close to whisper in my ear, "You sure you dare?"

And suddenly, I shiver. He sounds angry, yet he's the one who started this game. Whatever…this has the potential to get out of hand. I turn to stop him because I'm not going to throw myself at Ammo just to prove to Mr. Powers that I don't back down.

But it's too late, because I'm standing in front of them, looking up at the blond perfection who is one of the best electric guitarists of my generation.

Ammo smiles at me, his clear blue eyes roaming my face, then trailing down my body, and suddenly all I want to do is throw my arms around Jett.

But it's done. I can't back down now. Mr. Powers wants to play.

Let's play.

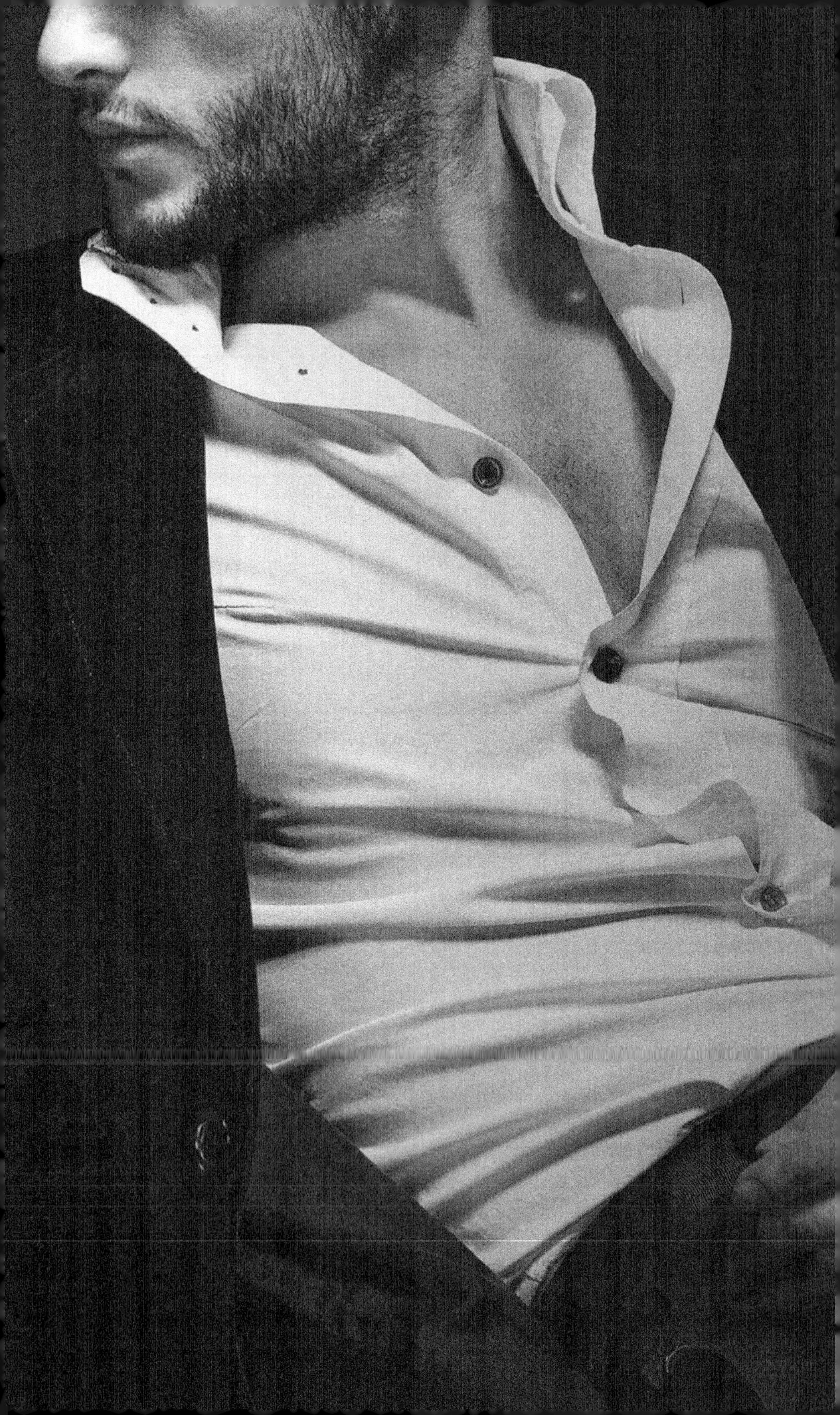

ten

JETT

I can barely see straight I'm so pissed. The fuck is she thinking? I'm not a man who cares what anyone does. In fact, it's my job not to ask questions that don't pertain to facts. But what started off as fun has turned into something else.

I should just leave her with the fucking tattooed guitarist. She's an adult. For a fucking woman who holds on to her virginity until she's nineteen, she sure as shit seems ready to try a new dick already.

Like mother, like daughter, I guess.

Why would I care? I never have before, but the moment her sapphire eyes lit up when Ammo walked in before us, my mood turned ugly, and it's getting worse as the seconds tick by.

"Jett Powers, how the hell are you?" Granger holds out his hand.

"Busy, fighting crime, being an all-American hero." I smirk, shaking his hand, then grab my Lolita and shove her in front of me.

"This is Raven. She's a huge fan." I feel her push back into me, but if she wants to fuck around, it's not my place to stop her. Ammo's eyes instantly dip to her tits, and why wouldn't he check her out? She's perfection. I bite the inside of my cheek, then smile as I turn to Gia.

POWER

"You keep getting better, Gia. You trying to bankrupt me?"

Gia throws her head back and laughs as she holds on to Granger's arm.

"Aw, Mr. Powers, you let me know which one you like, and I'll make sure they give you the family discount." Her green eyes twinkle. Like Tess, she's stunning, but they can't even begin to compare to Raven. A lone sparkling star in the deep, dark night.

That is, if she doesn't become a whore. My eyes narrow as I watch Ammo tilt his head toward Raven, using the excuse he can't hear her.

"Thank you." I down my champagne, needing something stronger.

"Let's get you a drink. Then I need to show you something." Ammo smiles, but he's not what I care about.

"Okay." Raven's voice sounds a little unsure, but she straightens her shoulders back and allows him to guide her toward the bar in the back.

"You okay, Powers?" Granger's voice makes me glance over at him and Gia. She's not even trying to hide her curiosity as she stares first at me, then at Raven's and Ammo's retreating backs.

"Fine." It comes out harsh.

Granger raises a dark brow, and removes his arm from Gia who's turning and squealing at someone entering the room.

"You're cool, right? Ammo will back off if she's yours." Granger's voice holds a warning.

I smile, because that's what I do, keep everyone off balance and guessing my next move.

"I'm cool. Excuse me." So what if he's frowning. I barely know Granger. I've taken care of some legal issues dealing with stalkers and such for the band. And then, of course, the Disciples case, but I owe him nothing.

I pull out my phone and text Iain to get the car ready as I walk up the stairs, the hairs on the back of my neck prickling.

If he's touching her... Christ, I need to get ahold of myself. I'm gonna need a lawyer for me if I'm not careful.

She's not at the bar. I casually walk to the side railing and look down, scanning the people milling around, laughing and enjoying themselves. What the fuck is wrong with me? If I was with Rachel, I would be one of those people drinking and laughing, but with Raven, this is different.

She's different. A flash of sapphire makes me lean my elbows on the railing because I've found her. She's smiling, but keeping a good distance from Ammo who is laughing. Why wouldn't he be happy? He's with my Lolita.

Fucking dick.

Watching her, I smirk. *Come on, baby. Look up for me. I'm right here.* She smiles again, and Ammo moves closer. She doesn't move back, but she does stare at the art, not him.

That's my girl. You know who owns your cunt. Come on, baby, show me those eyes. Look up like a good fucking girl.

She turns, and I eyeball every movement she makes. Every single breath she takes, I want for me. Irrational? Yes.

I take a breath and watch her slowly look around. The music has faded to a dull pulse as she searches for me.

Yeah, that's my girl. I'm right here. You can feel me, can't you? Look up and tell me exactly what you need.

As if she can actually hear me, she looks up, and time fucking stops. She doesn't move; her eyes tell me everything.

She's forbidden.

I know I'm gonna ruin her, not that I care because I want her like a dog needing to mark his territory. My eyes hold hers until Ammo dares to touch her chin, breaking her gaze. I straighten and look around as the room comes back into focus.

I see you. Now be a good girl and come for me. I click open the app and turn the vibrator on slowly. She instantly stiffens and takes a step back. When I smile at her, she looks back up at me. Ammo follows her gaze and frowns.

Fucking prick.

I nod at him and turn it up a notch more. *That's it, Raven. You breathe for me.* She looks up at me, then holds on to the wall as she starts to frantically talk to him. I smile again and head down the stairs. Fuck, my cock is hard. I walk toward them, a polite smile on my face.

"Everything okay?" I look down at my phone and turn it back on low. Raven looks almost desperate, her eyes the size of saucers as I smile at her, then Ammo.

"I don't know. No, I don't feel good," she moans.

"She thinks she ate something bad." Ammo's blue eyes actually hold some concern, and I have to relax my grip. I'm gonna break my phone if I don't.

"I'll take her home." I nod at him.

"Exactly who is she to you?" His tan, tattooed hand moves to stop me from taking what's mine.

Mine.

I look down at my chest, then slowly up at him. He's the same height, and not backing down at my stare, which makes me smile. Only an arrogant, fucking punk like him would think he's as powerful as me.

He's not.

He's also out of his league. I fight dirty.

"I'm her fucking daddy. Now back away," I calmly say straight to his face. His eyes narrow, darting from mine to hers, but he drops his hand and backs away.

"Oh God." Raven groans.

I smile at Ammo and turn to her. "Let's go, sweetheart." I grab her arm and weave us through the crowd and out into the paparazzi again.

"Jett... Mr. Powers, please, I'm gonna..." Panting, she grabs my bicep.

Pulling her close, I murmur in her ear, "That's it, Raven. Show me how you come for me." My hand holds her steady as I watch her. Her eyes close, but her face... if I live to be a hundred, I will always remember how absolutely exquisite she looks at this moment.

Her lips are red, puffy, and parted as she tries to stay quiet. Her smoky eyes flutter, and nothing in this second could tear my gaze away.

The world could stop spinning, but this second, this moment, it's just her and me.

"Open your eyes, beautiful." She blinks up at me, and I see the second she goes over.

"That's my girl." I pull her in tight, turning the vibrator off as she buries her face in my chest, her breath shaky.

"Let's go," I say, moving us past the cameras and questions. All of this means nothing. I don't hide, and I don't give a fuck what they print. They know better than to slander me. But Raven doesn't need assholes following her around. She slides into the car, and I follow.

"Where to, Mr. Powers?" Iain looks back at me, respectfully ignoring my Lolita sitting quietly next to me.

"Home." The car pulls out onto Melrose Boulevard, and I pull Raven into my arms.

"Open your legs, baby." I kiss her forehead and she obeys. My hand slides up her thigh to pull the small vibrator out.

She turns so she can see me. I caress her cheek. "Are you a monster or a good guy?" It's almost a whisper, a small puff of sweet air.

"Jury's out on that." My thumb gently rubs and dips in and out of her slick, wet core. She tries to shut her legs and move away as she points at Iain. I cock my head, then pull her completely onto my lap, my legs spreading her open as she tries to stay quiet. Iain knows better than to turn around.

"Quiet." Lightly biting her earlobe, I slide my fingers deep inside her. One hand grabs my forearm as the other one makes sure her dress is covering my hand.

In and out, I finger fuck her tight, sweet pussy. She may be staring straight ahead, but her greedy pussy, which I'm just starting to train, knows what it wants and grabs on to my fingers. I pick up speed, then pull out and rub her wet juices on her swollen nub.

"Iain? Can we have some music, please? Anything but the Stuffed Muffins." She's biting her lower lip so hard, trying to be silent, but her cunt is wet. And with every stroke in and out of her, you can hear it in the soundless car.

I kiss her cheek as Billie Eilish spills through the back of the Mercedes, the speakers so clear that I growl with satisfaction.

"Mine, this is mine." She stiffens as if unsure as to what she should do. Her hands reach forward to grab the seat in front of us.

"Me, Raven, I'm all you need." My two fingers are thrusting deep into her hot, swollen core. My cock is leaking, but her release is more important.

"Close your eyes." She nods, taking small, quiet gasps, her nails digging into my wrist.

"Come," I whisper, biting and sucking on her earlobe.

Her pussy latches onto my fingers and holds them, pulsing in waves. Grabbing the back of her hair tight, I say, "Kiss me." I groan into her parted lips and her breath seems to be only for me. Her cherry lips taste like sweet wine, and our tongues twist together, my fingers staying deep inside her as she continues to contract.

"Sir, we're here." Iain clears his voice as I break away.

Slowly I pull my fingers out of her. She slides off my lap, smoothing her dress.

"Thank you, Iain. Sweep the property, and I'll see you tomorrow." He doesn't look back and exits the car.

Iain keeps the fucking crazy people away from me and what's mine. He doesn't ask questions, and is not afraid to get his hands dirty. I pay him a fortune. He's worth it.

I turn to look at Raven, a wave of possessiveness coming over me as she tries not to yawn.

"Come on, let's go to bed." I open the door and she reluctantly scoots out. Before she can protest, I sweep her up, ignoring Patty's shocked face. She holds the door for us, and I carry Raven up the stairs, two at a time. I'll take her to her room since she stayed with me last night. That's enough.

She sighs as if she knows my thoughts, and my arms tighten. That possessive, almost caveman-like feeling sweeps over me again.

Goddammit. I'm hesitating… the fuck is wrong with me? I don't hesitate, don't question my needs.

I take.

This will end, but fuck it, I'm a shit. A selfish dick. She feels good, and I want her right now.

It's as simple as that.

I. Want. Her.

Turning, I kick open my bedroom door. I have zero intention of ending us yet.

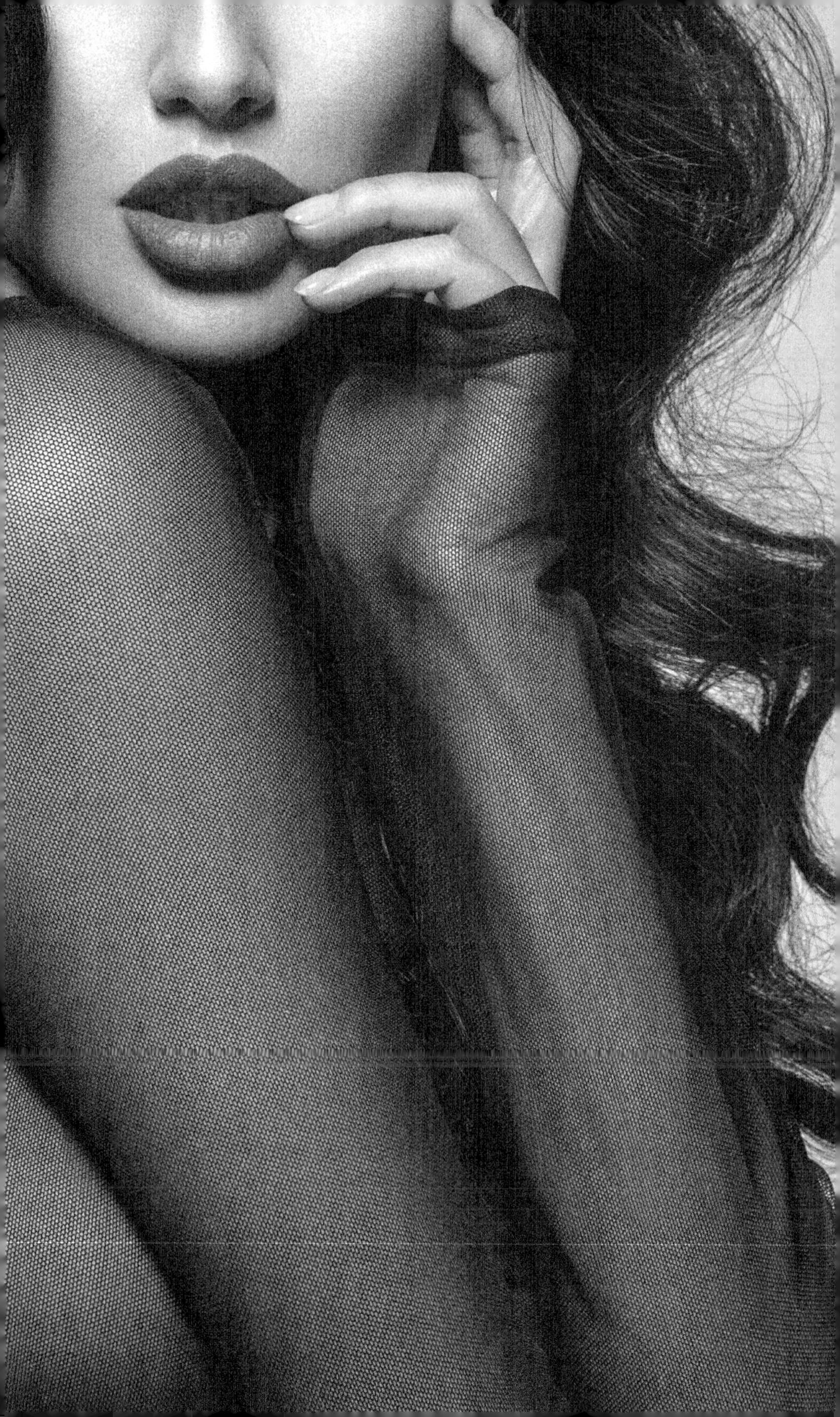

Eleven

RAVEN

"Raven?" I groan. My eyes feel like they have weights on them. "No, it's too early. I'm on vacation, summer break," I mumble as I roll to his side of the bed and snuggle my nose in his pillow.

"I've got to go to work. Kiss me." His voice reminds me of a gravelly, delicious, caramel crunch bar. You just sigh and lick your lips waiting for more. I can feel myself smirk at my ridiculous thoughts.

"Raven, come on baby. Kiss me." I blink my eyes open to see charcoal-colored slacks that hug his muscular thighs. God, he's way too beautiful. Pure male perfection.

"What time is it?" Sitting up on my elbows, I gaze up at him.

"Early." Although the curtains are open, it's still pretty dark in here. I can see him, but it looks kind of overcast. I toss off the comforter, get on my knees, and move into his arms. Wrapping my hands around his neck, I can feel his still-wet hair.

He inhales as if my scent is the one he likes. I squirm, rubbing my hard, sensitive nipples on his chest as I brush my lips on his.

"Morning, Mr. Powers." Smiling, I momentarily let myself fantasize about waking up to his blue eyes every morning.

He smiles back at me, and my stomach flips. Instantly, I'm wet.

"I'll be done early today," he says. "Be ready to go out for dinner. I've laid out what I want you to wear."

My core throbs at his words. Would he do this every day if we were actually together? Dress me, pet me, fuck me?

His eyes narrow and he grins. "I have to go. I'll call you later." I sit back, bringing my hair up into a messy bun as he reaches for his suit jacket.

"Do you dress my mom?" As soon as I say it, I wish I hadn't because I hate her, and if he says yes...

"No," he says dryly, reaching for his phone.

I nod and try not to smile. Though I really have nothing to be happy about, I am happy anyway. The reality that my mom will be returning at any time can come later. I'm about to crawl toward my phone when he grabs my ankles. As I flop on my stomach, he pulls me to the end of the bed.

"On all fours." He slaps my ass.

"Ow, Jett, that hurt." Because it did.

"I want this ass." He almost purrs it as he caresses one cheek. And I stiffen. *Is he talking about anal?*

"What do you mean?" My voice goes up a notch, and I'm now completely awake.

"I want to fuck you here." He leans over and bites my ass cheek.

"What?" I scream, because holy shit.

"You... your penis," I whisper the *penis* part as my whole face gets red. "Would never fit."

"Cock, baby. My cock would never fit," he corrects me and I almost sigh, because he's teasing me.

"Say it." Suddenly he releases me, and I turn, watching him go into his closet.

"Your cock," I yell, because he really is filthy. "Your cock is way too big for my ass, Mr. Powers." I smile at myself and cross my leg.

"Agreed." He walks out, and my smile fades. He's not even trying to hide the lube and what looks a plastic bullet thing.

"I'm late. On all fours, I don't want you to take this out unless I say so," he commands as I just blink at him, then swallow and shake my head.

"I... you can't be serious." My voice cracks. He squeezes a big dollop of lube on the clear bullet thing.

"Raven. Now, trust me, I will make you feel so good, but I don't have time to prepare this ass, so turn and let the plug work."

"Oh my God." Again, I don't move and simply try to breathe.

"What if I say no?" I ask, staring at the toy, plug, whatever it is.

"Raven." I jump and look at him. "Have I ever not made you feel good?"

I shake my head.

"Then why are you acting like this?"

It feels like I'm being scolded, and I raise my chin.

"Because your cock is huge," I fire right back as our eyes lock and his lips twitch.

"Fair enough." He shakes his head and laughs.

"Really?" Because for a second I'm disappointed, which is insane I know, but he's right. He does always make me feel good, and if I'm ever gonna try anal, it should definitely be with him.

"No."

"No?" I stand.

"Get on all fours, my love." His voice doesn't remind me of a candy bar anymore. I look at him. His eyes are intense, like the bluest sky. He's dead serious about this, and my gut says I need to get on the bed.

"Fine, but only because I'm actually curious," I snip, climbing on all fours.

"Fuck, I want to take my belt to your ass for making me wait, and for your sassy mouth," he growls. "Lean forward."

I obey, resting my head on my crossed arms. He places a knee on the bed, and the bottle of lube drops on the mattress next to the pillows with a thud.

"Breathe, Raven," he demands.

When I take a breath, I feel the tip of the plug circle my rosette hole. Gently, he dips it in and out.

"Rub your clit, baby."

I take another breath and turn my head, rubbing my embarrassingly slick clit. Why am I so turned on? I mean, this is probably gonna hurt, yet I can't stop the moan from escaping.

"Yeah, you're gonna love my cock in this ass. In and out, I'll fuck it while my fingers make you come."

"Oh my God." Is all I can say.

Slowly he pushes the plug in and out of my small hole, and it feels so good.

"Harder. Rub, Raven," he demands, and I do, feeling myself start to pulse.

"Can I come?" My voice sounds far away as I feel it go in fully. Then I'm gone, spiraling into a million pieces as both holes seem to contract, even though only one is still full. I turn to my side and try to catch my breath.

Jett is texting on his phone. If there wasn't a huge bulge in his slacks, I'd be insulted.

"I have to go. Don't touch yourself or remove it unless I say so." He looks up and pockets his phone, his eyes caressing my face, then traveling down my body.

"Stand up," he commands.

I slowly move off the bed and into his arms, thinking it might hurt, but it doesn't. It's just full and different. Jett leans down and his lips take mine. It's almost loving, tender, and for a second I'm terrified.

Because lines are getting blurred, things that I never thought I'd like, I do, and this has only been a couple of days. How am I going to survive when my mom comes back? I'm setting myself up for a major fall, but I'm not about to stop myself, because in the back of my head, I know he feels something too.

"Have a good day." My voice is soft. I lick my lips, letting my hand slide down his chest to grab his erection.

He smirks, reaching down to help my hand rub him, then backs away as he turns, saying over his shoulder, "Go put a robe on. I have Patty bringing you breakfast."

Then he's gone, and the room is just a room. Jett's what makes this house feel so good—it's all him. Smiling, I reach for his robe. The thought of wearing anything my mom has touched makes me sick.

"Knock-knock." Patty stands outside the door, smiling at me. She always looks so neat and put together. Last night was the only time I saw her actually look surprised.

"Good morning." I return her smile.

"Mr. Powers said you wanted French toast this morning with strawberries and blueberries."

"Sounds delicious." I walk over to the balcony and stop. Should I go to my room?

"Patty? Do you know when my mother is coming home? I mean, I can try and lie to you, but that would be insulting to both of us." I look straight into her dark brown eyes. They hold no judgment.

"I think tomorrow." She breezes past me to the balcony. "And thank you."

I nod and follow her. I guess I'm staying here.

Three hours later, I've eaten way too much, showered, and used a skin scrub that is making my skin glow. The one thing I can say about my mom is she does not skimp on herself. All her skin products are the best: creams, serums, and exfoliants. You name it, she has it. Thank God, their bathroom is huge and has a beautiful shelf for all of it.

Everything about Jett Powers is perfect, including his bathroom. It has hardwood floors that heat up, along with heated towel racks, and it's so big it even has a couch.

POWER

If this were my house, this would be where I spent most of my time. With the giant skylight, the natural light is amazing for putting on makeup.

With a sigh, I step back to look at myself.

Makeup looks good. I went light, with pastels on my eyes and lips, although I did use a lot of mascara, making sure my eyes pop since my lips are a neutral pink.

Jett picked out a white summer halter dress, and it's one of my favorites. My breasts look fantastic in it.

He even laid out the panties he wants me to wear, which are white lace, and new, high-heeled Prada sandals—I love them.

I'm getting spoiled. I sigh and pull my straightened hair over to one shoulder as I wait for him.

Because of the plug, I'm avoiding sitting, so I'm trying really hard not to snoop around.

Really hard.

My eyes drift around the large room and focus on the art. The room's warm lighting is almost the color of the foam on cappuccinos. All of it is unique, different. And it's all his. My mom has never owned more than a painting or two at a time. Her decorator used to come and switch them up every couple of years.

But this art is large, vibrant. It sucks you in. Most of the paintings are oil and abstract, although he does have some charcoal nudes in the bathroom.

Taking a deep breath, I peer at his nightstand. Screw it. He'll never know, and I want to know what makes him tick.

I walk over and look over my shoulder, which is stupid. The door is locked, and it's just me.

A rush of adrenaline runs through me. Is this bad? It feels bad. What if I find a diary? Would I read it?

"Fuck, yes, you will," I whisper, tugging open the drawer. I don't know what I was expecting, but definitely not a gun.

"Holy shit." I straighten up. It's in a holster, *but that is a gun.* I swallow and lean down to look at what else he's got. Pens, a ton of condoms, and a box.

Again, that nagging feeling sweeps over me. Is this bad? Am I crap? Because I'm completely invading his personal property. Not moving, I simply stare at it.

I should shut the drawer.

I should.

"Stop, he's got a butt plug in your ass. You've earned the right to look." Not even caring that I'm talking to myself—it soothes me—I take the velvet sapphire box out and smooth my fingers over it. It's about the size of a small shoe box with a latch.

If this box was really important, it would be locked, I reason with myself. The snap clicks open easily.

"Shit." I take a breath and exhale, slowly sitting down on the bed to look inside.

Sketches? Interesting. I pull out a handful. There have to be more than a hundred on all sorts of paper, in ink, crayons, and pencil, and they are… stunning.

"Are these Jett's?" My hand traces the mountains and sunset done entirely on a white paper napkin, in what looks like black pen. Another shows flowers wrapped around a woman's leg, almost climbing onto her, using nothing but crayon and white paper, folded up. Sketch after sketch, I view each one, my head spinning. Who did these? They're not signed. They have to be his, right?

I'm obsessed. If these are his, the man has a true gift. I look up at the giant oil painting wondering if that one's his also. Like is this his true passion, and he's only a lawyer to pay the bills?

"Ms. Stewart?" I scream and bolt up, spilling a ton of drawings on the floor, and stare at Patty.

"Oh my God, you scared me." Sinking to my knees, I try to pick up the sketches so she doesn't see them, which is absurd. It's obvious I'm checking them out. That doesn't mean she can.

"Here." She hands me a cell phone.

"Oh." I blow some hair out of my face. "Um, thank you. I was just…" My voice trails off because, again, this woman is not stupid. Clearly, she sees a lot of things in this house, so hope-

POWER

fully she doesn't say anything to Jett. Should I ask her not to? Would that make me sound guilty?

"Raven." Her voice makes me jump. "The phone." She wiggles it at me. I try to stand, holding his treasures, doing my best to act casual and still not bend them. It doesn't matter that seventy percent of them are on cheap paper, folded and ripped already.

"Thank you, Patty." My voice sounds curt. Nodding, I take the phone. She nods back, a small smile on her lips as she walks out and shuts the door.

"Hello?" I brace myself for my mother's voice.

"Are you a snoop?" And I almost drop everything, phone, drawings, my stomach...

Because it's not my mother.

It's Mr. Powers.

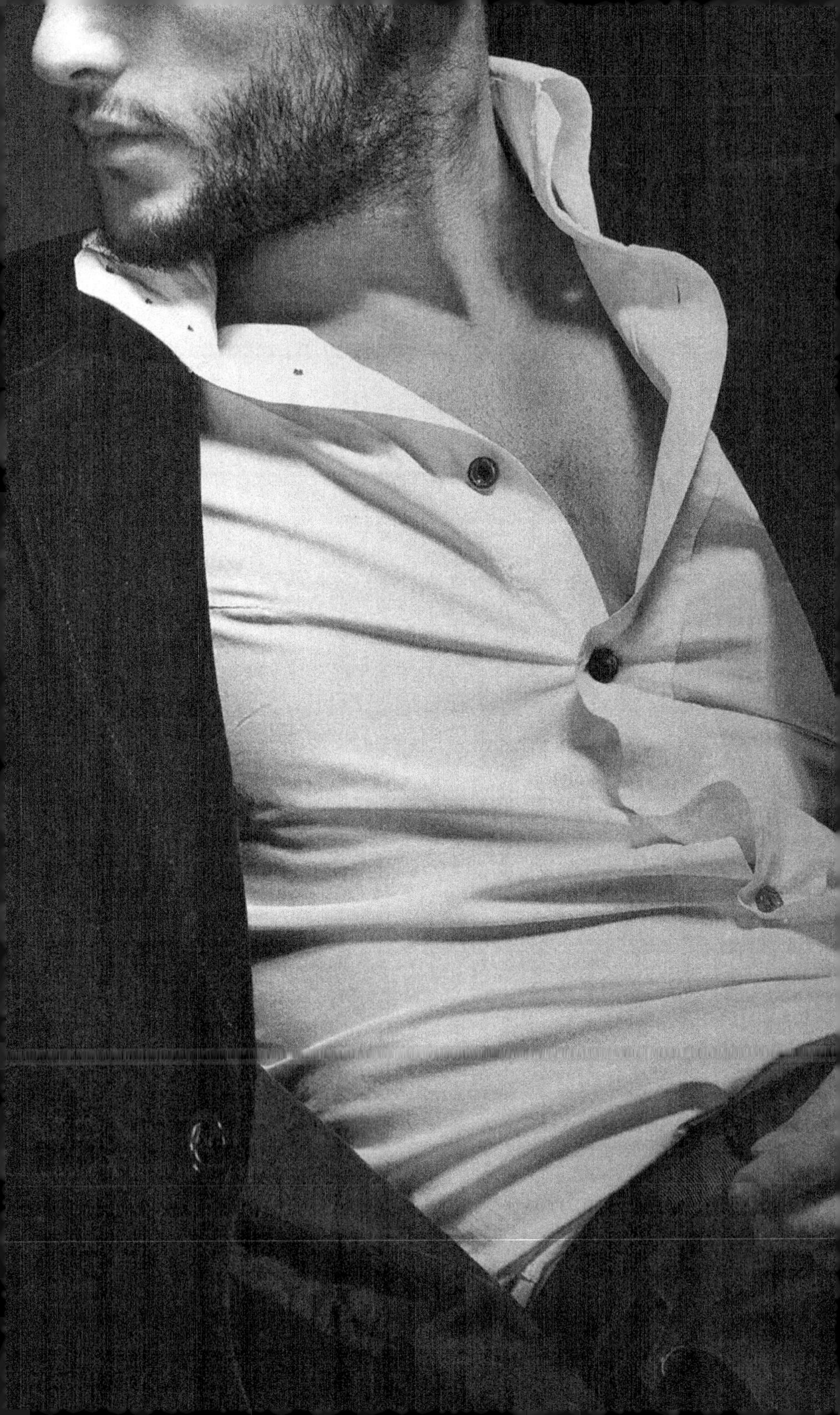

Twelve

JETT

Seated in my guest house, which is actually for my security team, I watch one of the screens intently. I have at least one bodyguard on my property, twenty-four-seven. They take care of everything, all the shit that comes with making enemies.

I've had plenty of death threats. I'm not the kind of man who plays. I pay my team a fortune, and in return I sleep better at night. My guest house is a two-story, 2,300-square-foot, four-bedroom, three-bath house, and one of the rooms is nothing but top-of-the-line security monitors and computers, allowing them, and me, to keep an eye on everything.

There are five men on my security team. I've handpicked either ex-CIA or Navy SEALs. They're on a schedule, so one is here every day.

Right now, I'm the only one in the room as I watch my Lolita behaving like a very bad girl.

"What?" Her voice sounds breathy as she looks around, my sketches falling out of her hands as she spins around, looking for the cameras.

She won't find them. They're in the paintings, but watching her horror at being caught makes my lips twitch.

"Are you a snoop? A bad girl who invades others' property?" My voice is almost a whisper as I zoom in on her face.

POWER

She's so beautiful, it almost takes my breath away. She closes her eyes, then opens them as she unknowingly faces the camera.

"Yes." Her voice cracks.

"Yes, what?" I adjust myself, because this fucking need I have for her seems to be growing, not dissipating. Like a man obsessed, I was in and out of court today and didn't even go back to the office afterward. Instead, I had Rebecca fill me in on the way home.

I came in here to have Zack bring me up to speed on anything new. And I updated him to have all the guys keep eyes out for the paparazzi. After last night, and the pro football player, they tend to come around. And I just had a feeling that my girl would be snooping. I would... fuck, I'm doing it right now.

But she doesn't need to know that, or that I have all her health records, grades, anything and everything. See, I knew I'd fuck her the second I heard her sassy mouth and saw her long legs as she leaned over my island. I knew she was on the pill, which is why I'm not wrapping up my dick. The virgin part was a surprise, though.

"Yes, Mr. Powers." She licks her puffy lips and I grin, because I was gonna wait until later to fuck her, but plans change.

"And?" I growl, cutting the feed to my bedroom.

"I'm a bad girl..." Her voice catches at the end, and I feel like a fucking teenager as I leave the room.

Nodding at Zack, I say, "Be ready," then hang up and walk across my yard, almost feeling her mind race. She wants to run, yet she has the same fucked-up craving. We both need each other to ease our aches. This *need*? That's our fix.

My cock is her drug, same as her pussy is mine, and I'm starting to already think of how I'll fuck her when Rachel comes back. When I open the back door, the house is silent. A faint smell of lemon and mint fills the room. I go straight up the stairs and swing my bedroom door open.

She sits on my bed, hands clutching my comforter on both sides in a death grip.

I walk in and pull off my belt, filling the room with a loud snap. She jumps.

"I... I'm so sorry," she announces, her head held high, and for a second, I let her scent and beauty distract me. Then I snap my belt, causing her to scream. Turning, I lock the door.

"Lie on the bed, dress up," I hiss as I march toward her. She holds her hands up, as if that could stop me, but whatever she thinks I'm gonna do, I'm not.

"Wait. I... how do you even know." Her chest rises and falls. She looks terrified, and I smile.

"Raven, would you like it if I went through your personal stuff?" My voice holds judgment, but there's that irony: I've done way worse; I literally know how many yeast infections she's had.

"No. I..." She takes a breath. "This is not me." Her eyes dart to mine, then the belt, then back to me. "I pride myself on... Oh my God." Her eyes widen as I toss my belt on the bed. It looks like a black snake against the starched white comforter cover.

"I'm not sure what you think you saw or heard—"

"Bed. Panties off, dress up, relax and breathe." Turning, I remove my suit jacket.

"Now, Raven," I say. She nods and shimmies out of her panties.

"Do you want my sandals on or off, Mr. Powers?"

I turn, removing my tie. "On."

She nods.

"Lift your dress." She slowly does, and her long legs tease me. Christ, she's like candy. No matter how much I eat her, I want more.

"Show me." I pull my shirt off, my eyes dipping to her pussy. She's waxed, but unlike a lot of women who have all the hair removed, Raven has chosen to keep at least a landing strip.

The room crackles with our energy. It's almost violent. She tries to breathe through her fear. I have to go slow so as not to hurt her because, for some reason, Raven makes me want to care for her, spoil her, control her...

"Fuck. You're ready." Unzipping my slacks, I watch her eyes widen. A small gasp escapes her when my cock springs free, extending up past my belly button.

"I..." She licks her lips again as if she doesn't know what to say.

"Get on the bed on all fours." She hesitates as I kick off my slacks and tower over her.

"I don't like to wait." My tone is soft. I stroke my cock. Jesus Christ, have I ever been so turned on? She obeys, and my eyes feast on the clear plug sitting in the spot where my cock will be very soon.

"Jett?" She freezes, realizing her mistake, and I almost take pity on her. Her eyes fill with tears.

"I mean, Mr. Powers."

"Shhh." I reach for my belt. Her nails dig into the comforter. Grinning, I toss it to the floor and she sighs.

"Raven, what you need to understand is that I know what you want. I know what you need. If I spank you, it's because why?"

"You know what I need?" I almost grin again. That was not part of our agreement. If anything, she's been so obvious about disobeying me, she's only saying those words because she's scared I'll use my belt on her.

When I lean forward, I'm so pent up my body heat probably scorches hers. "A little fear is good, right, Raven? Adrenaline rushes right here." Grunting, I snake my hand around to her slick pussy and rub her clit back and forth.

"It's like snooping. You know it's wrong, but you do it anyway because it feels good..." I stop stroking her greedy pussy. Yeah, she's ready. Her breath stutters in disappointment when I sit up, leaving her cunt to focus on her perfect ass. My hands move to caress her cheeks while I listen to her breathe, my nostrils flaring as I inhale her fucking scent.

"Spread your legs more. And tell Mr. Powers why you snooped." Watching her, for a second I wonder if I should jack off first, mark her ass with my cum, then fuck her tight hole. Because, Christ...

"I wanted to know you better," she says it fast as my thumb gently rolls the plug in a circle.

"Something tells me by the end of the day you'll know me." I remove the plug, not fast, just smoothly, causing her to whimper.

"That's it, baby. You just breathe and let me take care of you." I reach for the lube I left on the nightstand this morning, and squeeze a good amount onto my index finger, then cover her hole with it.

"Is this gonna hurt?" she whispers.

"No." I leave her ass to coat my cock with lube. "Some women like pain. That's not you," I tell her.

"Oh, thank God." Her voice cracks as she watches me stroke myself.

"Relax and breathe. The plug has you ready, but I'm thick. Lean forward and let me bring out what you were born to be." My hand rests on her hip while I add more lube, then line the tip of my cock at her virgin rosette hole and glide in slowly.

"Raven." My voice tenses. Christ, she's tight and hot. My chest is already covered in sweat. I pull out and ease in again. "Breathe, baby." She does and I push in farther, marveling at how fucking amazing she feels. Has it ever been this good?

"Fuck, your ass feels so good. I'm inside you." I pull out and go back in again as I growl, "That's it. Keep breathing." I open her ass cheeks wide so I can watch my cock slowly glide in and out of her small hole.

"Talk, Raven," I grunt, prepared to jet my load already, and she hasn't even taken half of me yet. But she's going to.

"I... it kind of hurts, burns, but not really... oh fuck." She pants, her hands clenching the sheet as I push in more, watch-

POWER

ing my cock slide fully into her at last. I can't move; the pleasure is like no other.

"Jesus Christ, that's it. You're perfect, Raven," I say gruffly, pulling out so I can thrust in again and again while she moans.

"Raven, you're doing so well," I praise her. My head spins, and my hands dig into her hips as I fuck her, slowly.

"This ass is mine, your cunt, *mine*. Say it, Raven." I'm fucking undone. The pleasure of my cock going in and out of her tight, sweet hole makes spots dance before my eyes.

"Yes, I'm yours," she chants.

"Touch yourself, baby. I'm gonna come," I hiss, feeling her fingers frantically rub her swollen clit.

"That's my girl, make yourself come, so you can squeeze Daddy Powers's cock." My eyes roll back in my head as she does just that.

"Mr.... oh God, Jett, I'm going to come..." Her cunt pulses and contracts, making her ass milk the last bit of my restraint from me. I let go, soar, eyes rolling back in my head as I find nirvana, holding her hips tight while pumping my release into her. Slowly I pull out and try to catch my breath.

Looking down at her, when I'm taking my last breath, this is what I hope to remember. Raven, panting on all fours, dress around her waist, tits spilling out as my cum drips out of her ass.

I wasn't lying. Raven was made to be a submissive, although she probably would never have known it had she not met me.

She looks behind her and our eyes lock. This is getting complicated, but not really. My future is mapped out. Marry Rachel—she's the right wife for me. We will work, climbing our way to the top of whatever I want to achieve.

I'll fuck other women, and she'll look the other way or join in. Simple. I'll see Raven for holidays.

She'll show up, and I'll look at her like I am doing right now, and we will both know that I own her...

"Come here. Let's get you cleaned up, then I'm taking you to Bar Moruno." I turn her and she glides sweetly into my arms. Kissing her eyes, stroking her hair, I whisper how fantastic she felt taking my cock.

She sighs and clings to me. Tightening my arm around her, I lift her up and walk us into the bathroom, ignoring how good she feels in my arms.

I'd like to say it's because she's fresh, new, but I've fucked too many women to believe that. There's something about Raven that speaks to me, calls to me...

Bad timing.

If I were ten years younger, I might have considered everything. I kiss the top of her head, inhaling her scent. Funny how life throws things at you when you're not looking.

But at the end of the day, I am who I am. She'll go back to school, and I'll stand in front of three hundred of my best friends and let them watch as I say, *I Do...* to her mother.

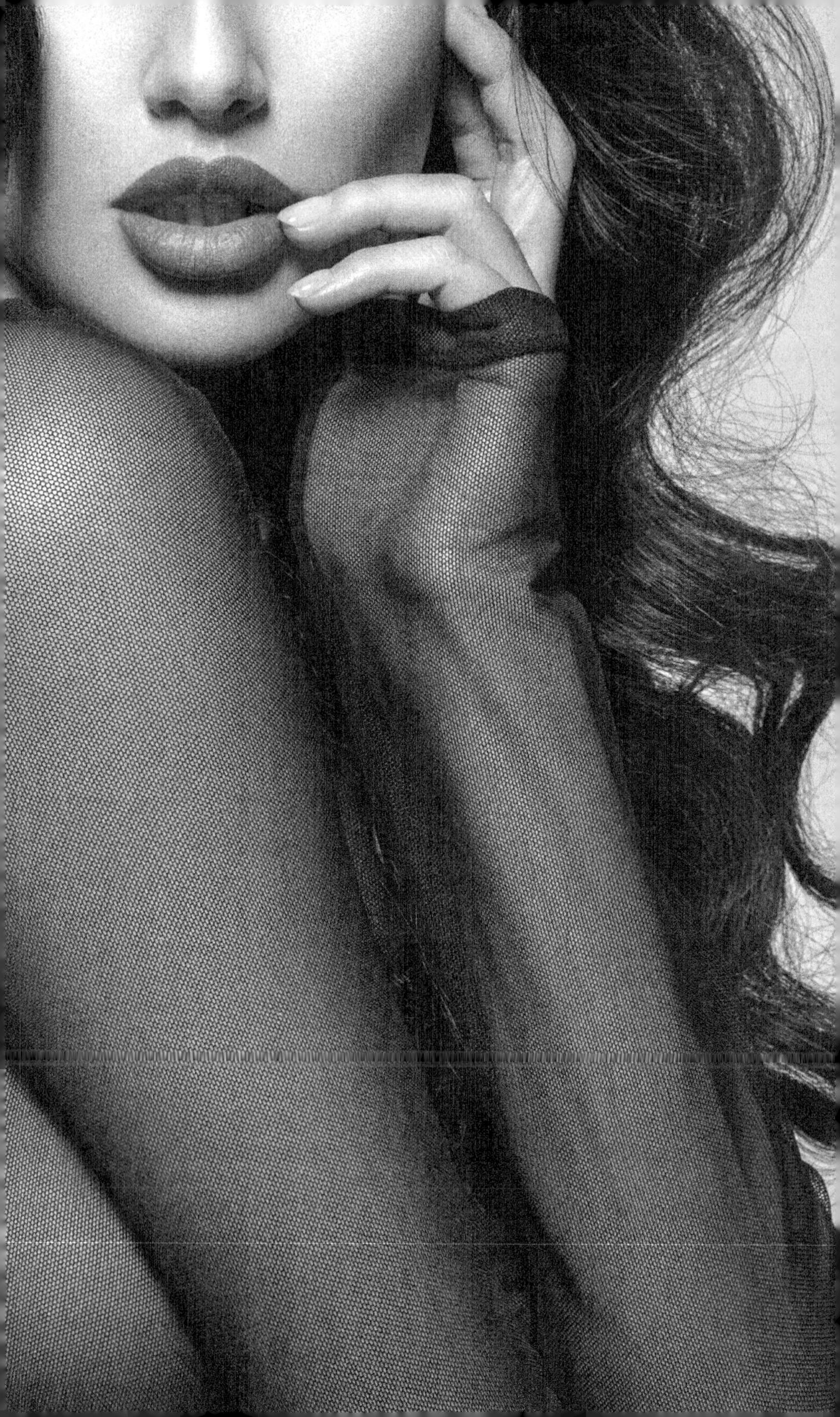

Thirteen

RAVEN

"Are you ready for me to take your orders?" The pretty tattooed waitress smiles at us. Looking over at Jett, I smirk and set my menu down.

"Yes, let's go with the Minerva spicy tuna, setas con huevos, and the pan tostado. You know what? Give us a pan con tomate also. Raven loves bread, and..."

I sit back and cross my legs while Jett keeps ordering. Apparently, we are not only having the rotisserie chicken, but also the prime rib eye.

So. Fucking. Hot.

He's wearing a black button-down shirt, sleeves rolled up, and dark jeans. No wonder he's made millions defending people. I mean, if I was on a jury, I'd vote not guilty.

The man is not just beautiful, he's mesmerizing. The waitress must think the same thing. Her hand is shaking as she nods nervously at him and types the order into her small computer.

"Anything else?" Her face is flushed.

"No, that's good for right now." He graces her with his panty-melting smile, and I almost feel bad for her since she stands there frozen, staring at him, then spins around almost plowing into another waiter.

I shake my head, unable to hold back the smile as I reach for my water.

"What's so funny?" His tan hand takes mine as I swallow. "Have people always responded to you this way?"

He laces his fingers with mine. "You have beautiful hands, you know?"

I blink at him. He just completely ignored my question. I'm starting to figure this voodoo of Mr. Jett Powers out. He's a master at changing things his way.

Genius, really.

"Thank you. Can you answer my question, please?"

He raises a dark brow at me and his lips twitch. "You know, Raven, I can't decide which part of you I like more: your sassy mouth or when you submit."

Letting go of my hand, he picks up his gin and tonic again. My eyes dip to his neck, and I watch the way his muscles move as he swallows.

Jesus, focus, Raven.

Placing my elbows on the table, I rest my chin on my hands. "I know how you do it, Mr. Powers. I was just wondering if you have always been like this."

A small grin appears as he glances at his drink and sets it down. "Do you?"

"I do." I waggle my eyebrows. "*You* control the conversation. *You* make people crave your attention." I sit back dramatically. "Which then makes everyone submit to you in some way." I smile because I'm right and he knows it.

For example, kissing my fingers. If I don't do what he wants, he stops and takes his attention away. It's basic mind-fuck psychology. What I am surprised about is how much it turns me on that he's that powerful. Maybe he's right. I am a submissive... but I think I just get off on his control.

He leans forward. "What else?"

I squirm, becoming wet. "Well, you're... attractive."

My lips twitch as he full-on smiles, and I notice a tiny dimple on his right cheek. "And you know it."

I motion with my hand at him. "Add that, with your intelligence and charisma, and it makes you deadly."

"Deadly." Our eyes lock.

"I like that." Neither of us moves.

"Anything else, Ms. Stewart?"

"Yes. I'd like to see you in front of a jury. I watched a little of that Disciples' member's trial. Did you plan to have that witness wait to take the stand and basically perjure herself?"

He leans forward. The waitress comes over with the bread and what looks like roasted feta cheese.

"Thank you." He smiles and waits for her to leave before he continues.

"First. You always keep them guessing," he says, placing a piece of the roasted bread on my plate. "If they are confused, they're weak, and that's when I strike. After that… they trust you, and once you have trust, everyone sees it the right way." He winks, then lounges back in his chair.

Winks.

My heart skips, and I try to remember what we're talking about. Because all I want is to spread my legs and let him eat my slick, throbbing pussy. Wrap my hands in his hair, knowing that I have Jett Powers on his knees.

Instead, I say, "Which is your way."

"Absolutely." He smirks and stares at my breasts, causing my nipples to harden.

"At the end of the day, it's always about winning, Raven." He looks into my eyes as if he knows what I'm thinking.

"And, if you dare," I say, watching his eyes turn almost black.

"Well, that's what separates the average from the great." He brings a piece of bread to my lips.

Holy fuck. My heart is racing. I lean forward to eat from his hand.

"Good girl. And, I'm in court Monday. You'll go with me."

"I'd like that." I slowly chew. The flavors of the grilled bread make me groan, *literally.*

"I was waiting." He laughs, scooping up some baked feta, smearing it on the toasted bread.

"Try this." Again, I take a bite from his hand and taste a burst of lemon along with olive oil and salt combined with the toasted bread.

"Oh my God." I reach and take the bread from his hand. "I can eat ten pieces of this."

"That's what I like to hear. How are you doing, Mr. Powers?" A tall, dark-haired man dressed in all black sets a dish down. "I know how you love the roasted sweet potatoes."

"Chef Chris." Jett looks up and fist-bumps the man. "This is Raven."

The chef smiles at me. "Nice to meet you. I hope you enjoy the food."

"It's so good," I gush, because it really is. Jett's eyes caress my face, making me grow warm.

"Chris is a fucking incredible chef," he informs me.

"Well, thank you, man." The chef laughs, motioning for the waitress to put down the chicken and steak. The smell instantly makes my mouth water.

"You two enjoy. Let me know if you want anything else." He flashes us a cocky grin, then moves to the back area where I can see the wood-fire oven built into the wall.

"Best chef in Los Angeles. Fuck, maybe the States. I've known him for years. He caters my parties." He grabs a knife and fork and cuts a small piece of perfectly cooked steak, holding it out for me.

"So good." I groan again. "I love all this." Picking up my own fork, I motion at the table full of food, trying not to completely stuff my face in front of him.

Jett leisurely cuts bites for us, telling me stories about all the places he's traveled to. It's like he's the perfect man, beautiful and surprisingly funny. I never want this to end.

Sighing, I sit back. "I'm full, but I can't stop eating. And now, I miss Spain. I guess if I get sick of everything in the States, I'll just take off and move to Costa del Sol, live on the beach." I grin.

"No, you're going to Stanford, then maybe Harvard for law." He takes a bite, and I laugh.

"Um, I would never get in, and I'm fine at NYU." I look at him, eyebrows raised. He can't be serious. Shit, he looks serious. I can't go to Stanford. I need my bestie. Look what happens when Cher leaves me alone.

"I've already spoken to the dean and three of my professors. They can't wait to meet you."

I blink at him, and my voice goes up a notch. "What?" My pulse races.

"NYU is not right for you." He says this as if we're talking about the menu, not my life.

"Jett. I'm not going to Stanford," I state firmly, then pick up my fork to inhale the last of the sweet potatoes. Surprisingly he doesn't say anything, which makes me stop.

"I'm not. I love New York—"

"No one loves New York. They just say that, but we're done talking about this tonight."

"Good." I drop my fork, needing to change the subject. "So. Back to the Disciples trial."

He throws his head back to laugh, then motions for the check.

"I'd love to tell you, but that's classified." He smirks.

"Classified? What are you, the CIA?"

He grins, handing the waitress his American Express Black Card, and looks at me. "Let's go home. I can think of ways you can try to earn access." And my heart aches. He's so gorgeous, and fun, and not mine...

"I'll do my best, Mr. Powers." I bite my lip while he signs the credit card slip.

"Let's go, my beauty." He stands, holding out his hand for me.

"Thank you for dinner. I had no idea you were so charming."

Again, he starts laughing. "That's classified too." His hand goes to my lower back as he nods at the chef.

"I think you should smile more in pictures. The tabloids portray you as an asshole."

"I am an asshole." He escorts us out onto the crowded sidewalk, wrapping his arm around my shoulders as my whole body tingles.

Breathe, just breathe.

"And I rarely laugh." He kisses the top of my head. My stomach dips. We look like a real couple, on a date, just walking to our Tesla.

"Tonight was unexpected." Again, my stomach flips. I need to be careful. I'm starting to want things that are more than likely not going to happen for me. I might be starved for love, but stupid *I'm not*. I'm also not delusional. Simply because we had a lovely date does not mean I'm special to him. The man just admitted his number one rule is to keep everyone guessing.

Except, I see the way he looks at me. I feel the connection we have when he touches me.

I feel it.

He wants me.

He's exciting, brilliant, and when I'm with him, everything seems easier.

"What are you thinking about, beautiful?" Jett's voice brings me back to the now as he motions to Iain, indicating he's already opened the car door for me.

"Just that I loved that restaurant." I smile and slide in. Yeah, I'm falling for him, but who wouldn't? He enters next to me, pulling me onto his lap, stroking my hair.

He's marrying your mother.

His arms tighten around me as he kisses my neck. His lips dip to my ear and I shiver. Everything I should be concerned about evaporates.

My mom.

His marriage.

Everything.

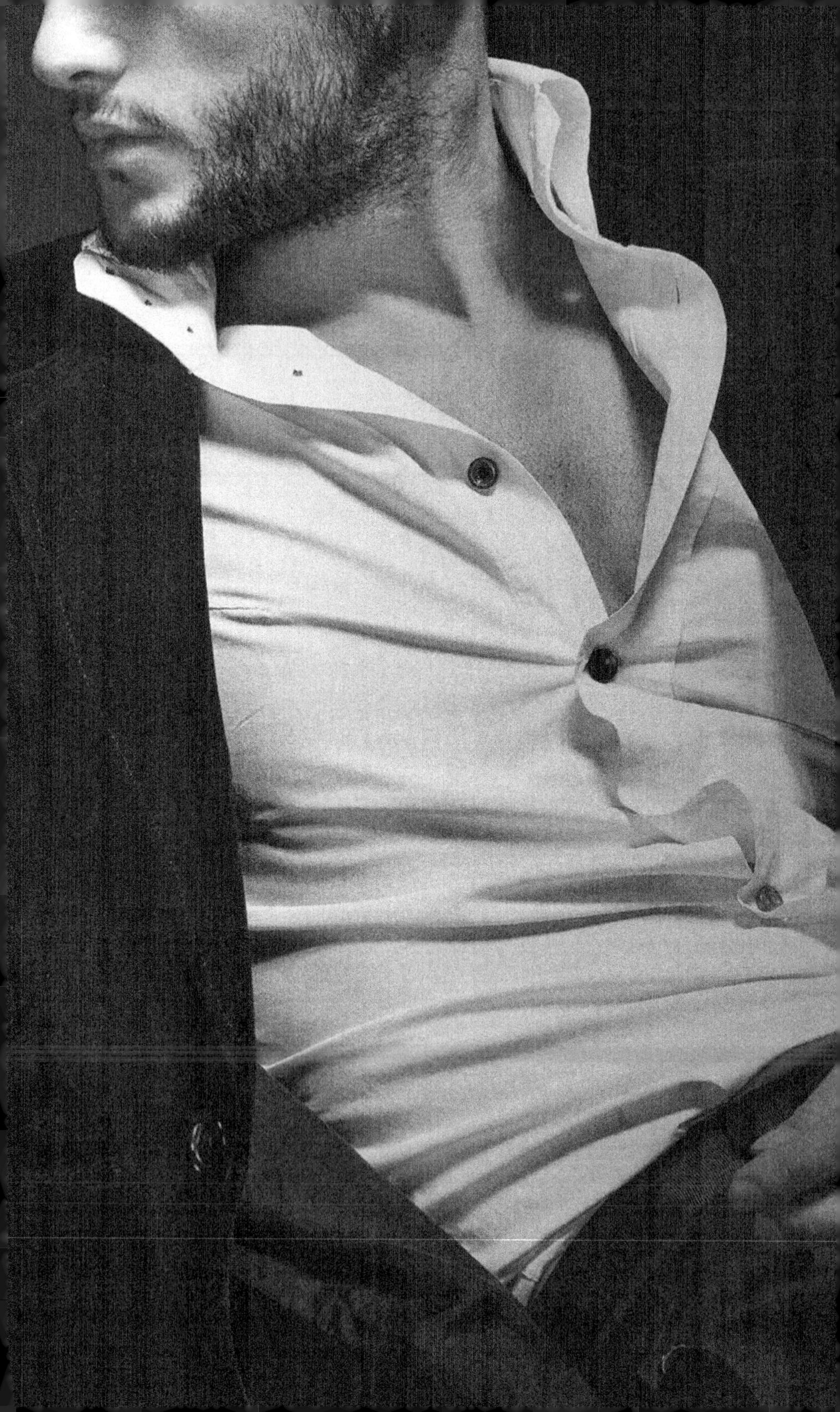

Fourteen

JETT

"I want you upstairs, naked, lying on my bed, waiting for me." I lightly bite her earlobe as we enter through the front door.

"Yes, Mr. Powers." She grins at me.

"And don't touch yourself. I need to make a phone call." Letting her go, I reach for my phone. It's been vibrating in my pocket the whole ride home.

"Fuck," I mumble, seeing six missed calls from Rachel... and no texts.

"What?" Raven looks back at me.

"Nothing." I push on Rachel's number, admiring Raven's ass as she moves toward the stairs. A loud ringing of a phone makes us both freeze and look around.

"Mom?" Raven screams first, grabbing ahold of the stairwell as Rachel slithers out of the corner holding a martini in nothing but a black slip.

"Christ." I press end on the call, stopping the annoying ring.

"Yes, Mommy is home," she snaps at her, then hisses as she passes. *Literally*, her red nails form a claw at Raven, like a cat ready to scratch.

"Oh my God." Raven stares somewhat in horror, somewhat in humor at her mother.

POWER

I've seen Rachel like this many times. She has a three-drink maximum. After that, she gets mean and belligerent, then passes out. She never mentions it in the morning, and to be honest, I don't care. She's probably an alcoholic, but she's a functioning one, so as long as she doesn't embarrass me around important people, I couldn't care less if she medicates herself with cocktails and pills.

Still, I am not about to tolerate her lashing out at Raven.

"Surprise." She continues toward me, holding up her arms, the martini spilling on the floor. "Where the fuck have you two been?"

I toss the key fob on the foyer table and reach out to steady her before she slips on the drink.

"Dinner," I state, wrinkling my nose at her scent. Jesus, she's had way more than three. She smells like a bar…and a funeral with her overpowering, flowery scent.

"*Dinner?*" She swings her head to stare at Raven.

"Yes. We're people. We have to eat," I say dryly as I walk her up the stairs. She stumbles, then giggles.

I clench my jaw, aggravated that she's home and a fucking train wreck. Her mascara is smudged under both eyes. Her ballooned-up lips are covered with smeared red lipstick, making her resemble a female Joker.

"I tried to get ahold of Erin." She hiccups.

"Not now, Rachel," I say, propelling her up the stairs.

"She didn't answer. And don't worry." She takes a sip from the empty martini glass. "I didn't leave a message, but on Monday I'll see if she's free next weekend to fuck us both again." She waves the glass, then sets it on my Chippendale buffet while I open our door.

"Let's talk about it in the morning." When I let go of her arm, she tries to walk in without weaving.

"Thirty minutes," I instruct Raven, not bothering to explain more as I shut the door.

"I missed you, baby." Rachel turns to face me, tossing off her slip.

"Time for bed." I guide her over, unable to disguise my distaste, which isn't fair. It's not her fault I'm borderline obsessed with fucking her daughter.

She smiles as she slips under the covers.

"Are you joining me?" She cocks her head, waiting for me.

Sighing, I turn off the light and get undressed.

"I want to suck your cock," she announces in the dark.

"Later." I get into bed, thankful she's smashed. I easily remove her cold, clammy hands.

She mumbles something, then passes out, a loud snore the only sound in our room.

The fuck is going on with me?

I look up at the dark ceiling and replay dinner. I haven't enjoyed a night like tonight ever. Not only is Raven smart, but she's also got a sweetness combined with a sassy mouth that makes me want to kiss her, then spank her ass red.

I turn to look at Rachel. Even in the dark I can see her red clown lips. I roll her onto her side and reach for my pants on the floor, retrieving my phone.

Then I send a text that confirms my spot in hell, if you believe in that.

ME: Come to my room. NOW.

Three dots appear... then nothing as my cock gets hard at the thought of her trying to decide whether she'll obey.

I grin and shoot her a text: **Do you dare?**

I toss my phone on the nightstand and wait for her.

She'll come, because whether she likes it or not, were both obsessed.

Sick, really.

But fuck it. No one's perfect.

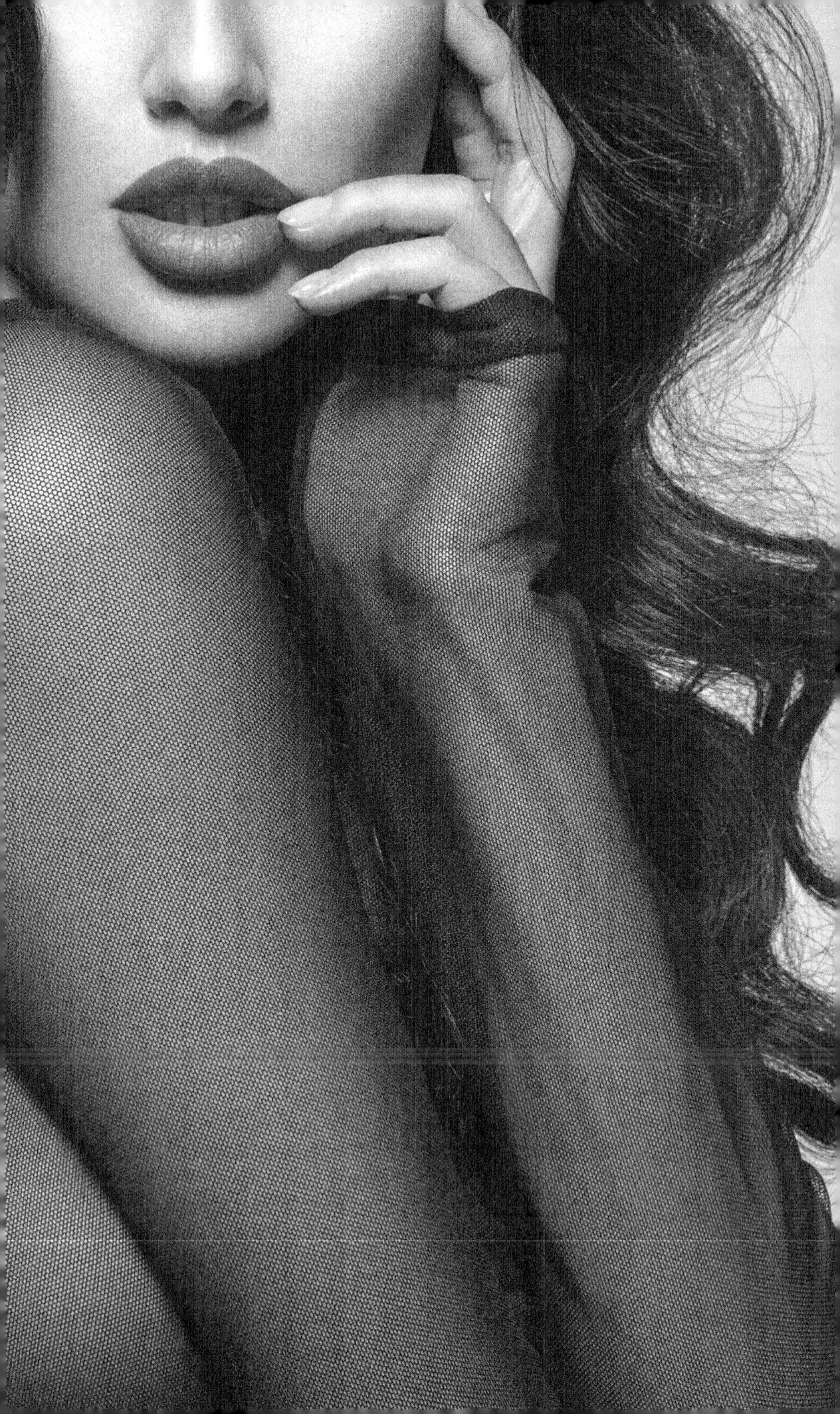

Fifteen

RAVEN

JETT: Come to my room. NOW.

That text is the first thing I see after getting out of the shower. Seeing my mom and Jett together made me feel dirty. And I can't really pinpoint exactly what it is. I don't regret Jett, but I guess it's the reality of seeing her with him, which slammed it home. He's not mine; he's not going to be mine. And my mother is acting more bizarre every day.

This sucks!

God, what was that creepy comment about someone named Erin fucking them this weekend? What are they, into threesomes?

What the hell?

I grab my phone and start texting "Fuck off, sicko," but before I send it, he texts me again.

JETT: Do you dare?

"Goddammit," I growl, looking up at the ceiling, then over at myself. I'm flushed from the hot water, or maybe because I'm in heat, literally burning for him.

Needing him.

I should press send and go to bed.

Don't do this, Raven. Go to bed. It's like I'm possessed. Am I really considering going to him?

POWER

Like in his room, where my mother is?

Maybe they both want to tell me something. Or he wants to cancel me going to court with him on Monday.

I sigh, slipping on one of the T-shirts I like to sleep in, and quietly shut my door.

"Jesus, what are you doing, Raven?" I whisper to the dark house as I make my way to his room, my hand hesitating on the door handle.

This is wrong.

Bad, so bad. If I actually open this door, I'm crossing a line I can't ever come back from.

"Walk away," I whisper, taking a step back. Swallowing, I listen for any movement.

Nothing. Maybe they're asleep? Dream on. He's taunting me, especially with the *do you dare* part...

Before I can talk myself out of this, I open the door. The room is dark, but since it's giant-sized and the bed is easy to spot, I freeze.

Fuck.

They're both in bed. My mind is going off like an annoying alarm. *Run...* She's right there. Licking my suddenly dry lips, I try to stay quiet, then almost scream as he kicks the sheet off of him.

Dead.

I'm actually concerned I might faint, because I can barely breathe. My eyes take in his beautiful body. The lights from outside almost twinkle on him. He lies there, stretched out, arm behind his head, showing off his perfect bicep and fucking eight-pack.

All that would be bearable if I could just look away from his giant cock, which he's stroking slowly with his other hand.

"Oh my God." I gasp and cover my mouth while his eyes remain fixated on me.

Everything stops.

The world, my conscience, everything, as I give in.

Forfeit.

I'm clearly not a good person because I've never been more turned on in my life.

I walk toward him as the moonlight touches the side of his face. He stops stroking himself and reaches for me. In one fast jerk I fall onto him. A small whoosh escapes my lips.

My mom mumbles something and flips onto her back. I can't breathe. Holy fuck. I'm going to get caught... and Jett's going to have to call an ambulance for me.

"Breathe, Raven," he whispers in my ear, then positions me so I'm straddling him.

"Yes." Inhaling, I try to calm my racing pulse.

"That's a good girl. Now take your shirt off," he demands, and I blink at him.

Slowly I pull my shirt off, letting it drop to the floor.

"Rachel, turn to your side." He speaks *loud,* causing my mom to snort, but she rolls to her side, her back to us.

This time I really have stopped breathing. My nails dig into his chest. He watches my mom for a second, then turns his face to me, relaxing back, his hard erection reaching past his belly button.

He's never been more powerful, more exciting than in this moment.

"What if she wakes up?" I whisper.

He grins. Jesus, he had to have made a deal with the devil—no one can be this gorgeous.

"I guess she'll watch you fucking me." His voice is not even that quiet, just rather soothing.

My core clenches.

"Oh my God. I can't do this." I shake my head, but his hands easily hold me in place.

"Sit on my cock, Raven." He wraps one hand around my neck and places the other on my hip.

"This is so bad." I groan.

"Fuck me," he demands.

POWER

One of my hands reaches for the wrought iron headboard as I look down at him.

"Do it... oh, Raven... yeah, that's it, baby." His eyes hold mine as I slide my slick, swollen pussy onto his hard cock, unable to stop myself from moaning.

"Yeah, that's my naughty girl," he growls when I lift myself up and pound down on him.

I try to stay quiet while he holds me still, and I feel his thick cock deep inside me.

"Such a naughty girl. You like fucking Mr. Powers, don't you?" His one hand digs into my hip, guiding me as I rub my clit back and forth on him.

"I do," I whisper, reaching for the headboard with my other hand, so I can fuck him as deep as I can take him.

"I'm inside you." His other hand tightens on my throat as he controls the tempo. "Easy, baby, I can feel your cunt wanting to come, and we're just getting started."

"Please..." I whisper, almost frantic to orgasm. What if my mom wakes up?

He lets go of my neck and lifts me off him. "No." I almost burst into tears. What the hell?

"Shhh, you don't want Rachel to wake up, do you?" He rolls me under him.

"Jett..."

"Quiet." His lips take mine and his tongue invades my mouth, claiming me.

Strong.

Controlling.

Fucking mesmerizing. And I'm gone. A piece of me will die tonight, a piece that I'll give to him.

"Wrap your legs around me, baby." He thrusts into me as we both groan at how good it feels.

Arching my head back, I stifle a moan while he sucks on my neck.

"Christ, I've never wanted anyone like I want you," he grunts, looking up into my eyes, fucking me hard.

In and out, I feel everything, my body tightening, climbing, preparing to soar.

"That's it, Raven. *Now come for Daddy*," he murmurs into my lips.

"Oh my God." My nails dig into his back as I go over, my core pulsing and spasming while he kisses me through it all.

Undone is as close as I can come to describing this wild, uncontrollable feeling. Sounds are gone, but I feel his cock swell, then jerk deep inside me.

I submit to this debauchery.

I make no excuses, nor do I have any more guilt.

He is and always will be my dark obsession.

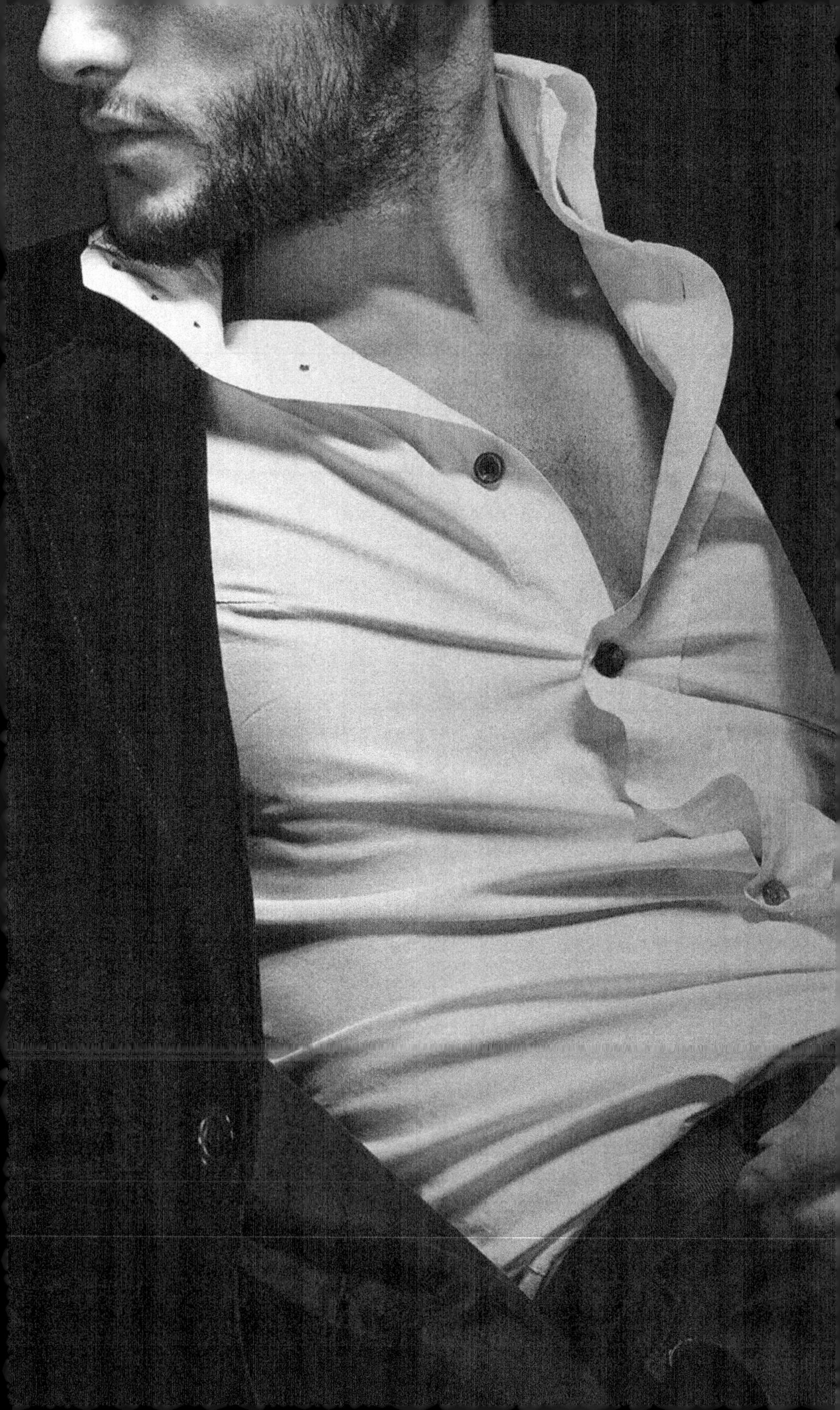

Sixteen

JETT

"Are you mad at me about last night?" Rachel sets her coffee cup down, looking every bit her age this morning.

"No, why?"

I'm gonna burn in hell.

"I feel like you're... avoiding me." She sighs, then looks up. At least she's taken a shower, her face washed clean of that Joker look.

"You were tired. I tucked you in and went to sleep myself."

Yep, definitely burning in hell.

I stand, leaning down to kiss the top of her head, which feels coarse from too much dyeing, and move to the refrigerator for some orange juice.

"So what dress should I wear tonight?" Rachel tries to break the uncomfortable silence, and the fact that I'm completely distracted.

She's right. I am avoiding her, like pretending to sleep when her hands went roaming this morning and my dick stayed soft.

I'm trying to console myself that my cock is just worn out from last night. Because, fuck, that was hot, and wrong, and completely depraved. And I loved every second of it.

The fuck was I thinking?

"Jett?" Rachel's voice brings me back to her, and the acknowledgment that she's not Raven. What am I doing? I'm pushing forty. This has to stop.

"You look lovely in anything you wear," I say automatically. Spewing compliments is my forte. They easily spill from my lips: *you look gorgeous, you're stunning.* Yet there's only one woman who takes my breath away.

I need to get my head examined and think about staying away.

Her wet cunt squeezing my cock as she came, over and over, both of us wrapped up in our own world, heightened by the allure of being caught.

Not that it was unfeasible—once Rachel passes out, she's out. But Raven didn't know that, and fuck, it was good.

It's a new day, though, and this obsession has run its course. I need to focus on my fiancée.

"I'm gonna go for a quick run, and then you want to go to the farmers' market? Or do you want to nap? I can always work." Sitting back down, I give her my full attention, forcing myself not to compare her tanned, lasered skin to Raven's fresh, natural glow.

"How about we take a nap together?" Rachel glides the tips of her pointy, clawed nails up and down my forearm, her red silk bathrobe hanging open on purpose, so my eyes can feast on her large, fake breasts. And I do. I stare, waiting, no, praying for an erection.

Nothing.

"Sure." I move my arm away and kiss her nose because she's frowning. "Let me go run, and I'll meet you upstairs." Maybe exercise will help. That, or I can use the excuse I wore myself out with my run.

Jesus, pathetic.

"What's going on, Jett? It's been days. You never go days without fucking." Her eyes latch onto mine.

I smile. Does she honestly think she can find anything? Like I would ever let that happen. She is a devious bitch, though, so I do need to fuck her just to get her off my ass.

"I've been jacking myself off so much my hands have calluses."

"So let me take care of you, baby."

I fight back my distaste at her calling me *baby*, and I'm done with her fucking stale floral scent.

She drops to her knees, scooting between my legs. "Does Mr. Happy want to come out and play?" She reaches to pull down my sweatpants, but I stop her.

"I'm gonna change your perfume." Grabbing her hands, I continue, "And your daughter could walk in any second."

Dead silence.

Literally, all I hear is the neighbor's gardeners mowing their lawn. That's how much I've killed the vibe.

"What? Since when?" she finally speaks. Her eyes narrow, causing her face to look borderline ugly as she stands.

"Since I found a new perfume for you." Great, now I have to go perfume shopping. Nah, I'll get Rebecca to sell me hers. It doesn't repulse me.

"Oh-kay." She holds up a hand. "Let me get this straight. You got me perfume, and you're worried about my daughter seeing us?" She cocks her head.

"Exactly." I stare straight back at her, daring her to question me. Her eyes narrow, but she must feel I'm done because she rubs her forehead.

"Look, I'm just tired," she snaps. "I had to hold Courtney's hand the whole three days I was in New York. She's a fucking prima donna. It's exhausting building people up, and then leaving you with Raven... worrying you wouldn't get along..." Her voice trails off as she leans back in the chair watching me.

I have to bite the inside of my cheek not to smile. What am I gonna say? *Oh, we got along. She's the best fuck I've ever had. And I get off on corrupting her, controlling her, oh, and my cock seems to only want her...*

Yeah, somehow, I don't think that would go over well.

"Morning." The object of our conversation appears at the doorway. And my cock instantly hardens.

POWER

"Hello, Mother, did you have a nice trip? Happy to be home?" She smiles, wearing a tiny black bikini, hair pulled into a messy bun, and her lips glossed up.

I try not to stare as she goes to the cabinet for a mug. Looking at my phone, I hear her pour herself a cup of coffee.

"*Home?*" Rachel spits out. "This is not your home." She snorts.

Slowly I look up and catch her rolling her eyes. I almost strangle her.

"What's wrong with you?" I grumble.

Rachel might be a fucking cunt, but she should know when I've reached my breaking point. And I'm done.

Instantly, she picks up her coffee and laughs over the rim. "Oh, stop it. I was just kidding." She shakes her head and takes a sip.

"I was going to take a swim. *If* that's okay, Mr. Powers?" Raven holds her head high and stares at her mother, then turns to face me, her cheeks flushed.

"You never need to ask." Our eyes lock, and for a moment I lose myself in them. Raven puts on a good act, but she craves love. It's why she responds so well to me.

Rachel humiliating her is disturbing on so many levels. The first is how hard my heart is pounding. The second, why I can't seem to control these feelings.

"I was joking, Jett. We're going to be married, so of course Raven is welcome," Rachel says tightly.

Again, dead silence. I need to get out of here and take Raven with me.

"I'm going for a run." I look down at Rachel. "You should take a nap. You need to get rid of those bags under your eyes. Try ice—maybe that will help."

Her mouth opens and closes and her cheeks flush in embarrassment.

Fucking cunt.

"Jett... please." Her voice cracks as her hands instantly go to her face. I don't wait to hear more. Quite frankly, I'm considering canceling going out tonight so as not to be near her. I stop at the doorway and motion for Raven to go ahead of me. She sets her cup down.

We don't say anything as we walk. I open the door to the backyard leading to the pool area before I grab her arm.

"No. Let go, *Mr. Powers*," she sneers.

Ignoring her, I drag her into the pool house. There's a sauna inside and a separate room set up for my massage therapist.

"I said, let go of me. I can't deal with her, or you." She rips her arm free as soon as we're inside.

Grabbing her face with both hands, I force her to look at me. "Raven, she's a bitter—"

"Stop. I know exactly what my mother is. What I'm wondering is what's wrong with you?" Her eyes are shiny with tears, looking like deep, dark pools of rain.

"I'm not going to discuss my relationship with you," I inform her.

"Why? Have I not earned it? Because sorry, I don't think I have any more holes left for you to fuck," she yells, frustrated tears spilling down her pink cheeks.

The monster inside me becomes unleashed.

I like her like this, needy, vulnerable, mine to corrupt, mine to build back up.

"She's a vile, horrible person. She hates me, you know?" Tears of what I'm sure are years of neglect and humiliation spill from her eyes.

My cock hardens almost to the point of pain. And before I can stop myself, I have her in my arms, pulling her hair tight until her neck falls back.

"Fuck, Raven." My tongue licks her tears; they taste like sweet taffy, making me groan. Kissing her, loving her, forcing her to submit, that's what turns me on.

Deep inside she knows who she belongs to. No matter what happens, she'll always be mine. I'm in her head, in her heart. I crush my lips down onto hers, destroying not only her, but us.

POWER

Burning in hell... I accept it. As long as she comes with me. I lift her up and walk her back to the massage table as I deepen the kiss. I want all of her, her smiles, her laughter, fuck, I want her soul. She moans and our tongues twist, my hand going to her neck as I devour her.

Setting her ass on the massage table. She's panting. One breast has fallen out of her bikini, and I lean down to bite it, licking when she hisses.

Her hands wrap tightly in my hair, and I place both her legs over my shoulders, dragging her to the edge of the table.

"Fuck me, Mr. Powers." She arches into my mouth, and I lick her clit, then suck.

Hard.

Wild.

Obsessed.

Her scent... fuck, I pull down my sweats so I can jack off while sucking on her clit.

"Why you?" she whimpers. "Why does it have to feel so good with *you*?" Her voice cracks. It's as though she wants to hate me yet knows she can't.

"I can't get enough of this cunt." I spread her legs wider, sucking, licking, fucking, drowning in her juices. She whimpers, her hands tightening. Moving up and down, she screams as she orgasms into my mouth.

I stand, letting her juices run down my chin, bringing her face to mine. "You're mine. I was the first."

My tongue shoves inside her mouth and she sucks on it. Pulling away, I flip her around.

"I need to be inside you." Kicking her legs apart, I hold her still by the back of her neck. "This," I growl, thrusting into her, "is why you will always be mine." Her hands go to hold the top of the table as I rut into her.

It's raw, frantic, she's everywhere on me, as I pound into her, fucking her, branding her...

"I can't get enough," I say with a groan as my stomach muscles tighten and her cunt contracts, squeezing my cock so hard I see black dots.

Then I lean forward and grab her hair by the roots, grunting while I move in and out. My balls tighten and I let go, fucking release everything inside her slick walls.

This is how I want her, under my me, controlled always. I should get her a diamond-and-sapphire choker. Fucking collar her so the world knows who she answers to.

"*Jesus Christ.*" I pull out. What am I thinking? My breathing is harsh and I try to focus. I'm in too deep. This has to be it.

I'm marrying Rachel, not collaring Raven.

She turns to stare at me, her eyes showing me everything a man like me should never see.

"I need to go." I pull my sweats up. This is over. It's not fair to her. "Raven?"

She cocks her head, her hair that was up has found its way down. Her eyes look like sparkling gems, and her lips are slightly parted while she tries to steady her breath. She's breathtaking, which makes her a target with her mother, and I guess me.

I reach up to stroke her lips.

I didn't plan this, but I started it, and now I'll end it.

Control.

It's what makes me, *me*. The more I have, the more powerful I feel.

"What? Nothing?" She shakes her head. Her hands tremble slightly as she straightens her bikini top. "Just go, Mr. Powers. Your secret is safe with me," she snaps, reaching down to tie her bottoms.

Go. I need to. I am marrying her mother.

"You can call me Jett from now on." I step back, knowing those were the words she needed to hear. She doesn't look at me, just nods, then brushes past me.

"I'm going to swim, *Jett*. Enjoy the rest of your day." Her voice is almost thick with held-back tears.

I fight the temptation to reach for her.

Tell her the truth.

"Raven?" She stops but doesn't turn.

"Make sure you lock your bedroom door tonight." Her back straightens. She reaches to pin her hair up again, and the door shuts behind her.

And I'm alone, with only her scent.

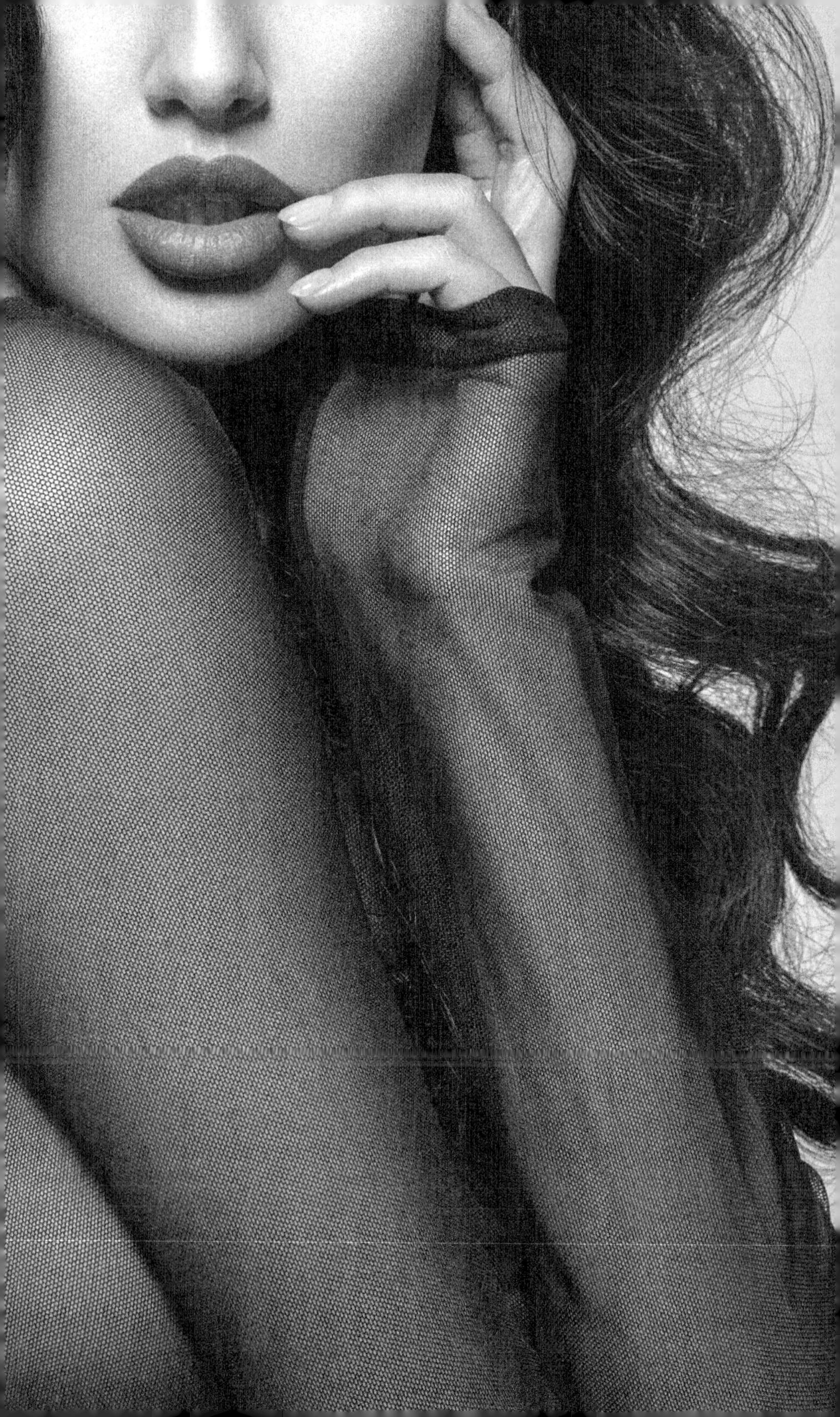

Seventeen

RAVEN

Turns out I didn't need to lock my door. He hasn't tried it once. It's been three nights and nothing. Monday came and went. I didn't go to court with him.

Maria did show up though. Apparently, her car took longer to fix than expected. She seems to be my personal jailer slash spy who reports daily to my mother. Or maybe it's Jett. I don't even care. I've got nothing to hide. Two emotions consume me: emptiness and rage. They alter depending on the time of day.

I've read three books, sunbathed every day, and if I don't get out of this house, I might go mad.

"Maria? How would you like to go to the beach? Maybe we could have a late lunch-early dinner on the boardwalk? Buy some cheap, completely unnecessary stuff? What do you think?" I smile, but I know she's on to me.

"What beach?" Her voice holds a note of caution.

"I don't care, just away from here." I close my eyes, trying to gather some patience. This is hardly Maria's fault.

"Sorry, I'm used to being more active." I puff out some air, and my mind goes to Jett. He can go all night.

"Why don't you use Mr. Powers's gym? Or maybe I get you a massage—"

"No," I almost scream. Jesus, can you imagine? The pool house? I sit at the end of my bed to think.

"I have to go out. I really don't care where we go."

Again, she frowns and looks at her watch. "When is Ms. Cher coming back?"

"Two-and-a-half weeks. Who else do I know who'd go out with me besides Brody?"

Looking at Maria, I want to burst into tears. When did I lose touch with my high school friends?

"I don't know. But Mr. Powers told Ms. Rachel to leave you alone. Why would he say this?" With her wise brown eyes, she looks at me as though she can discover everything she missed this past week.

"So I take it you don't want to go to the beach?" I grumble, opening the balcony doors. The blast of hot air promptly makes me slam them shut.

"My knee is acting up, and that sand…"

"Never mind. You shouldn't be babysitting me. I'm hardly a child." I sigh, aggravated.

Asshole.

What an idiot I was. Because this stings, and I'm mad at myself for even having a glimmer of hope. I guess I thought he was better than what he is. That a man of his intelligence would see through my mom and acknowledge she's a terrible person.

And then what? We'd ride away into the sunset? *My ass.*

Thankfully, I've only had to see my mom once. She ignored me; I ignored her back.

And Jett…

I can't think about him. Otherwise, I'll start crying. Screw that. He doesn't get my tears. He gets nothing.

"Can I have some privacy, Maria?" I sit on the end of my bed. It's time I bite the bullet and call Cher—I need her. I was waiting, in case Jett… Well, it doesn't matter. He didn't. So I can safely tell her everything.

I look over at Maria who hasn't moved. Instead, she stands there, watching me and frowning. I grab my phone.

"Maria? Please." I hold up my phone.

Narrowing her eyes, she walks toward my door. "I'll be downstairs," she grumbles. Instead of being comforting, it sounds like a threat. I know she's trying to protect me from my mom and Jett, but it's too late for that.

I smile at her as she shuts my door.

I have to get out of here.

I despise not having my own money. I mean, I have my American Express card, but my parents take turns paying it off every month.

Maybe I should look for a job? Although, who's gonna hire me without a car? And I'm only here for another month. I'd have to have Maria chauffeur me around.

"God." I groan, flopping back on the bed, instantly seeing his face. Bolting up, I push on Cher's number. I've been pretending I lost my phone charger. That's why I've ignored her calls and texts.

Taking a breath, I wait, listening to the funky overseas ringtone, my mind wandering.

Is he fucking my mom?

"Of course he is, stupid," I grumble. *I hate him.*

"Of course who is? And it's about fucking time. Ciao, bella," Cher's voice blasts into my ear. Without a doubt, she has the worst Italian accent, but she doesn't care.

I wish I was Cher.

"Sorry, I told you I had to get a new charger. Maria's car broke down." I bite my lip, wondering if I should wait to tell her everything in person. It's not like she can really help; she's in fucking Italy.

"What's happening? Jesus, I really am psychic. I knew something was wrong," she huffs, and I almost start laughing. It's either that or cry. Cher loves to think she is gifted in the supernatural.

A couple of years ago, she became a witch. Apparently if you're a real witch you don't tell anyone. Cher found that information out after she'd informed our whole senior class. Thank God her dad is famous. No one even cared.

POWER

Now, if I had announced that I was a witch, they'd have probably tried to throw me in a bonfire after a football game.

"You finally got Brody to fuck you and it was terrible?" She sounds concerned. "Listen, it sucks the first time and, well, a lot of times after that. Tell him to watch lots of porn. And don't worry. It's just because a lot of men have a hard time knowing where the clitoris is—"

"I didn't sleep with Brody," I say, cutting her off. I can't handle a sex education class from her, especially since my first time was fucking amazing.

Jett definitely knows where the clit is, along with every other spot that makes my eyes roll back in my head.

"How?" she wails.

"Cher! I swear to God, my ear is ringing," I shout. I love her but she's making me rethink confessing.

"I'm just so disappointed for you. Please don't get down. I'll be home soon, and I swear, I will get you—"

"I slept with Jett."

Dead silence.

"Cher?"

"*Daddy Powers?*" Her voice is a whisper until the end, when she screams.

"Don't call him that," I retort, mostly because my heart skips a beat and face flushes as I hear his voice growl, *"That's it, Raven. Now come for Daddy."*

"Cher, listen, this is not at all what you're thinking. You have no idea—"

"Holy fuck. You lucky bitch. Was he... Oh my God, is he as good as he looks?" I flop back on the bed and want to crawl into a ball. Just saying his name out loud hurts.

"He is, was." My voice cracks.

"Oh dear." Cher exhales. "Wait. What happened to Brody?"

I snort. Memories of that night, which seems so long ago, but was only a little over a week ago, run through my head. Jesus, I feel like I've aged ten years.

"Brody came over, and while he was sloppily trying to find my clitoris, Jett Powers walked in on us and took over." I vomit this out so fast, I toss my arm over my eyes. Again, the phone line is quiet.

"He took over in front of Brody?" Cher sounds as horrified as I feel.

"What?" I sit up.

"You said he took over," she says.

"Oh my God, I meant, he kicked Brody out, then took over. Does it even matter? This is my life," I yell, completely frustrated. She doesn't get it. No one can.

"Wow," she whispers.

"Yes." I stand and start to pace. "And then we just... kept at it. He's so controlling, in the best way, and exciting. You have no idea how nasty he is..." I let my voice drift. It seems I've rendered Cher speechless, which has to be a first for her. Who knows what she'd do if I told her the rest.

"I just... fucking Daddy Powers. I knew it," she squeals again. "You lucky bitch."

"Cher, are you insane? He's marrying my mother," I scream into the phone.

"Wait, still?" Again, she sounds shocked, and that hysterical feeling like I might start laughing and never stop is coming.

I clear my voice but can't help it. I laugh and choke out, "Still."

Which promptly makes me cry because Cher loves me so much, she can't imagine that he wouldn't break it off.

"Okay. Just take a breath and let me think." She tries to sound calm.

Nodding, I look up at the ceiling.

"So are you still fucking him? And does your mom know?"

"No, and no." I keep pacing, switching my cell to my other ear. "Or maybe she does. She's a crazy person, so you never know." My voice sounds bitter, and I know it. "Why would he be with her, Cher? Why?" I bite the inside of my cheek before I say more.

"Oh, Raven, you're in love with him," Cher declares, and my heart burns at her words.

I can't be. I won't allow it.

"Stop it. I'm not in love with him. I barely know him. It was hot because he's forbidden, and he's experienced. That's it," I explain slowly.

"So what are you? I'm confused. If he's gonna be with your mom, you can't keep fucking him. I don't care how hot he is."

"Well, we don't have to worry about that. He's been ignoring me since the day after my mom got back from New York," I snap, as if she should know all this.

"Okay. Good." I can hear her lighting up a cigarette. "So here's what you need to do."

I stop pacing.

"You need to take a shower, and then go out, pick up the hottest man, and fuck him. I'm telling you that's the only way you will ever get Daddy Powers out of your system."

I turn and blink at my reflection from the balcony doors, barely recognizing myself. I'm tan from days of sun, but it's my eyes that look so different.

I look kind of savage. Instead of crying, I'm taking my life into my own hands. Screw Jett Powers and my disgusting mother.

I breathe out. "I agree."

"You do?" She sounds shocked.

"I do. Fuck Jett. He can have my mom. They deserve each other. I'm going out." I spin around, marching to my closet.

"Are you okay? I'm a little concerned. Maybe you should wait until I come home." Cher's voice reminds me I'm still on the phone with her.

"Nope, you're right. I'll text you later."

Then I hang up on her loud, "Wait."

This is exactly what I need. I shiver, feeling goose bumps. Two weeks ago, I'd never have done anything like this. Now… My phone vibrates and I glance down.

CHER: CONDOMS?!!
ME: Don't worry.

As I turn off my phone, my mind races. *Shit, condoms.* I'm on the pill, and Brody was tested, so, until this second, I haven't even considered I might have gotten an STI from Jett.

"Oh my God." I cover my mouth. What if I did and it's just marinating, getting ready to explode in the next week or so? Just because I'm clean does not mean Jett is, although he does have that giant box of condoms in his nightstand drawer.

Clearly, he doesn't use them, since he didn't think twice about wrapping up his dick with me. Jesus, what if he gave me herpes? I mean, he fucks my mom. And that whole threesome comment.

I feel sick.

Stop thinking about him and worry about how you're gonna get rid of Maria. Maybe she'll be off. She's been here all day. Doesn't matter. I intend to get drunk and have sex.

I jerk my red spaghetti strap dress off a hanger and grab my new Prada wedge sandals. This should all work. My dress clings to my form, and my heeled sandals make my legs and ass look fantastic.

It's two thirty. That gives me plenty of time to get ready, steal some of Jett's condoms, call an Uber, and find a hip place on Sunset Boulevard for happy hour.

I have a credit card, fake ID, and killer shoes. What more do I need?

I take a breath, my hands slightly shaking with adrenaline. I'm actually doing this. He's not the only one who dares.

I pull open my nightstand drawer to look at the card he wrote to me.

Do you dare?

Oh, Mr. Powers, you have no idea.

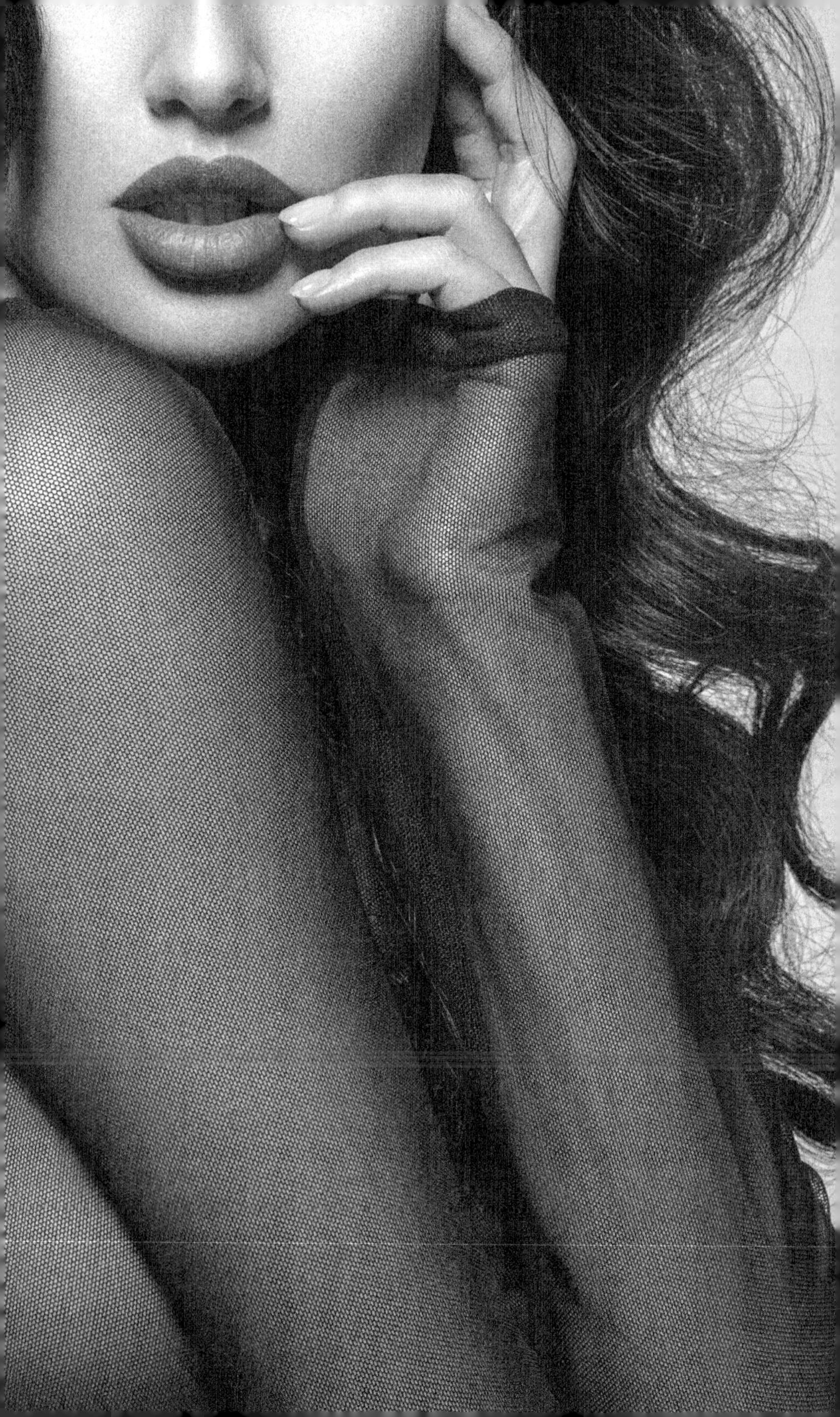

Eighteen

RAVEN

I lean forward, finishing my eye makeup. As an environmentalist, I always try to keep my showers around five minutes or so to save water, but today, I'm kind of being a rebel, and I took a long hot shower.

I did a face mask, used my favorite orange peel sugar body scrub, and shaved everything that needed to be touched up—since I wax all the time, it wasn't much.

Now done with my makeup, I step back to look at myself. If I were a man, I would want to fuck me.

Next, I need to sneak into Jett's room for the condoms. First, I order an Uber. It says ten minutes.

Perfect.

I peek my head out my door. It's around 4:00 p.m., so besides Jett's random assistants and Patty or Maria, it's just me.

I take a deep breath. What is going on with my nerves? *Calm, just relax,* I repeat in my head, then walk to his door and tap lightly.

Nothing.

"Okay, in and out." I look around, then swing the door open and slip inside. Everything is perfect as usual. It's hard not to look at their bed.

"Assholes," I snarl, marching to his side of the bed and jerking open his nightstand drawer. Hmm, the gun is gone, but the condoms are still there. Of course they are. He doesn't use them.

I grab a few, looking for his box with his sketches, but it's gone also.

Great.

A small twinge of guilt plagues me. Clearly, he moved it because of me. *Leave it, Raven. It's none of your business.* I slam the drawer shut and easily slip out, trying not to breathe in my mom's perfume. I don't care that it cost her thousands of dollars. There's something with her and that scent I've always disliked.

My phone dings. Zander, my driver, is here. I take the stairs as fast as I can in my heeled sandals. God, the last thing I need is to fall. I'd be stuck in my room for weeks.

But so far, so good. No sign of Maria. No sign of anyone, really. Could I be this lucky? My hand is on the door handle when it swings open, and I almost plow right into my mother.

"What the hell, Raven?" she screams. I guess she's as startled me.

"I didn't see you." I try to go around her, only to be stopped by her claw of a hand.

"Where are you going?" Her eyes take in my appearance. It's times like this when I wish I had at least inherited her height. Even with my heeled sandals, she looks down at me.

"Out." I cock my head, daring her to say anything.

"With your boyfriend?" Her eyes swing to the poor Uber driver in his Ford Focus.

"Sure." I stare at her, then pull my arm free and move toward the car. I can sense her watching me, but she doesn't stop me again. I slide into the back.

"Where to?" Zander, who has to be in his mid-forties, smiles back at me.

"Take me to the hippiest bar on Sunset Boulevard." Settling back in the car, I try hard not to second-guess my decision.

Cher's right. I need to do this, take my power back. I almost start laughing because he's now ruined that word for me, *dick*.

"Well, I'm a dad of three and I don't get out much, but I do know a place that a lot of customers go—"

"Perfect," I interrupt him, because not gonna lie, seeing my bitchy mom has kind of thrown me.

"My son has to start summer school tomorrow..."

I plaster on a smile as I completely tune out the chatty Uber driver. Was that a sign that I shouldn't do this tonight? Like a bad omen or something? I cross my legs and look out the window, barely even seeing the scenery of Beverly Hills pass me by.

I'll just do my three-strike rule. Strike one, running into my mom. If I get two more strikes.

Boom. I'm out.

Easy.

There, I feel better already. Always good to have a plan.

"Okay. Here we are, and let me give you my number if you need a ride home. Need to keep food on the table." He laughs, maneuvering us over as the valet guy instantly opens the door for me.

I quickly give him a fifty-dollar tip, not that I listened to ninety percent of his rambling about his kids. But since my mom pays for my card this month, I smile at the thought of her seeing the credit card statement.

"Thank you," I say and slide out, looking around. Yep, this is perfect.

"Excuse me." The valet looks over as he opens the door to the Town Car. "Where's the bar?"

"All the way to the top." He smiles.

I nod, entering the lavish hotel. Maybe I'll just get a room? That way if the bar pickup plan doesn't work out, I can still enjoy myself.

I'll drink champagne in the bathtub, rent a movie... Great, now that sounds way better than picking someone up. Who can even try to compete with Jett Powers anyway?

POWER

You have to at least get a drink. If it's boring, leave and get a room, but you spent hours getting ready, so go.

I step into the elevator as three girls dressed in short dresses and heels rush in before the doors can close on them.

"Holy shit, Ashley is saying he's at the bar." One of the girls with a nose ring looks at her phone. The other two reapply their lip gloss.

One drink, I chant in my head. Then back to the lobby for a room. Maybe I'll do a mindless *Friends* marathon… or *The Office*?

The elevator doors open and Rihanna's "Live Your Life" spills from the speakers. The girls behind me push forward, beelining straight to the bar. It's crowded and elegant, shaped like a square, with dark blue neon lights. I go forward, noticing the rest of the bar has booths and tables. A large wall water fountain is lit up with multicolored lights trickling down with the water.

I should leave. I'm super nervous, and why torture myself? I wanted to get out of the house. *I'm out.* Now I want to watch *Friends* and order room service.

One drink. I make my way to the bar, ignoring all the laughter and the throng of gorgeous people. This is cliché LA. Cher would be in heaven.

I squeeze my way in, ignoring the man who my right arm is touching, and lean forward to get the bartender's attention.

"What can I get you?" A pretty dark-haired girl in a black tuxedo-like halter top smiles at me.

"Belvedere martini, with blueberries instead of olives if you have them. If not, olives are fine," I yell.

"ID." She wipes her hand on a bar towel as I fish through my bag, my face heating up as I hand her my fake one. Cher insisted we get them. It had better work; they were not cheap. She looks at it, then me, and smiles. "Blueberries it is."

When she walks away, I take a deep breath and exhale, tossing my ID back into my bag.

"You okay?" the man next to me asks. I place both hands on the bar and go to give him my bitch glare, then remember the whole reason I'm here is to meet a stranger and let him fuck me.

"Fine." I tilt my head and smile, then kind of falter, because he's hot. Tall, wearing an expensive navy suit, with dark auburn hair.

"Here you go." The bartender breaks my stare as she places my martini in front of me. "Twenty-two dollars."

"Put it on my tab, and three more Pappy's." He grins down at me. My red alert alarm goes off in my head. This one is no good. In fact, he might be my strike two, reminding me a little too much of Jett with the whole I'm-God's-gift-to-women thing.

"What's your name, beautiful?" He leans his elbows forward so I can really see his handsome face. Tan skin, light freckles cover the bridge of his nose, *definitely a no.*

"Cher," I easily lie, picking up my drink to get away from him.

"Wait for me. I need to introduce myself to you before you run away." That stops me. Am I jaded? Ridiculous? Because this guy is nothing like Jett. He's playful, and there's a twinkle in his eyes, not the dark intensity that robs me of breath and speech.

Maybe this man is the perfect distraction for me. He's gorgeous and looks like he knows where a clitoris is.

"Cher?" He arches a brow at me. "Tell me you are over eighteen?"

And... he's strike two. Already asking way too many questions.

"I'm twenty-one. Thanks for the drink." I move to shimmy out of the crowded area, but he grabs the three highballs, following me.

"Come join me and my friends. I just got into town, darlin'." He motions with his head toward the left side of the bar where the booths are.

This time huge warning bells are full-on ringing. Not because I think he'll rape me, but it feels like I'm gonna regret this.

He must sense my resistance because he gives me a smile that I'm sure has convinced way too many women he is the man of their dreams.

Unfortunately for him, it does nothing to me, except remind me that I already met the man of my dreams...and he's fucking my mother.

"Come on, I'll protect you from all these assholes in suits." He waggles his eyebrows, and I can't help but smile.

Why not? He's charming and gorgeous, hopefully not married, although I have no intention of seeing him again, so who cares. I look at my shoes, then back at him.

"Fine. One drink, then I have to meet my girlfriends." I start to follow him. This is what I came here for after all.

"I'm Andrew." He grins, walking ahead of me, stopping at a booth. "And this is Jax Saddington and Jett Powers." He sets the drinks down on the table and I freeze.

He did not just say that name?

I'm hearing things. My eyes dart to the two men sitting, laughing.

I'm going to throw up, or at the very least, faint, because this can't be happening.

It. Can't. Be! As my eyes find the one man who's not supposed to be staring at me.

What are the odds? One in a million?

Strike three, Raven.

You're out.

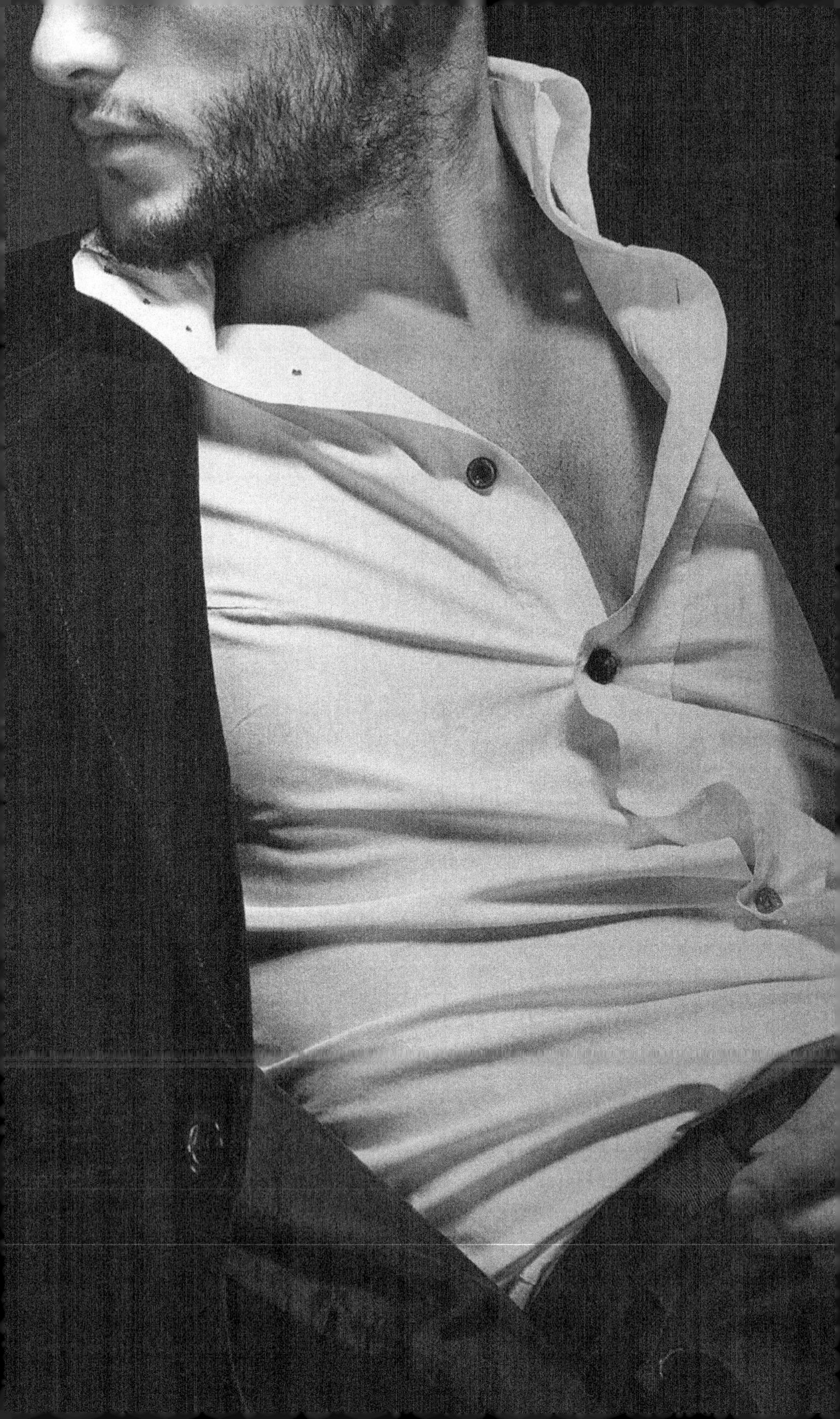

Nineteen

JETT

If I was in a foul mood the last four days, staring at Raven with a smiling Andrew has me seeing red.

Red.

For a second I glare, my nostrils flaring, confirming that this is indeed *my* Lolita.

In this bar.

Alone.

What the hell? I'll give her this; she's got balls. Anyone with any sense would run, but not Raven.

No, she stands, shoulders back, cherry-stained lips parted, eyes like giant sapphire gems as she stares at everyone but me.

Yeah, you can try to ignore me, but you're fucked, Raven. I almost throw my head back and laugh at how the universe has decided to play with me.

I've spent days white knuckling my urge to go to her, like a boozer craving a drink. I've avoided her like the plague, upping my workouts, jerking off in the shower, fucking avoiding my fiancée because of this piece of poison.

And here we are.

My eyes dip to her delicate neck, focusing on her rapid pulse that's pounding just under her jaw.

POWER

There's only one reason for her to be here. She's here to get fucked. For her to have the bad luck of picking Andrew, one of the few people I call a friend, is her own karma slapping her in the face.

I don't know why I'm so surprised. Clearly, she has more of Rachel in her than I thought.

Like mother, like daughter.

My eyes take in her full tits, showcased magnificently in her tight red dress as she tries to breathe.

"Cher. Sit, I promise we don't bite." Andrew flashes her a grin.

My fists clench. Though I remind myself this is not Andrew's fault if he thinks he can touch my Lolita...

I stand, and she takes a step back, almost bumping into a group behind us as I reach for her arm, causing her to gasp.

"Then again, maybe we do."

"I have to meet someone," she blurts out, her big eyes aimed at Andrew and Jax as if they can save her.

No one can save her now. I rarely, if ever, lose control, but tonight? This? I'm done.

"Don't listen to Jett. He's become a jaded man." Andrew smirks and motions for Jax to move.

I hold up my hand, stopping Jax from getting out.

"She can sit here. I'm not staying long." I smile as our eyes connect.

She must see I'm barely holding back my temper because she wisely slides in, setting her drink down in front of her. I slide in next to her and place my arm behind her, resting it on the booth.

"So, *Cher*, where are you from?" My voice barely hides my anger.

"Spain," she fires right back, staring at Andrew.

"Spain?" Andrew nods, leaning back in the deep red leather booth. "Really? My family has a house in Marbella."

"Lovely," is all she says.

Jax grins, looking from me to her as Raven brings the martini to her lips.

"So, Cher... I take it your parents are big fans of hers?" Andrew smiles as he takes a sip of his drink.

"Clueless," she says over the rim.

"Excuse me?" Andrew cocks his head.

"*Clueless*, the movie." She looks at them. "Alicia Silverstone and Paul Rudd..." Both Jax and Andrew simply stare.

"Great movie. You should see it. Anyway, that's who they named me after." She sets her glass down and starts to fish out a blueberry.

"Another one?" Andrew chuckles.

"Please." She nods, biting her lip, and I can feel my jaw clench as Andrew flashes her a grin and moves out of the booth. Christ, can he be more obvious?

"So, Jax..." She scoots a little away from me and crosses her legs. "I met your brother and his wife Tess."

Jax smiles. Fucking Saddington twins. We run in the same circles. I think Jax is seeing someone. Not sure, though. I only got here about ten minutes before Andrew dumped my Lolita on us. Before he can answer, I say, "Where?"

Her eyes slant over at me but stay focused on Jax. "It was at Gia Fontaine—"

"Actually, I think she goes by Granger, now," I say, cutting her off.

This time she does turn to glare at me. "If I'm not mistaken, she's kept her maiden name professionally." She blinks at me, and I can't decide if I want to shove my cock down her throat or spank her ass.

I shouldn't engage. But screw it, I want to see her squirm. "Small world. I was there also." Not caring in the least that Jax is watching us as if we are an amusing movie, I briefly reflect on how much his stupid dimples aggravate me.

"Really? My *daddy* brought me so..." She smiles sweetly at me, and I almost choke on my bourbon.

"Here you go, my angel." Andrew places another martini in front of her and settles back in the booth.

"What'd I miss?"

"Oh, not much." Jax motions with his glass of bourbon at Raven.

"Apparently, Cher has a Big Daddy who took her to the Gia Fontaine-Granger exhibit, where she met my brother and Tess." Jax nods as he covers his laughter by drinking his bourbon like a shot, then stands.

"Good seeing you, Powers, and good luck." His eyes drift to Raven while he walks past us toward the end of the bar.

"Wait. You're kidding me?" Andrew sits up. "Do you know each other?"

"I need to use the restroom," Raven snaps as Andrew glares at me.

"Of course." Sliding out of the booth for her, I look over at Andrew who is not even hiding his disapproval.

"You're fucking shitting me?" He leans back in the booth. "Well, I guess I don't need to ask how things are with you and Rachel." He shakes his head, mumbling into his drink.

"We're fantastic." My eyes follow her tight ass as she exits the bar; then I reach for my own glass of bourbon and slam it.

"I need to go," I say tersely.

"Of course." Andrew shakes his head. Not that I give a shit.

I weave around people, my mind on autopilot.

Livid.

Not sure if it's more at Raven or myself. She came here to get fucked.

Fucked.

By a stranger, and I've been using my hand? The fuck is wrong with me? Bringing out my phone, I text Iain to bring the car up front. I'm done. My head is pounding. Heaven help her when I find her, considering the mood I'm in.

I turn the corner, and there she stands with her credit card in her hand at reception. A blond moron in a suit stands smiling at her. Apparently, she thinks she's getting a room.

"There you are, sweetheart." I walk up and slide my arm around her. She stiffens but stays quiet. The moron behind the long marble counter looks completely disappointed.

"Sorry, we won't be needing the room. I just got a phone call." I smile down at her.

She hesitates, then clears her throat, reaching for her card.

"Let's go." My hand digs into her hip and I move us away.

"You fuck," she seethes. "You've got some nerve."

"Keep walking, my love, if you know what's good for you," I growl into her ear. My hand leaves her hip to take her cold hand. I don't trust either of us right now, but I have no intention of dealing with any of this until we're alone.

Iain pulls up, just as we exit, and the warm night air caresses my face. I jerk open the car door and look down at her.

"Get in, *now*." My voice sounds flat. My eyes take in her flushed cheeks, dipping down to her hard nipples.

She shakes her head but obeys, sliding into the back as I follow.

Neither of us talks. Our energy is almost stifling in the car. I want to shake her, kiss her, fuck her so hard she will never think of another man's cock.

Ruin her.

Then I'll toss her away. Because *she went to get fucked by a stranger*. Unbuttoning my suit jacket, I look out the window. The pretty houses of Beverly Hills swirl by, one after another, all trying to compete for best-in-town status.

Why do I feel like I've been gut-punched? It's got to be a control thing. In my subconscious, I wasn't done with her, so I still want to control her.

"Am I under arrest?" Her voice makes me turn and look at her. "Because you do realize you have no right to interfere with anything I'm doing, right?" she snaps. "You're not my real daddy, *Jett*," she sneers, then turns to look out the window.

"You want to be a whore?" The words echo around us, ugly and dirty.

She gasps, her eyes snapping to mine. "How dare you?" Her voice cracks.

"Dare? I *dare* anything. That's not the question. You're underage, in a place you shouldn't be, dressed like a whore." She looks like I've slapped her. I loosen my tie.

"I just wanted to get out of the house," she screams. It ricochets around the car. We stare at each other.

God, I hope Rachel isn't home. Because she needs her ass spanked.

"You needed to get out of the house?" I cock my head.

"Yes. I have basically been holed up in that room, not that you would know or care." She bites her bottom lip as I glance over at Iain who's pulling into my driveway.

"God, whatever, you caught me." She puts her head back on the leather seat. "I just wanted to get out, have some fun, and maybe not think about you." She puts her hands over her face.

And for a second, I just sit, letting her words swirl around me. She's fearless, breathtaking, and manipulative.

Which makes her dangerous.

This might have started out as a game, a moment of weakness on my part, wanting the forbidden fruit, but now... I'm not thinking rationally.

"Goddammit," I mutter, throwing the door open. *This shit is the very reason I don't have relationships. It's why Rachel is my fiancée.*

No feelings.

No drama.

Nothing but respect for each other's accomplishments.

Not this.

Not feeling like I may do bodily harm to anyone who dares to look, touch, or breathe near her. *Christ, you need to get your ass upstairs and fuck Rachel. Leave Raven. She can find her way back to her room.*

Seconds tick by as I fight a battle that's pointless. But I know who and what I am, and as long as I'm able to sleep at night, that's all that matters.

One delicate leg steps out, followed by another when I reach my hand out to her. She looks at it, and just like the day we first met in the kitchen, she makes me wait, as if she, too, is trying to stop this madness.

But this is beyond madness. It's fucking mayhem.

Leave her, plays over and over in my head like a broken record, until I feel her hand in mine. Electric energy makes my fingers tingle. I bring her close and inhale her scent.

She pulls back, and our eyes collide, do battle. If I was obsessed before, I'm now barely able to keep myself in check.

"Jett—" The floodlights spill on, lighting up the entire front part of the property. Rachel steps out, a cigarette in her hand.

"What the hell?" She looks at Raven, then me. I don't know how much she saw, if anything.

"I ran into Raven at the bar. I brought her home." I shut the door as Iain pulls the car around the back toward the garage.

"You expect me to believe that?" she spits.

"It's true." Raven rolls her eyes at her mother as she walks up the steps.

"You're stalking him, aren't you?" She goes to follow her, but I grab her arm.

"She's not stalking me, Rachel. She was there to fuck a stranger," I snarl, my eyes taking in her cigarette.

"Then why is she home?" Her voice doesn't hide her contempt.

"Because she's underage, and the stranger was *Andrew*." I stare at Rachel who takes one more inhale and walks to the kitchen to run water on the end.

"Andrew Carrington?" She still sounds doubtful, but I'm sick of her, this day, and not being able to come home in peace. I spent a lot of money making my home a haven for me. I usually like coming home. Lately, I dread it.

"Yes, Andrew Carrington."

"Why?" She shuts the water off and turns to face me.

"Why, what?" I growl, going around her to the refrigerator.

"Why would you care? I mean, for someone like Andrew to even look at Raven… In all honesty, she's borderline attractive. I've seen the women he dates. She could only be so lucky."

I shut the refrigerator door slowly as my mind tries to process her words. "Let me understand what you just said. You think I should have left Raven to get fucked by Andrew *and* be grateful for it? Have you lost your mind?" My eyes remain focused on her face.

"Have you? Because all I know is that ever since my daughter moved in, you haven't touched me. In fact, you act like I'm beneath you. And don't try that lawyer shit," she screams, slapping the marble island for effect.

"I'm tired." I snort, walking around her toward the stairs.

"Don't you dare walk away from me, Jett Powers. What is happening?" She runs after me.

"*I'm* going to bed." I turn and look at her. She's right. I have zero interest in her sexually, and haven't for a long time.

"And"—I take a step on the stairs—"Raven will be going to work with me. She can intern. Clearly, she needs to keep busy even if her mother doesn't care whether she fucks random men. *I do*. It's bad for my name, your name. I refuse for it to go around our circle that your daughter is a whore." That shuts her ugly red lips that were getting ready to spew more jealous venom. Turning, I take the stairs two at a time.

"Jett, I'm sorry. I didn't think about it like that. You're right. She can't be screwing around. I'm mortified." She pants after me, but I'm done with her tonight. Too fucking raw.

I need a shower and sleep. I'll deal with everything in the morning when I don't feel like I'm ready to murder someone.

That includes my Lolita.

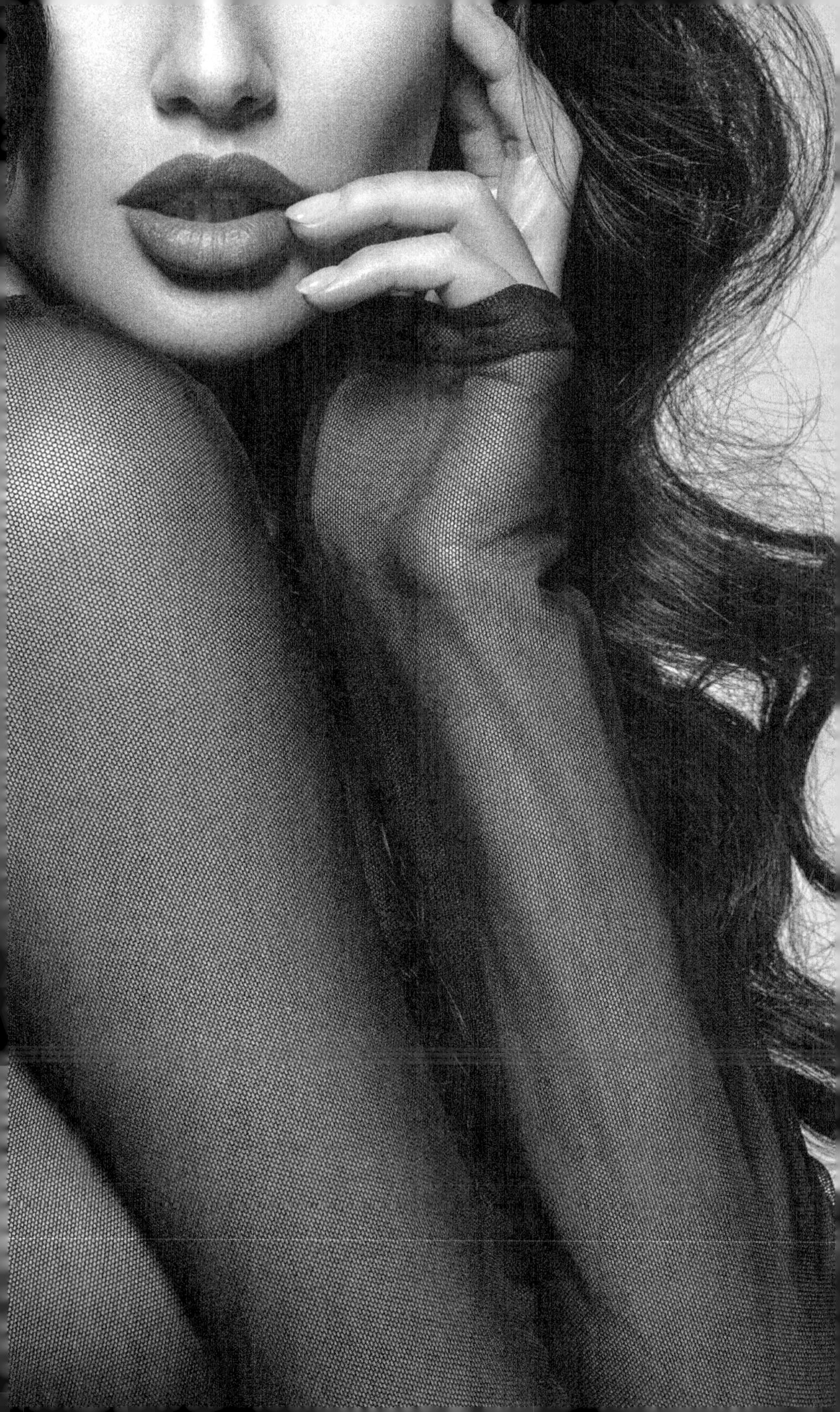

Twenty
RAVEN

"**G**et up."

I blink my eyes open. "Oh, God, that's a lot of light." Rolling to my back, I fling my arm over my eyes to shield me from the morning sun Jett let into my room.

"We're leaving in forty-five minutes." His hypnotic voice makes me peek up at him. He's dressed in a starched white dress shirt, sapphire-colored tie, and black suit slacks. My face instantly heats when I remember the dream I was just having about him.

"Wait, what?" I stop as the debacle of last night rolls over me. One second I'm peaceful, the next I want to roll up in a ball and hide.

The bar… how? Out of hundreds of bars, that's the one I picked? Then the redhead, Andrew, and Jax Saddington.

Jesus, Raven.

Why didn't I simply get a room? I could have gotten drunk watching *Friends*, not having Jett Powers glaring down at me, saying something about forty-five minutes. Did I agree to something and I'm not remembering?

No. I wasn't that drunk. Tipsy, yes. I did slam two large martinis on an empty stomach, but I still remember… *unfortunately*.

I wonder if I pretended I was drunk from earlier, and that's why I went to the bar. Because my thinking was impaired. No, that won't work. My bitch of a mom saw me before I left. Also, it was clear I was there to hook up with someone. *Oh God.*

"Raven. Get up and take a shower," he demands.

My eyes dart to his, and I nod, not sure what I'm agreeing to, but it involves him, so that makes me breathless. The last thing I heard last night was my mother screaming that he hasn't touched her since I showed up.

"Good. Wear what I've laid out for you." Again, it's a demand, but his eyes caress my face. He turns to leave.

"Holy shit." I sit up. My head is pounding, and my mouth is in desperate need of water, but even feeling like shit, I can't stop the butterflies in my stomach.

He hasn't slept with her.

At all, since me. That has to be positive. I throw the covers off to stand and stretch. The clothes he wants me to wear are draped perfectly on my huge leather chair.

Hmm, black slacks and a black sleeveless turtleneck with heeled black pumps. I take a breath and exhale, then look at my phone. Eight thirty in the morning. I reach for my bag to dig out some Advil, trying hard to block out last night, and grab a bottle of water off my dresser.

With that look on Jett's face when Andrew moved away to introduce me, I honestly thought I was going to faint. Either that, or he was going to strangle me.

"So bad." Turning on the shower, I find it impossible to turn my brain off. Still, I wash myself, my mind going over last night's events. Jax Saddington's handsome face, laughing when I said my daddy brought me. And Andrew... poor Andrew, although something tells me there's nothing poor about any of them. I turn off the water and step out. I feel a million times better already. If I hurry, maybe I can slam a couple of cups of coffee.

I'm dressed and my makeup's on in under ten minutes. It helps that I just pinned my wet hair up in a tight bun and threw on some red lipstick. I grab my handbag and phone and shut the door, rushing toward the kitchen, only to stop when I see my mom lounging in her red silk robe. It hangs open, and I try not to look at one of her large, fake breasts.

She tried to make me get fake ones at fourteen when it was obvious mine were not going to be huge. That, and she wanted me to get my ass done, saying, "Men don't like skinny asses. Look at the Kardashian girls."

Like I would ever want to look like the Kardashians? I take a deep breath. Jett is sitting on the other side of her. Was that why her robe is open? Was he touching her?

"Do I have time for a cup of coffee?" My voice is laced with contempt, which again is wrong. He's marrying her, not me. Jesus, I've never been a jealous person, always thought it was pathetic. Look at me now.

"No." He stands and pulls his black suit jacket off the chair to put it on. Leaning over, he kisses my mom who clings to him until her phone starts ringing.

"Hold on." She rudely tells whoever's on the phone, then looks at me. "I expect you to not embarrass either Mr. Powers or myself, do you understand, Raven?"

"Excuse me?" Because, I could have chugged a cup of coffee already. As for my mom, I have no idea what she's rambling about, nor do my hangover and I care.

"Last night, the bar, the men—" She stares at me, and I notice her face is completely made up, although she's still in her robe.

"I'll explain everything to her, Rachel." Jett says dryly as my mom's eyes narrow on me. She brings her phone back to her ear.

"Lunatic," I mumble, rolling my eyes and following Jett outside. "Christ." I groan again, way too hungover for no coffee and any more lectures. God, maybe I can take a quick nap. I dig in my bag for my sunglasses.

"Where exactly are we going?" I slide into the back of the car this time.

POWER

"You're going to intern for me until you go to Stanford." He sits next to me as the car pulls out of the driveway. I don't respond, but rub my temples, wishing to God the freaking Advil would do its magic.

"Wait. What?" I sigh, turning to him. He seems absorbed with whoever he's texting because he's ignoring me. My eyes take in his handsome profile. Why does he have to be so damn hot?

"Let's pull through Starbucks and get Raven and the others some coffee." He looks up.

"You got it, Mr. Powers." Iain nods. Does the man ever get a day off? Even if Jett isn't working, Iain is still around.

"Jett?" I ask.

He continues to text, not looking up.

"Mr. Powers?" My voice gets louder, causing him to arch a dark brow at me.

"What? You don't want coffee?"

"Yes, I want coffee." I almost laugh, because he really is the master manipulator, but this is his second comment about Stanford. He needs to stop.

"I'm not going to Stanford. As for interning, I would love to." Because it's true; being able to have Jett Powers, Attorney at Law on my resume is golden.

He stops texting to look at me. "Darlin', the only reason you're going to work, and believe me this will be work, is because I will not tolerate you fucking around. You want to be a whore, you can do it when you're at Stanford." He states this like he's speaking about the weather or asking me to pass the bread at a restaurant.

Trying to breathe, I blink at him. My headache just spiked to another level, and for a second I actually want to slap his arrogant, smug face. I dig my nails into the leather seat and feel a satisfying tear. His eyes trail down, then back to my face, the only emotion a slight tic on his right jaw.

"I'd think about it," is all he says, then turns to order several coffees and bagels, along with some croissants and breakfast sandwiches.

I need to pull it together. I'm all over the place, and his mood has not improved from last night. If anything, he's getting darker. The window zips shut as he settles back in the seat.

"You'll start trailing Rebecca. If she asks you to scrub the toilets, you do it, understand?"

"Completely. But I'll be ruining really expensive clothes." I smile, hoping to lighten the vibe, but he ignores me and answers his phone as Iain passes me a coffee and bagel.

"Thank you," I whisper, taking the coffee, trying not to groan out loud at how good the first sip always is.

"Doug, I thought I said no and good luck," Jett says into the phone.

The paper crinkles loudly when I take my bagel out and I freeze, looking over at him. My heart flips. I'm in over my head. The way he watches me leaves me... breathless.

I bring the hot coffee to my lips while he listens on the phone. Clearly this is some big case. His blue eyes caress my face.

"That's a crime of passion, Doug. You know how I feel about those cases," Jett informs him while reaching for my bagel.

"Do they have the murder weapon yet?" I almost gasp, because I'm trying not to look like I'm eavesdropping, but to be involved in what goes on in a murder trial is too good to be true.

"You know what? Send me your files. *If* I decide to take over, that's exactly what I will do. I run everything, you stay on as co-counsel, but this will be my show. Please tell your client, Mrs. Hopper, that." He hangs up and takes a bite of the bagel.

And all I can do is watch him. He's always hot, but when he's in his element, he's fucking immortal.

A god among men. God, I'm so wet, if I rub my legs together, maybe I could come? I mean, Iain is pulling into a dark parking garage.

"You okay?" His voice makes my eyes widen, but I actually groan out loud when his large, tan hand touches the inside of my leg.

I shake my head *no*. Because I'm not. I'm on fire; I want him. It's like I'm sick or something. But I don't trust myself to speak. The car stops, and suddenly, as if I wished it, Iain is gone and it's just me and Mr. Powers.

Fucking Mr. Powers.

"Spread your legs," he says, and I move so fast and feel so desperate I barely register the sting of hot coffee on my hand.

"Give me the cup. You look a little frantic," his voice coaxes as I try to breathe. He saves me any further humiliation by gently taking the coffee out of my hand.

"I don't know what's wrong with me," I whisper.

Please, fuck me. Please.

He looks down at me, his eyes trailing up and down my body as his hand slides up my thigh. Why did he make me wear slacks? Why?

"I know exactly what's wrong. Now tell Mr. Powers what it is, Raven." His voice is demanding. His hand cups my swollen, wet pussy.

"I want you to fuck me, Mr. Powers." I buck up as if that will actually do anything.

He leans in, his mouth close to mine, as his fingers rub circles on my clit, the material of my slacks adding an almost frustrating pressure, enough to feel good, but not enough to get me off.

"That's the problem, my pretty baby." He takes his hand away, turning to open the car door.

"What?" I sit up, reaching for him, but he's already out. All I see are his thighs in his dark slacks.

"You'd fuck anyone. Now let's go." His voice sounds cold now, almost like an echo in a cement tomb. If he had slapped me, I think that would hurt less than his words. It's like he just sliced a piece of my heart out.

He's not a fucking god; he's a vicious antichrist.

"Go ahead, I'll be up in a minute." I grab my bag, trying to shield myself from him.

"Get out, *now*." He doesn't move, and my face heats up as the humiliation of being played makes me blink back tears.

"Fine." I sniff, grabbing my coffee from the cupholder in the front, not caring the least that I spill more.

I step out and look up, hating that I'm so much smaller than him. Doesn't matter, though. He thinks he can bully me. The thing is, I grew up with the worst bully alive, a fucking viper for a mother. I've got years and years on him.

"You're a manipulative bully, Jett Powers. You're the bad guy. I'm just the sucker who fell for you. Now show me who Rebecca is, and don't ever think you can mind fuck me again." I start to walk, only for him to grab me and pull me with so much force I drop the coffee. The hot liquid saturates most of his shoes and pant leg, but that's nothing compared to the force of his lips on mine.

It's primal, fierce, and for a second I let myself submit as his tongue tangles with mine. Then I dig my nails into his forearm and neck, causing him to lift his face, his eyes dark. He smiles.

"That's it, Raven. Fight me," he growls.

"Fuck you, Jett."

"I intend to." He grabs my arm, jerking me along as he slams the deserted stairwell door open, and I'm not gonna lie, as much as I hate him, I also like the rush. The door slams shut with a loud bang, and he pushes me forward, my hands grabbing the metal railing. His hands jerk my hips tight on his erection, and he rubs it against my ass.

"Tell me, Raven, were you gonna let Andrew fuck your ass?" His other hand goes to the back of my neck. "No one gets you but me." His other hand snakes around to my stomach and into my pants.

"You don't own me. I can fuck whoever I want." I smile, then gasp as his two fingers stroke me.

POWER

"That's my little whore. You're so wet," he whispers and bites my ear. "Unbutton your slacks." And suddenly his hands are gone as I hear him unbuckling his belt. I should try to at least make an effort to get away. I just called him out for being a bad guy and a bully, but I want him.

It's just sex. It means nothing. I undo my slacks.

"Take them off," he demands.

I kick off my heels and let them fall to the cement, praying the floor is somewhat clean while I step out of my panties.

"Wait. What if someone comes down the stairs, or… Jesus." His fingers are back inside me, rubbing, stroking, so deep.

"Fuck, this cunt is tight." And all I can do is hold on to the railing while he rubs that magical spot and I start to climb.

"Jett. I'm going to come." My voice is almost frantic.

"Not yet," he grunts. "I need to eat this cunt." His fingers are gone, and I almost scream. Maybe I do. I'm beyond caring.

"Jesus Christ." When he looks at me, his blue eyes are almost black.

Spreading my legs, I lower my ass till I'm sitting on the edge of the cold concrete steps.

"You can come. I want you to come in my mouth." He kneels, and everything slows. It's just us, our breathing, his mouth. I lean my head back and arch up as he starts to suck on my clit. Nothing, no one in this world, will ever be able to make me feel like this.

"Oh fuck," I whimper.

He grabs my hips, using his tongue to fuck my slick core, in and out, before it returns to my clit.

One hand grabs the railing as my body tightens. Every single cell is tingling as I go over. Wave after wave of unending pleasure flows through me as he watches me come undone.

He stands, unzips his slacks, and brings out his cock. Barely able to breathe, I lick my lips at his thick, pulsing member.

"Turn around." His voice seems strained.

Somehow I make myself grab on to the next step while his hand caresses my ass.

"This ass is mine. You're mine." A loud smack is what I hear before my brain actually registers that my right ass cheek is stinging.

"Mine. You don't go to bars." He slaps the other cheek, and this time, I feel everything, and it fucking hurts.

"I'd think better about moving, Raven. You're gonna take it, take whatever I give you." He continues to spank me, but at this point, the stinging is gone, and all I feel is a warm burn.

"I should take my belt to this ass." In one hard thrust, he's inside me, and we both groan. I fall forward. His cock is that big, and at this angle... holy fuck. My breasts are smashed onto the steps, my knees have to be bruised, but all I feel is him—and his cock inside me.

Inside me. I never want it to end.

"Tell me, Raven. Say the words as I fuck this cunt of mine raw," he grunts, his anger almost an aphrodisiac. If he's this upset about the bar, that means he's jealous.

"I won't go to bars," I pant, sensing his thumb at my tiny hole.

"Yeah... what else?" His thumb slowly slides into my ass, and fuck...

"Jett—Mr. Powers. I..."

"Take it." He picks up speed.

In and out, I feel his thumb in my ass and his cock so deep inside me.

"Tell me," he demands.

"You're the only one who can fuck me," I scream, unable to stop the orgasm. It crashes over me, and I dig my nails into the stairs.

"Fuck, Raven, fuck," he whispers as my pussy contracts and my ass pulses. I think I might be screaming or chanting his name when he pulls out. Warm spurts of his release cover my ass, and he comes, loud, guttural, echoing around us.

"Christ." His voice is ragged. He sounds slightly out of breath. "Don't move yet." I lean my head on my arm, trying to catch my own breath as everything comes back into focus.

Suddenly I'm aware of smells, sounds. "Oh my God." My face is on the dirty stairwell? What is wrong with me?

I look back at him as he zips up his slacks and jerks off his tie, leaning down to clean up as much as he can, which is absurd. He came so much, it's trickling down my right thigh.

"I can't believe you." My cheeks are on fire. I turn and follow his eyes as they take in my swollen, bruised knees.

"Look at me. I can't go inside like this. Oh my God." I bring up my hands, which are black, including my forearms.

"Take it easy. I have a shower." His mouth twitches, and he briefly looks down at my feet, then back at my face.

"What did you do to me?" I cover my mouth with my hands, only to have him grab them.

"Let's not touch your face, babe." He reaches for my slacks and shakes them out as my tiny black panties land in the corner.

I blink at him. His mouth twitches, and then he throws his head back to laugh.

"Baby, I'm sorry, but you look... amazing." He keeps laughing.

"So much so that you're laughing?" I cock my head but feel my own lips twitch.

He pulls me into his arms. "You look thoroughly fucked." He kisses my lips. "I like you filthy and hot." His lips trail to my eyes.

My head falls back. How does he do this? One minute, I hate him, the next moment he can do no wrong.

"Come on, let's get you dressed."

My gaze shifts to my panties.

"Let's not worry about them." Again, his mouth twitches.

"You're the worst." I pull away, taking my slacks from him, using his hand to steady me since my legs are shaking.

"Here." He crouches down, and I watch as he gently puts each of my dirty feet in my fabulous Louboutin pumps. I could cry feeling the dirt on the clean leather.

"There. All better." He looks up, and for a second I gasp for air.

Breathless.

That's the only word that comes to my mind. With his dark hair and full lips forming a broad smile, he's *breathless*. His blue eyes hold me hostage. Every time I look at him, I lose a bit of myself…but gain a bit of him.

God, my heart is pounding so loud, he has to hear it. He stands. I swallow. His eyes change, and he isn't smiling anymore. *Can he feel this?* Does he know that together we're complete?

Jett has become my everything. Brilliant, controlling, my missing piece.

This is the moment I accept my truths.

Somehow, some way, I've fallen in love with him despite knowing he's not mine.

Holy fuck.

I'm in love with Jett Powers, my mother's fiancé.

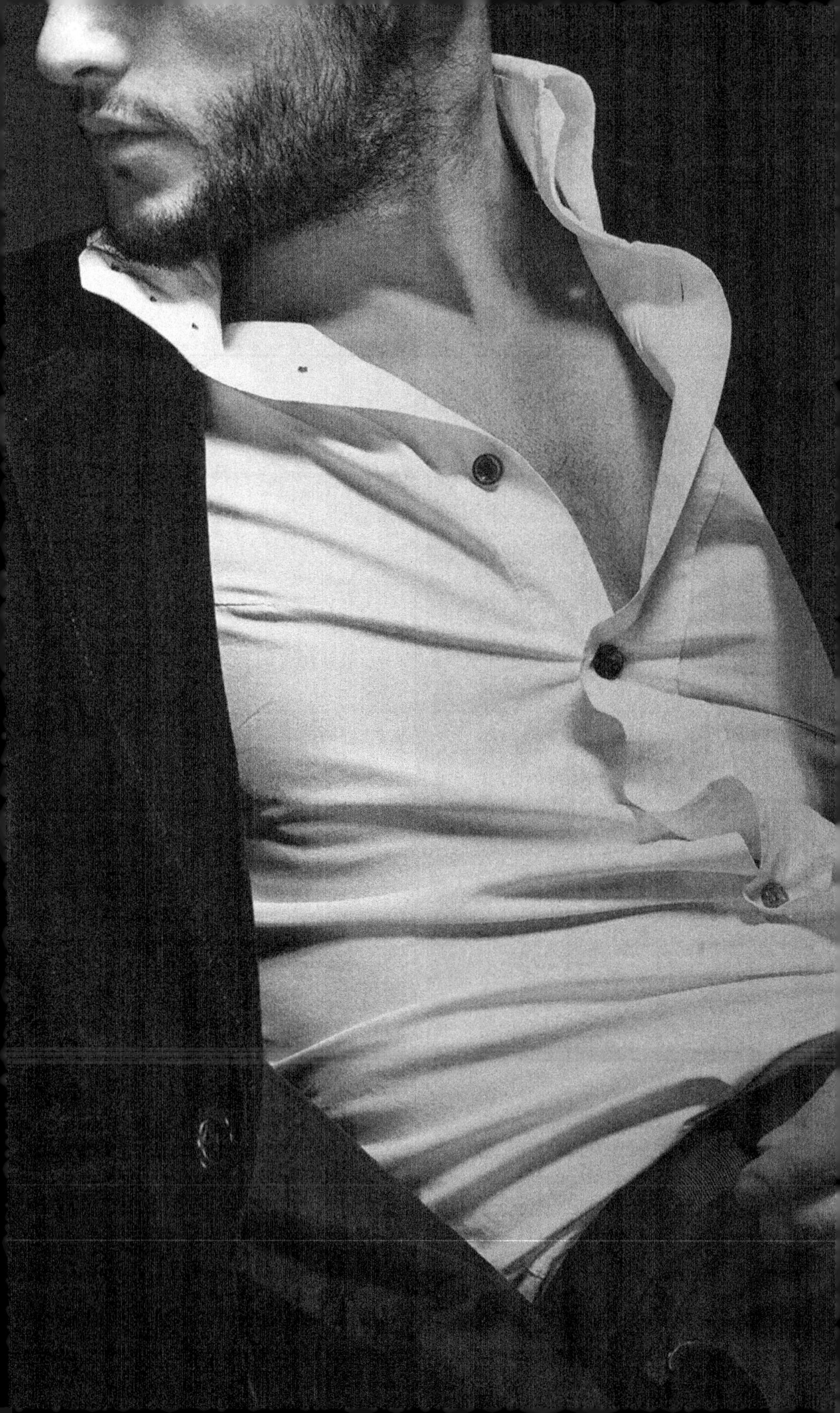

Twenty-One

JETT

I don't know what possessed me to think it was a good idea to bring Raven not only into my office, but now to the courtroom where she sits next to me.

It feels too intimate, but after the stairwell incident, everything has become heightened.

I gave up trying to deny myself of her. I've rationalized that I will end it. She's going back to school in a month. Until then, I'm a selfish bastard who might be fucked, because we're getting into a routine. She's up and ready to leave by seven in the morning. We're out the door and stopping for coffees and shit for my office by seven thirty, and I'm at my desk working by eight.

My office is getting spoiled. Screw that, I'm getting spoiled.

She's taken over going through my depositions and highlighting anything that's off.

Christ, I walked in on her yesterday schooling Mike, one of my best lawyers, on environmental law. He had to ruin it by asking her out. I almost fired him on the spot, but he was saved by Raven saying she had a boyfriend.

Boyfriend.

It's almost comical. I guess that's me. Considering how many hours we spend together, you'd think she'd start to aggravate me. I adore Rebecca, but even with her I have a ten-minute tolerance time span. After that, I'm done.

POWER

Apparently, that rule doesn't apply to Raven. The more time I spend with her, the more I like her. And this is not just her tight pussy. I'm borderline obsessed with her mind. She's incredibly sharp. She keeps up with me, challenges me, then submits.

My phone vibrates. I look over at her, typing on her laptop as she glances up and flashes me a smile that makes my chest hurt.

The fuck is happening to me? I'm hardly a kid. These kinds of things like smiling and touching are for other men, not me. She's wearing her hair down today. Long, dark chocolate waves spill over her shoulder. My hand almost tingles with the need to touch the silken strands.

Goddammit, my cock is hard, *again*. I shift in my chair. This is getting out of hand. I just dragged Raven into the shithole public bathroom not twenty-five minutes ago. I fucked her up against the door.

Epitome of class, Jett.

Shaking my head, I glance at my phone. Rachel. I hit decline. What the hell is she thinking calling me? She should know I'd be in court, or maybe not. Raven and I have been staying out late and getting up early… When's the last time I actually sat and had a conversation with her?

Jesus Christ, I'm a dick.

I look over at my client. He's a big star, but had an older client not asked me to represent him as a favor, I would have said no. It's easy money, though. Cut and dry. A stupid actor getting caught with ecstasy, first offense.

Bobby leans over. "How much longer do you think? And with the community service stuff, can I pay someone to do it for me?"

I stare at him. Good thing he made it. He's stupid.

"No, you can't pay someone to do your community service, and if I were you, I'd stop laughing at your phone and focus on looking mournful." He looks at me blankly, and I marvel at Hollywood. Only industry in the world where you can literally be an idiot and a drug abuser and get paid for it.

"She's looking at us," he whispers.

I glance up at Judge Anderson, clear my throat, and hiss, "Stand." Smiling at her, I button my suit jacket.

"In the case between the People versus...." I'm barely listening as she gives him thirty-two hours of community service and a fine of one-hundred-thousand dollars, which is actually pretty steep considering I pleaded it down to a misdemeanor.

"Good luck." I nod at him.

"Is that it? I'm free?" He smiles and waves at the reporters.

"Yes, I'll have one of my staff pay the fine and take care of everything. All you have to do is show up for community service and pay my bill." I place my laptop and papers in my leather briefcase, then reach for Raven.

"You're so cool." She smiles as she slips her sunglasses on.

I can't help but smirk. "Damn right, I am." I grin at her and push the doors open.

"No comment." I hold up my hand and smile at the paparazzi, but keep walking to the parking lot.

"Okay, so Rebecca just texted." Raven reads from her phone. "You have a big day tomorrow and... my mom has called her three times." She bites her lip when I open the door for her and she slides into my Ferrari.

I was in such a good mood this morning; I gave Iain the day off. Something tells me that may end tonight. Three calls. I walk around to the driver's side, noticing Bobby exiting the courthouse with his bodyguard.

I should bill him extra for being stupid.

I sink into my seat and start my Ferrari. It purrs like a kitten, reminding me I should drive it more.

"Did your mother leave any messages?"

"No." She stares out the window.

I press the button and instruct the car to call Rachel. It goes straight to voicemail.

POWER

"Call Rebecca."

"Hello, Mr. Powers," Rebecca answers on the first ring.

"Am I supposed to go anywhere tonight with Rachel?" I snap, then take a breath. It's not her fault I've found myself in this situation. "I'm sorry, Becca."

"Please, you're the best boss ever. It looks like you're open for tonight, but you had a dinner scheduled with the mayor and his wife last night and Rachel asked me to cancel it."

"Really?"

"Yeah, she asked me to cancel it a couple of days ago."

"Hmm, you can take off. I'm not coming back in today." I disconnect the line and stay quiet as I drive. Maybe I should have Tina, one of my assistants, go to Tiffany's or Cartier and get her something. Christ, that can't be any more obvious that I'm fucking around. The funny thing is, Rachel doesn't care if I have snatch on the side, but *this* isn't that.

This is starting to be more, something that I'm not capable of having, especially when I'm getting married in less than five months.

"Has Rachel always been like this with you?" I glance over at her.

She sighs and keeps looking out the window. "I don't talk about her, especially with you." She rubs her forehead.

I nod. "Well, we're beyond that, but I'm not going to force you." My hands tighten on the steering wheel.

She shrugs. "Some women should not have children, and she's one of them. Maria basically raised me." Her voice is raspy with emotion. She's been traumatized by both her parents, tossed around, neither of them really wanting her, though Rachel's ex at least tried, and she had Maria. Guess the mystery as to why Rachel insisted on keeping Maria when she moved in is solved.

We stay silent the rest of the ride while I try to wrestle with my conscience. I need to pull back. No matter how much I want her, we can't ever be. She's young, beautiful, and deserves the world. I can't give myself to her. Not really. I'm not built for it. My job, career, are my great loves, but Raven is still young enough to find someone who will always put her first. Someone who will drop everything just to have her smile. Yeah, my Lolita deserves to have it all. She can make a difference.

I pull into my driveway, looking for Rachel's car. It's not there, but she might have put it in the garage.

Raven barely waits for me to stop and swings the door open, sprinting upstairs past a concerned-looking Maria who stands holding the front door open.

"What the fuck?" Sighing, I grab my briefcase, then glance at my phone. Nothing new, just work stuff.

It's almost four. Maybe I'll order a pizza if Rachel is gone. Crack open a bottle of red, and Raven and I can watch a movie, maybe take a swim.

Silence greets me as I walk in. "Rachel?"

"She's gone out." Maria stands in the kitchen doorway.

"When is she coming back?" I say tightly, not in the mood for Maria's disapproving stare. I'm trying to have patience since she basically raised Raven, but I won't put up with her interfering.

"She didn't say, just that she was going out."

"Thank you. You can go home." I toss my briefcase on one of the tables and push on Rachel's number. Again, it goes straight to voicemail.

"I was thinking I'd take Ms. Raven with me tonight." She raises her chin, her arms crossed.

That stops me. I look up from my phone. "Excuse me?"

"Yes, I wanted to make her homemade tacos. It's one of her favorite meals."

I cock my head. "Well then, you should definitely make them for her. But not tonight." I toss my phone on my kitchen island and take off my suit jacket.

She hesitates.

"Something else you need to tell me?"

POWER

"Yes, I already made the tortillas fresh—"

"Thank you, Maria, but not tonight. You can go. I'm tired."

I fling open my takeout menu drawer and ignore her as she fidgets. I glance up at her from the menu.

"I can wait until Ms. Rachel comes home." She raises her chin. Again, anyone else would have been fired, but since she's trying to protect Raven, can I blame her?

That being said, I'm ordering pizza and going upstairs to fuck.

"No need, I'm home." Smiling, I pick up my phone. "See you tomorrow."

She nods, looking miserable, but I've never seen her look happy. She picks up her purse, mumbling as she walks out. At least Raven has one person in her corner.

While ordering the pizza, I hear the front door shut. After I grab a bottle of my favorite red, I take the stairs two at a time, going straight to my Lolita's room.

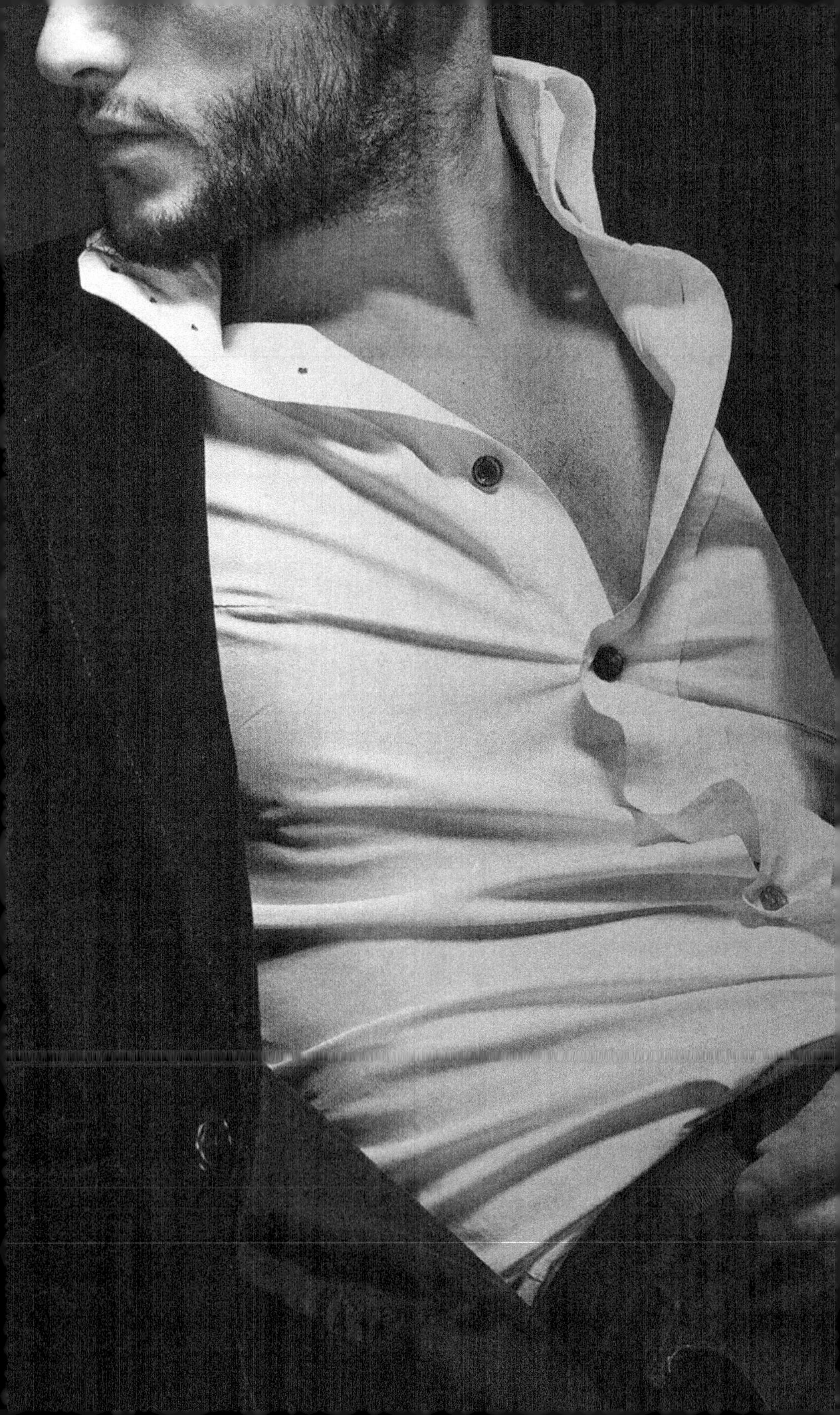

Twenty-Two

JETT

"Pizza's here." Raven leans against the door frame in my white robe, one leg peeking out of the opening. Her hair is up, and small ringlets cascade around her neck.

I step out of the shower and reach for a towel. "Where do you want to eat?" I grin at her as her eyes dip to my cock.

"How about the backyard?" She stares, my dick hardens, and her eyes meet mine as I dry myself off with the towel.

"Perfect." I look down at her. "You okay?"

She nods.

"Words, Raven." I tilt her chin up, losing myself in her pools of sapphire.

"I'm fine." She sighs, her finger tracing a droplet of water running down my chest.

"To be honest"—she takes a breath—"I despise being reminded that you're with my mother." She spits out mother, then turns to leave.

"I don't think so." I grab her and pull her into my arms. "Look. I'm a bastard. But I had no idea this was going to happen." It's as close as I will admit to myself, or her, that this, *us*, is something.

She looks at me, her eyes showing me everything that she's not jaded enough to hide.

POWER

"When we're together, it feels right, you know? And..." She shrugs, staring at my chest rather than my eyes.

"I think... I might be falling for Mr. Powers." She grins and bites her bottom lip, peeking up at me. My chest thuds, almost aches. Christ, just looking at her almost hurts.

"Well, don't. I'm not the right man for you, baby." I kiss the top of her head, step around her, and walk out into her room, wrapping the towel around my waist.

"Why?" she demands.

I look over my shoulder, and for the first time in a long time, I hesitate. Which is insane—I just had this very conversation with myself.

"I'm too old for you, and I'm married to my job." I lift up the lid to the pizza box and smell the pepperoni and jalapeños. Raven loves spicy food. If you'd asked me what kind of pizza Rachel likes, I wouldn't have a clue.

"You have your whole life ahead of you. You'd tire of me." I shut the box and grin at her.

"I think you're wrong." She walks toward me.

My eyes narrow and my nostrils flare at her mesmerizing scent; it complements the aroma of our dinner.

She's dangerous, becoming my very own kryptonite. Cocking her head, she stops right in front of me. "And I think you know it."

Our eyes lock. How has my fucking Lolita somehow gotten the better of this situation?

"I had a really good day today. That is, up until my bitch of a mom started calling. But she's not here, and she can't hurt me anymore. I'm free. I make my own decisions." She turns and picks up the bottle of red I brought in with me and walks out of the room.

"Fuck me." I stare after her. I'm a big enough man to give credit where credit is due, and she just dominated this conversation.

Lifting the pizza box, I follow her down the stairs to my backyard. The sun is starting her descent; reds, oranges, and pinks fill the sky. Los Angeles has her flaws, but her sunsets are not one of them.

"The night is gorgeous. I love it out here." She smiles at me as I set the pizza down on the large table.

"Glasses and the wine opener are over there." I motion with my head to the outdoor kitchen. "I need to talk to my head of security for a second."

"Oh, right. I always forget about that." She looks around at my numerous cameras.

"I told you, I'm an ass. I seem to make enemies," I call over my shoulder and open the guest house door. Iain sits on the couch, holding up a hand as soon as I enter.

"I turned them off. Let me know when you're done." He stares at the TV, not looking at me, with a stupid grin on his face.

What the hell? I shut the door because if I'm not careful, I'm gonna start trying to defend myself. Screw that.

I turn and head toward her. Standing, she shimmies out of my robe, letting it fall onto the large lounge chair, a deep orange and purple sky behind her.

Danger.

It's like an alarm going off in my head. I'm entering into something I have no control over. For the life of me I don't understand why I don't walk away.

That's a lie, I think, as my eyes devour her naked, fucking hard nipples and juicy tits. Sipping her wine, she waits for me.

"Everything good, Mr. Powers?" Her voice is slightly raspy.

My eyes caress her face. How have I developed a weakness? It's almost laughable. All the shit talk I've said about the schmucks I know getting pussy-whipped? Yet here I am.

Raven is my weakness. No matter how much I tell myself to walk away…

I won't.

And she knows it. What's worse, I don't care if she does. All I want is to bury my mouth in her cunt, suck her nectar until she screams my name, then slowly savor her all night.

Fetching the wineglass from her, I take a sip, hold the glass to her puffy lips, and watch her drink the thick, chocolate-berry blend, tilting the glass more until the deep red liquid spills over the sides. Her eyes widen as it trails down her neck to her breasts.

"Fuck, lie down, baby." Setting the glass on the table next to us, she lies back, her hands stretching up slightly, hanging over the top. She squirms.

Merely looking at her makes me grin. She's perfection. Suddenly, all thoughts about anything besides this woman are gone. The slight warm breeze and the fragrance of lavender and jasmine cocoon us.

"Spread your legs." My nostrils flare as she slowly plants each foot on the edge of the lounger. I let my towel fall.

"You are beautiful." Stroking my cock, I stand over her like a fucking god, preparing to claim what is mine. She licks her wet lips stained with the wine, and I move in between her legs to suck and lick the wine off her right breast.

"Oh God." She groans and arches up while my tongue flicks her hard nipple.

When I move to the other, this time I suck and bite. Her nails dig into the cushion. I lift my head and she slowly opens her eyes.

This is our moment. This second as our eyes connect, it's all there, her love, her needs, her wants. No matter what happens, she will always fully and completely be mine.

"Jett," she whispers.

"Yeah?" I blow on her nipple. "What do you need?" I reach over for the wineglass.

"You. I only need you," she moans as I pour wine on her belly button.

"You've got me. I don't even know how." I dip my head to lick the liquid. Her breathing picks up speed.

"Tell me, tell Mr. Powers, where you want to be sucked on next?"

"My pussy," she screams and arches up.

I can't help but smile. I barely got the question out.

"This is my *cunt*. You understand, Raven, no one else touches it, including you, unless I say so."

"Yes." Her eyes flutter as she watches me trickle more wine onto her pink, wet core.

"Ohhh." She leans up on her elbows, her head falling to the side as she watches me lower my head.

"That's it, baby. Watch me suck on your cunt." Instantly my tongue licks her sweet clit back and forth.

"Fuck, you taste good. Tell your daddy exactly what you need." My own breathing becomes harsh. I bury my face in her, latching onto her delicious nub as she chants my name.

"Oh God," she whines, weaving her hands through my hair.

I rub her juices all over my mouth, needing her scent like I need oxygen.

"Jett... Daddy..." Her hands tighten. "I need to come." She gasps. "I need to come in your mouth." While she pants, I keep sucking on her clit, feeling her whole body tighten. Spiraling over, she jerks against my mouth.

"Fuck, I can't get enough." I give her clit another lick, then slide up her warm body, thrusting my cock deep inside her tight, wet pussy.

"Jesus," I growl.

Her cunt tightens around my thick shaft as if it wants to squeeze every drop out of me.

"So tight and wet and mine." Pulling out, I slide in again, her nails digging into my back as I start to lose sight of everything but this fucking pleasure.

In and out, I pound into her. All the while, she scratches and claws my back and chest.

"That's it, beautiful," I praise her.

Leaning up, she bites my lip, then sucks on the bottom part.

Wild, untamed, almost violent, yet tender all wrapped together. Taking her hand, which is digging into my chest, I lace my fingers with hers.

"I'm going to come," she pants out.

My mouth takes hers. Our tongues tangle and my stomach muscles tighten.

"Jett, I'm going to come," she screams and I let her, not caring who hears us.

"That's it, Raven. Come, baby. Let that fucking cunt milk me." My eyes hold hers. And as I claim the last bit of her soul, I watch her die and become reborn. She whimpers as her pussy contracts in pulsing beats.

"Fuck, that's it. I'm gonna fill you up." My own breathing is harsh as her slick, warm cunt pulses so hard it forces my cock to spit out my seed, over and over.

"Christ." I grab hold of the back of her head and jerk it, letting my mouth suck on her pulse, feeling everything, the pleasure so intense it's tingling in my toes while I stay deep inside her.

Connected.

Our eyes remain locked. She tries to catch her breath, and I try to steal it. When I let go of her hand so I can thrust in one more time, she smiles.

Sighing, she laces her hands in my hair as I kiss her eyelids, her nose, her ear…

The fuck? Did something just move behind the garage? I lift my head, but don't pull out as I search for whoever was watching.

"What's wrong?" Raven turns her head.

"Nothing, I thought I saw someone." I look back at her and kiss her berry lips.

"Wait, what? Who?" She tries to look again, but I see nothing, and I'm still riding the high of having one of the best orgasms of my life.

I'll have Iain check the property to be sure. Right now, I'm gonna eat pizza, drink wine, and cuddle with Raven. I slowly pull out as she groans in protest.

"It was nothing, baby." I kiss her again, because I can't seem to stop, and stand. Reaching for our wineglass, I walk over to the brick outdoor oven where the bottle sits and look over at the spot where I thought I saw something.

Nothing.

I flick on the bistro lights, still nothing. Grabbing the bottle and glass, I return to Raven who is smiling, her legs crossed, looking so beautiful and happy. A feeling of contentment flows over me as my eyes caress her face.

"Put your robe on, my love. I'm gonna have Iain turn the cameras back on and walk the property."

"Really? I wanted to go skinny-dipping." She pouts, and for a moment I almost say fuck it. But Rachel could come home anytime.

"Not tonight." I hand her the wine and pick up her robe as her eyes peruse my body.

"You're so hot." She grins. Sitting up, she places one leg on each side of the lounger. My eyes dip to her wet pussy on display for me, and my cock is hard already.

"Robe, Raven," I hiss.

"Oh, alright." She takes a sip of the wine.

Gritting my teeth, I watch her neck as she swallows. She's testing me. My hands ball into the robe. I'm ready to spank her ass, then make her gag on my cock. Maybe we should go back upstairs to her room?

Finally, she stands and takes the robe. "I'll be back. Let me get some clothes." Not waiting to see the look on her face—I don't need to—I can feel her disappointment.

I rush up the stairs. This is the right thing to do. Rachel may be a bitch, but she doesn't need to see me with Raven.

I frown, kicking my door open and grabbing my sweatpants and a T-shirt. Christ, when did I become a hypocrite? I don't give a fuck if anyone sees me fucking. But it's different with Raven. The need to share her is not there. In fact, it's the opposite, if I'm honest. I've developed an almost animalistic rage at the thought of anyone touching her besides me.

Control, Jett.

Get these urges contained.

Rachel is your fiancée, and Raven... you shouldn't even be thinking about anything more than having pizza and watching TV with her.

This is what you want, I keep telling myself as I walk down the stairs.

This life, my job, everything that I've worked so hard for. No worries, no feelings, no drama.

Order.

So why do I feel robbed that I can't go skinny-dipping in my pool with Raven?

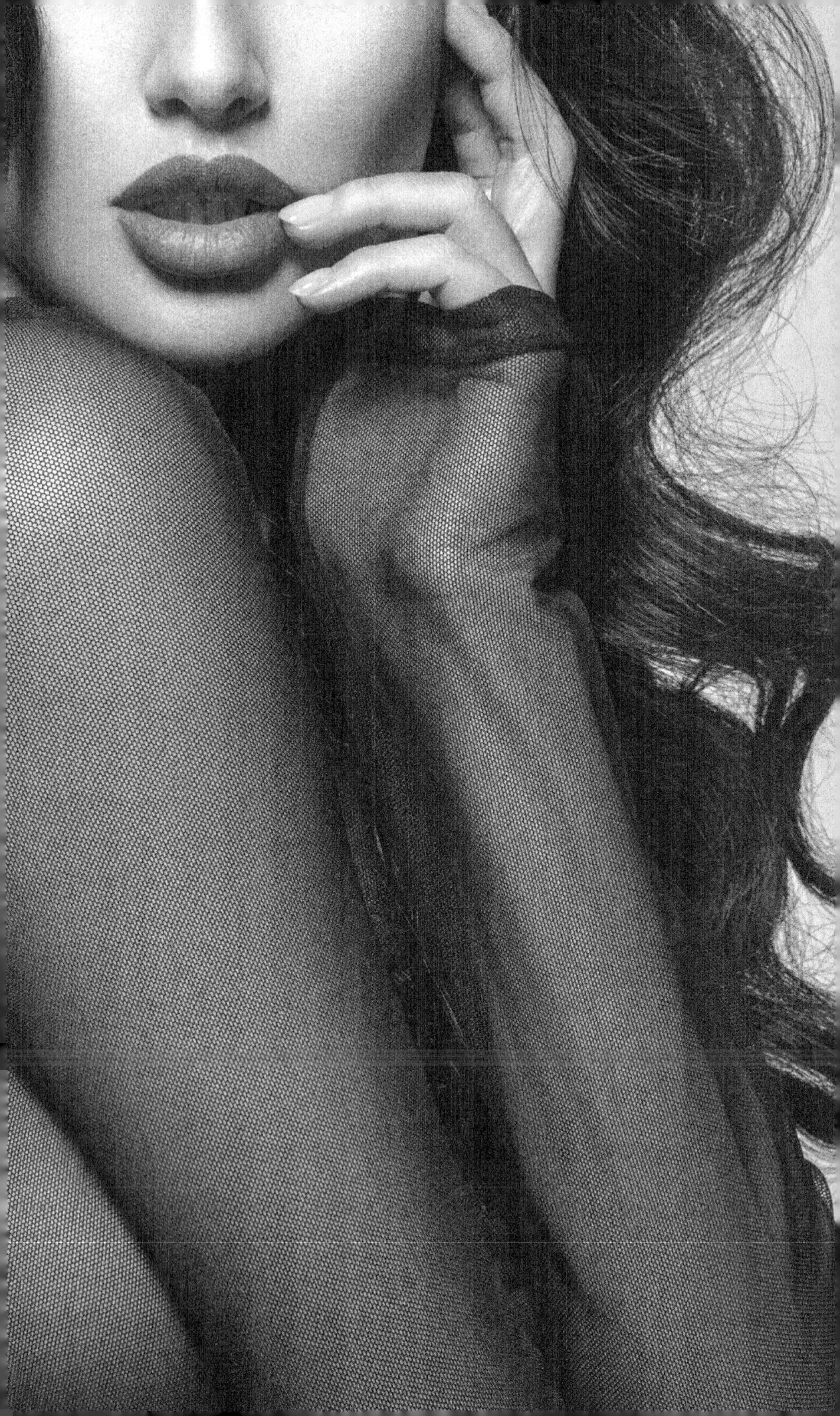

Twenty-Three

RAVEN

I turn over and open my eyes. Something woke me. Blinking again, I try to clear away the cobwebs from the wine and get my mind to focus.

Something's wrong. I sleep like the dead. Sighing, I prop myself up on my elbows. My mind replays last night. Jett and I made love. He was mine, connected, kissing me, loving me. I probably didn't need to be so transparent about my feelings for him, but whatever. I'm sick of lying. I'm crazy in love with him, and he needed to know.

"Why are you smiling?" Someone sitting in the corner chair leans forward.

Bolting up, I grab the sheet.

"What the fuck, Mom?" My heart and head pound. "Seriously, what are you doing in my room?" My voice is getting louder. What the hell?

"*Your* room?" She stands and walks over to the window. This is creepy, even for her. Like this is a whole 'nother level of crazy.

"Yes. *My* room." I toss off the covers, only to remember I'm naked as my skin pebbles with uncomfortable goose bumps.

She looks like she hasn't gone to bed yet. Her makeup is a mess; her perfect clothes are wrinkled. God, how long has she been sitting here, watching me?

"This is not your room." She slants me a look.

I try to rationalize things and calm my terror. Surely Jett will save me if I scream.

"Whatever." I straighten my shoulders back.

She turns to full-on look at me, as though she's just now taking me in.

"I have no idea what's going on, but get out." I spin around, moving to my dresser for a bra and panties.

"You stupid, delusional girl." Her voice is low. She lights up a cigarette.

Wow, she's got to be plastered. Jett hates smoking, and my mom knows it. She never lights up in the house.

I take a deep breath, my eyes shifting to the door. When did this room get so big? It feels like that door is miles away. I can still yell...

Stop it.

She's your mother. She's not going to hurt you. *Pull yourself together, Raven,* I repeat over and over. Biting my bottom lip, I slip my panties on.

"You come into my house and try to steal my man? Oh, sweetheart, I think we need to have a mother-daughter talk." She blows smoke up at the ceiling, and my heart thuds. This is bad.

"Excuse me?" I say slowly, grabbing the first shirt I see in my drawer. Screw the bra.

"Oh, save the innocent act for Jett." She snorts. "I knew you were seducing him for a while, you little *traitorous cunt*," she screams. Her red lips look bizarre, like she has four balls injected in them, two on top and two on the bottom. Jesus, she reeks of booze.

"You're drunk, so I'll pretend this didn't happen, okay?" I snap back while pulling out some black yoga leggings. I just want to get clothes on, some kind of barrier from her madness.

"Oh, I don't think so. You need to go. Here." She tosses what looks like an American Express Black Card on my bed.

"Take the card and get out. You don't need to bother showing up for the wedding." She takes another drag.

Ugly words, hurtful words.

She's got to be the worst person alive. To be honest, I don't think she ever loved me, but this, buying me off, it's almost laughable. My heart skips. If she is this desperate to get rid of me, that must mean she thinks I'm special to Jett.

I take a breath. "Mom, I'm not doing anything with Mr. Powers besides going to work with him. I have no idea what this is all about."

She takes a step closer to me, and I despise being short, or as my father lovingly says, petite...whatever that is. Though I try to move away from her, she reaches for me with that claw of a hand.

"Mine. *He's mine.* Don't think I won't do anything and everything to keep him." She shakes me.

"Get off me, you old hag." I rip my arm away. My face is on fire with humiliation and anger. I'm done with her. This abuse stops now.

"Hag? How dare you—"

"I dare everything. You have zero idea who I am." I face her, and her eyes widen.

"You really are a stupid girl," she sneers, smoke dancing around her pale face, making her look cartoonish.

"I'm far from stupid. Now, take your bribe money and get out of my room." I look at the bed and the card.

"Maybe use it to get some more shit injected in your face. You're looking a little tired today." It's petty and beneath me, but she's a terrible person, and I have no intention of letting her destroy me anymore.

Straightening, she brings the cigarette to her mouth and inhales deeply. The smoke escapes her nostrils. "Well, well, well. It looks like you just might have some of me in you. But you're playing a game you can't win. You think you know Jett?"

She smiles, and I want to cover my ears because I know what she's going to say will hurt me.

"You think you can actually keep someone like him interested?" My mother shakes her head. "Has he shared you yet, Raven?" She smirks as my brain starts to buzz, like little bees trying to protect me from what's coming next.

"Because that's what he likes. He gets off watching, and fucking, other women. It's what he does. So you thinking you're special is kind of laughable." She licks her lips, dropping the cigarette and putting it out with her heel.

"This, my stupid little girl, is why he'll never leave me. Because I like it too." She saunters to the door, then turns. "You don't believe me? Make sure you're home tonight, my love. You'll see firsthand exactly who and what Jett Powers really is and what he likes."

She walks out, her heels clicking on the floor, or maybe it's my teeth. I'm shaking.

"What the fuck?" I look around as if the room can answer me, give me the strength I need to compete with someone so awful.

"Think, Raven, think," I say, closing my eyes, then opening them.

I need Jett.

I rush over to my phone and stare at it. What am I going to say? *My mom might finally have snapped. You're engaged to a bad person who says you will want to share me. Oh, and by the way, I'm in love with you in case you didn't get that last night...*

"Oh my God." I drop my phone and pace the room. Okay, I need to get ready for work. I can do that; then I'll get some coffee and try to talk to Jett.

"Perfect." I march toward the bathroom. I'm in and out of the shower, barely even remembering it, my mind is spinning so much. What did she mean about tonight? Are they planning some kind of... what? Orgy? Threesome? I grab on to the sink because I refuse to believe her. He's not like that. He can't be.

She's just trying to scare me. I look up at myself in the mirror and stare. Somehow, I look different. I don't know what it is, but I'm certainly not the same person who showed up a month ago.

Clearing my throat, I straighten and grab some lip gloss. I'm pale now that the horror has worn off, so I apply some light blush... I need to talk to someone.

Cher.

I need her. There's no way I can handle this alone.

After tossing all my cosmetics back into my bag, I pull my hair into a tight bun and get dressed for the day, secretly hoping he's sitting in the chair my mom was in, waiting for me.

He's not. Of course, he's not. Quickly, I put on some flared dress slacks and a white starched shirt, then roll up the sleeves. I slip on a pair of plain black pumps and reach for my phone. Huffing in and out in short breaths, I call Cher.

"Pick up, Cher," I grumble as the phone just rings. Finally, I hang up and text.

ME: I can't begin to get into how fucked I am. Where are you?

She's probably not gonna see this for hours, and I need to go to work. How am I gonna sit next to him and pretend I'm fine? Should I tell him what happened?

I grab my bag and slowly walk out, looking to make sure my mom isn't around, then speed walk down the stairs, almost colliding with Jett. I scream.

Frowning, he holds me. "You okay?"

"I—"

"Oh, there you are, Raven. Jett and I were just discussing our date night tonight. I'll have Maria make you dinner. You don't mind, right?" She's wearing her stupid red silk robe again, hair wet and off her face, but she's reapplied her makeup.

"Rachel." Jett sighs as he lets go of my arms. "Raven can eat with us." He walks over to grab his suit jacket.

"Why would she? That would be... uncomfortable." She slithers over to him as he looks down at her. Bile rises in my throat. Watching him, with her, is making me physically ill. What can he possibly see in her? Because all I see is a manipulative, hateful person.

"I'm not feeling well," I announce, watching my mom smile up at him, then glance over at me, eyes narrowed. My hand is tingling. Jesus, for a second I actually saw myself slapping and clawing at her fake face.

"Let's go. We're late." He buttons his suit, frowning at me.

"I really don't feel well *at all*." I was wrong. I can't be near him right now. It hurts too much.

I need to think, regroup, get a plan, because this one has matured into a situation my heart can't seem to handle.

Not after last night.

"Oh dear." She cocks her head at me. "Jett, Raven should stay home today. If she has something, you don't want her giving it to everyone."

I barely hear my mom's voice as I stare at Jett. His beautiful blue eyes search my face, and for a split second he looks like he might actually touch me. Instead, he nods.

"Get some rest. You're pale." He turns to leave.

I don't wait to hear anything more, not from him, or my mom. I take off my pumps and dart up the stairs, slamming my door and locking it. In a moment of almost paranoid terror, I rush over to the giant leather chair my creepy mother was sitting on and push it in front of the door.

"What are you doing?" I drop into it, trying to catch my breath as my phone starts ringing.

"Shit." I reach for my handbag, praying it's Cher, but deep inside I know it's not.

"Breathe, Raven." I shouldn't answer this phone call, should ignore all calls from him, but it's like a compulsion. I need him, or at least that's what it feels like right now.

"What?" My voice sounds like I'm ready to cry, which I am, but he certainly doesn't need to know that.

"What's wrong with you?" His voice is so strong, powerful. I close my eyes, feeling the tears already trickling down.

"I... just don't feel well," I whisper.

"You've been taking your birth control, right?" His voice, which only seconds ago seemed magical, makes my eyes bolt wide open.

"I never said I was on the pill." And I know I haven't. I've been surprised he never once questioned me about any sort of birth control. Actually, I figured he'd had a vasectomy. Clearly not.

"Do you think I'd come inside you if I didn't know you were on birth control? I don't want kids. I always wrap it up." Again, his voice is so calm, in control, I almost want to lie and say I haven't been taking it just to hear some sort of emotion rather than his sanctimonious tone.

"What are you talking about?" I'm two seconds from losing it. "How could you know that I'm on the pill?" I demand, covering my mouth with my hand. My leg starts to bounce.

"I have all your medical records."

"So you spied on me?" Though I'm tempted to scream, or lose it, I keep my voice steady.

"Of course," he says like it's no big deal.

And I start laughing. It's either that or break down and sob. "Why?"

"You know why." His voice is calm, almost soothing. It's how he always wins. He stays calm, controlled, no surprises.

I shake my head and stare out the window. I'm completely in over my head with a man who seems to have zero conscience. Strike that. I'm in love with him, even knowing exactly what he is: an asshole.

What's wrong with me?

Shaking my head, I close my eyes and speak slowly. "Jett, I'm not sick because I'm pregnant... I'm in love with you."

There, I did it.

It's out there, and I don't regret it. If anything, his silence actually makes me smile. Slumping back in the large chair, I wait as the seconds tick by.

"Did you hear me? I'm in love with you, and seeing you with my mom makes me sick. I want to throw up, probably will. Thinking about you, and how you feel when you're inside me, and knowing you're doing that with her..."

"I'm not." His deep voice makes me sit up.

I try to calm my racing heart, but can't breathe. Holy shit, this is it. He's going to say the words I need to hear.

"We will talk about this later." His voice is clipped, almost annoyed sounding.

"That's all you're going to say? *I'm not?* I'm not what?" I demand, because I've come this far, so why stop now?

"I'm *not* discussing this on the phone." His voice is full of warning.

Inhaling deeply, I nod, then let the hysterical laughter come out.

"Well, at least you don't have to worry about pregnancy. You have a good day, Mr. Powers." That's enough humiliation for today, or any other day. I'm about to hang up.

"Raven." His voice stops me.

"What?"

"I haven't been with your mother, or anyone else, since the day I took your virginity." And then the line goes dead.

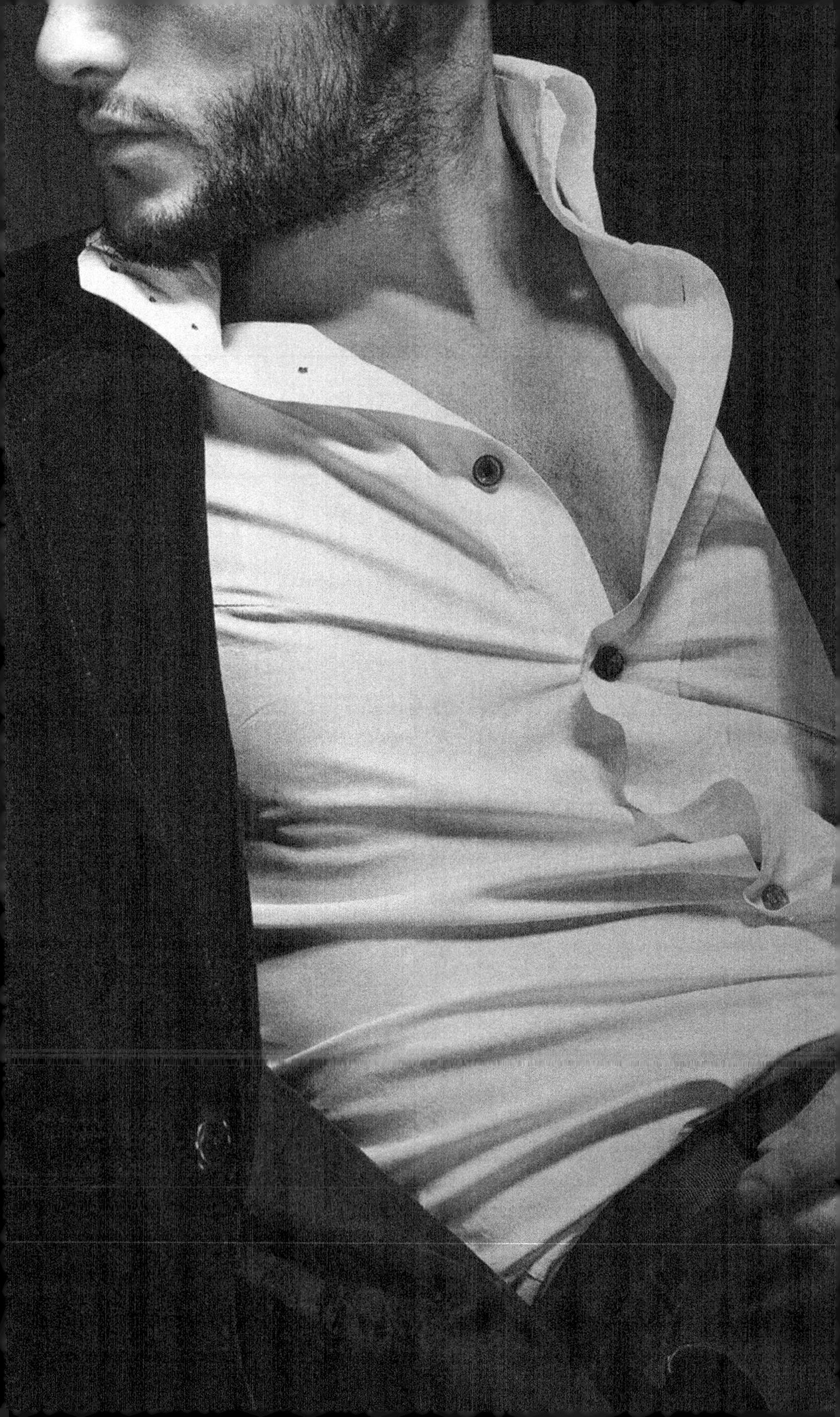

Twenty-Four

JETT

"Becca, call Doug Jefferson and tell him I'm passing on the Hopper case." I walk past a stunned Rebecca who jumps up from her seat as if I've scared her.

"Yes, of course. Do I give him a reason?"

Glaring at her, I swing my massive office door open.

"I'm so sorry. Coffee?" she calls after me as I shut the door. She'll bring me coffee and every kind of Danish since she knows she fucked up by questioning me.

I should just call it a day, I think, looking at my Rolex. It's almost three. I spent way longer than I wanted to today in court, only to be hit with nonstop messages about taking this murder case as soon as I got out. It's the type of case I should jump at: wealthy woman killing her husband of twelve years. She said it was because he had just found out he was dying and that it was a suicide. I can definitely work that, even with the lack of weapon or any real concrete testimony saying that he was indeed terminal.

It will be a major event. Paparazzi will eat it up. They need something since the Disciples case is over. Young, beautiful Mrs. Hopper, a former Playboy bunny, found depressed, older husband dead because he couldn't handle going through a lengthy death.

POWER

Yeah, I'd kill it, but since I've fucked myself into a predicament, literally, the thought of work doesn't hold any allure at the moment.

Raven.

My little Lolita, speaking her truths, not letting anything stop her.

Fucking balls.

I admire that. Today she put it all on the line, and I know I need to end it. Standing, I walk to my liquor cabinet and grab a bottle of whatever is closest, then drop back into my chair and spin around to look out of the giant office windows. I unscrew the top of the bottle and drink as though it's water instead of fucking whiskey burning a path from my throat down to my esophagus.

Truths.

Secrets.

Lies.

I slam the bottle down and watch it mark my perfectly shined cherrywood desk. My phone vibrates. I ignore it. This is my time.

Right now. I need to sit here and drink and think. Leaning my head back, I envision her dropping her robe, her cherry lips parted...

With a snort, I sit up, reaching for the bottle, and bring it to my lips as I come to peace with what I'm finally ready to do.

"Mr. Powers?" Rebecca's voice makes me spin my chair to face her. Her usual pleasant, nothing-fazes-me façade has evaporated.

"Yes?"

"I'm so sorry to bother you." She clears her throat, and her eyes widen when I drink straight from the bottle.

"It's just that... I mean, Rachel, that is, Ms. Stewart, is trying to reach you." Her brown eyes hold concern, which makes me smile.

"You can go," I say, propping my feet on the edge of the desk.

"Can I get you a glass? Or maybe call for Iain to bring the car for you?" She takes a step closer, and for a second, her thin form reminds me of Raven's if I really squint.

Except she's not.

"Did my fiancée leave a message?" After bringing the bottle to my lips, the warm burn starts to make me feel more like the real me. Fuck all this drivel in my head. So we had great sex. She had a fucking untouched pussy; that's all this fascination was. And now it's over. I'll go home to Rachel. I'll fuck her, saturate myself in her cunt, and erase all those thoughts and the smell and taste of orange blossoms and coconut.

Rachel is who I deserve. She is on the same path. Raven... well, Raven deserves the world. She'll go to Stanford, make her mark.

"She said..." Rebecca shifts to another foot as if she's nervous, but to be honest I had forgotten she was there.

"She said, hurry home, she has a surprise for you," she blurts out, and her cheeks pinken.

"A surprise." I throw my head back to laugh. God, only Rachel is fucked up enough to bring in another woman when Raven is here.

"Perfect." I point the bottle at Rebecca and stand. "Yes, please call Iain."

"Yes, Mr. Powers." And for a second those words make my chest hurt, but they're mere words. So what if my Lolita said them like the good girl she is? I need to focus on the future.

"One more thing?"

"Yes?"

"Is Raven coming in on Monday? I heard she wasn't feeling well, and she wasn't here today—"

"No. Raven is done interning. If you need more help, hire someone," I seethe with visions of tossing the glass bottle out the window and shattering everything.

POWER

Shattering.

The way my chest feels when I think of giving her up. I close my eyes and take a deep breath. This is over. I need to tell Raven the truth—that I have never considered not marrying Rachel.

I never lied to her.

She only thinks she's in love with me. She's nineteen, for fuck's sake, caught up in the excitement of having sex with an older, experienced man.

I walk out of my office, ignoring the startled gasps and stares, push the elevator button, and loosen my tie.

Love.

Christ, it's not even a real emotion. It's nothing more than two people connecting and then mistaking that feeling as love. It wears off, as all connections do. They break up, and boom, they start all over with another person.

Snorting, I bring the bottle to my lips. This is why Rachel is the one for me. I already can't stand her. How fucked up is that?

"Mr. Powers." I turn toward the voice.

"Your car is ready for you." Iain stands with the door open.

"Thank you." I slide in and lean my head back, letting the warmth of the bourbon flow through my veins. And just like that, I feel better than I have in weeks.

It takes ten minutes from my office to my house. In thirty minutes, I'll be balls deep inside whoever the surprise is that Rachel has arranged.

And in an hour... well, in an hour, everything will be back to normal.

"Mr. Powers?" Iain's voice makes me blink and I slowly look over at him. His usual calm expression has changed, his eyebrows knit together as if he, too, is concerned. Clearly, he's been standing with the car door open while my mind races.

Nodding, I step out and gaze up at my house. "You believe in love, man?" I say, turning before I walk up the steps. The question seems to have caught him off guard. Pain swirls in his dark eyes. I guess that's my answer.

"Absolutely." He takes a breath and nods. "Fuck yeah, I do." He steps to the front of the Mercedes.

As I start to walk up my front steps, I reflect on this. Even Iain believes in love, has clearly been in love. For all I know, he's in a happy relationship, though I somehow doubt that if the haunted look in his eyes is any clue. Yeah, that's a man who has demons, someone who's been hurt. I open the front door and enter my foyer, instantly smelling food.

"Rachel?" I call out, setting my bottle down.

"Upstairs," she yells back.

The house seems deserted. She probably dismissed everyone. I take the stairs, hearing music coming from my bedroom as I walk to the left toward Raven's room, stopping myself before I knock.

It's like I have weights on my chest, like I'm fighting something. This is a battle that can't ever be won.

Screw knocking. Why pretend you're something you're not? I enter, my eyes instantly finding her. It's as if I've stepped into a different universe, because in this universe all is moving slowly, as if time is trying to give me a second to catch up.

Raven stands. The book she was reading falls to the floor. Her eyes are red as if she's been crying. But all I can do is stare at her.

She is my weakness, but I don't have to be her downfall.

"It's over." My voice comes out strong. Our eyes connect, and I let myself become trapped in her sapphire pools as they blink back tears.

"What is wrong with you?" Her voice cracks. As she walks toward me, her scent of orange blossoms wraps around me. When I die, this will be my last smell—I know it. Her face and this smell will wrap around me as I take my last breath. Jesus Christ, I need to stop drinking. I'm thinking crazy, or maybe she's just that dangerous.

Her eyes, which at first held tears, are now almost black. "What. Is. Wrong. With. You?" she repeats.

"I told you I'm an asshole." I unbutton the top two buttons of my dress shirt.

She snorts, covers her mouth, and nods, then points out the door. "You really are going to marry her? Do you have a fucking clue who, and what, she is?"

"I know exactly what she is, Raven." My voice is flat, and suddenly everything seems gray and dark.

"She's hated me from the day I was born. Why?" She throws up her hands. "I don't know, and you know what, Jett? I don't care, but you... I thought you were brilliant. I thought you were strong and..." Tears spill down her face. Pain, much like what I witnessed moments ago with Iain, flows out of her, making me uncomfortable, as if there's a noose around my neck.

"It's done. It was not my intention to hurt you, or for you to develop feelings for me—"

"Shut up. You're a fucking liar. Do you even see yourself? I know you have feelings for me. What the fuck happened to you?" She wipes her cheeks, and her eyes search mine.

My head is pounding. "You're wrong. I'm a one-person show. Your mother is the same. Together, we make sense."

"She fucked my high school boyfriend. She's like a black widow. How can you stand to be inside..." Her eyes widen as if she's picturing us together.

"I did not set out to hurt you." I turn.

"Well, *you did*," she screams at my back.

"Stay in your room, Raven." I shut her door, the music and laughter guiding me toward my bedroom.

Because this is it.

This is who I truly am. Leaning against my door frame, I steady myself and watch Rachel. Glass of champagne in one hand while she flicks her tongue over Emily's tight nipples. Emily's eyes dart to mine. Smiling, she parts her legs, showing me her wet cunt.

Nothing. I feel nothing. I grind my teeth at how fucking pathetic this is.

"Look who finally decided to join us," she coos as Rachel raises her head.

"Jett, baby, *finally*. I was beginning to wonder if you got lost." Her smile doesn't reach her eyes. There is no sparkle, no deep pools of sapphires to lose myself in. I never got her sapphires, never caressed her skin with her wearing nothing but them.

I never did a lot of things…

I push off the doorway and untuck my shirt, walking farther in. Rachel's hands move inside Emily's legs.

"I got her all ready for you," she says, watching me unbutton my shirt and toss it to the floor.

"Get up," I grunt.

Emily leaps up, making room for me to sit. Her scent is not as repulsive as Rachel's flowers, but it's not what I seek.

Like a king, I sit and let their hands touch me while I wait.

One.

Two.

Three.

I look up.

She stands in the doorway. Our eyes collide, and her pain almost drowns me, but that can't happen—I'm already dead.

And now, it's done.

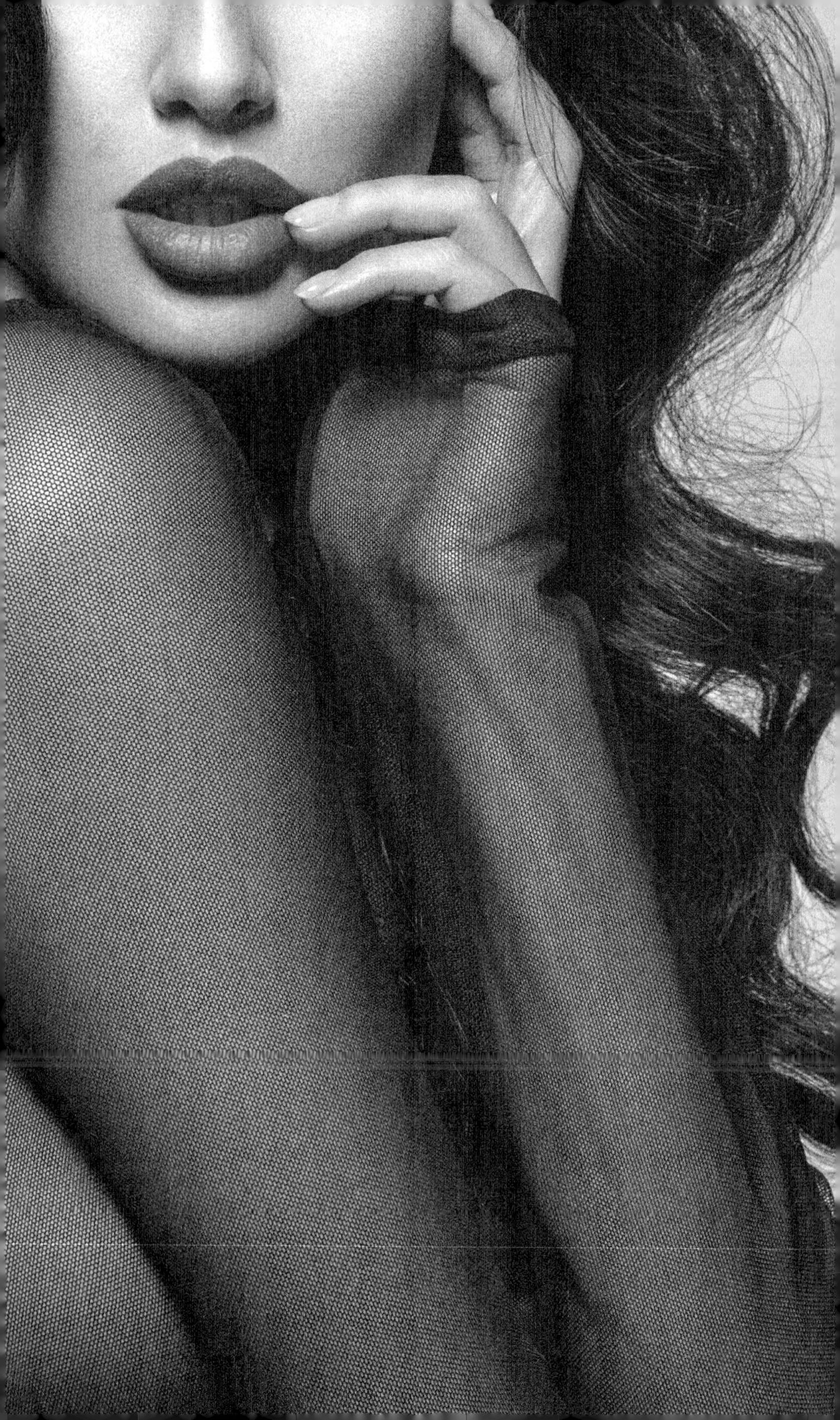

Twenty-Five

RAVEN

This can't be happening. My mind scrambles to my earlier phone conversation with Cher, when she told me this would happen, that I never should have told him I loved him if I didn't want it to end.

But I can't pretend that I'm okay with him being with my mom. He needed to know.

"I did not set out to hurt you," he says.

This might be the moment I finally snap. All my life, everyone has picked my mother and now, *even he has.*

He picked her.

Her!

"Well, *you did*," I scream, because I want him to bleed, feel something, not just speak in clichés. He didn't want to hurt me? How fucking pathetic.

I watch, almost frozen, as he turns and walks away, and my heart suddenly pounds in my temples. He's leaving me.

"Stay in your room, Raven." His voice is gravelly and strong, and the knife that has been hovering around my chest finally slices it open and penetrates.

"This is not real. I can't be that much of an idiot." Sinking back into the chair, I look around, but everything is blurry through my tears.

"No." I stand. "You're lying," I whisper, angrily wiping away my tears. The time for crying is over. I need to fight.

I can't lose him. I have to stop him. This can't be how it ends. I run to my door and swing it open, instantly hearing crappy music coming from his room. Goose bumps start on my neck and travel down my arms as I move closer.

"No." I choke on my words, because he told me to stay away, and for a split second I hesitate. Am I ready to face his truths?

"Jett, baby, *finally*. I was beginning to wonder if you got lost." My mother's voice makes me gag, but I continue, knowing that I should stop.

Stop, Raven.

Why won't I stop? This is going to hurt me, but it's as if I'm gone, on autopilot, placing one foot in front of another until I reach for the wall to steady me.

The door is open. The lights are on, and I take one more step...

That's when I see it all. I see him for who he truly is.

This is when I should leave, or scream, but I don't. I just stare at my mother in some red lingerie, licking the nipple of a blond woman sitting naked in a chair.

Frozen.

I stand, watching him untuck his shirt, demanding they move. And then he sits, and my world that has never been perfect, but was at least bearable, crumbles.

No, my world explodes. And not because of the hands reaching to unzip his slacks, or my mother reaching to touch the other woman's cunt.

No, all that is mere background drama in a horrific play. What makes me stop breathing is him.

His blue eyes are laser-focused on me. This is what will haunt me.

He wants me to see him. He wants to hurt me in the most vicious, primal way.

He wants us to be done.

Like a key fitting into a lock and clicking open, I feel my head snap, almost like the flash of a camera lens, as I back away.

He is a monster.

And I'm done.

Him, my mother, my life, in one click. It's over.

Somehow, I make it back to my room and move to my closet. *Monster.* I can almost hear them panting. My mind won't stop replaying it, and I doubt it ever will. It's hard to believe I once thought being humiliated and tortured by my ex was the end of the world when he laughed and bragged about fucking my mom. That seems so juvenile now.

"Darren just hurt you. Jett, just fucking destroyed you." God, I'm losing it. I'm full-on talking to myself. "Whatever." Pulling out my suitcase, I rip clothes off hangers and toss them into my bag. I must be crying. Can barely breathe or see as I move to my drawers and continue throwing clothes into my bag. Then I grab my handbag and start throwing my makeup in, but my hand freezes.

"Fucking bitch," I scream as I spot the American Express Black Card my mother gave me earlier, just sitting on top of my powder case.

I almost start laughing, but it's too sick, really. She planned all this. She wins. I'm taking her bribe card. She can pay to have me out of her life until I get on my feet. After that, I'll never see her again.

I bring out my phone and call Cher, trying not to hyperventilate while grabbing my various moisturizers and tossing those into the bag too.

"Hey, babe. I'm dying to hear what happened." Cher's voice is taken over by loud music.

"Fucking get to a spot where you can hear me," I scream, barely hanging on and not about to compete with a club.

"Oh shit. Hold on. Don't go anywhere. I'm almost out," Cher says as the music fades. "Oh God, what happened? Did you tell him what I told you to?" Her voice is coming in clear now.

"No. He broke it off with me, and I just walked in on him having a threesome with my mom and some blond bitch." My voice doesn't even sound like mine, and I wonder if I've snapped and am dreaming all this.

"Oh, Raven, oh no." Cher's voice cracks.

Nope, not dreaming, and this shit hurts, almost burns so much that I want to clutch my chest and curl into a ball. That can come later, though. First, I need to get the fuck out of here.

"I just... how could h—"

"Stop, Cher. I need to leave. Are you fucking listening? I need to get away, *now*." I take a breath and bring the phone down to look at the screen. *What am I doing?* Cher is in Italy. She can't help.

"I have to go. I'll call you later," I snap.

"Raven, wait, don't hang—" I press end and turn, looking at my door, and then I call the only other friend I have.

"Brody." I sniff. "Brody will help." With a nod, I scroll through my missed calls, ignoring that my hands are shaking. God, I have so many nice texts from him asking how I'm doing. And I never responded because *I* was fucking the monster.

Monster.

I push on his number and bite my lower lip, looking at my door again, wondering if the man who is currently having sex with my mother and some random woman will ever walk through this doorway again.

"Raven?" Brody's sweet voice is like cold, stinging water thrown in my face. It's the last straw, really, and I start sobbing.

"Raven? What's happened? Are you hurt?"

"Oh, Brody. Thank you for answering." I try to say more, but I'm crying so hard he stops me.

"I'm calling the cops. I can't even understand you."

"Noooo, no cops. I just need you. Can you come and get me, *please*?" I say, looking up at the ceiling, hoping that will help get me under control. At this point, I'm not certain I'm using complete sentences. I do know the cops should not be involved. I'm trying to get away...not locked up.

"Okay. I'm leaving now. Be outside the gate in a half hour. Can you do that?" His voice is calm and soothing. Any other time, it probably would have aggravated me, but right now, I cling to it.

"Thank you." I hang up and keep stuffing as much as I can in. For some reason, it feels like I have a lot more than what I arrived with. I should leave the expensive clothes and shoes. Where I'm going, I won't need them, other than to maybe sell them since I may never come back, at least not for years. It's hard to breathe. My nose is stuffy, and my eyes are so swollen and red, they feel like sandpaper.

Grabbing my bags, I ignore the music and other sounds coming from their room. If I focus on that, I'll throw up, and I need to get out of this shithole.

Not seeing anyone, I throw my carry-on and handbag over my shoulder and pull my large Louis Vuitton bag down the long driveway.

"Raven?"

Shit, it's Iain yelling at me. *Just keep walking, just keep walking*, plays in my head. Christ, I'm a mess.

"Hey, Raven. What are you doing?" He catches up with me. The floodlights come on.

"I'm leaving." I keep walking until I get to the gate.

"I'm assuming Mr. Powers has no idea you're going?"

"Look…" I heave my bags over to my other shoulder, trying hard not to start crying again. "Can you please open the gate? I have a friend coming for me."

He simply stares at me.

"Fine, here." I take off my Rolex, a gift from my dad when I graduated high school, and hand it to him. "Please, take it. Just fucking open the gate." I shove the watch at him.

He looks at the watch and then up at my face. "I don't want your watch. And you know I need to let him know."

"Do you?" My voice is getting loud. "Because he's busy fucking my mom and some other whore… and I can't… I can't stay here." And here come the tears again. It's like I can't stop or control myself.

"Raven." He sighs and looks over at the house. "I still have to." His voice is gentle.

"Please, take my watch. I don't have cash, but I can send you some when I get situated. But, Iain, I'm begging you, I have to get out of here." I try to hand him my watch again, but he shakes his head.

"Okay. Great, you do what you've got to do." I toss my watch into my handbag and look ahead, waiting for Brody. Maybe I should call the police.

"Where are you going?" he asks, his voice flat.

"I don't know, but I have friends. You don't need to worry about me," I say, still staring at the gate.

"It's my job to worry," he states as Brody comes speeding up in his BMW. He barely stops and is out of the car, his thin body looking like he's ready to do battle.

"Open the gate." Brody's typically calm voice sounds rather frantic.

"Iain." I look at him. "Please, let me go. Trust me, Jett and my mom don't care." I wipe my cheeks, trying to stop the insane tears from flowing.

His brown eyes go from me to Brody. "Do you need money?" He reaches into his wallet handing me a lot of cash.

"No. My mom was kind enough to give me an American Express Black Card so I'd leave. I'm good." My voice drips with sarcasm.

"Just take the cash. You never know when you might need it." He tucks it in my bag.

"Thank you. I'll pay you back." I sniff, and the tears that had slowed start right back up.

"Listen, man. This is unacceptable. Raven is not a prisoner. Open the gate or I'll call the police," Brody yells at Iain who smirks.

"He's rescuing you, huh?" He arches a brow at me but pushes a button on his phone and the large, wrought iron gate opens.

"Yep." I say over my shoulder as I walk toward Brody who grabs my luggage, tossing it into his trunk.

"Raven?" Iain calls out.

"Yeah?" I stop and turn, though Brody reaches for me.

"Cheer up. Things always work out the way they're supposed to." He smiles, then turns and walks up the driveway. The gate closes, and Brody puts his arms around me. I want to scream back at Iain, *What does that mean?* or *You don't understand*, but he's too far away and it's pointless. He doesn't get my pain.

"Jesus, Raven, you scared me. What happened?" Brody pulls back so his eyes can assess me.

"I can't talk about it now. Just get me out of here."

He nods and walks me over to the passenger seat as if I'm made of glass, so gentle... The complete opposite of Jett. He'd have pulled me in tightly and held me, letting his strength assure me that everything was okay, that he was there, and that I didn't need anyone but him.

Except Jett is a monster, not my knight in shining armor. How did I lose sight of that so fast?

I drop into the passenger seat and let Brody fuss over me, not really listening to his rambling, hearing bits and pieces of how he's gonna take care of me and I'll stay with him.

"I'm going to Spain, Brody." I look over at him. At least he looks like he's been in the sun, so his coloring is better.

"Spain? What about school?" He almost misses a turn.

"I'm done with school for right now." I look back out the window, leaning my head against the cool glass.

"But... I thought..."

"I'm going to Spain. Do you want to come with me?" My voice sounds far away, and I realize I don't really care if he comes with me or not.

I'm all alone.

I hate being alone, but I am, and no matter how much I'd like for Brody to be able to fix me, he can't.

"Now?" His voice goes up an octave.

"Yes."

"I can't. I mean..." He looks over at me, then back at the street. "Goddammit, Raven, why Spain?"

"Because that's where I'm supposed to be." I bring my knees up and wrap my arms around myself as if that can protect my heart from this pain.

But it doesn't.

It hurts, I hurt, and something tells me this might never go away.

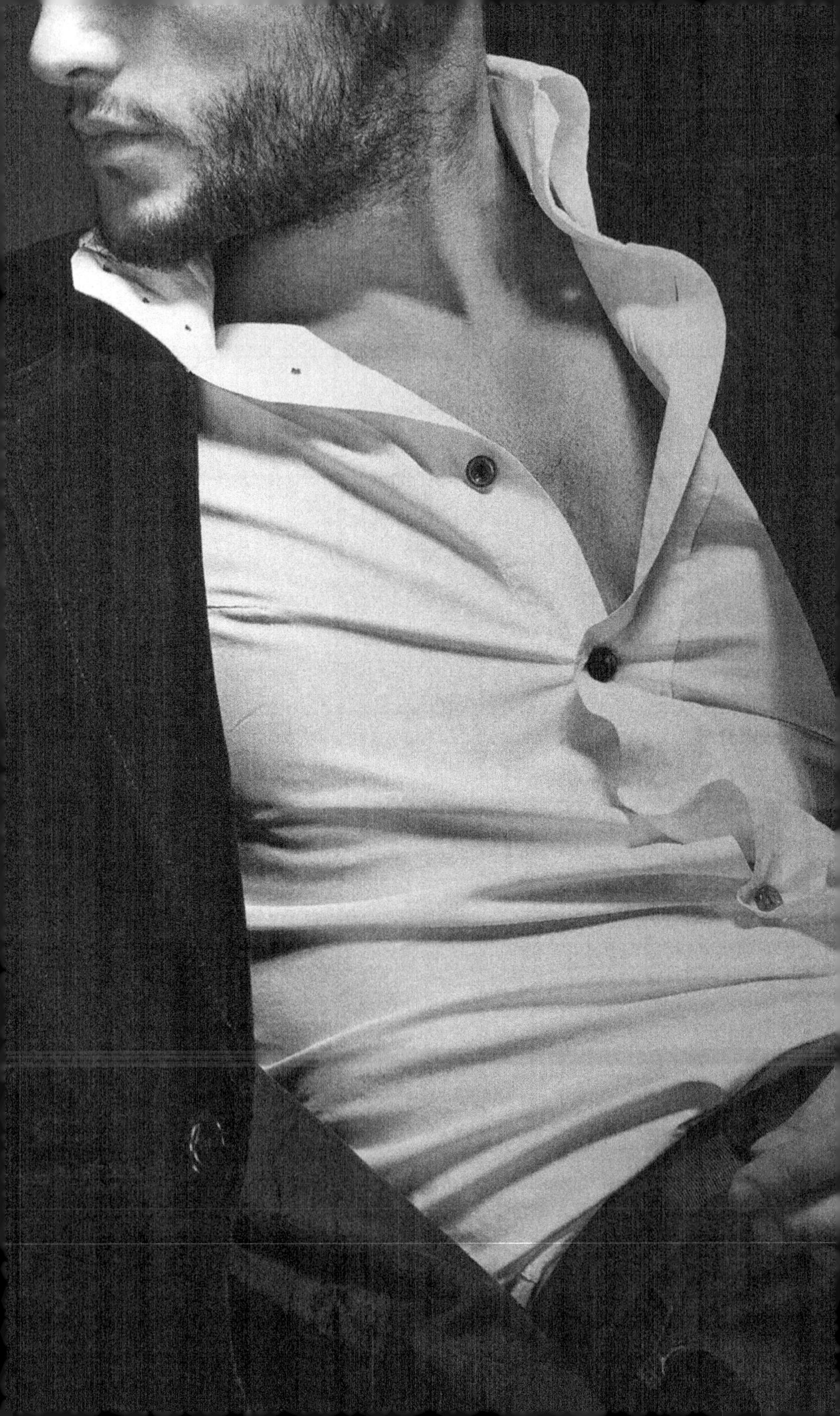

Twenty-Six

JETT

I roll over and squint at the blinding sun in my eyes. "The fuck?" Groaning, I sit up and blink away the black dots, then look over at a naked Rachel.

"Christ." I lie back, scrubbing my hands up and down my face. The events of last night flood my brain.

Raven. Her face, her lips, her fucking pain as she watched Rachel and Emily touch me.

"Fuck." I sit up and toss the covers off, then rest my elbows on my knees, ignoring Rachel's groans at being disturbed. My head is pounding and my mouth feels like I drank sewer water.

I grab the bottle of whiskey from my nightstand and take a swig. Definitely a hair-of-the-dog type of morning.

"Emily?" I call out. She must have left, not that I blame her. Last night couldn't have been more fucked up.

Standing, I slowly make my way to the bathroom to take a piss. Poor Emily. I need to call her and tell her none of what went down was her fault.

No matter how much she tried, I never got hard. I'd like to blame it on the booze, but it wasn't.

I know it wasn't.

I flush the toilet and stumble over to the shower, needing a cold one to wake me up enough to figure out my next plan.

POWER

What the fuck has happened to me?

Closing my eyes, I place my hands against the tiled wall, my head leaning down as I let the icy sting of the water distract me. But all I see is her, my Lolita, with her big blue eyes and puffy red lips. She hates me.

Christ, I hate me. Talk about fucking self-sabotaging, last night was ugly, dirty, and for the first time since I was probably ten, I feel... regret? Shame?

Maybe both, because I wanted to hurt her. She made me feel, laugh, and question my life, and for that I wanted to punish her. Add in a half bottle of whiskey, and yeah, that helps for making good choices.

I raise my head as the water hits my face. It's over. She will hate me, but at least maybe this madness can stop.

I don't want her love. I want things back like they were, where I was happily dipping my dick in wet, warm pussy and not caring. I want to get up and be excited to take a big case, not worrying about how I can sneak into Raven's room and fuck her before work.

My cock jumps to life at the thought of that. Turning, I grab the soap. I may have a real problem.

I mean, girl-on-girl action and I didn't even get hard? I sat and watched them get each other off, and my cock didn't even twitch with interest. But thinking about Raven? I'm hard as fuck.

I do a final rinse off and step out. I need to call Sam and have him come over and give me a B12 shot, at least, because my head is pounding, and my mood is turning darker the more awake I get.

After brushing my teeth, I pull on some jeans and a T-shirt, barely looking at Rachel as I text Sam. I need coffee before I check on her. Fuck it, I can't feel shittier. Might as well get it over with.

I walk down the hall, drenched in sweat as I make my way to her door and knock.

Nothing, but what did I expect? I pound again as my mind tries to block out the betrayal her eyes held for me.

"Raven." Still silence. I lean my arm up on the door frame and wait, my pulse starting to race. Twisting the door handle, I brace myself for her pain, her anger, anything but what I'm seeing.

I take a breath and glance around. For the second time in my life, I see red and grab an empty drawer, still open from her packing, and throw it against the wall, watching it crack and splinter.

"Raven?" I scream, kicking the bathroom door open. Her scent instantly envelops me, and I look up, seeing the shampoos and lipsticks she's left behind.

"Iain?" I bellow as I move to the window and look down at the sunny day.

"What's happened?" Rachel runs in, still naked, her face looking like she has two black eyes since she clearly passed out in her makeup.

"Where the fuck is Raven?" I roar.

She takes a step back. "How would I know?" Her words don't matter; her eyes tell me everything I need to know. She can't even try to pretend.

"Put some clothes on. I'm calling the police."

"What? Why would you call the police?" Her eyes narrow and she plants her hands on her hips, completely ignorant to the fact that my security team has their Glocks drawn and is rushing in.

"Get the footage. Raven is gone. How the fuck did this happen?" I turn to look at Eddie and Michael as Iain bursts into the room.

"Mr. Powers, Raven left last night." Eddie lowers his Glock.

My pulse is pounding out of my chest. "What? Why wasn't I notified?" I swing around to look at them. "You're fired. Get out."

"Mr. Powers?" Iain holds up his hands and motions for his guys to leave the room.

Iain is my main man, but if he allowed Raven to leave me...

"Did you let her go?" I walk up to him.

"I did. She said that her mother had given her a new American Express Black Card and that both of you were... occupied at the time. Seeing as she's an adult, and I was not instructed that she wasn't allowed—"

"I never said she could leave," I hiss as Rachel steps in between Iain and me.

"Jett, why do you care?" I look down at her. "I'm your fiancée, her mother, and if Raven wants to leave and go back to New York early, or go hang with people her own age, why would that be bad?"

I look at her, but I speak to Iain. "Get Larry to track Raven's phone. Find her, and make sure she is safe."

"I'll get on it right now." He moves toward the door.

Rachel peers at me cautiously.

"And Iain?" I finally look away from her and over at him. His brown eyes remain calm while he waits. "Please apologize to Eddie and Michael. I was taken by surprise. I thought something bad had happened to her. They still have their jobs."

"I will let them know." He leaves me with Rachel.

She licks her lips. "Do you have something you want to confess to me?"

"No," I retort, needing to get the hell out of this room and away from her. I can't believe she left. Yet, then again, I would have done the same thing if the roles were reversed.

"Jett. This is a good thing." Rachel follows me into our room.

I stare out the window watching a minivan pull up. She wraps her arms around me, and I stay silent. Sam steps out of the van with his bag of magical things.

"Leave it alone, Rachel." I step away.

"I saw you two," she snaps.

"What did you say?"

"I saw you with her. I watched the way you kissed her, looked at her. You're in love with her, and you don't even know it." My head is spinning. Maybe I've done some questionable things in my life, but is she actually telling me she watched me fuck Raven?

"You're mistaken." I need to get away from her.

"The great, mighty Jett Powers finally being brought down. How does it feel, my love?" She walks over to her purse and grabs her cigarettes.

"It meant nothing, Rachel, just sex." I clear my voice and the doorbell rings. "That's Sam." I walk out of the room.

"Don't worry, Jett. Eventually your pecker will work again." She lights her cigarette as my nostrils flare in distaste.

"Oh, I'm sorry. I forgot you dislike women who smoke. But since Emily is the only one getting me off right now..." She inhales as I leave her ranting and walk down the stairs.

"Sam's in your office, and all the footage from last night is cued up on your computer," Iain says while he types on his phone.

"Where is she?" I stop before I enter my office.

"Her phone is off, but the last spotting was at LAX. Do you want me to hire someone?" He straightens.

"Yes, and track all her credit cards," I demand, entering my office. I lower myself into my chair, barely speaking to Sam. He knows what to do. I hold out my arm.

"Cocktail, or just B12?"

"Both." I lean my head back, trying not to see her, but as soon as I close my eyes, she's there, her puffy lips forming a smile, almost taking my breath away.

The small prick in my vein, and the cool liquid filling my system will calm me, fix all this irrational thinking.

I breathe in and out as the cobwebs fade, and I open my eyes.

She's gone.

POWER

It's what I wanted, right? And as twisted as Rachel is, she's right. My cock will forget her.

And all will be calm and right. Work, friends, Rachel, I'll go back to how it was before I saw her face, before I tasted her and my life orbited out of control.

It's over, I made sure of that. So why do I feel like everything in my life before her was surviving, not living?

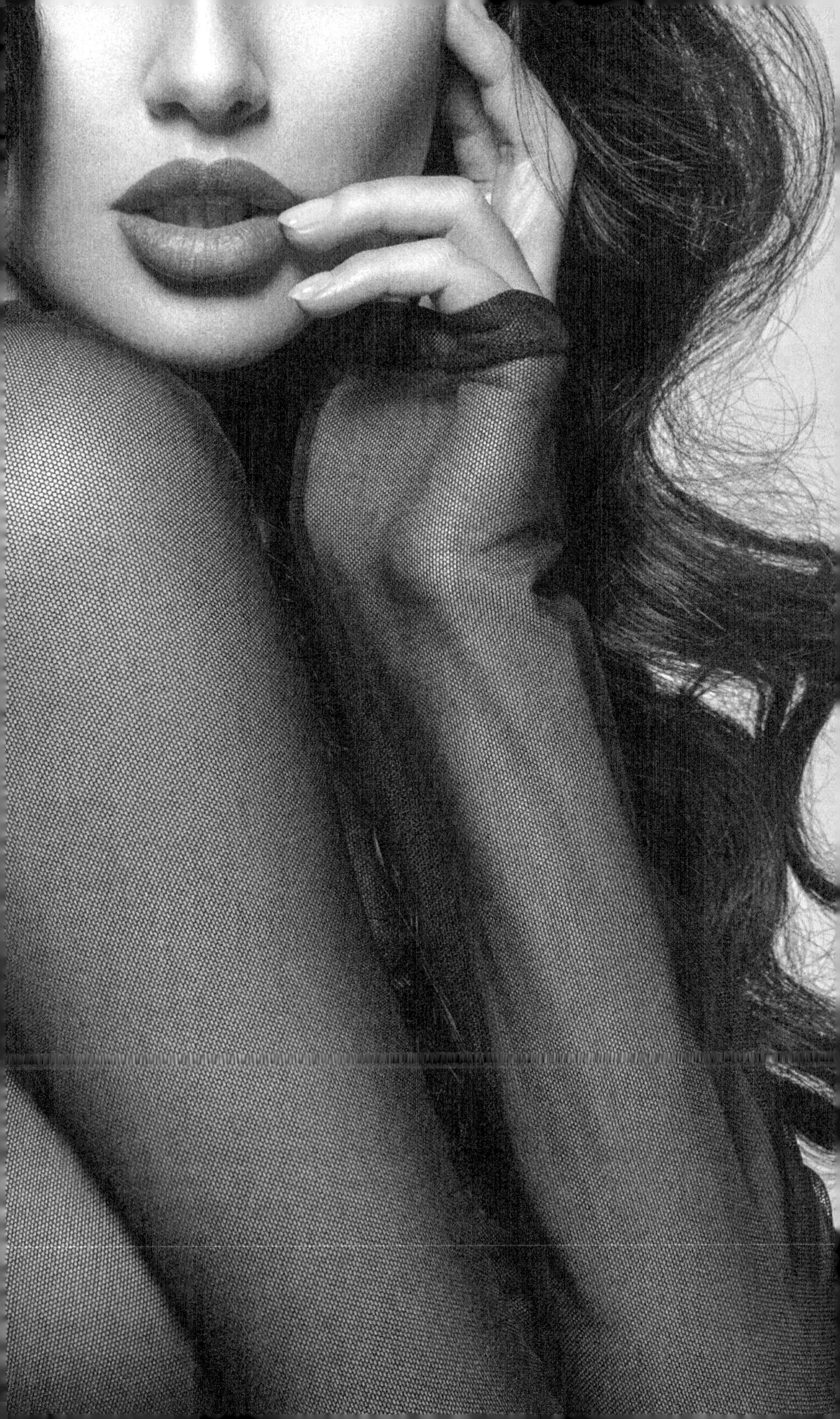

Twenty-Seven

RAVEN

Costa del Sol, Spain

"Raven? Earth to Raven?"

When I blink, Cher comes into focus.

"What?" I sit up straighter in my seat. "Sorry, I'm tired." I recross my legs and try looking interested, but the truth is I'm living in paradise with my best friend and Brody, and I don't think I could be more miserable.

"Oh, honey, it will get better, I promise it will. It's only been a couple weeks, right, Brody?" She reaches for my hand, her giant straw hat almost smacking me in the face. Brody mumbles something while he reads on his phone.

"Did we pay? Let's get a bottle of something and take a nap on the beach." I lean back, avoiding the hat. Cher turns to look at a couple of men who whistle as they pass. "God, men are pigs." I roll my eyes, and Brody glances up. "I mean, besides you, of course."

"No. This can't happen. I refuse to watch you become a bitter bitch. It. Will. Not. Happen. We're going out tonight to a club." Cher slaps the table.

Brody and I groan. "I'm not going to a club," I snap.

"Oh, yes, you are. Both of you." She points a finger at me, her nail perfectly manicured.

"Stop pointing." I slap her hand away.

"God, you two are literally no fun. Brody?" She turns to him.

He smirks, still looking down at his phone.

"You, Mr. Man, are not nursing a broken heart. You're going with me tonight." Cher leans forward, and I can't help but smile as Brody holds up his hand to block the killer hat.

"Christ, Cher, really? Control your hat." He frowns, his eyes darting to mine.

"You can't still be hung up on Raven, can you? You have to give up. She's mourning Daddy Powers."

I groan, because I adore her, but seriously? "Cher, please try to have a filter for once."

She sighs and sits back. "I'm only being honest for both your sakes." She looks at him, then me.

"And Brody only has another week with us. I refuse for your black cloud to bring Brody down." She smiles at me, picking up her drink and sipping from a straw.

I glare at her even though she's right. I'm hardly fun. It's like a knife has been inserted into my heart and left to fester and ooze. So yeah, I might be a little testy. And poor Brody. I know he only came to Spain because he was hoping I'd go back to him.

God, if only I could, but I'll never look at Brody as more than a good friend. I was kind of thinking he was getting it because only an idiot would try to follow Jett Powers.

"Okay." He sets his phone down and looks at us. "I'm thinking about staying."

"Wait, what are you talking about? This is your senior year—you can't stay." I look at him, then try smiling at the waiter when he brings the check. Heaving my big leather bag up on my lap, I fish out my American Express Black Card.

I take care of all the food, and pretty much anything we do that takes credit cards. Cher had to ask her dad to rent us the apartment. Apparently, they don't take Black Cards when you sign a lease.

It took us a solid week of searching, but we now have a cute two-bedroom apartment where we can walk to the ocean and shops. It even has a small balcony.

Unfortunately, it's only for six months. She could only convince her dad to let her to stay for that length of time. It's a miracle she talked her dad into allowing her a break from NYU. She somehow convinced him she needed this break to fine-tune her vision for her future fashion line.

He bought it, and here we are. Brody, on the other hand, was only supposed to stay for a couple of weeks.

"I can do my last year online, and to be honest, I'm sick of California."

We both stare at him.

"But our apartment only has two bedrooms," Cher says slowly as we both look at each other. Not that I really care. I don't have the energy right now.

"I'll keep sleeping on the pull-out couch." He picks up his phone again. "I already switched to online classes and just emailed my parents." He smiles as if he's doing us a favor.

"I just…" Cher's voice trails off as I kick her under the table.

"You stay as long as you like." I nod at him while Cher stares at me.

"Okay, but if we are going to be like *Three's Company*, you can't flip out when we have random men coming in and out of our lives." I close my eyes at Cher's lack of tact.

Brody frowns as if that did not occur to him.

"Fine, same applies to me." His eyes dart to mine. I don't have the heart to tell him I don't care who he hooks up with.

"Raven will be fine, and I highly encourage it." She nods, setting her drink down and looking around at the picturesque view.

Heaven. At least my version. I look over at the brick street, the sun kissing it with a slight glare, the smell of flowers hanging from the balconies filling the air.

This is where the wealthy come to play and dock their yachts. Celebrities can walk the streets without being harassed.

POWER

All I can do is drag myself out of bed and stumble down to the beach, where I fall asleep again until Brody wakes me up to turn onto my back.

I do need to work on my Spanish. Even though most everyone speaks English, I'm determined to master it since this is going to be my home. Brody staying might actually be a good thing. He can help pay rent after the six months are up.

"I'm gonna set up my office on the balcony." Brody smiles. "I need to write my thesis paper, and the view is perfect." He stands and stretches.

"Oh, perfect," Cher says dryly as she looks at me, like I can do anything.

A Ferrari speeds up the narrow street, and my face flushes and heart races. I lean forward, grabbing the table.

Please be him, please.

He gets out, and of course, it's not him. Not ever gonna be him. Because Jett is in Los Angeles with my mother, getting ready to marry her.

"God." I sigh and let go of the table, blinking away the tears, which are a regular occurrence. Lately they've been part of my daily routine.

Wow, that guy doesn't even resemble him. Aside from the dark hair, he looks nothing like Jett.

This is getting ridiculous. It's like he's haunting me. Either that, or I so desperately want him to appear, I think I'm seeing him everywhere.

Clearly, deep down inside, I hoped he was going to come after me. Which is pathetic, and I will never voice it, but even after everything he did, I still burn for him.

I've woken up every night sweating. It's horrible and torturous, and I've only now given up. I frantically use my fingers to fuck me, as I see him, feel him… let him guide me to my release.

And I hate him for that.

That still doesn't change the way I feel, and the truth that I'm terrified I'll never be free of him.

"Raven?" Cher's voice brings me back to the now.

"Yes?"

"Jesus. You've got to pull yourself together." She shakes her head and stands.

"Brody, you're gonna cook, and not just vegan crap." She loops her arms with both of ours, and we start down the street.

I stop listening as they both laugh together, because even laughter hurts. More than anything else, I'm just so sad, and watching them makes it harder. No matter what Brody says, he never felt this way about me.

Wasted love.

"I'm gonna go for a swim." I try to pull away.

"No, you're going to take a shower, and then we are all going out tonight, and we're gonna have *fun*."

I turn to look up at her. Having given up on heels, flip flops are my shoes of choice these days.

"If I go out tonight, you promise I don't have to go out again?"

"Um, no. But, if you go out tonight and have a smile and a laugh, then you don't have to go out again for another week." I roll my eyes at her.

"Again, it's like I'm dealing with ninety-year-olds. Actually, the elderly would be more fun than you and old man Brody." She shakes her head as both of us try avoiding the hat.

"For the love of God, we will go as long as you never wear this fucking thing again." He pulls her hat off and tosses it up in the air while she screams and laughs, both of them running to try getting to it first as it floats down the street.

I want to be them. I want to never feel like this again.

I want...

I take a deep breath and follow them, because at the end of the day, even feeling like my heart has been damaged, I have them, and they won't let me give up.

POWER

So, screw it. Cher wants to go clubbing? I will. Brody wants to stay and take over the balcony? It's his. Without them, I'm not sure I'll make it.

"Raven," Cher screams for me. Shading my eyes, I stare down the street at them. It looks like she's retrieved her hat, but Brody has tossed her over his shoulder.

I shake my head, and smile, yet I hear his voice in my head. *"Do you dare?"*

"Fuck you, Jett Powers, get out of my head," I say, putting one foot in front of the other. One day it won't feel like a chore. One day I'll wake up and he'll be gone.

One day...

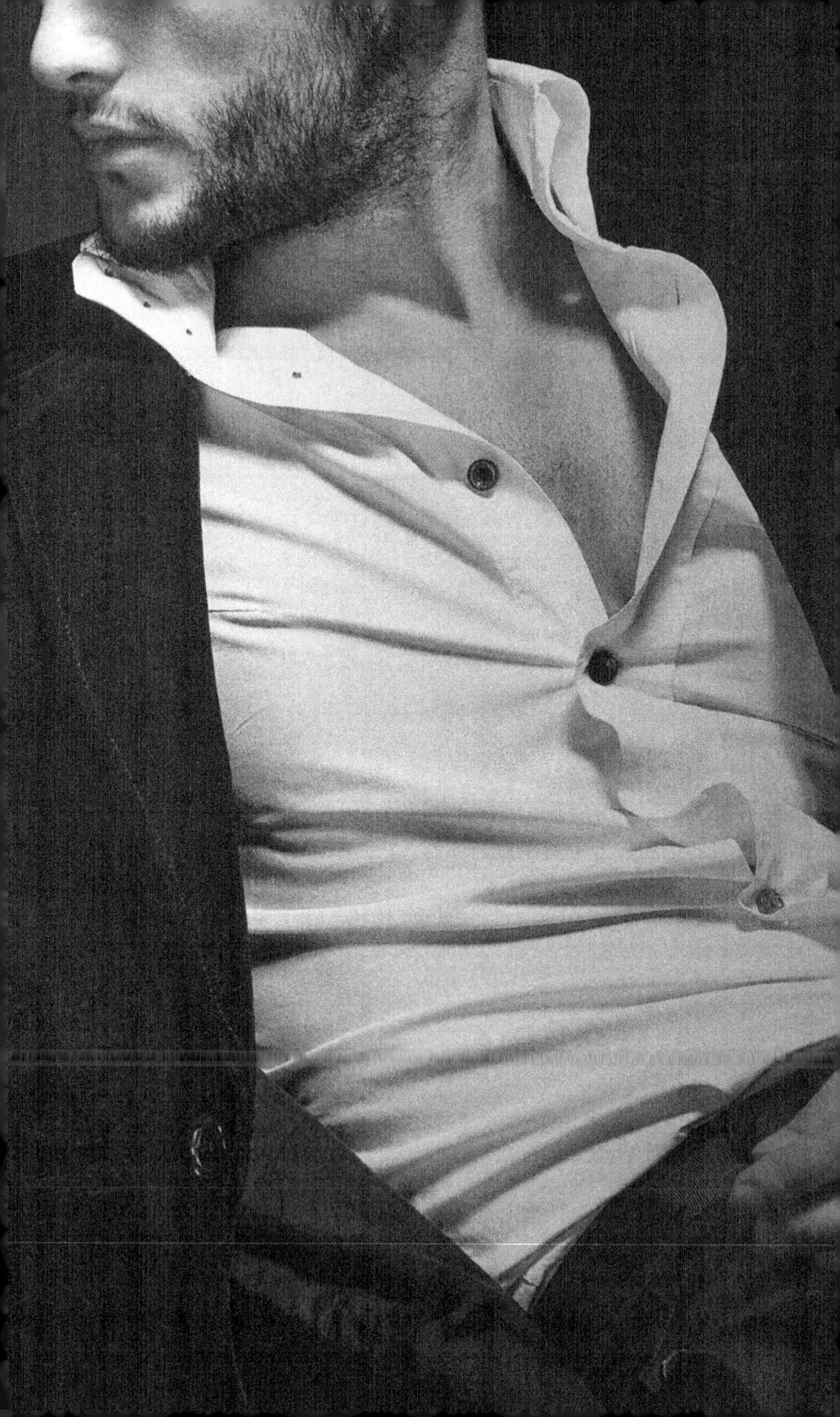

Twenty-Eight

JETT

Beverly Hills, CA

I'm fucking tired. My legs feel like I'm running with weights. Christ, I'm literally dragging my ass up my driveway, and I don't have the excuse of being hungover this time. I even went to bed early last night.

I'll have Rebecca schedule Sam to come to the office today and give me another B12 shot. I need something to get me going.

My mind goes over the ton of work piling up on my desk, which is making me angry, mostly at myself. Although, I did go off yesterday on a random delivery guy. Yeah, he fucked up, but he's a fucking delivery guy making fifteen bucks an hour and didn't deserve that type of treatment.

Poor Rebecca tries to humor me. My colleagues are avoiding me. I overheard Tim calling me the Grim Reaper. Fuck it—it's true. I'm not a pleasant person. I should buy the whole office lunch today.

"Jett?" Rachel's voice makes me grit my teeth when I enter from the front door. Ever since Raven left, I've avoided the backyard and, therefore, the back entrance. I run my hand through my hair. Christ, I'm drenched.

POWER

"Yeah, it's me." Feeling the cool air from the AC as I make my way to the kitchen, I contemplate taking a shower. Rachel just got home from her trip to Atlanta, though, so I guess I need to at least pretend to be interested.

Home.

What a joke. It's felt more like a prison lately. I'm tempted to sell it and start over. Too much shit I'd like to forget.

When I enter, my eyes take in Rachel's tight dress and heels. She smiles at me. The table is loaded with what looks to be Danishes, bagels, and fruit.

"Surprise." She walks up to me and runs her hands up and down my wet T-shirt. "Oh, sweaty."

I take a deep breath, forcing myself to have patience.

"Are you hungry? I had Patty create all this for you. I missed you." She leans in for a kiss. I give her a quick one, then walk to the refrigerator.

"I should take a shower." Opening the door to get some orange juice, I wonder if I'm getting sick. Nah, I never get sick.

"How was Atlanta?" Shaking the bottle of fresh-squeezed OJ, I don't even bother with a glass.

"It was Arizona," she corrects me.

I stop drinking the juice to look at her. "Right, Arizona. I knew it started with an A." Grinning, I put the lid back on the juice and shut the refrigerator.

Rachel's eyes narrow on me and we stare at each other. I almost use the excuse of needing a shower again because this is so fucking uncomfortable.

Yet I don't. Instead, I sit and grab a piece of pineapple. "So was Arizona hot?"

She clears her throat and sits herself. "It was one-hundred and twelve the whole week."

I nod, not caring. "And Courtney? She seems to be everywhere lately. I keep hearing her latest song on the radio." I heard it once, but whatever.

"Thanks to me. I told her this album was going to be the one."

She grabs the spoon and scoops up some fruit, then picks up her fork to eat it. I guess my picking at it with my fingers is beneath her.

"Well, this is what you are the best at," I say.

"It really is. She's the voice, but without me, she'd be nothing," she snips, cutting a piece of watermelon.

What am I doing? Am I really sitting here, trying to keep a conversation going with a person I can't stand, talking about things I don't care about?

Seriously, what the fuck am I doing?

I can't stand her.

My job, which I have always loved, has suddenly gone stale. And I hate myself for hurting the one person who actually made me feel something.

"Jett, did you hear me?" Rachel leans forward, reaching to touch my hand. I frown at her. "What?" She leans back.

"This, us, it's over. You know that, right?" I stand.

"Excuse me?" She looks like I've slapped her, but it's all a façade. Her eyes are dead. How am I just seeing this? Or maybe I always knew but didn't care.

But today... today I care.

"I need to take care of something." I go to move around her, but she grabs my arm as I pass.

"What has happened? Is this because your cock doesn't work? We can work thr—"

"My cock works just fine, Rachel, but not with you." I look down at her.

Standing, she turns to me. "What are you saying?"

"It's pretty clear. It's over, Rachel. Keep the ring."

"I don't accept this." She straightens. "We have the Beverly Hills Hotel booked for four months from now. Three-hundred of the most influential people will watch me become your wife."

"No, they won't. We're not getting married. It's over, Rachel." I begin walking up the stairs.

"You need to stop and think." Her voice is low, almost menacing. "Because I have it all on my phone. That night I watched you make love to my daughter." I stop and look down at her.

Turning, I narrow my eyes. "You did what?"

"I filmed you and her, just in case." She starts to walk up the stairs, a smug smile on her face. "I really don't get you. You made her leave, Jett. *You picked me.*"

Pain, almost a burn in my chest, which I try to ignore, spirals through me.

"What the fuck? Raven is your daughter." My hand goes to rub my chest, as if that can protect me from the truth that she's right: I did pick her.

I picked her, then destroyed Raven, thinking I was doing the right thing.

"She tried to take what's mine, and that I can't have." She takes the last step as we face each other.

I smile, because she's now crossed the line, and I'm done. "You are a fucked-up cunt. I used to admire that. I don't anymore. It's that simple. Keep the ring, and Rebecca will take care of canceling the wedding." My voice stays calm.

Turning, I continue up the stairs and step into my room. Rachel follows me.

"You're making a mistake." Her voice goes up a notch, and I can sense her becoming desperate.

"I. Don't. Care."

She might intimidate most people, but she's never gone up against me. I throw open my closet and crouch down to open my safe.

"Jett, think. Do you honestly think Raven will ever trust you? Forgive you? She won't. I know her—she never forgets." She laughs, but it's hollow.

I bring out my passport and some cash, then kick the safe shut.

"I'll take my chances. Either way, I'd rather be alone than spend another minute with you."

"Really?" She takes a step. "You have no idea how much damage I will cause. This is what I do, Jett! No one will side with you. Our friends will shun you."

My lips twitch. "You're right. You are the best at what you do, but you forget, I'm a goddamn legend at what I do. You believe I give a fuck about what anyone thinks?" I cock my head at her.

"I have TMZ on speed dial," she hisses.

Raven was right about her mother. She thinks she's got me, but I'm about to introduce her to the real Jett Powers.

"I just want to make sure I'm hearing you correctly," I say. "You're trying to bribe me with a sex video of Raven and me?"

She licks her lips and takes a step back as if hearing it out loud has made her hesitate. I smile—this is what I was born for, taking down people like her.

"I'd think twice before you do anything that might... not work in your favor. You can say whatever you want about me, but what you say you have on your phone gets erased."

"Fuck you, Jett," she screams. "I'm not being discarded like I'm nothing. I worked my ass off to get where I am, and if you think I'm letting her win..." Her face reddens.

Reaching out, I cup her face. She looks up at me with wild eyes.

"*You lost.* Now, you can walk away and keep your career, money, and life, or you can go to war with me. And, believe me, darlin', I'm not bragging when I tell you this. I will destroy you. And when I'm done, I'll give you the gun to end your miserable existence just so I can piss on your grave." My voice sounds like a caress, yet my hand tightens on her neck. She struggles, her nails digging into my chest.

"The choice is yours." I let go of her and she stumbles back, sitting down at the end of the bed.

"You wouldn't dare—"

"I dare everything. In fact, my cock is hard just thinking about it." I reach for my dick. "Now, pack your shit and don't be here when I get back."

As I move around her, she stares at me wide-eyed, fear keeping her ugly mouth shut.

"I'll delete it," she says at last, her voice flat.

The beast in me has been unleashed, though, and I almost want to thank her for making it happen.

"I thought you'd make the right choice," I say over my shoulder as I leave her.

Texting Iain, I make my way downstairs. I head straight to the kitchen and take her phone and purse, then walk to my office.

Iain is already there, along with Eddie and Larry, my assistant. "I want someone on her twenty-four-seven," I say to Iain, tossing her phone to Larry and setting her purse down.

"Transfer all her stuff, then strip it. Get into all her bank accounts." Larry looks up as he plugs her phone into my laptop.

"You want me to freeze the accounts?" He starts to type on the laptop.

"Just one. She's desperate right now. It'll send her a message that I'm not fucking around. We can reassess when I get back."

I look over at Iain. "I'll take the G6."

He nods. "I'll get the team ready."

Larry hands me back Rachel's phone and rummages through her purse.

I hand the phone to Iain. "Here, give this back to her. Tell her if she wants her business shit, she can talk to Larry."

He pockets the phone. "I'll take care of Rachel. You have nothing to worry about. Jerry's waiting to take you to the hangar."

Nodding, I prepare to push on Rebecca's number and look back at Larry. "Send me that video she has of Raven and me, please."

Poor Larry turns red, but nods. I grin. I'm a sick fuck, and the thought of being able to watch my Lolita come, on my phone, Christ, the mere thought of it is making me hard.

"Thanks, man." I walk out and press on Rebecca's number.

"Good morning, Mr. Powers."

"Morning, Becca. I need you to give all my cases to Mike."

"Is everything okay?" Her typically calm voice disappears.

"Probably not." Grinning, I slide into the back of the vehicle. "Please make arrangements for me to stay at Puente in Marbella, and I want the suite with the sea view. After that, I need you to cancel my wedding and alert all guests."

"Oh my God." Her voice grows louder.

"Becca, I'm leaving you in charge. I want daily accounts on everything, but as of right now, I'm not taking any cases, and I don't know when I'm coming back." I look out the window, watching everything blur past me.

"I just, okay, Mr. Powers. Is there anything else?"

"Yes, give yourself a raise, and I'll touch base when I land."

"Thank you." Her voice cracks. "This is shocking. You love your practice."

"I do, but we both know I've been struggling. I need to get away. I always said if found something I loved more than the law, I would go after it." As Jerry turns into the hangar, my pilot and a flight attendant are waiting.

"It's Raven, isn't it?" Rebecca's calm voice is back as I hear her typing on the computer.

"I need to go. Also, I have Rachel being watched, but if she drops by or you hear anything at all, you get ahold of Iain."

"Oh, don't you worry. She won't be getting by my desk. I'm already canceling everything for the wedding."

"Shit. One more thing." Getting out of the Tesla, I nod at my crew. "I need you to find someone to get me a whole new wardrobe. I need everything, suits and casual. I'm getting on the plane in sweats and a T-shirt."

"Not a problem, Mr. Powers."

POWER

"You're in charge." I grin, and it's my first real smile in more than two weeks.

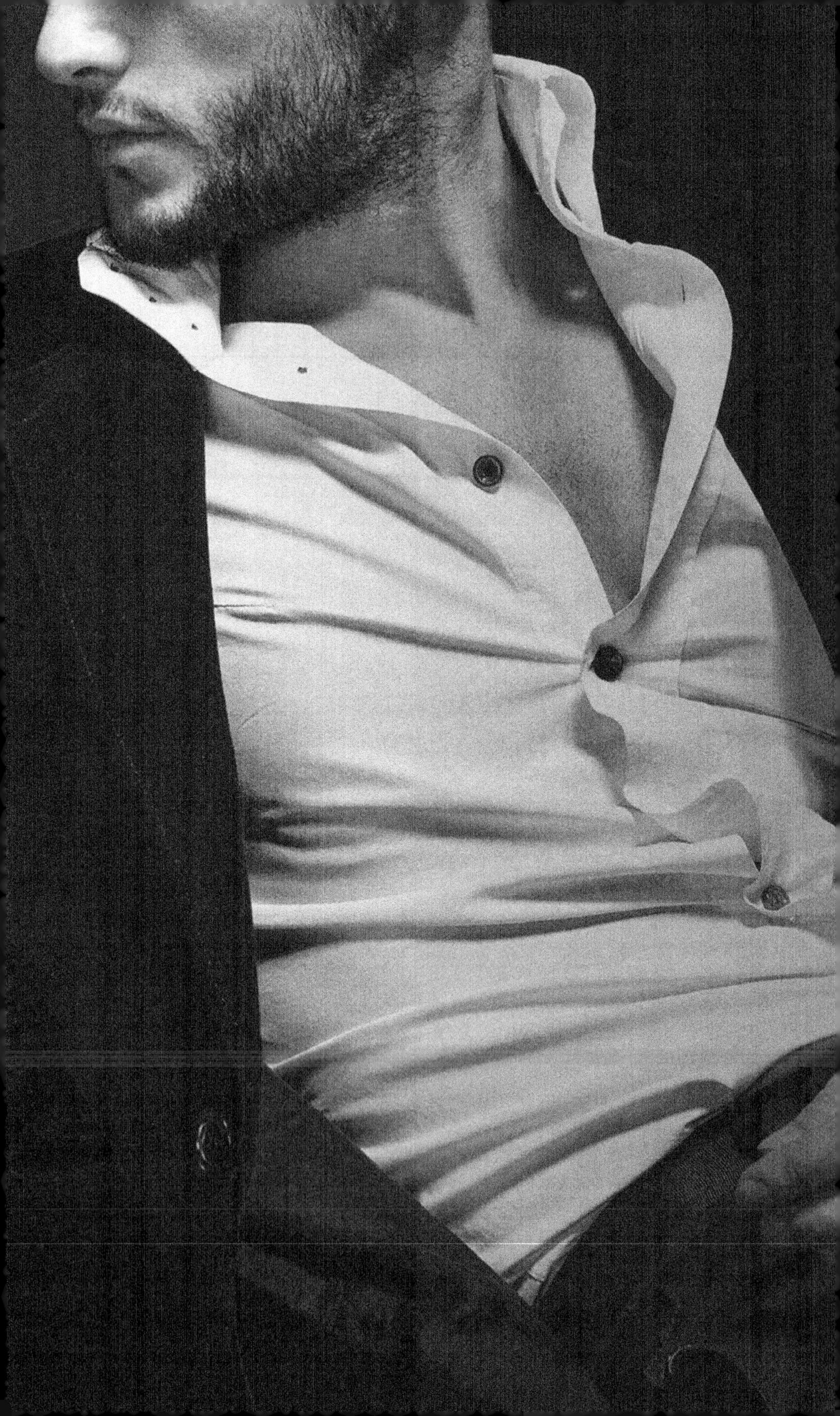

Twenty-Nine

JETT

"Can I get you anything else, Mr. Powers?" Payton, my flight attendant, smiles at me, her invitation obvious in her tone.

I smile back. "Yes, another Bombay Sapphire and tonic." I swivel my chair to look out the window. The blue sky is all that greets me, and I relax into the leather seat.

I rarely use my jet, and at certain times I've thought of getting rid of it. I can't very well be an environmentalist and fly around polluting our skies. But today, I am grateful to have it.

"Here you are." She sets my drink down, along with some Marcona almonds. Her blouse is open enough to give me a tease of her breast.

"Thanks." I grin, stretching my legs out. "How much longer?"

"Two more hours." She cocks her head at me.

I reach for my drink. Payton's a smart girl. She'll figure out I'm not gonna fuck her.

"Call if you want me." She walks back to the kitchen area by the cockpit. I take a sip and let the refreshing flavors wake me up.

I actually slept. I don't know how long it's been since I've gotten more than four hours of sleep in a night.

After boarding, I went straight to the bedroom and slept

POWER

for a solid seven hours. Didn't dream; just slept. Got up, took a shower, and here I sit, with a cocktail.

Fucking free. I grin and look over at the large TV, where a soccer game is on the screen.

My phone vibrates, alerting me that I'm getting several emails. For the first time ever, though, I don't check them. They all can wait.

Christ, what should my plan be? I can't just take her, lock her in my room with me until she submits.

Yeah, not an option, even though I want to.

I might have to do some groveling. My lips curve up—I've never had to grovel a day in my life. But I've also never felt like this before.

Love.

Rachel's spiteful face appears in my mind as I replay her words. *"I saw you with her. I watched the way you kissed her, looked at her. You're in love with her, and you don't even know it."*

"Shit." I bring the drink to my lips and take two big swigs.

Is that what this is?

Love?

Pansy-ass word, which I don't ever use, unless I'm talking about my mom, dad, or brother. Yet here I am in my private jet, chasing after this woman who's destroyed my peace, ripped my heart open, and made me question my very beliefs.

I've left my career and house, and dumped my fiancée all because when I close my eyes, she's all I see.

My addiction. Whatever, I now accept that I can't quit her. I want to wake up every morning inside her, and go to sleep every night the same way.

I don't even care if I ever step foot in a courtroom again. I've conquered that part of my life. I worked hard, tackled it, and won.

Because that's what I do. I win. But with Raven... I bring the drink to my lips and finish it. I fucked up. I wanted to hurt her, break her, and now I need to put her back together and fucking worship her. But first, I need to get her to forgive me.

What if she says no?

She can't say no. Not if I don't give up. That's one thing everyone in Raven's life has done.

No one has ever put her first: not her father and certainly not Rachel. *But I'm going to.*

I want to give her everything. And not just my money. I want her to know that I'm hers.

That I'd easily die for her, since living without her is not an option.

Is that love?

She's become my world...

My life.

Sweat beads on my forehead. I take my glass and suck on the last piece of ice.

Yeah, I'm fucked. That's love alright.

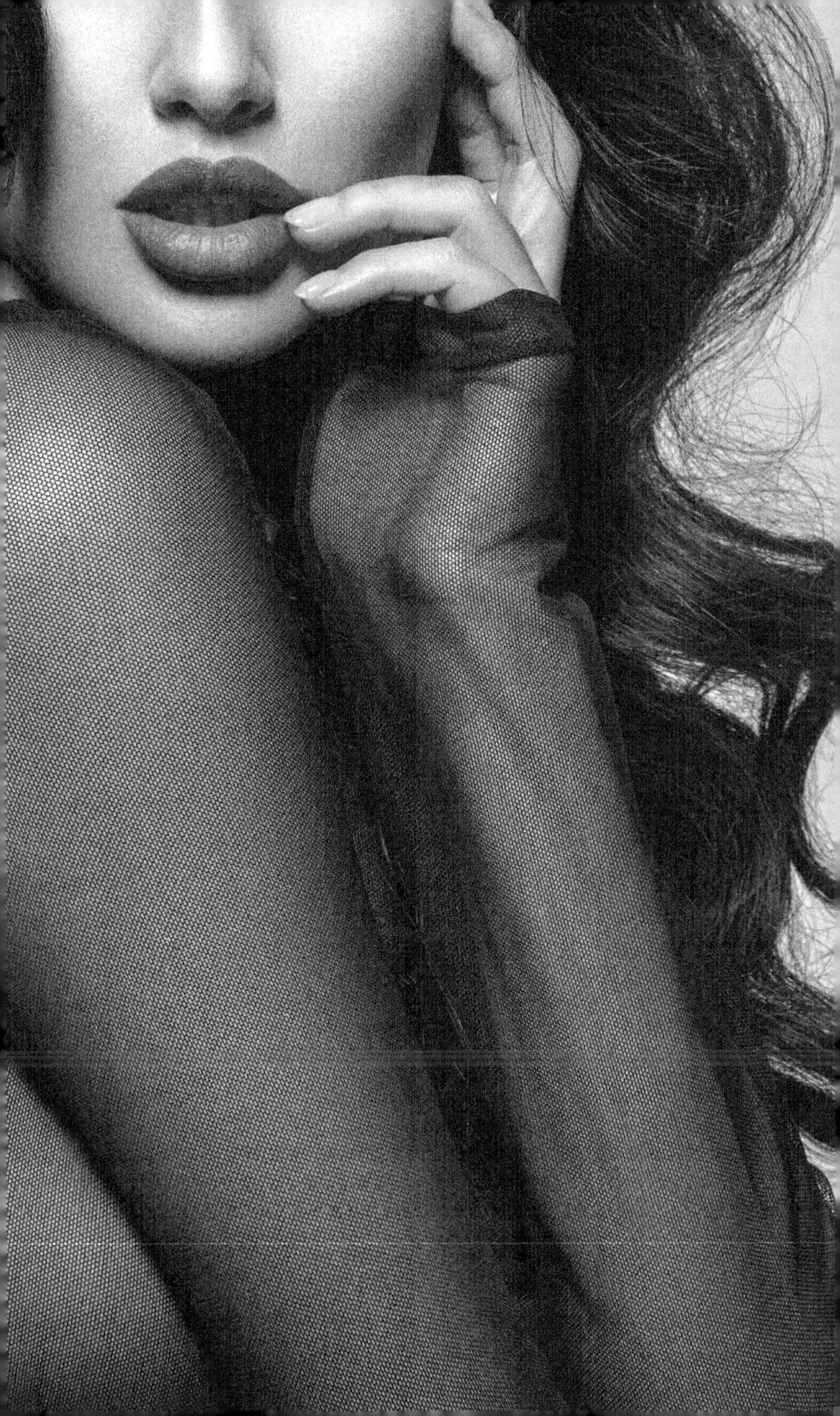

Thirty

RAVEN

Costa del Sol, Spain

"Are you ready?" Cher yells from her room to mine. I take a step back and look at myself in the full-length mirror. We went shopping today and got new dresses. Cher's is strapless and mine is a halter, both white to show off our amazing tans from three weeks of sunbathing.

I straightened my hair tonight, kind of shocked at how long it is, past my breasts. I like it, though. It's kind of got this wild, nasty vibe going on. And considering I've given up on anything to do with my past, I've decided to reinvent myself right now. Yep, I'm going for the free-bird attitude.

"I'm ready." I sashay out.

Poor Brody looks up from the TV. He got stung by a jellyfish this afternoon and is sprawled out on our couch, looking miserable.

"How's the foot?" I smile sympathetically.

"Wow. You look... amazing." He sits up on his elbows.

"Thanks." I flash him a saucy smile and step into the kitchen to grab the tequila from the freezer. I've found that alcohol helps numb the pain, and since my heart seems unable to stop burning, I'm working on drowning it.

POWER

"Dammit, I knew I should have gotten that dress. Let's trade?" Cher flounces in as I finish pouring three shots.

"No." I hand her the glass and walk over to Brody. "To us." I throw the shot back and promptly exhale.

"Okay, let's do this before I decide to stay home with Brody and watch TV." I grab my handbag.

"Again with the negativity. Did you not have fun the other night?" Cher puts the tequila back in the freezer.

"No, you had fun. I cried in the bathroom for as long as I could, then got yelled at by the owner." I roll my eyes.

"Yeah, don't do that tonight." Cher smiles at me.

We look over at Brody.

"Don't wait up for us." Cher throws him a kiss, as I mouth, *Help me.*

"Be careful. Don't take drinks from strangers," he calls after us.

I slam the door shut and we walk down the street, the tequila already making me feel nice and toasty.

"Okay, so don't get mad, but I invited Matteo and Danny to meet us tonight." Cher keeps looking straight ahead.

"What?" I grab her arm. "I told you I'm not ready for that." I specifically told her no. And now I'll have to keep a conversation going with a guy I have zero interest in because Cher wants Matteo.

"Relax, they know, but it's time you at least have a conversation with someone besides Brody and me."

We're still a block away, and I can already hear the nightclub's music. I take a deep breath, smelling the ocean. If it's really bad tonight, I'll ditch them and walk to the beach to sit and cry there.

"Okay, there they are. Smile." Cher pinches me as she calls out to them.

"God," I say with a groan as I walk behind her, hugging Danny first while Cher laughs at something Matteo said before he breaks away to kiss both my cheeks.

And nothing… not even the slightest flutter. What is wrong with me? Both these guys are young and hot, so even though I have nothing in common with them, I should at least feel some sort of energy when they touch me, right?

Jesus, maybe Cher's right. I really am turning into a ninety-year-old woman. If I wasn't getting myself off every night, I'd worry my sex drive was completely gone.

"Shall we party, my beauties?" Matteo motions for us to go first. There's already a line to get in, but he slips the bouncer some money, and we're in.

Purple and red lasers zoom across the club, smoke fills the air, and the loud beat of Drake makes my head pound.

"Drinks?" Danny yells as I turn away from his breath. He smells like an ashtray.

Perfect.

"Yes, we want drinks," Cher screams over the music.

Ignoring them, I look around. As always, it's packed. The red and black walls, along with tiny lights that look like candles in the large chandelier remind me of a haunted house, making me wonder why everyone deems this the club to be at.

"Let's dance." Cher grabs my hand, dragging me onto the dance floor right next to the speakers. It's loud, and a large disco ball casts down hundreds of bursts of colored lights as it spins.

"I told you to talk, Raven." She spins as I lift my hands to the beat.

"Like I can have a conversation in here," I shout back, then turn away, letting the tequila and music take over.

I love to dance. One of my big regrets was quitting my jazz classes when I went to college, but as soon as I moved to New York, I guess I got intimidated, which is silly now that I look back on it.

Cher says something, but Nicki Minaj's "Super Freaky Girl" is so loud, I can't hear. That, and the crowd on the dance floor seems to have multiplied.

POWER

Danny and Matteo show up with the shots after dodging hands and bodies to reach us.

"Shoot them quick. We don't want to get thrown out," Danny yells as he hands me mine, while Matteo gives Cher hers.

"Salud." We toss them back like its water and not the tequila that's burning fire down my esophagus.

"Yes, I like this," Danny says as his hands go to my hips, trying to match my grind. He's a bad dancer, but what guy isn't? I spin away from him, rubbing my back against Cher's. Turning, she laughs and grabs me as we both match the beat.

"That's it, my beauties," Matteo yells, leaning in close to our faces. "Now, who wants to feel really good?"

"We do," Cher screams.

Matteo smiles and winks, motioning for us to follow him.

"I told you we were gonna have fun tonight." She grabs my hand, her face flushed with excitement. "They have cocaine. Fuck yes, let's go."

I let her pull me because for the first time in my life, I don't care. God, maybe it will make me feel better. There has to be a reason people love it. I just want something, anything, to numb my pain.

We weave around the crowded dance floor, following Matteo and Danny toward a back room.

My eyes take in the dark club. It has to be close to capacity. Either that, or they don't care. Some guy plants his hands on my ass, then gives me a halfhearted apology. I glare at him, yet looking past him, I freeze. My whole body grows cold, then instantly breaks into a sweat. Gulping air, I try to catch my breath.

"Oh my God." I try pulling away. "Move," I scream at the assholes who just blocked my view.

"What?" Cher turns to glance down at me while I frantically try to move around the group to look for him.

"Jett's here, over there." I point to the dark corner.

"Where?" Cher stands on her tiptoes.

"He's there," I scream, my pulse pounding so hard I truly might hyperventilate.

"That's not him," she says dryly, grabbing my arm while Danny yells for us.

"Stop, it is." At last able to maneuver around the group, I look at the corner, but she's right. The man standing there may have dark hair, but he's definitely not Jett.

"Wait. I swear to God, he's here." My eyes dart around, but there are too many bodies.

Cher looks as well, then shrugs. "Raven, I don't see him, and I hate to have to tough love you, but he's marrying your mother, not chasing after you," she shouts over the noise.

My eyes instantly fill with tears.

"Oh no, don't cry. I was only trying to snap you out of it. Please, Raven, don't go all dark tonight, come on." She grabs my hand, but I shake my head.

My mind is racing. Maybe I've seriously snapped, like lost it. Why do I keep feeling like he's here? Am I that desperate?

"I have to get out of here," I yell and jerk away from Cher. "I can't breathe. He was here. He has to be here. Otherwise, I'm officially losing it."

Cher looks at me, knitting her brows. "Okay, take it easy. Let me tell them we're going." She rubs my arm, frowning at how sweaty I am.

"I need to go outside." I try gulping in a good breath, but I think that's just making the panic worse with all the smoke.

"Screw it, I'll text them. We can go to their dad's pool tomorrow. He owns a hotel."

She grabs my hand and moves people out of our way, the sounds of our names fading as we make our way outside. The warm air hits my clammy face.

"Just breathe, Raven. It's okay. I shouldn't have pushed you. Clearly, it's too soon." She rubs my back as I wheeze, glancing around at all the faces outside.

"I... do you see him?" I kind of spin, then look at Cher, who isn't even trying to hide her frown.

"Do I need to get a cab, or can you walk? He. Is. Not. Here. You thought you saw him, that's all."

"Let's walk. The air will help." I move forward and Cher follows, texting on her phone. The night air, and maybe walking, seem to help as I listen to the ocean on our uphill walk.

"Okay, so do you want to talk about this?" Cher pops her phone into her bag, and I hold my hand up.

"I'm feeling like you might not have to take me to the hospital, okay?"

"Fine. But this isn't healthy," she snaps.

"Are you kidding me? Healthy? I'm freaking out, Cher. My whole life has crumbled. It's like I'm in this black hole and I'm trying so hard to climb my way out, but I can't do it." I stop to face her. A lone dog barks at us from across the street.

"I know, honey." She goes to hug me, but I step back.

"You don't know. I feel like I've been gutted, and it will never end. Sooner or later, I will have to see him because, as you love to remind me, he's marrying my mother." The tears that I've been holding back spill down my cheeks.

Cher sniffs. "I... was only trying to help. I hate seeing you like this. I hate Jett Powers for doing this to you, and I hate that we're yelling at each other." She pulls me in for a hug. I cling to her and cry.

"I still love him. What do I do?" I look out at the ocean.

"You go to bed, and everything will be better in the morning." She sniffs back her own tears.

Pulling back, I nod and smile at my sweet, good Cher.

It won't be better tomorrow, but I love that she looks at things that way. We cross the street to our apartment building, and a song about how the sun's coming out tomorrow from *Annie* plays in my head.

"So you don't think I'm losing it?" I open the door for her.

"Nope." She smiles, wiping under her eyes, and we both walk in.

Brody's asleep with the TV on. I don't bother turning it off and walk into my room, kick off my heels, and drop into bed, hoping the sun truly does come out tomorrow.

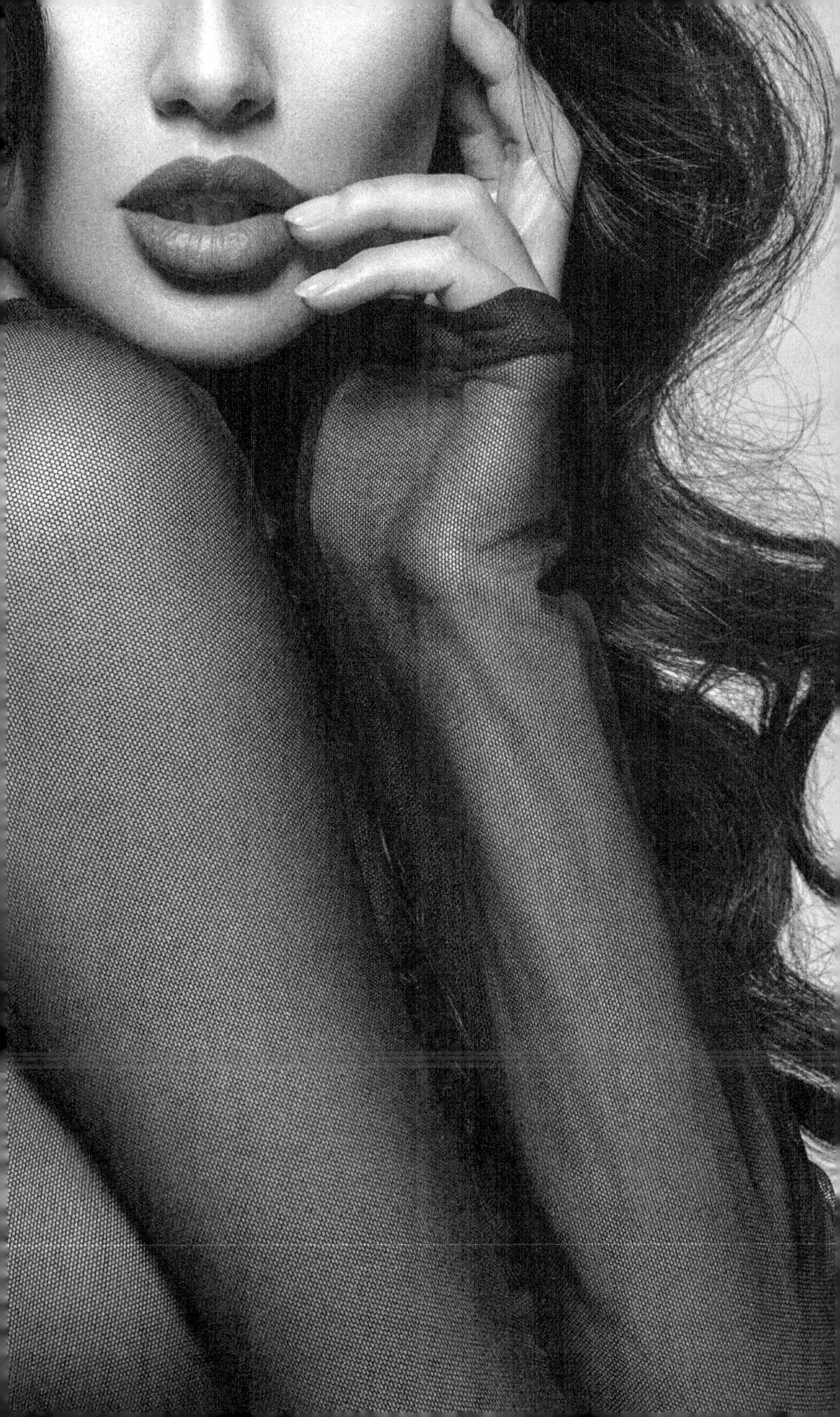

Thirty-One

RAVEN

What is that noise? I roll over and sit up. It sounds like the upstairs is coming down on us.

"Brody? Cher?" I call out. A loud groan comes from Cher's room, but nothing else.

"Are we having an earthquake?" Cher yells.

Leaving my room, I walk out to find Brody.

"No, I think it's construction." Moving to the window, I look down at a bunch of workers coming in and out of the building.

"Did we get a notice that the building is getting a makeover?" I call out. Looking out the window, I spot Brody crossing the street with coffee cups and a bag. Thank God for him.

Cher stumbles out, still in her clothes from last night also, looking like Spot the dog with one eye covered in mascara.

"Is that a jackhammer I hear?" She points to the ceiling.

We're a fucking mess, and I let out a snort. "Yep."

Cher is the worst morning person. "Well, we're moving if this carries on." She huffs and rubs her head.

Brody walks in. "What happened to you two?" He looks from me to Cher. "Rough night?" He laughs, dropping the bag from under his arm, then handing us each a coffee.

"You could say that." Cher yawns.

Brody grins and leans against the counter. I'm still amazed at what sun can do for a person. He looks like a different man.

POWER

His hair is growing out, and now that he's doing yoga on the beach, he's kind of got the lean surfer-slash-hip-professor thing going on.

If only I could fall back in love with him. Not that I was ever truly in love with him. It would be so much easier though. No more pain, just a mutual respect for each other.

"So." He takes a sip of his coffee and motions with his eyes to the ceiling. "The building got bought by a rich American. He's redoing all of it, apparently, starting with the upstairs, because he paid all four of the upstairs tenants a ton of money to move."

I choke on my coffee. "What?"

Brody reaches for my arms and says, "Raise them over your head," as if I'm a toddler choking on a toy.

"Who's the American?" My eyes dart to Cher's. It's hard to breathe. My eyes water and I try hard not to cough.

"It's not him." Cher holds up a hand at me and rolls her eyes, turning to face Brody. "So are we all going to have to move?" She pouts. "Because this is a prime spot. Although, the noise... how much did he pay everyone?"

"I don't know. I'll try to find out more."

It's not him, can't be him, right?

"How's your foot?" I say, trying to sound normal since inside I'm freaking out.

"Better. I bought you guys some bizcocho." He grabs his computer and heads to the balcony.

"Okay, I can't handle this noise. Let's go to Matteo's dad's hotel. We can pass out lying by the pool," Cher says, turning to me.

I take a small sip of coffee, hoping I don't have another coughing fit.

"Good idea." I nod.

Her eyes narrow. "What's wrong with you?"

"Nothing. I think that's exactly what we should do. Give me five minutes to put my bikini on," I say over my shoulder.

"Okay, but please, for the love of God, no drama today. My head can't take it—"

"Call a cab. I don't feel like walking," I interrupt her. The last thing I need is a lecture; I need to think.

After slipping into my pink-and-black polka-dot bottoms, I look at myself in the mirror. Not too bad. I'll splash some water on my face, lather on sun protection, and I'll be ready.

Thirty minutes later, I sit alone with a Bloody Mary. Cher convinced Matteo to give her a tour of the place, or the other way around. Either way, she dumped me as soon as we arrived.

Sighing, I take in the view. It's a gorgeous hotel, but everything in Costa del Sol is lovely. I sip my drink and debate whether I should swim first, then sunbathe, or go straight to sunbathing. I kick off my flip flops and stand, preparing to dip in the pool.

"Raven."

My eyes slowly lift to that voice as I grab the back of the wooden seat to hold me.

I'm not hallucinating.

He's here. Fucking Jett Powers is here. This time I truly am breathless.

I'm going to faint...

"I got you." His voice is strong, gravelly. He pulls me into his arms, and for a second, I cling to him, needing his fresh scent and strength to keep me standing.

His hand goes to my hair. When he jerks my head back, my eyes lock with his.

"Breathe, baby." His mouth hovers over mine as if he's giving me the very air I need to finally get my brain working.

He's here.

"That was you last night?" My voice sounds way stronger than I feel. His eyes change, and I know it was him.

I don't know if I'm more relieved I'm not crazy, or fucking livid that he would show up and... what? Think I'm just going to fuck him?

I put my hands on his chest to try pushing him away, but he's strong and shirtless, a beautiful combination.

I hate him.

Hate him.

"Take it easy."

He must get that my shock is wearing off. I go to knee him in the nuts, but he easily drops me on the cushioned chair, leaving my knee to connect with air.

"Relax." He glares at me and runs his hands through his hair.

My eyes take in his perfect physique.

"How did you find me?" I clear my throat, swallowing back the tears. I'd rather cut off my arm than cry in front of him right now.

"I've known where you've been all along." He sits down on the chair across from me as I force myself to think.

"Is my mom with you?" I turn my head right and left to check. If she's here, that might send me over the edge. Did they come here together? She to torture me, and he to... what?

"Raven. Stop it. We need to talk. Things need to be said. Do you really want to do this here?" He motions to the pool area, which is starting to fill up.

"We have nothing to say. You made things pretty clear, *Mr. Powers*," I snap, grabbing my drink, not caring that a good portion spills on the glass table.

"Raven, I broke it off with Rachel." He stands, holding out his hand.

Could he seriously think I'd be stupid enough to fall for him again? Though my heart just skipped at his words, I don't say anything. Instead, I keep swallowing the spicy tomato juice, praying the vodka will calm me enough to hide my true thoughts—that I'm fighting to hold on to all the pain he's caused.

"Look. I know I handled everything badly—"

And that's it—that's where I need to stop all this. "Badly?" I stand, setting the Bloody Mary down. "*You fucking destroyed me.*"

He drops his hand and looks over at a newly arrived family jumping into the pool with shouts and laughter.

"I have no idea why you're here, but stay away from me." I grab my bag, my eyes watering, my teeth sinking into my bottom lip. And all at once, his strong arm intertwines with mine. I gasp.

"Let's go." He literally drags me.

Struggling to get away, I don't care in the least if we're making a scene. He must not either because he lifts me up and tosses me over his shoulder.

"Are you completely insane?" I cough and wheeze. His shoulder presses against my diaphragm, and it's hard to breathe.

"Yep. I'm gonna talk, and you're gonna listen even if I have to tie you up." It takes all my strength not to drop my handbag while he walks us into the posh lobby and over to the elevators.

"Jett, put me down. I'll come with you. People are looking," I choke out, but he ignores me.

The elevator doors open, and he steps in. This is surreal. This can't be happening. I can't be alone with him.

"Sorry, on our honeymoon," he says to a woman in the corner.

All I can see are her toes.

"Oh, well, congratulations." She giggles and I bite my bottom lip again.

I should say I'm being kidnapped. Throw his ass in jail.

Instead, I stay quiet, saving my strength because I'm not the same girl who worshipped him. He killed that girl when he fucked my mother and that other skank.

Now I hate him.

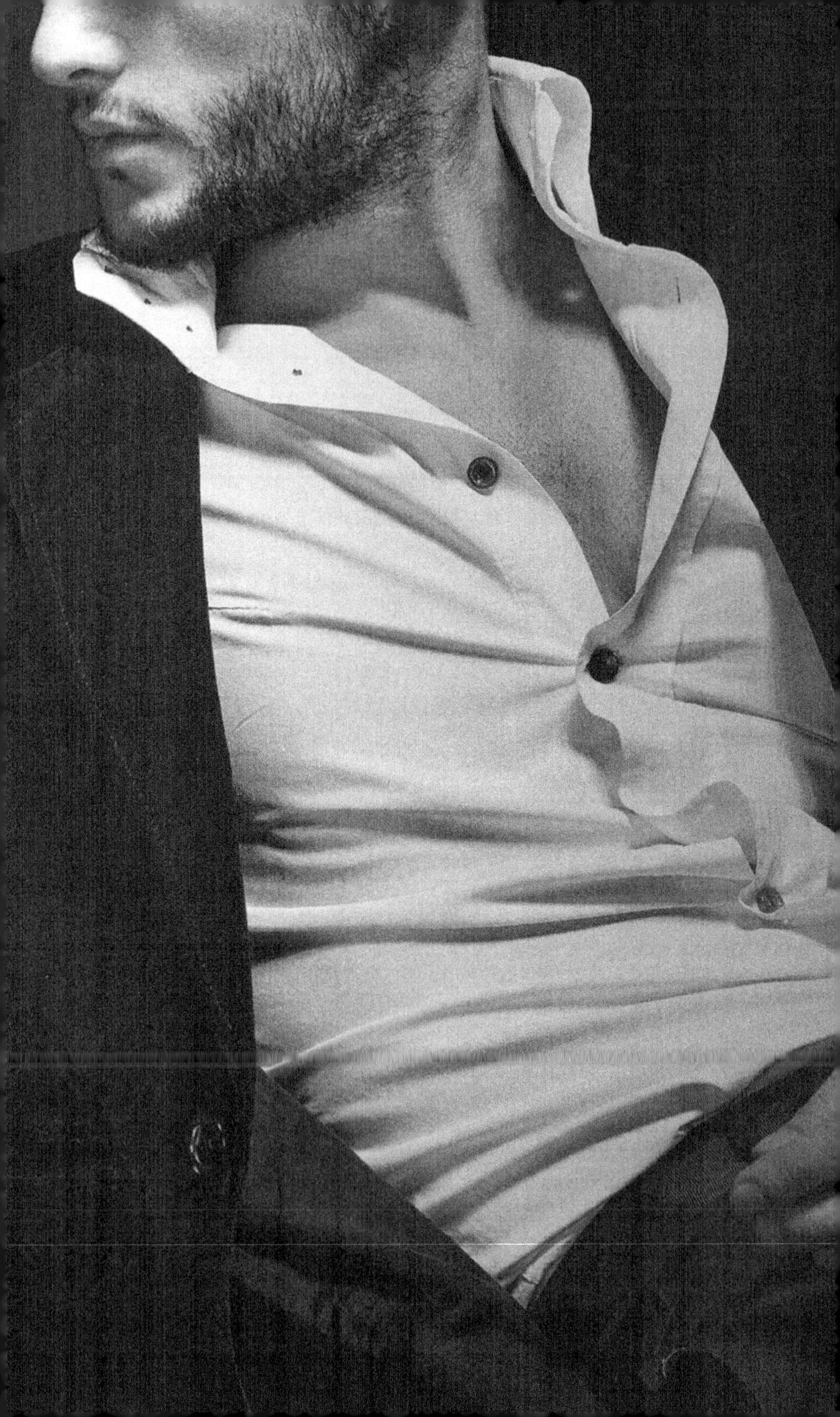

Thirty-Two

JETT

So much for patience. In my defense, she's making a scene, and we need an opportunity to talk.

Right, Jett, so you tossed her over your shoulder?

Using the key card, I unlock the door to the room I reserved as soon as I saw Raven and her friend heading toward the pool.

Probably better I'm taking her away because if that fucking punk from last night shows up, things will get ugly. Almost beat the shit out of the guy, but thankfully she left, and the loser ended up taking another woman home.

I set her down on the king-size bed and look around. In an instant, she jumps up.

"How dare you," she seethes, flinging her purse onto the bed. Her hair is wild, spilling around both shoulders, her face flushed from being carried over my shoulder. My cock, which was already aching, starts to leak. Turning, I open the minibar for a bottle of something—any liquor will do.

"Cocktail? And we both know I dare anything," I say dryly, grabbing two bottles of vodka and moving to the glass window overlooking the ocean. She doesn't need to mix liquor, and I don't need tequila making me crazy.

"I have nothing to say to you, so no, I don't want a cocktail."

"Well, I have a lot I need to say to you." I turn to look at her, and my fucking heart aches. This irrational need to keep her makes me unscrew the lid of the vodka and down it in two swigs, tossing it in the trash can.

"Why? What can you possibly think will ever change the fact that I saw you?" she shouts, her beautiful sapphire eyes glistening with tears as she looks up at the ceiling.

"First. You're right. I shouldn't have just... done that." I motion to her and the room and rub the back of my neck.

"You're unbelievable, and what's really sad is no one stopped you. I'm mortified, and my stomach hurts." She grabs a bottle of vodka from my hand, both of us looking at each other as the tips of our fingers touch.

"I'm sorry. I'm not thinking right, haven't been thinking right. But I'm hoping that can all change." My nostrils flare at her fucking scent. Jesus, all I want is to lean down, open her legs, and fucking suck on her sweet nub until she comes in my mouth, let her juices drip down my neck...

"What could you possibly have to say?" She shakes her head, twists off the lid, and takes a swig of the vodka, her whole body shaking.

"That I love you, and I came here to fight for you. Because I can't live another day without you." I look down at her. She's perfection, and suddenly I know that it doesn't matter if she says no today. I'll never stop. I'll wear her down until she has no choice but to forgive me.

"You... what?" She backs away.

"I love you, have always loved you. You had to feel it, know it." I walk toward her.

"You don't believe in love." She shakes her head. Her back hits the wall and I reach out, caging her in with my arms.

"That was true until this fucking Lolita came into my life and changed everything. I've given up my job because I can't think straight. I got rid of my fiancée. Left my country to come here. Why?" I growl. "Because I. Can't. Live. Without. You."

She looks up at me, her breathing harsh, her chest flushed, and I can smell her arousal.

She wants me.

I drop to my knees, and she plants both hands on the wall for support.

"It's too late... I hate you," she whispers.

Reaching over, I move the tiny strip of fabric off her pussy. It looks freshly waxed. "Fuck." I lean forward and inhale.

Panting, she says, "I need to go." Yet she whimpers when my tongue caresses her folds.

"Open your legs, baby," I murmur, helping her move one leg.

"That's it, that's my good girl. Now let's see if Daddy can make everything better."

Reaching up, I hold her still. Her head falls back against the wall.

"You can't. *I hate you,*" she says, her voice husky.

My mouth latches onto her clit, sucking on it. She's so slick and her cunt is so hot, almost burning, that I switch from sucking to fucking her with my tongue.

"Fuck, you taste good." I can't get enough of her taste, her smell. I grab her hips, holding her still. "Talk to me, Raven. Tell me how much you fucking hate me."

When her head rolls to the side and she looks down at me, time stops—so does the world, the room, and everything but us. Her chest is heaving, and I smile, leaning forward to lick her wet, swollen clit back and forth.

"Just make me come," she moans. Her hands, which were digging into the wall, grab my hair. She jerks my head closer, her breathing harsh.

"Say it," I demand, my mouth hovering over her wet cunt. I'm fighting the urge to pull my aching cock out and fucking impale her with it—but this is for her.

"I hate you," she screams, arching her head back.

"That's my girl. Now, come." And she does. Grabbing my hair with one hand, she digs her nails into my neck with the other and screams my name, her pussy convulsing in my mouth.

POWER

I lick my lips and inhale her scent, gently moving the bottom of her bikini back into place as I give her pussy another kiss and stand.

"Open your eyes," I grunt, grasping her chin.

She shakes her head *no,* but slowly opens her eyes to look at me. She can lie with her mouth, her tongue forming any words she wants, but her eyes tell me everything.

I own her and always will. She's fucking mine.

"I want you to listen carefully," I say.

She blinks and takes a deep, shaky breath.

"I'm not going away. I'm staying here for as long as this takes."

"You're wasting your time." She goes to pull away, but I continue gripping her chin, forcing her head back.

"I'm a fucking asshole, and I have done some questionable things, but this... you. The way it is with us, that's something we can never break free from. Believe me, my love, I've tried."

"Jett, I get that you think because you are you, everyone will just cave. But you hurt me, and I loved you. So what did you think was going to happen?" She jerks her chin away. "Did you think because you can make me come, I'll forgive you?" Her eyes fill with tears, but she holds her head high and shoulders back.

"I deserve more, and you may be right. I might never be able to shake you, but I also won't live in fear that you'll tire of me, or cheat on me, or fucking share me." She pushes against my chest.

I grab her and hold both her wrists. "I love you, I'm not going to share you. What the fuck, Raven?" My head pounds.

"Why are you doing this?" she yells. "Just why?"

I place her hand on my racing heart. "This is why. You feel it? Do you think I wanted this to happen? Never in a million years, but it did, and now I'm not leaving without you. If it takes forever, then forever it is. Because *you are mine and I am yours.*" I want to shake her, make that haunted look go away.

Her warm hand stays on my chest. The room is thick with our energy and pain, but more than that, I feel us, smell us...

"I need to go. I can't do—"

Suddenly a ringing sound comes from her bag. I almost take it and smash it, but something tells me that won't help me, so I clear my throat and back away.

"Go." I force myself to walk over to the window. This is the first time in my life that I haven't been able to talk my way out of whatever needed to be fixed. I turn, watching her grab her purse from the bed and walk to door.

"Raven? I meant what I said. I'm not leaving." My eyes lock with hers.

She cocks her head. "It's too late, Mr. Powers. I'll never be able to forget that you fucked my mother and that other woman."

I stare at her eyes, wondering if I should tell her the truth. Nah, she thinks the worst, not that I can blame her.

"It's never too late." I take a breath.

Her phone starts ringing again, and she looks down at her purse, then at me.

"For us, it is." Then she opens the door and I watch her leave, hearing her answer the phone.

"Fuck." I sit on the edge of the bed, then flop back and stare at the ceiling. "Do not go after her. You need to give her time," I grumble, rubbing my face, smelling her delicious cunt.

"Fuck this." I reach down inside my boardshorts, grab my thick, hard cock, and stroke it.

This was not how any of this was supposed to go. But I'm wound up too tight to think straight.

I jerk my shorts down and close my eyes. My breathing picks up while I jack myself off, hard, fast. And there she is, my Lolita. I grunt, envisioning her. Those beautiful lips open as her eyes dip to watch me pleasure myself.

"Yeah," I hiss as my hand picks up speed, and the need to come overtakes me. Licking my lips, I taste her cum.

POWER

"Fuck..." My body tightens as I let it build. "Raven," I call out. Hot sperm pulses out of me onto my stomach. I don't move, just stay still, letting my breathing return to normal. I consider my next move.

With a groan, I stand, pulling my shorts up and walking into the bathroom to clean the sperm off my chest, barely looking at myself in the mirror.

"Get your shit together, Jett." I turn the sink on to splash some water on my face, almost laughing at how all the women I've wronged in my life have finally gotten their revenge.

She said no.

She said it's too late.

I rip the towel off the rack and dry my face. Instead of throwing it on the floor for someone else to clean up, I fold it and lay it on the sink. Pulling my wallet from my side pocket, I leave a twenty-dollar bill on the extra folded towels.

Clearly, I need to rethink my tactics. Because she has to know *no* means absolutely nothing to me.

Christ, I'm completely thrown here. Flinging the door open, I take out my phone to track her. Good. She's traveling back to her place. I text her.

ME: I can still taste you.

Three dots appear, then stop and start again, but nothing comes through, and I smile.

ME: Dinner tomorrow? I'm cooking.

I grin, knowing that will get a response.

RAVEN: Please don't make me have to block you.
ME: Wouldn't matter. I told you I'm not going anywhere. Might as well have dinner.

The dots appear again, then stop. Though I wait, apparently she's not engaging anymore, so I walk out into the lobby.

This is just day one, Jett, I remind myself while I hand the key card to the woman at reception.

Give her time. The jury doesn't always come back with a decision right away.

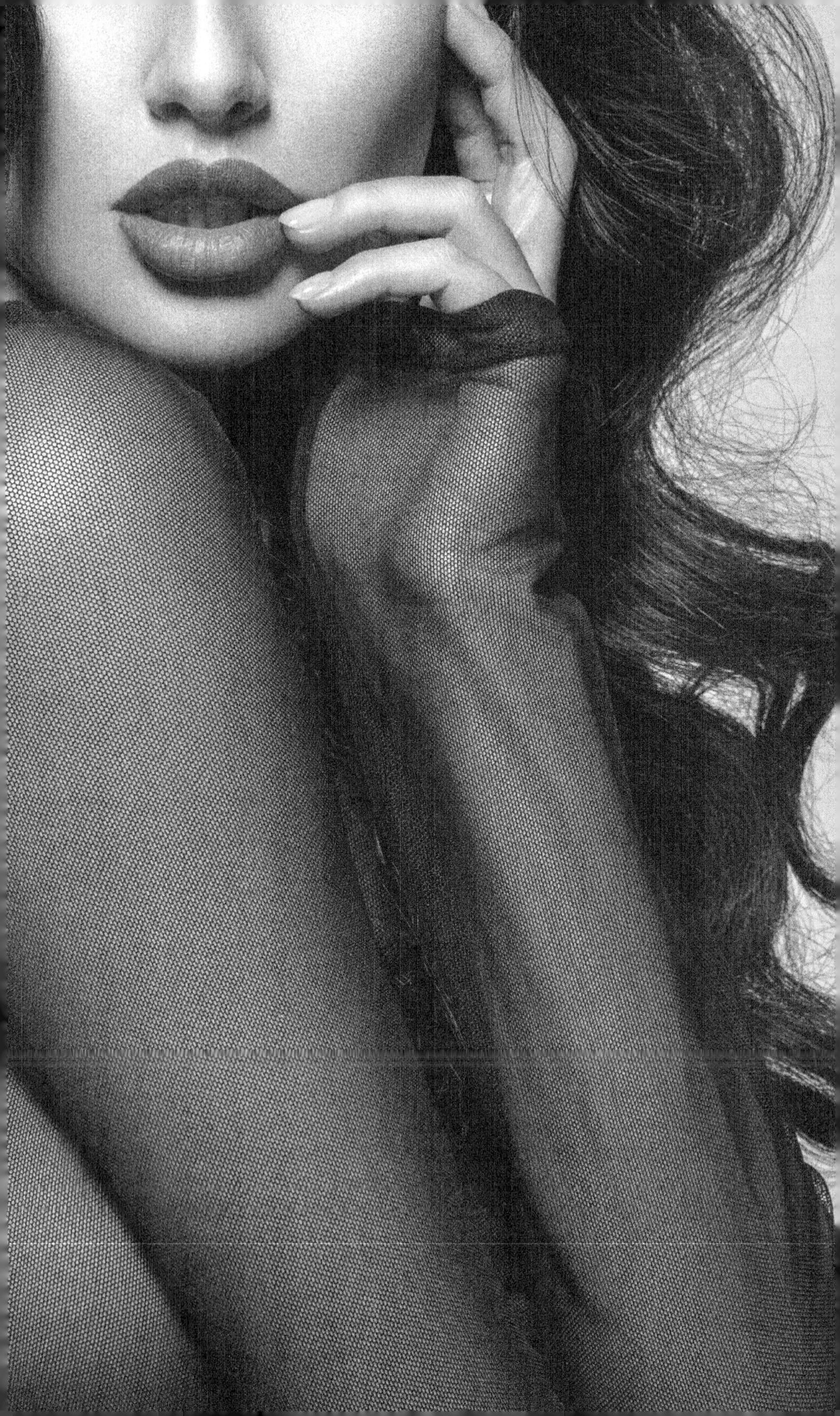

Thirty-Three

RAVEN

"Raven, wake up," Cher sings as she plops down on my bed, crossing her legs and smiling at me.

"Oh God." I groan and pull the pillow over my head.

Laughing, she grabs it. "Wake up. You have more groveling gifts."

I've never seen Cher happier about Jett sending me all these gifts that mean nothing to me. They started arriving the day after the hotel visit. The first day he sent six platinum, sapphire, and diamond bangles. Exquisite, but I've left them in their turquoise box untouched.

Day two was boxes, and I do mean boxes of apparently the best dark chocolate in the world.

Day three, flowers. So many, I had the delivery man hand them out to shops on the street.

Day four, silk, lace, and leather lingerie.

Day five... well, day five was kind of unfair since he knows I have a weakness for shoes. It still pains me to look at all those boxes from Jimmy Choo, Prada, and Louboutin. I had to give them to Cher. Now I can't go near her room because I see them, taunting me. Granted, my foot is a size six and Cher wears an eight. Whatever, she's savvy; she can exchange them.

And here we are on day six. I almost don't have the strength to look—it has to be amazing if Cher is singing.

POWER

I sigh and sit up, tossing my hair off my shoulders. My eyes feel like shit. I haven't left the apartment in days, and I cry myself to sleep. The annoying sounds of construction are my only company. Cher delivers the gifts to me in the morning, then leaves with Matteo. Brody is consumed with school. And I pace my dark room, haunted by memories of him. The way he smells, his smile, that small dimple on his cheek that I've decided is mine and only I can see.

It's like my heart that was bleeding is now racing, and I can't seem to stop it. I feel like I'm on a treadmill that won't stop.

"Just donate it. Did the restaurant come for the chocolate?" I'm not keeping any of this. It's one big fat no.

I get that he's rich, but does he seriously think I'm that shallow? That he can buy my love?

"Oh, honey, you won't be donating this." She hands me the long, rectangular turquoise box that has the famous Tiffany branding on it.

"Did you look at it?" I stare at her as I take the box. It still has the turquoise bow on it, so maybe she didn't.

"Stop it. I did not, but come on. Feel that baby. A guy with gloves delivered it. He even had a guard." She claps her hands and slides closer.

There goes my heart, racing again. I'm so stressed out, I don't even need coffee. It's like I can feel him thinking about me, touching me...

I look down at the box and rub my hands across the lettering. A teardrop lands on my finger.

"Take it. Call Tiffany's and return it. I don't want it." I sniff, wiping my poor sore nose on the shoulder of the T-shirt I was sleeping in.

"No." She looks at me. "And quite frankly, I'm getting a little sick of you ordering me around. You don't want your presents, call and get them removed yourself. Or better yet..." She stands and smooths her hand on her cute pink dress. "Call Daddy Powers and tell him to stop sending stuff. We're running out of room anyway." She turns and slams my door.

I jump. What the hell? Then I leap up and chase after her.

"You're unbelievable, Cher. All you do is hang out with Matteo. You've no idea that I'm barely staying afloat. Jett is here. *Here.*" I motion with my hands. "And I can't stop wanting him. It's like I'm sick and there is no cure. And you don't care." I'm screaming, because the sound of the electric saw being used upstairs has taken over, and she needs to hear this.

"Raven. Enough." Cher spins toward me. "You love him. He may be a shit, but either get rid of him and move on, or do us all a favor and give him a chance, because this"—she motions up and down at my appearance—"is pathetic. You want to know why I'm hanging out with Matteo?" She puts her hands on her hips. "Because I can't watch you quit on yourself."

She grabs her phone. "I love you, but I'm telling you this because I really hope you'd do the same for me if I was ever in this condition." Turning, she walks toward the door.

I go to open my mouth, but nothing comes out.

"Fight, Raven. Say what you will about Daddy Powers, but he fights. It might be dirty, but he fights to win." She grabs her big black sunglasses off the counter. "And call Maria back. She's been trying to get ahold of you for over a week," she snaps, putting her glasses on and stomping out the front door.

"Wow. Fucking calling you on your shit, huh?" Brody walks in to grab some of the chocolate.

"I just... I mean, she's wrong, right?" Using the Tiffany box, I point at the door.

"I'm not getting involved." He shakes his head and stuffs his mouth full of dark chocolate.

"And you can't donate this stuff. Jesus, have you tried it yet? Fucking amazing." He pops more into his mouth, closing his eyes like it's better than sex, and maybe it is for him. I'm starting to suspect Brody is asexual.

"But you should call Maria back and... take a shower." He grins and walks back to the balcony.

"Unbelievable." I march into the kitchen. God, this really is the first time I've been here in days.

Roses are everywhere. Boxes and boxes of chocolate are scattered all over the one counter, along with a small pile of envelopes, tucked neatly in the corner.

"What the hell?" I grab them. They all have my name on them, but they aren't open. Why didn't Cher give me these?

Because she's sick of you.

I grab them and a block of dark chocolate, then make my way back to my room and sit on the end of my bed. I put the Tiffany box next to me and pop some chocolate into my mouth, instantly moaning out loud.

Fucking asshole. He *had* to send crack chocolate. Now I won't be able to stop. It's like eating a mouthful of mouthwatering, creamy goodness with just the right amount of sweet bitterness.

I reach for another chunk, grab my phone, and dial Maria. I've been avoiding her because I can't handle the guilt. Now that I know Jett dumped my mom, I'm sure she fired Maria. I tried to get my dad to hire her, but he said no, so now I'm stalling until I have some way to get her here. Maybe she can cook for us?

Right, like you have that kind of money.

"Hello." Maria's voice sounds way better than mine.

I straighten. "Maria, I'm so sorry I haven't called you back, but I'm working on trying to get you over here. Don't you worry about anything. I have everything under control." I say all this so fast my face heats up.

"What are you talking about?" she snaps, and I can almost see her frowning at the phone.

"Well, I heard about Jett, I mean Mr. Powers, dumping my mom..."

"It's so wonderful, right?" She snickers, and this time I look at my cell. Did the phone cut out? Like is this bad reception?

"Raven? I've been worried. I expect you to return my calls." Her voice sounds like it did when I was a kid.

"I'm sorry." I sigh, looking up at the ceiling. "I just wanted to find a way to support you. Did my mom fire you?" When I say the last part, I shake my head, knowing she did.

"Of course." Again, Maria's voice sounds better than I've heard her… ever.

"I'm so sorry."

"Raven, what is going on? Your mother is a sicko. And don't you worry about Maria. I'm working for Mr. Jett. He said since I'm the one who raised you, I deserve my own house. And he set up a retirement plan for me."

After swallowing the dark chocolate, I shout, "He did what?"

"He bought me a house, and—"

"Oh my God." I look around my room as if my yellow walls can actually talk and tell me what to say because I'm at a loss. He bought Maria a house? Because she raised me?

"I can't wait for you to see it: two bedrooms, so you always have a home." Her voice brings tears to my eyes.

"That… I… that's very kind of him," I croak out.

"Yes, it was. I figure I'll hang around, and then when you and Mr. Jett have babies, I'll help."

I bite my lip. This is so surreal that I'm going to start laughing. It's like he's Mr. Wonderful, except he's not. If Maria knew what he did…

"Raven?" she snaps.

I jump. "I need to go. I'm not feeling well." I close my eyes. It's like in a matter of a week, he's completely turned the tables and made himself the good guy.

"Okay, but you call me sometime." She laughs.

"Maria, I need you to know, I'm not with Mr. Powers, no matter what you heard from my mom. I just… there won't be babies." I laugh, but it sounds bitter. "Jett doesn't want babies, and I can't forgive him." There, at least I said it. Now next time I call, I won't have to hear that ever again.

Silence greets me. "Maria?"

"Yes." She sighs. "He didn't tell you?" And goose bumps appear on my arms.

"Tell me what?"

"Are you talking about him with your mother and her assistant?"

My hand goes to my mouth, and I nod even though she can't see me.

"Oh dear." She sighs again. "He didn't touch them, Raven." She laughs. "Men. So stupid. Why didn't he tell you?"

"Maria? What are you talking about?" I hiss, preparing for the inevitable panic attack as that horrible night replays.

"Look, I don't particularly like Mr. Jett, but he loves you, so for that I give him a second chance. As for that night, your mom and that woman were together. Jett didn't touch them."

"How do you know this?" I demand.

"What? Are you kidding me? I know everything that goes on." She tsks.

I shake my head. "I saw them."

"You saw what he wanted you to see. That man has been a mess since the first day you stepped foot in his house. I knew he would be. It's why I tried so hard to keep you away, but..." Her voice drifts off for a moment. "Who am I to interfere with destiny?"

"Is this because he bought you a house?" My head is spinning. Everything is crashing around me, and if this is true, and Jett didn't sleep with my mother, can I forgive him?

"Raven." Maria sounds like she's getting mad. "Let me spell this out for you. Actions speak louder than words. Is Mr. Jett perfect? No. But I can see when someone is in love. I'm not stupid. Now I need to go." And before I can stop her, the line goes dead.

"Wow, Raven, you really are on a roll." I snort and drop the phone onto my bed. Looking at the envelopes, I pick one up and open it. At least it will distract me from having to deal with the truth that he didn't fuck my mom, that he never did since I came around, that he never wanted us to happen, but somehow we did...

We did. Slowly I open the first one.

Raven,

I was running this morning and stopped by a small shop. A man, a chocolatier, said he could make magical things happen if you eat his chocolate.

I did. As I tasted this piece of heaven, all I could think of was you. My mouth was filled with sweetness, with a slight edge of bitterness.

He told me to make a wish...

Love, your Jett

I drop the letter, grab the last piece of chocolate, which I brought to my room, and close my eyes as I pop it into my mouth. It tastes exactly like what he wrote.

This is who we are.

Sweetness and ecstasy, tested by bitterness. Do I dare wish for something that has the potential to be my downfall?

Do I?

I take a breath as I wish, then open my eyes, reaching for the next envelope.

Raven,

I've never had to win someone. I've never had to fight for someone. But I do for you. I saw these bloodred roses and they made me think of you.

My heart bleeds red, but only for you.

Love, your Jett

POWER

I rip open another.

Raven,
I will spoil you every day, for all our days.
Love, your Jett

"Oh my God." I cover my mouth, drop the letter, and reach for the Tiffany box. Jerking the ribbon off, I open it.

"Jesus, Jett." I stare at the sapphire-and-diamond choker, then scan the area around my bed to find the letter that goes with it.

Raven,
I had a vision.
I saw sapphires spilling all over you, running down your breasts in a sparkling river of gems.
It was that vision, that second, that my life changed. I might not have said it, but deep inside I knew.
You are my forever.
Love, your Jett

Forever.

I look around. "What do I do?" I whisper. Grabbing the choker, I run to the bathroom, rip off my T-shirt, and put the necklace on. It's cool on my skin. I take a step back, so I can see more of myself.

It's like this necklace has branded me, chained me to him, our souls intertwined together. To be honest, the letters mean more to me than any of the gifts. It has never been about money; it's about trust. Can I really trust him not to hurt me again?

"Can you trust yourself?" I whisper, because that's what all this is boiling down to. I lost a piece of myself that night, seeing him in a way I never thought possible.

What does your gut say?

I walk over and turn the shower on, removing the choker. Slowly, I wash myself while my mind tries to work through all this. He's not messing around. He wants it all. Can I give him that? I deserve it, and so does he.

I turn the water off and step out, wrapping a towel around my chest.

Do you dare?

It rings in my head, and I freeze. Suddenly I can breathe again. *It doesn't have to be this difficult, Raven. He asked this question in the beginning, and your answer is still the same. It will always be the same. Because at the end of the day, he's right.*

There is no choice. He is my forever, and I am his.

"Holy fuck." I almost trip over a pile of clothes trying to get to my phone on the bed. Jesus, my hands are shaking as I start to text.

ME: Are you free?

Exhaling, I wait.

JETT: Only for you.

My mouth twitches as I type.

ME: I need to talk
JETT: I'll be there in ten.

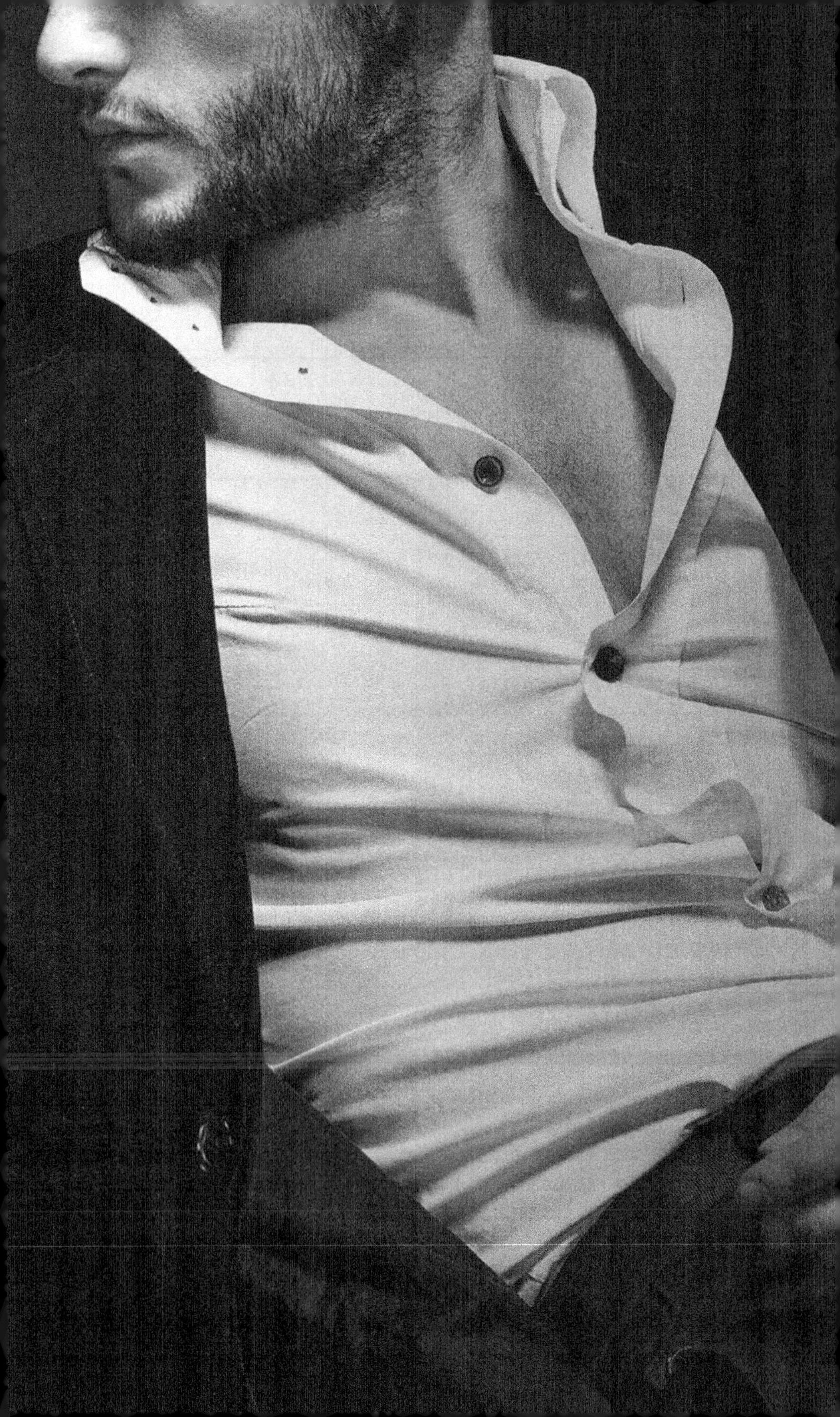

Thirty-Four

JETT

I knock on her door. It's been a week since the hotel room incident. I left her alone, gave her space, and waited for this very text.

Not gonna lie; it hasn't been easy, but I knew if I was ever going to get her to actually hear me, I needed to give her space.

I've thought about myself a lot, trying to figure why I am the way I am. Which is bullshit at the end of the day. We can't change the past, but we can change the future.

And my future is her. Do I delude myself thinking everything is going to be easy and perfect? No, but that's okay, because that's our journey.

"Coming," she calls out and swings the door open. Seeing her stand there in a pale-yellow dress, her wet hair pushed back from her exquisite face and hanging long down her back, my heart aches.

But it's her eyes that capture me, rendering me speechless as she looks up at me and I know she's ready.

"Hi," she says on an exhale. Her cherry red lips curve into a smile.

"Let's take a walk on the beach. I have something for you." My eyes caress her face, and I barely notice my choker on her neck. It seems almost dull compared to her.

"Okay." Nodding, she steps out.

I hold out my hand. Only this time, she doesn't hesitate. This time she takes it, and that electric charge that is just us—our energy—zings through the tips of our fingers up my arm.

"Jett," she whispers.

Smiling, I shake my head and lead us down the hallway and out into the sunny day.

I dip my head as we walk hand in hand in silence, enjoying her nearness. And I let myself have this.

This moment.

This woman.

This is all I will ever need. Yes, money helps, but it did me no good without her. As I stop at the beach, her eyes search my face, then travel down to the box under my arm.

"I'm not sure I should leave or stay with you when you open this." I grin at her, handing her the box. She cocks her head. I gaze out at the ocean rolling in and out.

"You need to stay with me," she says.

Reaching up, I brush off a strand of hair that has decided to caress her face.

"What's in there, is..."

"You?" she finishes for me.

Putting my hands in the pockets of my jeans, I nod.

"Everything you need to know is in that box." I feel exposed. Without a doubt, this is the most intimate thing I've ever done. Christ, is it too soon?

She reaches for my hand, taking it out of my pocket, kicks off her flip flops, and drags me onto the sand.

"Here. This is the perfect spot." She sits. It's close enough to hear the waves, but far enough away so we don't get wet.

I stay standing, and as I look away and take in the sea, I hear her rip open the paper.

Then silence. Nothing but the ocean, seagulls, and my own breath as I wait... wait for what? There is no more waiting. This is it. I gaze down at her.

She sits, her head down, her hands caressing my drawings. "All of them are in there, even the ones from when I was a kid." I grin, picking up a primitive drawing of a superhero.

"I called him Time Machine. He had the power of stopping time." My voice sounds hoarse. Shaking my head, I reach for one of her. She's laughing in this one, and I hand it to her.

"Beautiful, inside and out."

She bites her lip as she watches me, her eyes swimming with tears.

"Jett, this is you. Your hopes, dreams... everything." She shakes her head and scoops them up to hold them to her chest.

"I have nothing like this to give to you." The tears that swim in her sapphire-blue eyes spill down her cheeks, and I reach over to brush them away with my thumb.

"Yes, you do. It's you. All these drawings, if you place them in order, all lead to you." My eyes caress her face.

"I thought I had it all figured out, Raven. I'm an arrogant ass who knows nothing except this." I hold her face with both hands so I can look into her eyes.

"I will not take another breath without you by my side."

She bites her lower lip and nods.

"I will die first because living without you is pointless."

She exhales a shaky breath as I continue.

"And I will spend every moment cherishing you, loving you, because you're my gift, Raven." My hands tighten on her face, and my eyes turn blurry. When I take her lips, she leans into me, and I deepen the kiss, unable to tell if I taste her tears or my own.

Because I'm finally free.

Love.

It's what humans seek from the time we are born until we draw our last breath. It's more powerful than any other emotion we feel. It can cause unlimited damage and pain, but it can also be our savior.

POWER

I thought I was too old for her, too old for love, but I guess that's not how it works—at least not for me. If I had to wait until I was ninety, I would.

All my life I've known my path, knew what I wanted and how to conquer it. Then this woman came and ripped me open and showed me what I really am. The future is unclear, except that I have her, and that's all I will ever need.

"I love you, Mr. Powers." She sniffs. When I look down at her, her eyes are swollen from crying, her lips are puffy from my kisses, and all I can think is she's never been more stunning.

"You are my forever," I say, knowing for the first time in my life that I speak the truth.

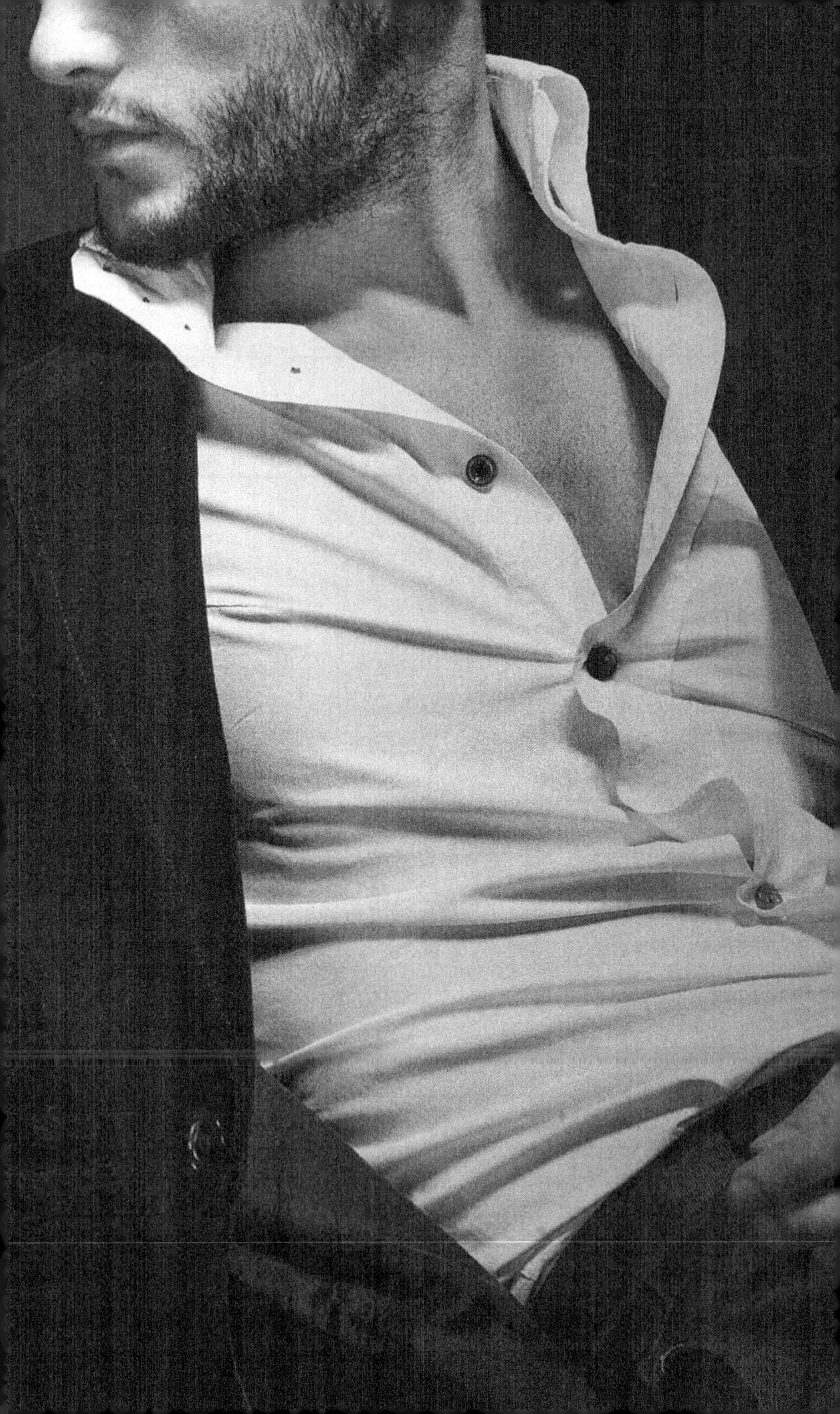

Epilogue

JETT

I stand looking down at her and smile. She sits, hair up in a messy bun, wearing nothing but a black blindfold.

I dangle the strawberry on her lips as she tries to reach up and bite it.

"Pretty confident this is something you like, huh?" I bring it back, caressing the bottom of her lip with the tip of the berry.

"Jett, I can smell it." She laughs and bites the tip. I can't help but grin and lean down to steal a kiss while she chews.

"Don't get cocky," I murmur.

"I wouldn't dream of it."

She gasps when I bite the fleshy part of her bottom lip. Taking her hand, I guide it to my hard erection. She smiles, trying to slip her hand into my waistband to get a better grip.

"Greedy this morning." I move away, hearing her huff. This is our last day in Spain. I got talked into coming back to the States to take a case. It will be eight months since I've stepped foot in a courtroom.

It's time. As much as I want to never return to reality and just fuck Raven, sunbathe, and take siestas, at some point we do need to return. I either had to shut down my practice or go back and take this case. I've got Brody moving up to our place. He's going to manage the building while Raven and I come and go.

POWER

Which allows my men the opportunity to update his apartment. It's the last one left to be renovated.

Raven and I turned the whole building green, complete with a communal vegetable garden on the roof.

Cher's back in the States, so that will be good for Raven. I think she needs to think about college. Her mind is too brilliant to waste. But she seems content doing her environmental work, which I support. A happy Raven makes a happy Jett, simple as that.

I turn and open the refrigerator, grabbing some whipped cream and a bottle of champagne. When I open it, she squeals at the loud pop and squirms in her chair, her nipples hard, waiting for me to suck on them.

"Open, my love." I pour a glass and take a sip. As I watch her slowly open her legs, my nostrils flare.

"That's a good girl, but I meant your mouth." She grins and licks her lips, thinking she's getting champagne. Instead, I bring a sliced piece of bell pepper to her lips and pop it in her mouth. Her smile stops, and she tries to spit it out.

"Don't you dare," I murmur.

"Oh my God, you know I hate bell peppers." She swallows, but not without a dramatic shudder.

I pull down my sweats and take my cock out. "Don't gag." Before she can speak, I grab the back of her head and guide it into her mouth. She instantly gags and I laugh.

"I told you not to get cocky." I pull out and thrust in again. Christ, no matter how many times I fuck her, it's never enough. In and out, she does her best to take me. Saliva drips down her chin and onto my balls.

"Yeah, that feels good. You like my cock in your mouth?" I growl, pulling her head back, sensing a slight tingle from the pepper on my cock.

She smiles. "Yes." She licks her lips, one hand digging into the table.

I grab the honey. "Open," I demand, watching as she takes a deep breath, probably thinking it will be my cock. Instead, I squeeze the honey into her mouth. She gasps and tries to swallow, but I keep squeezing, letting the golden liquid drip out of her mouth and down her chin to her tits and stomach.

I kneel. "Let's see if Daddy can help." I lower my head and latch onto one hard nipple, licking and sucking while she moans.

"Oh God." She reaches for my hair, and I smile, trying to decide whether I want her cunt or ass this morning.

"Tell me what you want, my love." I lick the honey that's dripping down her abdomen, then reach for her neck to hold her still.

"You. I want you." She pants as I lower my head to lick her sweetness—it's sticky and slick.

"Spread your legs and don't come until I say so, Raven," I command. "Now inch that ass to the edge." She shimmies down. With a grin, I suck on her, sliding my two fingers deep inside her, rubbing her G-spot.

"Oh fuck." She grabs my hand. "I'm going to come. Can I come, please?" I pull my fingers out and lift my head.

"I said you can come when I say so." I blow on her clit, licking her from top to bottom, going all the way to her rosette hole.

She moans while I lick it. "That's a good girl. You want me to fuck you here?" My thumb goes in and out of her small hole.

"Oh God, I... Jett," she whimpers.

"Yes or no?" I demand, watching her pussy already starting to contract. She's not even trying to hold back this morning.

"Jett, please..."

"Since you are already coming, yes." I lean down and let my tongue take her over as she screams my name, her ass and pussy pulsing. She grabs my hair and pulls.

Standing, I lift her up and sit in the chair. She straddles me.

"Jett, take the blindfold off." She rubs her wet cunt on my cock as I slap her ass hard.

"Turn around."

She hesitates, but I lift her up easily and set her back down, admiring her back and small waist.

It's been a while since I fucked her ass, but we need lube. No matter how ready and aroused I get her, my cock is just too thick. When I pull her back, my hands go to her tits, and I pinch her nipples. She's covered in sticky honey. Lifting her, I push her front on the table. My hands are now covered in honey. Grabbing my cock, I lean over her.

"You trust me?" I go to hold the back of her neck.

"I love you," she says, panting.

"I love you too. But that wasn't the question," I grunt, spreading her legs with my feet.

"I trust you... *forever*," she screams.

I grab my cock and thrust into her slick, wet core.

"Hold on to the edge," I hiss, the pleasure so intense I feel like I'm ready to shoot my load already. Pounding into her, I grab her hips to keep her still.

"Fuck, Raven, it's so good with us. You feel me getting ready to come?" My stomach muscles tighten.

"Yes, fuck me," she shouts.

I slap her ass, and her cunt grabs my cock. The adrenaline rush goes straight to my head. Everything is heightened, the pleasure making my eyes roll back as I gasp for breath, not wanting it to end.

"Say it," I grunt, our bodies smacking together.

"I love you," she screams while her pussy pulses, milking my cock.

"So. Fucking. Good." I do one last thrust, then let go, fucking fly, my body jerking my release into her.

"Jesus." I pull out and turn her so I can kiss her sugared lips and slip off the blindfold. She's a mess, the honey covering her entire chest. Somehow it has found its way to her hair. I'm covered in sweat and cum. There couldn't be a better moment.

This is us.

She's a little unsteady, so I drop to my knee and hold her waist. But when I look up at her and grin, I know the time is right.

"I love you," I say.

Her eyes become wide, and all she seems to be able to do is nod.

"Raven Stewart, love of my life, woman who has done the unthinkable... will you marry me and be my wife?"

She blinks at me, and I lean over to grab the turquoise box from the counter. As she covers her mouth, I open it.

"Oh my God." She stares at it. A giant princess-cut sapphire surrounded by diamonds twinkles before us. Slowly, her eyes meet mine. "Yes, Jett Powers, I would love to be your wife." Her eyes instantly fill with tears.

Pulling the ring out, I slip it on her finger. "You are my forever, and I want everything with you."

She stands on her tiptoes, tears spilling down her cheeks, which are smeared with honey-sweet tears. "I just want you, and babies, and..." She throws her arms around my neck and kisses the very tip of my mouth.

Holding on, I breathe her in.

"Did you just say you want babies?" I can't stop smiling while she continues to kiss me.

"Of course. Not now, but someday."

Lifting her up, I walk us toward the shower.

"Maybe I'll consider one," I murmur into her lips.

"We need at least two." She wraps her legs around me.

"Hmm, I love a good counter-offer," I say.

"Let me see if I can convince you." She slides down my body and all is forgotten—it's just the two of us.

The world can pause for all I care. Babies, jobs, and life can wait as she takes my cock into her mouth and everything fades.

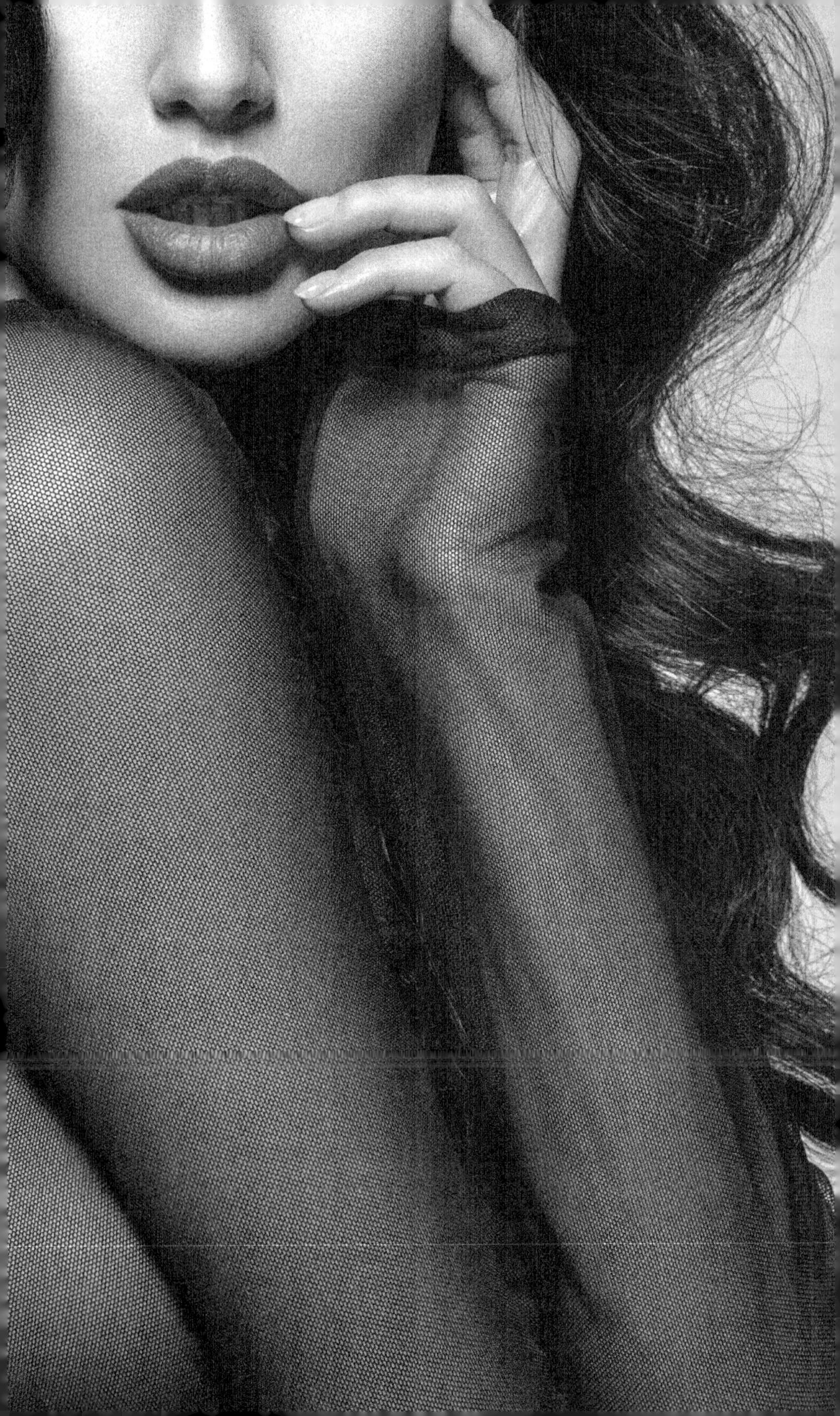

Extended Epilogue

RAVEN

One year later, Costa del Sol, Spain

"**O**kay, blot your lips," Cher says, demonstrating in front of my face.

"Like this?" I exaggerate my lip blotting and laugh at her expression. But come on, this is the third time she's shown me.

"Raven, I swear to God—"

"Sorry, but you have to stop. If I'm not ready by now, I'll never be." I breathe in some much-needed oxygen and glance around the small courtyard where I'm about to get married.

"I just... we should have flown Dante in to do your makeup. I mean, I did the best I could on your eyelashes—"

"Cher." I reach for her hand, which is patting more powder on my forehead. "The reason I didn't fly Dante in is because I want you. You're better than any professional." She stops patting and looks down at me.

"Stop it... Really?"

"Yes." I shake my head, grinning as she nods and takes a step back.

"I just don't understand why you're so calm." She runs a hand through her long blond hair, her eyes focused on something over my shoulder, a flirty smile on her face.

"Because I'm trying to enjoy today. I'm getting married only once. What are you doing?" I turn to see who's holding her fascination, but the giant flower arch is impeding my view.

"You need to make sure I'm sitting next to Brett at dinner," she says, not even looking at me.

"Cher, for fuck's sake, focus." I roll my eyes and take in a deep breath, only to exhale when I feel the tape holding my breasts in place so they don't escape my plunging V-neck. I'm wearing a one-of-a-kind Alberto Ressario gown. He personally hand-stitched the lace and pearls on the tight bodice.

I asked for a gown that was special. He created a masterpiece. White silk with a long train and a slit on my right leg, so when I walk, my sapphire garter shows. It's stunning.

"Is he seeing anyone?" Cher walks around me, absently smoothing my dress.

"I'm sure he is. Brett always has a ton of women." I smile up at the photographer who's been discreetly following my every move.

"He's beyond hot, and he just screams nasty, like I want him to—"

"Oh my God, you do know I'm about to get married, right?" I have to stop her because when Cher gets going, who knows what she'll say, and there're people staring at us.

"I have to have him." She pouts. "You owe me this."

"If he hasn't shown interest, I would not..." My voice trails off as I turn to smile at my dad, who's walking toward us looking rather dashing in his black tuxedo. He and my new stepmother and baby sister showed up yesterday, but with all the preparations, I haven't been able to spend much time with him.

Cher stands there staring at me like I'm the crazy one for not understanding that she's Cher and can have anyone. But the truth is Brett's a lot like Jett. They can't be manipulated. He's also, well, Brett.

"Fine, I'll find out the dirt, but I'm warning you: you need to stay away from him," I mumble, then turn and throw my arms around my father.

"What does that mean?" she snaps, her brown eyes narrowing on me as I sway back and forth with him. Great, now I just upped the stakes. I know her. She's gonna want him more because he's a challenge.

"Sweetheart, let me look at you." My dad pulls back to look at me, and for the first time I notice he's going gray around the temples, and his eyes seem tired. I wonder if things aren't as good as he's been saying when we've talked on the phone.

"You okay?"

"I'm fine. Just so proud of you." His eyes fill with tears. "I feel like I somehow failed you, you know, leaving when I did, with your mother..."

I have to bite my tongue not to say, *Well, you kind of did.* But in the end, everything that happened to me in the past has led me here.

To Jett.

He's my future, all I'll ever need, and I wouldn't change a minute of my past pain. If anything, it makes me grateful for what I have now.

"Oh, Mr. Stewart, please don't make Raven cry." Cher steps in. "I spent hours on her eyes."

We both look at her, then back at each other, and burst out laughing.

"You're right. No getting all mushy on your big day." He clears his voice and steps back, allowing Cher to move in between us, her eyes assessing my face, but I know it's more than that. Cher was there with me when everything went down. She remembers how painfully vicious my mom was... is. I push all those thoughts aside. She doesn't get to invade my thoughts. Not today.

"*You* are beautiful inside and out, Raven. You're kind of my hero." She bites her bottom lip and grabs my hands, squeezing them.

I shake my head and repeat the same thing I've always said. "I have no idea why..." We both break into a smile.

"Goddamn it." She throws her arms around me and I look up at the sky, trying to hold back my tears.

"I really am happy for you." She hugs me tight.

"I know." I pull back to look at her because I do know. Things have changed, which is normal. My life revolves around Jett, and Cher is busy with her clothing line. We see each other as much as we can, but today, my wedding, it's kind of just slamming it all home that things are different, but in a good way.

"Beautiful. Hold that pose for a second, ladies." The photographer walks around us snapping pictures as he talks, completely breaking the moment, but it's probably for the best since the soulful sounds of flamenco guitar are now playing in the background.

"That's your cue." Cher sniffs and wipes under her eyes as she smiles supportively.

"Yes." I exhale. This is it. The sun is setting, and the sky shows off massive amounts of reds and oranges and a splash of purple streaks. Hundreds of tiny bistro lights strung from one side of the courtyard to the other twinkle and sway in the warm evening breeze. The air smells of the ocean along with the night-blooming jasmine that climbs the trellis. Bloodred and sapphire roses are strategically placed all around, their petals sprinkled across the white carpet I'll walk on when I step toward Jett to say my vows.

The priest, Father Garcia, waits, smiling and talking with Jett's parents in the first row of seats. He's a dear friend who agreed to marry us, even with me and Jett not belonging to his church. I adore him. We first met him a couple of years ago when his church was hosting a fiesta to raise money for the elementary school down the street that needed a new building. We ended up dancing and laughing most of the night. The next day, Jett donated so much money they named the building after him. We've stayed close, and he's the only one I'd ever choose to marry us.

"It's time, Raven." My dad holds out his arm to me as I take another deep breath, only to feel the tape on my right breast snap.

"Oh no...God, no." I gasp and turn, my eyes frantically seeking Cher.

"What?" she hisses, then reaches to touch up my face.

"Stop that. I just felt the tape on the right side break." I motion to my breast as both my dad and Cher stare at me.

"Impossible. I put too much on. You're fine. Go." She smiles and nods.

"Honey, you look stunning." My dad looks confused. And it's not like I can say I'm worried my right boob is going to burst out any second. It's my dad, for fuck's sake.

"Thank you." I nod and almost take another deep breath but catch myself.

"Let's do this." I loop my arm with his and let him guide us forward. If I live to be a hundred, I don't think I will ever forget this feeling as we slowly move.

Terror.

And not because I'm about to get married, but because of what Jett will do if anyone sees my breast burst out. One step in front of the other, we walk. The guitar music fades, and I look straight ahead, ignoring all the well-wishers, the whispers of how beautiful I am.

It's as if the world has stopped as I blink my eyes and stare only at him.

Jett Powers.

Beautiful.

Powerful.

And *mine*. Excitement floods me, and I'm instantly wet, my nipples hardening. His blue eyes sweep me up and down, then lock onto mine. His full lips break into a smile.

Jesus, I need to breathe. I dig my nails into my father's suit as if that can steady me.

POWER

Nothing can. This feeling, this amazing pull I have with him is real. I move closer as his eyes narrow, but it's the slight flare of his nostrils that makes me bite my lip, as if he can smell my arousal, my almost primal need for him.

My father stops and gives my hand to Jett's, and that jolt of electricity I get every time he touches me almost makes me shudder. I vaguely acknowledge Father Garcia approaching as Jett's warmth infiltrates my body, like heat from a fire on a cold day.

I'm sure I'm speaking, repeating the words that Father Garcia is saying. I feel surreal, almost as if I'm in a trance, as I hear myself say, "I do."

Jett steps closer. His hand reaches for my chin, tilting my face up. His eyes caress me, and suddenly everything is clear as he says, "I do."

I do.

My breath stutters, and my eyes fill with tears.

I do. It means so much. Those two words that humans have been saying as part of a ritual for hundreds and hundreds of years. I never really thought about them. It's just what you say when you get married.

But I get it now. *I do* give myself to him. *I do* promise to love him, to take care of him in sickness and in health...

I do.

"Breathe, my love. I've got you." Jett's voice sounds strong and confident.

He's got me... and I've got him. I watch him place the diamond-and-sapphire wedding band on my finger and he smiles.

I smile back as Father Garcia says, "I now pronounce you husband and wife." And then I'm in Jett's arms, his lips on mine as I cling to him, letting his mouth claim me.

The loud sound of clapping and cheering makes Jett pull back, his eyes robbing me of what little oxygen I had as he guides me toward the church.

"Congratulations, my friends. I wish you joy and happiness." Father Garcia beams and walks with us as our small sphere of family and friends explodes around us.

"Thank you, Father. I need to have a small word with my wife. You don't mind if we take a moment inside." It's not a question.

My cheeks flush and I smile at the blur of people as we walk by.

"What are you doing?" I spit out as I continue to smile like I'm in a beauty pageant.

"Bathroom, now," he growls, his one hand at the base of my back, the other pulling open the old wooden door.

"Jett? We have guests," I puff out. My eyes instantly adjust to the dark church. The only light comes from the rays of color spilling in from the stained glass windows.

"My love, your tits are falling out." He grabs my hand and weaves us around the pews.

"What? They are not." I look down. They're spilling forward, but no nipples have escaped.

"Jett—" My voice drifts off. I try not to catch my heel in the cracks on the wood floor, almost bumping into him as he stops at a door.

"Inside. I'm gonna fuck you."

JETT

To say I've lost all patience would be an understatement. We purposely picked Spain so we could have a casual, family-and-close-friends' wedding.

Somehow, I didn't factor in that would mean entertaining. It went from me being able to fuck Raven anytime I wanted to hanging out with my parents and brother who surprised us by flying in early. Then came Maria and Cher, along with Raven's father and his new wife and baby...

That was all fine. I get that we have family and friends. It wasn't until brunch the other morning, when my mother and Maria were talking about how romantic it would be if Raven stayed in a separate room the night before our wedding, that I started getting aggravated. Then, Cher chimed in that it was a must, that we had to respect the tradition. Otherwise, it was bad luck. I laughed, thinking they were not serious.

Apparently, they were and got Raven on board. I've been using my hand on my cock for the last day and a half while my fiancée was in the hotel down the street with Cher. So, seeing my Raven walk toward me, looking more beautiful than any bride could ever wish, has me a little undone.

I savored the moment.

I let myself say my vows to love and cherish her, and I intend on doing just that, starting now.

Do I care that I've dragged Raven away from everyone minutes after Father Garcia legally pledged our souls together?

Not. At. All.

Raven is mine.

Mine.

I'm not waiting a second longer. My hand tightens on hers as I maneuver us through the small, dimly lit church. My eyes take in the confessional booth, then shift back to the exquisite gown my wife is wearing. As much as I'd love to sneak us into that small booth, rip off her panties, and have her sit on my cock...

That can't happen.

"Jett—" Raven gasps as I stop at the bathroom door, my hand pushing the hard wooden door open.

"Inside. I'm gonna fuck you," I hiss. Christ, I'm wound up so tight my hands are shaking.

Obsessed.

I can feel my pulse in my temples. My dick is throbbing, and I can't think straight.

"But... we have family." Her voice sounds breathless because she wants my cock inside her swollen pussy as much as I do.

Pulling her into the small room that's nothing but a toilet, sink, and small window, I shut the door and lock it.

"Jett…" She puffs out some air as I back her to the edge of the sink and lower myself to my knees.

"Oh my God." Her hands snake into my hair.

Smirking, I glide my hands up her tan legs to pull her panties down.

"Step out, baby. I need to eat *my* cunt," I growl.

"Wait, we… the…" she whispers but obeys, lifting one leg so I can slip the silk G-string off, pocketing it as I unbuckle my slacks.

"Pull the dress up, and spread your legs," I order, releasing my leaking cock, jerking on it hard as I lean forward to lick her sweet, slick core.

"Fuck, you taste good." My tongue moves back and forth on her swollen nub. Sucking on it, I gaze up and watch her nipples harden.

She groans loud and leans back on the sink. Grabbing one leg, I put it over my shoulder and let my tongue fuck her. Her hands tighten in my hair and she chants my name, her greedy pussy already pulsing.

I pull back and her eyes pop open, and I can't help but smile as I grab my cock and jack myself off. If we didn't have to go back out and be social, I'd shoot my load on her pussy and dress.

"Talk to me. Tell Daddy exactly what you need," I demand, my mouth right at her wet cunt, inhaling her scent as she tries to arch back into my mouth.

"Jett… please," she begs.

After another quick lick, I stand, grabbing the back of her leg to spread her open. I grip my cock and rub the tip back and forth on her clit.

"Look at this pink, wet cunt. Does this feel good?"

"Yes. Fuck me, Daddy," she cries out. It echoes around the small bathroom, and I smile.

POWER

"Such a nasty mouth on such a pretty face. Let's see if I can't help you out, Mrs. Powers." While I thrust my thick cock deep inside her, we both groan in pleasure.

"Jesus Christ," I grunt, pulling out slightly, then impaling her again and again, fucking her hard.

Primal.

I'm past caring about anything other than sating my need, this all-consuming lust I've been holding in check for almost two days. Right now, nothing in this universe can stop me as I slam into her. Her satin dress bunches up, filling the sink; her one breast is spilling out as I pinch her nipple.

"Jett... oh God," she whimpers and arches so as to stare into my eyes. And everything fades. In and out, our bodies slap together, building, climbing...

"I'm going to—can I come?" Her voice becomes louder as her core clenches and clamps onto my dick.

"Fuck, you feel good. I'm inside you, baby," I grunt.

My hips pick up speed and her hand reaches for me as I watch her shatter, fucking soar, and I never want this to end.

"I love you," she cries out, her nails digging into my neck while the other holds on to my tuxedo.

"Jesus, Raven," I groan, pounding into her, fucking her through her orgasm. My nostrils flare at her scent, and her slick juices drip down my balls, causing my cock to thicken.

"So fucking tight. I'm gonna come." My fist hits the wall and I let go, exploding into a million pieces as my eyes roll back in my head. My body jerks, and my cock pulses, shooting my seed deep inside her.

"Christ." I lean my forehead on hers, trying to catch my breath. Raven entwines her hands in my hair and kisses my eyes and my lips. If I died right now, I'd be fine because this is my heaven.

"Hey, man?" A loud bang on the door makes me freeze.

"You need to wrap this up." My brother's voice booms in. "Father Garcia is getting ready to give a tour, and Mom needs to use the restroom, so..."

"Oh my God," Raven whispers as her nails dig into my neck. I can't actually be hearing my brother's sanctimonious voice. Right? I mean, what the hell?

"Holy shit," Raven mouths, her eyes the size of saucers as I slowly pull out.

"Brett, I'm a little busy right now," I call out, watching Raven. Her dress, which I spent a small fortune on, lays bunched up in the sink. The faucet, which appears to have a small drip, is saturating part of it. Her tan skin is flushed pink, and her lips are puffy from my mouth. She's truly breathtaking. I almost reach for my heart because it's aching. Each day I go to bed thinking I can't love her more, yet I wake and am proven wrong.

"Fuck, I love you." My voice is almost hoarse with emotion when I reach and lift her ass off the edge of the sink.

"Wait, my dress." Her one hand still clutches my arm for support; the other tries to gracefully pull her dress out of the sink.

"Oh my God, *no*," she wails, holding up the dress where there are two good-sized wet spots on the white silk.

"Jett…" Her voice sounds accusatory. She grabs ahold of the edge of the sink to kick out the long train from behind, looking over her shoulder, then back at me.

"That might be from the faucet." I'm doing my best not to laugh at the play of emotions on her face.

"Are you kidding me?" she hisses. "So, if it dries, we know it's water, and if it gets stiff, we know it's—"

"I hate to interrupt again, but the good Father and our mother are coming this way." Brett's annoying voice filters in as Raven covers her mouth, shaking her head no at me.

"For fuck's sake, Brett, just give us five minutes," I growl, reaching around Raven to grab a bunch of paper towels.

"On it, and don't worry. I'm asking them to put tequila out along with the champagne, because from what I just heard, all of us, including you two, are gonna need it." Brett laughs as I grit my teeth, hearing him walk away.

POWER

"I swear to God he's lucky I just came and it's our wedding day. Otherwise, I'd punch his arrogant face." I kiss the top of Raven's head and she spins to face me, looking glorious in her horror. I pull up my slacks and zip them.

"Jett." Her voice goes up a notch and her cheeks turn pinker.

"Babe, relax." My lips twitch as I turn on the old faucet, saturating the towels to clean her up.

"*No*, you don't understand. We can't go back out there. I look like... *you know*," she whispers, tucking her breast back into the dress. She smooths her hand up and down the seam, trying to get the tape to stick again.

"Shhh, you look exquisite." I squat down to clean her up. She's right though—she does look like she just got fucked. I smirk. Can't help it. Leaning forward, I inhale her candy-smelling cunt that's creamed up with my seed and her cum, and my cock instantly twitches. Ignoring it, I concentrate on my task.

"Perfect." I shoot the paper towels into the trash and reach into my pocket for her silk panties.

"Step," I order.

She lifts one heeled foot, then the other, and I slowly stand, pulling her G-string up.

"There, all fixed." I rub my nose on hers.

She bites her lower lip, trying not to smile, and wraps her arms around my neck.

"I love you." My lips caress hers.

She sighs and smiles. "I love you more."

"Not possible," I grunt into her mouth, slowly tilting her head back so our eyes connect. "You're mine, Raven Powers. My wife, my soul, my reason to live. Thank you for making me the luckiest man alive today."

"Jett..." Her voice cracks with emotion as her sapphire eyes fill with tears. She opens her mouth, then shuts it abruptly when we hear a voice.

"This door? This is the restroom?" My mom rattles the doorknob. "It's locked," she calls out.

Sighing, I say, "Mom, I'm in here." I hold Raven tight since she's trying to escape.

"Oh, Jett, there you are. I don't want to be rude, honey, but your guests are waiting, and I need to use the—" I grab Raven's hand and unlock the door as both of us smile at my mother, her eyes instantly narrowing as she looks at both of us.

"I'm assuming I'll be a grandmother soon…" She eyes me as I walk us out.

"I'll see what I can do, Mom," I say over my shoulder, guiding Raven out into the church and moving us back toward our reception, which seems to be in full force.

"You know what this means, don't you?" I look down at her.

"What?" She bats her eyes up at me innocently.

"I guess it's time I knock you up."

"I guess it is." She smirks, and my chest aches as I bring her hand to my lips.

"We'll need a lot of time to practice," I murmur, watching her eyes darken. With a wink, I walk us out, guiding us down the small steps and into the courtyard, the smell of fresh tortillas and carne asada fragrant in the air.

Cher rushes over with a glass of champagne. Brett raises his glass of tequila and I take a second to soak this all up. Ultimately, we never know what can happen in the future.

All we have is the present.

I pull Raven tight to my chest. Her head falls back and she laughs. I swing her around in my arms, kissing her cherry-stained lips.

She's the one. My soulmate if you believe in that.

I do.

I do…

I hope you loved Jett and Raven's story as much as I did. If you want to see Jett Powers, famed defense attorney, in his first appearance, pick up *Force*! Meet my dangerous and unbelievably hot enforcer, Ryder, and his secret obsession.
I love my Disciples!

FORCE

I love my Rock Gods!

Did you catch the cameo from The Stuffed Muffins? Stage dive into Rhys and Gia's uncontrollable attraction in *Rise*!

RISE

I'm so excited to announce that I'm heading back into TSM's world of sex, drugs, and rock 'n' roll!
Coming Spring 2023

ROCK GOD SERIES 2

ALSO…

I'm co-authoring *Filthy Disciple* with the incredibly talented Serena Akeroyd!
For all my loyal fans who worried Cindy wouldn't get her story…
It is on!

FILTHY DISCIPLE

Want to read more by me?

All my books are available in Kindle Unlimited and Audio!

The Disciples Series
LETHAL
ATONE
REPENT
IGNITE
FORCE
FILTHY DISCIPLE

The Entitled Duet
THE ENTITLED
THE ENLIGHTENED
THE ENCOUNTER

ROCK GOD SERIES
RISE

***

LETHAL
Blade McCormick is not a nice guy.

He's pure adrenaline and smells like smoke and leather—the kind of guy you look at and know he's going to be a combination of nasty and irresistible. The moment I allowed myself to touch his hot skin and kiss his full lips, I. Was. Done.

Like currency, I've become part of a transaction. Blade took me to *pay off a debt*. I try to tell myself, *Eve, you should hate him. He's a bad guy.* But then again, I'm not a good girl. Blade's the president of the Disciples, the notorious motorcycle club. I should be frightened, yet somehow, he doesn't scare me. If anything, I think I scare him.

It takes a lot of work to become the club's Queen, but I'll stop at nothing to have the King!

ATONE

I don't apologize or regret the destruction I'm about to cause. I'm at peace with what I must do... nothing can or will stand in my way. Not even the raven-haired beauty with golden eyes who haunts my dreams.

No one is innocent in the story of my life. Fairy tales don't exist!

I. Make. No. Excuses.

Everyone needs to *atone*, and I'm the man who is going to see to it.

REPENT

There are two sides to every story.

I fell in love with a redheaded boy, a boy who was kind and good.

Until he wasn't.

He broke my heart once, twice... I've lost count. Like a dark god, he haunts me. He smells like smoke and cinnamon, with danger seeping from every pore. He is my savior, my lover, exciting and addictive.

I should've seen it coming...

Never trust a Disciple. You have to sell your soul to the devil to get one to love you. I would.

I did.

My name is Dolores Dunghart, and I might have done the unforgivable.

I don't care if you judge me... I've judged myself.

But this is how we live.

And this is our love story.

Edge and Dolly forever.

IGNITE
ANTOINETTE

Axel Fontaine has a giant...

At least that's what everyone says. Unfortunately, it's true. All. Of. It.

He's dangerous, scary, and addictive. Without a doubt, the last person I should fall for is the VP of the Disciples MC.

I'm out of my league.

He's a six-foot-four, blue-eyed biker god.

I'm an ex-ballerina turned stripper who should run away.

But how do you escape the one man who ignites your body and consumes your very soul?

Axel doesn't do relationships. But I'm betting on ME to change his mind.

AXEL

I don't do relationships. I don't do drama, and I definitely don't do love.

I'm not Prince Charming. I'm the VP of the Disciples and the club is my family.

The last thing I need is a violet-eyed enchantress who smells like candy and has some sort of voodoo chemistry that's messing with my mind.

She needs to go.

She's a distraction... a weakness I can't have.

Men like me fall in lust, not love.

So, why is she still here?

FORCE

I've made two impulsive decisions in my life, and both have involved the notorious enforcer of the Disciples MC.

The first, I humiliated myself by spying on him.

The second, I decided to throw caution to the wind and show up at probably the worst possible time.

He's dangerous, demanding, and able to consume me with just one look.

He's also on trial for murder, and no one in his club trusts me.

You'd think I'd run. I mean, the cards are stacked against us.

But I can't escape my need, this all-consuming pull I have with him.

He may be wrong for me, but he's the very force that brings me to life.

Meet my deliciously HOT Reed Saddington! Venture into my angsty, billionaire world of *The Entitled*.

THE ENTITLED

People say you can't find your soulmate at eight years old. I did.

I found Reed and loved him more than I loved myself. We were young... beautiful... *entitled*.

Money and private schools, our families' lavish parties and posh, New York City apartments—it was all mere window dressing. What was real was our obsessive love, which grew right along with us as we moved toward adulthood. It consumed me, and only in his arms did I feel wanted and safe.

But I have a secret. It's big and to some, unforgivable. And it's why I let Reed destroy me, or maybe I destroyed us. Either way, I'm worse than broke—I'm broken.

Once upon a time, we were happy... Yet privilege has an ugly underside, and in the blink of an eye, my world crashed down around me.

I don't feel *entitled* anymore.

The Entitled is first in *The Entitled* duet. Reed and Tess's story concludes in *The Enlightened*.

THE ENLIGHTENED
My secret's out. Reed knows the truth.

The destruction's done. There's no taking it back.

Reed took all my firsts like a shiny present. He made promises with silky words I greedily kept as truths. But the moment I faltered, he took away everything.

Now we're both guilty of sins.

As we come together for Grandfather Ian's funeral, it's time to face what I've done—what we've done. The boy I've loved since age eight is now a man, his rage palpable, his turquoise eyes piercing me with an intensity that sets me on fire. Each delicious kiss seems to peel away our ugly past—a past we're desperate to escape.

They say forgiveness comes from within. Can I trust him to forgive me? Have we both been enlightened?

I used to believe in the fantasy of a happily ever after. Trouble is my life's not a fairy tale.

Meet Reed's twin brother, Jax Saddington
The Encounter

I don't know her name. All I do know is when she walked by, I felt something...

A dark, consuming need.

She's alluring, haunted, and full of secrets.

One night is all she's willing to give me. I'll take it... and her.

I'm Jax Saddington, heir to the Saddington empire, and this elusive temptress is about to discover one thing: the rules don't apply to me.

Jax & Ava's full story is coming in 2023!

Add it to your TBR

***Who's ready to stage dive into
Rhys and Gia's uncontrollable attraction?***

RISE
I know what I want.

So when opportunity knocked, I took it. I grabbed my shot, willing to do anything to make it happen.

From the beginning, I knew I was destined to be with the six-foot-four, bourbon-eyed Rock God. Only back in the early days he wasn't a god.

Rhys Granger was my brother's friend, the boy next door who wrote verses and played his guitar in our garage. He was talented. Exciting. Damaged. The kind of guy who made all the girls cry...

Except for me. I thought I was special. Turns out I'm not.

And now... *I despise him.*

He's the lead singer of the Stuffed Muffins, one of the biggest bands in the world, with dark hair, full lips, and a body to die for.

Unfortunately, he's a dick.

Not, that I care anymore. I have my own career. I'm successful in my own right. So, when offered another once-in-a-lifetime opportunity, I happily turn it down.

But the universe has other plans, and I'm forced back into the savagely glamorous world of rock 'n' roll. Thrust into battling his seductive smile, his dangerous kisses, and my own addictive needs.

He might be a Rock God, but he's also a man. And I'm the woman he never saw coming.

**Don't forget to follow THE STUFFED MUFFINS on Instagram for VIP ACCESS!
Stalk the naughty bad boys of rock 'n' roll!**

Connect

Website: http://www.cassandrafayerobbins.com
TikTok: bit.ly/CassandraRobbinsTT
Instagram: bit.ly/CassandraRobbinsIG
Facebook: bit.ly/CassandraRobbins_FB
Facebook Reader Group: bit.ly/CassandraRobbins_RE
Twitter: bit.ly/CassandraRobbinsTW
Goodreads: bit.ly/CassandraRobbins_GR
Newsletter: bit.ly/CassandraRobbinsNL
BookBub: bit.ly/CassandraRobbins_BB
Amazon: bit.ly/CassandraRobbins_AMZ

Acknowledgements

First and always, to my husband and my two beautiful children. Their patience when I'm trying to figure out how to do this self-publishing journey is amazing. I love you guys more than you can imagine.

My brother Chris, my baby brother Duke, and my cousin Jake: I'm so lucky to have you. My dad, my Minnesota family: thank you for all your support.

To my editor Nikki Busch: You are the best at what you do. You truly make all my stories incredible. Not only are you a wonderful friend, but I would be lost without you.

Michelle Clay and Annette Brignac: What can I say besides you two complete me! I'm beyond honored to be part of our tribe, but also to call you both my best friends. When I ask for 100 percent, you give me 150 percent, and I love you both so much.

To Candi Kane PR, my master at calm: You're simply fantastic! To my incredibly talented cover designer Lori Jackson: Thank you for bringing my deliciously hot Jett Powers to life. Elaine York: you're a genius at making the insides of my books look so stunningly beautiful. Betty at Tease Diaries – Ms Betty's Design Studio, you know my vision and make the most beautiful teasers. Thank you to my incredible photographer, Michelle Lancaster. We've been together for a long time and I'm in awe of you. Thank you to Richard Deiss for being the perfect Jett Powers!

I have, without a doubt, the best betas: Michelle, Annette, and Rea, thank you from the bottom of my heart.

A very special thank you to Annette for giving me just the right inspiration. You're amazing! Not only are you a dear friend, but your honesty and support mean the world to me.

Another special thank you to Kelly and Robyn. You know what you do for me, and I appreciate you both so much.

To my incredible team: Without you I could not do this. You're all so special to me. Darlene, Megan, Kelly, Teresa, Melinda, Cameel, Heather, Cat, Cindy, Erin, Gladys, Rebecca, Stephanie, Tammy, Jennifer, Robyn, Myen, Chayo, Stracey, Violet, Nichole, Mandy, Melissa, Tiffany, Laura, Lucia, Danielle, Clayr, and Sophie: Any magic that happens to me, just know that all of you are part of it. Your friendships and support mean the world to me. Love you all so much.

To my reader group, Robbins Entitled: I adore all of you and am honored to be able to get to know you all. It makes my day to get up and talk to you.

Huge thank you to all the amazing bloggers, IG bookstagrammers, and TikTokers who supported this release. I'm beyond grateful for your sharing of Jett and Raven.

Lastly, and most importantly, I thank you, *my readers*. You're what matters most.

XXXX
Cassandra

About the Author

Cassandra Robbins is a *USA Today,* Amazon Top 20, KDP All-Star, and international bestselling author. She threatened to write a romance novel for years, and finally let the voices take over with her debut novel, *The Entitled*. She's a self-proclaimed hopeless romantic, driven to create obsessive, angst-filled characters who have to fight for their happily ever after. Cassandra resides in Los Angeles with her hot husband, two beautiful children, and a fluffy Samoyed, Stanley, and Goldendoodle, Fozzie. Her family and friends are her lifeline, but writing is her passion.